The Narrative of
Arthur Gordon Pym

and Other Tales

Edgar Allan Poe

ALMA CLASSICS

ALMA CLASSICS
an imprint of

ALMA BOOKS LTD
60 High Street
Wimbledon Village
London SW19 5EE
United Kingdom
www.almaclassics.com

Represented by:
Authorised Rep Compliance Ltd
Ground Floor
71 Lower Baggot Street
Dublin, D02 P593
Ireland
www.arccompliance.com

For the publication details of the individual stories in this collection see the relevant note to each title

This edition first published by Alma Classics in 2025

Cover: Nathan Burton

Edited text, Notes and Extra Material © Alma Books Ltd, 2025

Printed in Great Britain by CPI Group (UK) Ltd, Croydon CR0 4YY

MIX
Paper | Supporting
responsible forestry
FSC® C013604

ISBN: 978-1-84749-932-5

Contents

The Narrative of
Arthur Gordon Pym

and Other Tales

THE NARRATIVE OF
ARTHUR GORDON PYM
OF NANTUCKET*

PREFACE*

Upon my return to the United States a few months ago, after the extraordinary series of adventure in the South Seas and elsewhere, of which an account is given in the following pages, accident threw me into the society of several gentlemen in Richmond, Va., who felt deep interest in all matters relating to the regions I had visited, and who were constantly urging it upon me, as a duty, to give my narrative to the public. I had several reasons, however, for declining to do so, some of which were of a nature altogether private, and concern no person but myself; others not so much so. One consideration which deterred me was that, having kept no journal during a greater portion of the time in which I was absent, I feared I should not be able to write, from mere memory, a statement so minute and connected as to have the *appearance* of that truth it would really possess, barring only the natural and unavoidable exaggeration to which all of us are prone when detailing events which have had powerful influence in exciting the imaginative faculties. Another reason was that the incidents to be narrated were of a nature so positively marvellous that, unsupported as my assertions must necessarily be (except by the evidence of a single individual, and he a half-breed Indian), I could only hope for belief among my family, and those of my friends who have had reason, through life, to put faith in my veracity – the probability being that the public at large would regard what I should put forth as merely an impudent and ingenious fiction. A distrust in my own abilities as a writer was, nevertheless, one of the principal causes which prevented me from complying with the suggestions of my advisers.

Among those gentlemen in Virginia who expressed the greatest interest in my statement, more particularly in regard to that portion of it which related to the Antarctic Ocean, was Mr Poe, lately editor of the *Southern Literary Messenger*, a monthly magazine, published by Mr Thomas W. White, in the city of Richmond.* He strongly advised me, among others, to prepare at once a full account of what I had seen and undergone, and

trust to the shrewdness and common sense of the public – insisting, with great plausibility, that however roughly, as regards mere authorship, my book should be got up, its very uncouthness, if there were any, would give it all the better chance of being received as truth.

Notwithstanding this representation, I did not make up my mind to do as he suggested. He afterwards proposed (finding that I would not stir in the matter) that I should allow him to draw up, in his own words, a narrative of the earlier portion of my adventures, from facts afforded by myself, publishing it in the *Southern Messenger under the garb of fiction.* To this, perceiving no objection, I consented, stipulating only that my real name should be retained. Two numbers of the pretended fiction appeared, consequently, in the *Messenger* for January and February (1837), and, in order that it might certainly be regarded as fiction, the name of Mr Poe was affixed to the articles in the table of contents of the magazine.

The manner in which this ruse was received has induced me at length to undertake a regular compilation and publication of the adventures in question, for I found that, in spite of the air of fable which had been so ingeniously thrown around that portion of my statement which appeared in the *Messenger* (without altering or distorting a single fact), the public were still not at all disposed to receive it as fable, and several letters were sent to Mr P.'s address, distinctly expressing a conviction to the contrary. I thence concluded that the facts of my narrative would prove of such a nature as to carry with them sufficient evidence of their own authenticity, and that I had consequently little to fear on the score of popular incredulity.

This exposé being made, it will be seen at once how much of what follows I claim to be my own writing, and it will also be understood that no fact is misrepresented in the first few pages which were written by Mr Poe. Even to those readers who have not seen the *Messenger*, it will be unnecessary to point out where his portion ends and my own commences – the difference in point of style will be readily perceived.

A.G. PYM

NEW YORK, JULY 1838

CHAPTER I

My name is Arthur Gordon Pym. My father was a respectable trader in sea-stores at Nantucket,* where I was born. My maternal grandfather was an attorney in good practice. He was fortunate in everything, and had speculated very successfully in stocks of the Edgarton New Bank,* as it was formerly called. By these and other means he had managed to lay by a tolerable sum of money. He was more attached to myself, I believe, than to any other person in the world, and I expected to inherit the most of his property at his death. He sent me, at six years of age, to the school of old Mr Ricketts, a gentleman with only one arm and of eccentric manners – he is well known to almost every person who has visited New Bedford.* I stayed at his school until I was sixteen, when I left him for Mr E. Ronald's academy on the hill. Here I became intimate with the son of Mr Barnard, a sea captain, who generally sailed in the employ of Lloyd & Vredenburgh – Mr Barnard is also very well known in New Bedford, and has many relations, I am certain, in Edgarton. His son was named Augustus, and he was nearly two years older than myself. He had been on a whaling voyage with his father in the *John Donaldson*, and was always talking to me of his adventures in the South Pacific Ocean. I used frequently to go home with him, and remain all day, and sometimes all night. We occupied the same bed, and he would be sure to keep me awake until almost light, telling me stories of the natives of the island of Tinian,* and other places he had visited in his travels. At last I could not help being interested in what he said, and by degrees I felt the greatest desire to go to sea. I owned a sailboat called the *Ariel*, and worth about seventy-five dollars. She had a half-deck or cuddy, and was rigged sloop-fashion* – I forget her tonnage, but she would hold ten persons without much crowding. In this boat we were in the habit of going on some of the maddest freaks in the world, and, when I now think of them, it appears to me a thousand wonders that I am alive today.

I will relate one of these adventures by way of introduction to a longer and more momentous narrative. One night there was a party at Mr Barnard's, and both Augustus and myself were not a little intoxicated towards the close of it. As usual, in such cases, I took part of his bed in preference to going home. He went to sleep, as I thought, very quietly (it being near one when the party broke up), and without saying a word on his favourite topic. It might have been half an hour from the time of our getting in bed, and I was just about falling into a doze, when he suddenly started up, and swore with a terrible oath that he would not go to sleep for any Arthur Pym in Christendom, when there was so glorious a breeze from the south-west. I never was so astonished in my life, not knowing what he intended, and thinking that the wines and liquors he had drunk had set him entirely beside himself. He proceeded to talk very coolly, however, saying he knew that I supposed him intoxicated, but that he was never more sober in his life. He was only tired, he added, of lying in bed on such a fine night like a dog, and was determined to get up and dress, and go out on a frolic with the boat. I can hardly tell what possessed me, but the words were no sooner out of his mouth than I felt a thrill of the greatest excitement and pleasure, and thought his mad idea one of the most delightful and most reasonable things in the world. It was blowing almost a gale, and the weather was very cold – it being late in October. I sprang out of bed, nevertheless, in a kind of ecstasy, and told him I was quite as brave as himself, and quite as tired as he was of lying in bed like a dog, and quite as ready for any fun or frolic as any Augustus Barnard in Nantucket.

We lost no time in getting on our clothes and hurrying down to the boat. She was lying at the old decayed wharf by the lumber yard of Pankey & Co., and almost thumping her sides out against the rough logs. Augustus got into her and bailed her, for she was nearly half full of water. This being done, we hoisted jib and mainsail,* kept full, and started boldly out to sea.

The wind, as I before said, blew freshly from the south-west. The night was very clear and cold. Augustus had taken the helm, and I stationed myself by the mast, on the deck of the cuddy. We flew along at a great rate – neither of us having said a word since casting loose from the wharf. I now asked my companion what course he intended to steer, and what time he thought it probable we should get back. He whistled for a few minutes, and then said crustily: "*I* am going to sea – *you* may go home if you think proper." Turning my eyes upon him, I perceived at once that, in spite of his assumed nonchalance, he was greatly agitated. I could see him distinctly by the light of the moon – his face was paler than any marble,

and his hand shook so excessively that he could scarcely retain hold of the tiller. I found that something had gone wrong, and became seriously alarmed. At this period I knew little about the management of a boat, and was now depending entirely upon the nautical skill of my friend. The wind, too, had suddenly increased, as we were fast getting out of the lee of the land – still I was ashamed to betray any trepidation, and for almost half an hour maintained a resolute silence. I could stand it no longer, however, and spoke to Augustus about the propriety of turning back. As before, it was nearly a minute before he made answer, or took any notice of my suggestion. "By and by," said he at length. "Time enough – home by and by." I had expected a similar reply, but there was something in the tone of these words which filled me with an indescribable feeling of dread. I again looked at the speaker attentively. His lips were perfectly livid, and his knees shook so violently together that he seemed scarcely able to stand. "For God's sake, Augustus," I screamed, now heartily frightened, "what ails you? What is the matter? What *are* you going to do?" "Matter!" he stammered, in the greatest apparent surprise, letting go the tiller at the same moment, and falling forward into the bottom of the boat. "Matter... why, nothing is the... matter... going home... d-d-don't you see?" The whole truth now flashed upon me. I flew to him and raised him up. He was drunk – beastly drunk – he could no longer either stand, speak or see. His eyes were perfectly glazed, and as I let him go in the extremity of my despair, he rolled like a mere log into the bilge water,* from which I had lifted him. It was evident that, during the evening, he had drunk far more than I suspected, and that his conduct in bed had been the result of a highly concentrated state of intoxication – a state which, like madness, frequently enables the victim to imitate the outward demeanour of one in perfect possession of his senses. The coolness of the night air, how-ever, had had its usual effect – the mental energy began to yield before its influence – and the confused perception which he no doubt then had of his perilous situation had assisted in hastening the catastrophe. He was now thoroughly insensible, and there was no probability that he would be otherwise for many hours.

It is hardly possible to conceive the extremity of my terror. The fumes of the wine lately taken had evaporated, leaving me doubly timid and irresolute. I knew that I was altogether incapable of managing the boat, and that a fierce wind and strong ebb tide were hurrying us to destruction. A storm was evidently gathering behind us; we had neither compass nor provisions; and it was clear that, if we held our present course, we should

be out of sight of land before daybreak. These thoughts, with a crowd of others equally fearful, flashed through my mind with a bewildering rapidity, and for some moments paralysed me beyond the possibility of making any exertion. The boat was going through the water at a terrible rate – full before the wind – no reef in either jib or mainsail* – running her bows* completely under the foam. It was a thousand wonders she did not broach to* – Augustus having let go the tiller, as I said before, and I being too much agitated to think of taking it myself. By good luck, however, she kept steady, and gradually I recovered some degree of presence of mind. Still the wind was increasing fearfully, and whenever we rose from a plunge forward, the sea behind fell combing over our counter,* and deluged us with water. I was so utterly benumbed, too, in every limb, as to be nearly unconscious of sensation. At length I summoned up the resolution of despair, and rushing to the mainsail let it go by the run.* As might have been expected, it flew over the bows, and, getting drenched with water, carried away the mast short off by the board.* This latter accident alone saved me from instant destruction. Under the jib only,* I now boomed along before the wind, shipping heavy seas occasionally over the counter, but relieved from the terror of immediate death. I took the helm, and breathed with greater freedom as I found that there yet remained to us a chance of ultimate escape. Augustus still lay senseless in the bottom of the boat, and as there was imminent danger of his drowning (the water being nearly a foot deep just where he fell), I contrived to raise him partially up, and keep him in a sitting position, by passing a rope round his waist, and lashing it to a ringbolt in the deck of the cuddy. Having thus arranged everything as well as I could in my chilled and agitated condition, I recommended myself to God, and made up my mind to bear whatever might happen with all the fortitude in my power.

Hardly had I come to this resolution when, suddenly, a loud and long scream or yell, as if from the throats of a thousand demons, seemed to pervade the whole atmosphere around and above the boat. Never while I live shall I forget the intense agony of terror I experienced at that moment. My hair stood erect on my head – I felt the blood congealing in my veins – my heart ceased utterly to beat, and without having once raised my eyes to learn the source of my alarm, I tumbled headlong and insensible upon the body of my fallen companion.

I found myself, upon reviving, in the cabin of a large whaling ship (the *Penguin*) bound to Nantucket. Several persons were standing over me, and Augustus, paler than death, was busily occupied in chafing my

hands. Upon seeing me open my eyes, his exclamations of gratitude and joy excited alternate laughter and tears from the rough-looking personages who were present. The mystery of our being in existence was now soon explained. We had been run down by the whaling ship, which was close-hauled,* beating up to Nantucket with every sail she could venture to set, and consequently running almost at right angles to our own course. Several men were on the lookout forward, but did not perceive our boat until it was an impossibility to avoid coming in contact – their shouts of warning upon seeing us were what so terribly alarmed me. The huge ship, I was told, rode immediately over us with as much ease as our own little vessel would have passed over a feather, and without the least perceptible impediment to her progress. Not a scream arose from the deck of the victim: there was a slight grating sound to be heard mingling with the roar of wind and water, as the frail bark which was swallowed up rubbed for a moment along the keel of her destroyer – but this was all. Thinking our boat (which it will be remembered was dismasted) some mere shell cut adrift as useless, the captain (Captain E.T.V. Block, of New London*) was for proceeding on his course without troubling himself further about the matter. Luckily, there were two of the lookout who swore positively to having seen some person at our helm, and represented the possibility of yet saving him. A discussion ensued, when Block grew angry, and, after a while, said that it was no business of his to be eternally watching for eggshells; that the ship should *not* put about for any such nonsense, and if there was a man run down, it was nobody's fault but his own – he might drown and be d—d – or some language to that effect. Henderson, the first mate, now took the matter up, being justly indignant, as well as the whole ship's crew, at a speech evincing so base a degree of heartless atrocity. He spoke plainly, seeing himself upheld by the men, told the captain he considered him a fit subject for the gallows, and that he would disobey his orders if he were hanged for it the moment he set his foot on shore. He strode aft, jostling Block (who turned pale and made no answer) on one side, and, seizing the helm, gave the word, in a firm voice, "*Hard-a-lee!*" The men flew to their posts, and the ship went cleverly about. All this had occupied nearly five minutes, and it was supposed to be hardly within the bounds of possibility that any individual could be saved – allowing any to have been on board the boat. Yet, as the reader has seen, both Augustus and myself were rescued, and our deliverance seemed to have been brought about by two of those almost inconceivable pieces of good fortune which are attributed by the wise and pious to the special interference of Providence.

While the ship was yet in stays,* the mate lowered the jolly-boat* and jumped into her with the very two men, I believe, who spoke up as having seen me at the helm. They had just left the lee of the vessel (the moon still shining brightly) when she made a long and heavy roll to windward, and Henderson, at the same moment, starting up in his seat, bawled out to his crew to "back water". He would say nothing else – repeating his cry impatiently: "*Back water! Back water!*" The men put back as speedily as possible, but by this time the ship had gone round, and gotten fully under headway, although all hands on board were making great exertions to take in sail. In despite of the danger of the attempt, the mate clung to the main-chains* as soon as they came within his reach. Another huge lurch now brought the starboard side of the vessel out of water nearly as far as her keel, when the cause of his anxiety was rendered obvious enough. The body of a man was seen to be affixed in the most singular manner to the smooth and shining bottom (the *Penguin* was coppered and copper-fastened), and beating violently against it with every movement of the hull. After several ineffectual efforts, made during the lurches of the ship, and at the imminent risk of swamping the boat, I was finally disengaged from my perilous situation and taken on board – for the body proved to be my own. It appeared that one of the timber bolts having started and broken a passage through the copper, it had arrested my progress as I passed under the ship, and fastened me in so extraordinary a manner to her bottom. The head of the bolt had made its way through the collar of the green baize jacket I had on, and through the back part of my neck, forcing itself out between two sinews and just below the right ear. I was immediately put to bed – although life seemed to be totally extinct. There was no surgeon on board. The captain, however, treated me with every attention – to make amends, I presume, in the eyes of his crew, for his atrocious behaviour in the previous portion of the adventure.

In the mean time, Henderson had again put off from the ship, although the wind was now blowing almost a hurricane. He had not been gone many minutes when he fell in with some fragments of our boat, and shortly afterwards one of the men with him asserted that he could distinguish a cry for help at intervals amid the roaring of the tempest. This induced the hardy seamen to persevere in their search for more than half an hour, although repeated signals to return were made them by Captain Block, and although every moment on the water in so frail a boat was fraught to them with the most imminent and deadly peril. Indeed, it is nearly impossible to conceive how the small jolly they were in could have escaped destruction

for a single instant. She was built, however, for the whaling service, and was fitted, as I have since had reason to believe, with air boxes,* in the manner of some lifeboats used on the coast of Wales.

After searching in vain for about the period of time just mentioned, it was determined to get back to the ship. They had scarcely made this resolve when a feeble cry arose from a dark object which floated rapidly by. They pursued and soon overtook it. It proved to be the entire deck of the *Ariel*'s cuddy. Augustus was struggling near it, apparently in the last agonies. Upon getting hold of him it was found that he was attached by a rope to the floating timber. This rope, it will be remembered, I had myself tied round his waist, and made fast to a ringbolt, for the purpose of keeping him in an upright position, and my so doing, it appeared, had been ultimately the means of preserving his life. The *Ariel* was slightly put together, and in going down her frame naturally went to pieces; the deck of the cuddy, as might be expected, was lifted, by the force of the water rushing in, entirely from the main timbers, and floated (with other fragments, no doubt) to the surface – Augustus was buoyed up with it, and thus escaped a terrible death.

It was more than an hour after being taken on board the *Penguin* before he could give any account of himself, or be made to comprehend the nature of the accident which had befallen our boat. At length he became thoroughly aroused, and spoke much of his sensations while in the water. Upon his first attaining any degree of consciousness, he found himself beneath the surface, whirling round and round with inconceivable rapidity, and with a rope wrapped in three or four folds tightly about his neck. In an instant afterwards he felt himself going rapidly upwards, when, his head striking violently against a hard substance, he again relapsed into insensibility. Upon once more reviving he was in fuller possession of his reason – this was still, however, in the greatest degree clouded and confused. He now knew that some accident had occurred, and that he was in the water, although his mouth was above the surface, and he could breathe with some freedom. Possibly, at this period the deck was drifting rapidly before the wind, and drawing him after it, as he floated upon his back. Of course, as long as he could have retained this position, it would have been nearly impossible that he should be drowned. Presently a surge threw him directly athwart the deck, and this post he endeavoured to maintain, screaming at intervals for help. Just before he was discovered by Mr Henderson, he had been obliged to relax his hold through exhaustion, and, falling into the sea, had given himself up for lost. During the whole period of his struggles he had not

the faintest recollection of the *Ariel*, nor of any matters in connection with the source of his disaster. A vague feeling of terror and despair had taken entire possession of his faculties. When he was finally picked up, every power of his mind had failed him, and, as before said, it was nearly an hour after getting on board the *Penguin* before he became fully aware of his condition. In regard to myself, I was resuscitated from a state bordering very nearly upon death (and after every other means had been tried in vain for three hours and a half) by vigorous friction with flannels bathed in hot oil – a proceeding suggested by Augustus. The wound in my neck, although of an ugly appearance, proved of little real consequence, and I soon recovered from its effects.

The *Penguin* got into port about nine o'clock in the morning, after encountering one of the severest gales ever experienced off Nantucket. Both Augustus and myself managed to appear at Mr Barnard's in time for breakfast – which, luckily, was somewhat late, owing to the party overnight. I suppose all at the table were too much fatigued themselves to notice our jaded appearance – of course, it would not have borne a very rigid scrutiny. Schoolboys, however, can accomplish wonders in the way of deception, and I verily believe not one of our friends in Nantucket had the slightest suspicion that the terrible story told by some sailors in town of their having run down a vessel at sea and drowned some thirty or forty poor devils had reference either to the *Ariel*, my companion or myself. We two have since very frequently talked the matter over – but never without a shudder. In one of our conversations Augustus frankly confessed to me that in his whole life he had at no time experienced so excruciating a sense of dismay as when on board our little boat he first discovered the extent of his intoxication, and felt himself sinking beneath its influence.

CHAPTER II

In no affairs of mere prejudice, *pro* or *con*, do we deduce inferences with entire certainty, even from the most simple data. It might be supposed that a catastrophe such as I have just related would have effectually cooled my incipient passion for the sea. On the contrary, I never experienced a more ardent longing for the wild adventures incident to the life of a navigator than within a week after our miraculous deliverance. This short period proved amply long enough to erase from my memory the shadows, and

bring out in vivid light all the pleasurably exciting points of colour, all the picturesqueness, of the late perilous accident. My conversations with Augustus grew daily more frequent and more intensely full of interest. He had a manner of relating his stories of the ocean (more than one half of which I now suspect to have been sheer fabrications) well adapted to have weight with one of my enthusiastic temperament and somewhat gloomy although glowing imagination. It is strange, too, that he most strongly enlisted my feelings in behalf of the life of a seaman when he depicted his more terrible moments of suffering and despair. For the bright side of the painting I had a limited sympathy. My visions were of shipwreck and famine; of death or captivity among barbarian hordes; of a lifetime dragged out in sorrow and tears upon some grey and desolate rock, in an ocean unapproachable and unknown. Such visions or desires – for they amounted to desires – are common, I have since been assured, to the whole numerous race of the melancholy among men; at the time of which I speak I regarded them only as prophetic glimpses of a destiny which I felt myself in a measure bound to fulfil. Augustus thoroughly entered into my state of mind. It is probable, indeed, that our intimate communion had resulted in a partial interchange of character.

About eighteen months after the period of the *Ariel*'s disaster, the firm of Lloyd & Vredenburgh (a house connected in some manner with the Messieurs Enderby, I believe, of Liverpool*) were engaged in repairing and fitting out the brig *Grampus** for a whaling voyage. She was an old hulk, and scarcely seaworthy when all was done to her that could be done. I hardly know why she was chosen in preference to other good vessels belonging to the same owners – but so it was. Mr Barnard was appointed to command her, and Augustus was going with him. While the brig was getting ready, he frequently urged upon me the excellency of the opportunity now offered for indulging my desire of travel. He found me by no means an unwilling listener – yet the matter could not be so easily arranged. My father made no direct opposition, but my mother went into hysterics at the bare mention of the design, and, more than all, my grandfather, from whom I expected much, vowed to cut me off with a shilling if I should ever broach the subject to him again. These difficulties, however, so far from abating my desire, only added fuel to the flame. I determined to go at all hazards, and, having made known my intention to Augustus, we set about arranging a plan by which it might be accomplished. In the mean time I forbore speaking to any of my relations in regard to the voyage, and, as I busied myself ostensibly with my usual studies, it was supposed that I

had abandoned the design. I have since frequently examined my conduct on this occasion with sentiments of displeasure as well as of surprise. The intense hypocrisy I made use of for the furtherance of my project – an hypocrisy pervading every word and action of my life for so long a period of time – could only have been rendered tolerable to myself by the wild and burning expectation with which I looked forward to the fulfilment of my long-cherished visions of travel.

In pursuance of my scheme of deception, I was necessarily obliged to leave much to the management of Augustus, who was employed for the greater part of every day on board the *Grampus*, attending to some arrangements for his father in the cabin and cabin hold. At night, however, we were sure to have a conference, and talk over our hopes. After nearly a month passed in this manner, without our hitting upon any plan we thought likely to succeed, he told me at last that he had determined upon everything necessary. I had a relation living in New Bedford, a Mr Ross, at whose house I was in the habit of spending occasionally two or three weeks at a time. The brig was to sail about the middle of June (June 1827), and it was agreed that, a day or two before her putting to sea, my father was to receive a note, as usual, from Mr Ross, asking me to come over and spend a fortnight with Robert and Emmet (his sons). Augustus charged himself with the inditing of this note and getting it delivered. Having set out as supposed, for New Bedford, I was then to report myself to my companion, who would contrive a hiding place for me in the *Grampus*. This hiding place, he assured me, would be rendered sufficiently comfortable for a residence of many days, during which I was not to make my appearance. When the brig had proceeded so far on her course as to make any turning back a matter out of question, I should then, he said, be formally installed in all the comforts of the cabin – and as to his father, he would only laugh heartily at the joke. Vessels enough would be met with by which a letter might be sent home explaining the adventure to my parents.

The middle of June at length arrived, and everything had been matured. The note was written and delivered, and on a Monday morning I left the house for the New Bedford packet, as supposed. I went, however, straight to Augustus, who was waiting for me at the corner of a street. It had been our original plan that I should keep out of the way until dark, and then slip on board the brig, but, as there was now a thick fog in our favour, it was agreed to lose no time in secreting me. Augustus led the way to the wharf, and I followed at a little distance, enveloped in a thick seaman's cloak, which he had brought with him, so that my person might not be

easily recognized. Just as we turned the second corner, after passing Mr Edmund's well, who should appear, standing right in front of me, and looking me full in the face, but old Mr Peterson, my grandfather. "Why, bless my soul, Gordon," said he after a long pause. "Why, why – *whose* dirty cloak is that you have on?" "Sir!" I replied, assuming, as well as I could, in the exigency of the moment, an air of offended surprise, and talking in the gruffest of all imaginable tones. "Sir! You are a summat mistaken – my name, in the first place, bee'nt nothing at all like Goddin, and I'd want you for to know better, you blackguard, than to call my new obercoat a darty one." For my life I could hardly refrain from screaming with laughter at the odd manner in which the old gentleman received this handsome rebuke. He started back two or three steps, turned first pale and then excessively red, threw up his spectacles, then, putting them down, ran full tilt at me, with his umbrella uplifted. He stopped short, however, in his career, as if struck with a sudden recollection, and presently, turning round, hobbled off down the street, shaking all the while with rage, and muttering between his teeth: "Won't do – new glasses – thought it was Gordon – d—d good-for-nothing saltwater Long Tom."*

After this narrow escape we proceeded with greater caution, and arrived at our point of destination in safety. There were only one or two of the hands on board, and these were busy forward, doing something to the forecastle combings.* Captain Barnard, we knew very well, was engaged at Lloyd & Vredenburgh's, and would remain there until late in the evening, so we had little to apprehend on his account. Augustus went first up the vessel's side, and in a short while I followed him, without being noticed by the men at work. We proceeded at once into the cabin, and found no person there. It was fitted up in the most comfortable style – a thing somewhat unusual in a whaling vessel. There were four very excellent staterooms, with wide and convenient berths. There was also a large stove, I took notice, and a remarkably thick and valuable carpet covering the floor of both the cabin and staterooms. The ceiling was full seven feet high, and, in short, everything appeared of a more roomy and agreeable nature than I had anticipated. Augustus, however, would allow me but little time for observation, insisting upon the necessity of my concealing myself as soon as possible. He led the way into his own stateroom, which was on the starboard side of the brig, and next to the bulkheads. Upon entering, he closed the door and bolted it. I thought I had never seen a nicer little room than the one in which I now found myself. It was about ten feet long, and had only one berth, which, as I said before, was wide

and convenient. In that portion of the closet nearest the bulkheads there was a space of four feet square, containing a table, a chair and a set of hanging shelves full of books, chiefly books of voyages and travels. There were many other little comforts in the room, among which I ought not to forget a kind of safe or refrigerator, in which Augustus pointed out to me a host of delicacies, both in the eating and drinking department.

He now pressed with his knuckles upon a certain spot of the carpet in one corner of the space just mentioned, letting me know that a portion of the flooring, about sixteen inches square, had been neatly cut out and again adjusted. As he pressed, this portion rose up at one end sufficiently to allow the passage of his finger beneath. In this manner he raised the mouth of the trap (to which the carpet was still fastened by tacks), and I found that it led into the after-hold. He next lit a small taper by means of a phosphorus match, and, placing the light in a dark lantern,* descended with it through the opening, bidding me follow. I did so, and he then pulled the cover upon the hole, by means of a nail driven into the underside – the carpet, of course, resuming its original position on the floor of the stateroom, and all traces of the aperture being concealed.

The taper gave out so feeble a ray that it was with the greatest difficulty I could grope my way through the confused mass of lumber among which I now found myself. By degrees, however, my eyes became accustomed to the gloom, and I proceeded with less trouble, holding on to the skirts of my friend's coat. He brought me, at length, after creeping and winding through innumerable narrow passages, to an iron-bound box, such as is used sometimes for packing fine earthenware. It was nearly four feet high, and full six long, but very narrow. Two large empty oil casks lay on the top of it, and above these, again, a vast quantity of straw matting, piled up as high as the floor of the cabin. In every other direction around was wedged as closely as possible, even up to the ceiling, a complete chaos of almost every species of ship furniture, together with a heterogeneous medley of crates, hampers, barrels and bales, so that it seemed a matter no less than miraculous that we had discovered any passage at all to the box. I afterwards found that Augustus had purposely arranged the stowage in this hold with a view to affording me a thorough concealment, having had only one assistant in the labour, a man not going out in the brig.

My companion now showed me that one of the ends of the box could be removed at pleasure. He slipped it aside and displayed the interior, at which I was excessively amused. A mattress from one of the cabin berths covered the whole of its bottom, and it contained almost every article of

mere comfort which could be crowded into so small a space, allowing me, at the same time, sufficient room for my accommodation, either in a sitting position or lying at full length. Among other things, there were some books, pen, ink and paper, three blankets, a large jug full of water, a keg of sea biscuit,* three or four immense Bologna sausages, an enormous ham, a cold leg of roast mutton and half a dozen bottles of cordials and liqueurs. I proceeded immediately to take possession of my little apartment, and this with feelings of higher satisfaction, I am sure, than any monarch ever experienced upon entering a new palace. Augustus now pointed out to me the method of fastening the open end of the box, and then, holding the taper close to the deck, showed me a piece of dark whipcord lying along it. This, he said, extended from my hiding place throughout all the necessary windings among the lumber, to a nail which was driven into the deck of the hold, immediately beneath the trapdoor leading into his stateroom. By means of this cord I should be enabled readily to trace my way out without his guidance, provided any unlooked-for accident should render such a step necessary. He now took his departure, leaving with me the lantern, together with a copious supply of tapers and phosphorus, and promising to pay me a visit as often as he could contrive to do so without observation. This was on 17th June.

I remained three days and nights (as nearly as I could guess) in my hiding place without getting out of it at all, except twice for the purpose of stretching my limbs by standing erect between two crates just opposite the opening. During the whole period I saw nothing of Augustus, but this occasioned me little uneasiness, as I knew the brig was expected to put to sea every hour, and in the bustle he would not easily find opportunities of coming down to me. At length I heard the trap open and shut, and presently he called in a low voice, asking if all was well, and if there was anything I wanted. "Nothing," I replied. "I am as comfortable as can be – when will the brig sail?" "She will be under weigh* in less than half an hour," he answered. "I came to let you know, and for fear you should be uneasy at my absence. I shall not have a chance of coming down again for some time – perhaps for three or four days more. All is going on right aboveboard.* After I go up and close the trap, do you creep along by the whipcord to where the nail is driven in. You will find my watch there – it may be useful to you, as you have no daylight to keep time by. I suppose you can't tell how long you have been buried – only three days – this is the twentieth. I would bring the watch to your box, but am afraid of being missed." With this he went up.

In about an hour after he had gone I distinctly felt the brig in motion, and congratulated myself upon having at length fairly commenced a voyage. Satisfied with this idea, I determined to make my mind as easy as possible, and await the course of events until I should be permitted to exchange the box for the more roomy, although hardly more comfortable, accommodations of the cabin. My first care was to get the watch. Leaving the taper burning, I groped along in the dark, following the cord through windings innumerable, in some of which I discovered that, after toiling a long distance, I was brought back within a foot or two of a former position. At length I reached the nail, and, securing the object of my journey, returned with it in safety. I now looked over the books which had been so thoughtfully provided, and selected the expedition of Lewis and Clark to the mouth of the Columbia.* With this I amused myself for some time, when, growing sleepy, I extinguished the light with great care, and soon fell into a sound slumber.

Upon awaking I felt strangely confused in mind, and some time elapsed before I could bring to recollection all the various circumstances of my situation. By degrees, however, I remembered all. Striking a light, I looked at the watch, but it was run down, and there were, consequently, no means of determining how long I slept. My limbs were greatly cramped, and I was forced to relieve them by standing between the crates. Presently feeling an almost ravenous appetite, I bethought myself of the cold mutton, some of which I had eaten just before going to sleep, and found excellent. What was my astonishment at discovering it to be in a state of absolute putrefaction! This circumstance occasioned me great disquietude – for, connecting it with the disorder of mind I experienced upon awaking, I began to suppose that I must have slept for an inordinately long period of time. The close atmosphere of the hold might have something to do with this, and might, in the end, be productive of the most serious results. My head ached excessively; I fancied that I drew every breath with difficulty; and, in short, I was oppressed with a multitude of gloomy feelings. Still I could not venture to make any disturbance by opening the trap or otherwise, and, having wound up the watch, contented myself as well as possible.

Throughout the whole of the next tedious twenty-four hours no person came to my relief, and I could not help accusing Augustus of the grossest inattention. What alarmed me chiefly was that the water in my jug was reduced to about half a pint, and I was suffering much from thirst, having eaten freely of the Bologna sausages after the loss of my mutton. I became very uneasy, and could no longer take any interest in my books.

I was overpowered, too, with a desire to sleep, yet trembled at the thought of indulging it, lest there might exist some pernicious influence, like that of burning charcoal, in the confined air of the hold. In the mean time the roll of the brig told me that we were far in the main ocean, and a dull humming sound, which reached my ears as if from an immense distance, convinced me no ordinary gale was blowing. I could not imagine a reason for the absence of Augustus. We were surely far enough advanced on our voyage to allow of my going up. Some accident might have happened to him – but I could think of none which would account for his suffering me to remain so long a prisoner, except, indeed, his having suddenly died or fallen overboard, and upon this idea I could not dwell with any degree of patience. It was possible that we had been baffled by headwinds, and were still in the near vicinity of Nantucket. This notion, however, I was forced to abandon, for, such being the case, the brig must have frequently gone about, and I was entirely satisfied, from her continual inclination to the larboard,* that she had been sailing all along with a steady breeze on her starboard quarter. Besides, granting that we were still in the neighbour-hood of the island, why should not Augustus have visited me and informed me of the circumstance? Pondering in this manner upon the difficulties of my solitary and cheerless condition, I resolved to wait yet another twenty-four hours, when, if no relief were obtained, I would make my way to the trap, and endeavour either to hold a parley with my friend, or get at least a little fresh air through the opening, and a further supply of water from his stateroom. While occupied with this thought, however, I fell, in spite of every exertion to the contrary, into a state of profound sleep, or rather stupor. My dreams were of the most terrific description. Every species of calamity and horror befell me. Among other miseries, I was smothered to death between huge pillows, by demons of the most ghastly and ferocious aspect. Immense serpents held me in their embrace, and looked earnestly in my face with their fearfully shining eyes. Then deserts, limitless, and of the most forlorn and awe-inspiring character, spread themselves out before me. Immensely tall trunks of trees, grey and leafless, rose up in endless succession as far as the eye could reach. Their roots were concealed in wide-spreading morasses, whose dreary water lay intensely black, still and altogether terrible beneath. And the strange trees seemed endowed with a human vitality, and waving to and fro their skeleton arms, were crying to the silent waters for mercy, in the shrill and piercing accents of the most acute agony and despair. The scene changed, and I stood, naked and alone, amid the burning sand plains of Zahara.* At my feet lay crouched a fierce

lion of the tropics. Suddenly his wild eyes opened and fell upon me. With a convulsive bound he sprang to his feet, and laid bare his horrible teeth. In another instant there burst from his red throat a roar like the thunder of the firmament, and I fell impetuously to the earth. Stifling in a paroxysm of terror, I at last found myself partially awake. My dream, then, was not all a dream. Now, at least, I was in possession of my senses. The paws of some huge and real monster were pressing heavily upon my bosom – his hot breath was in my ear – and his white and ghastly fangs were gleaming upon me through the gloom.

Had a thousand lives hung upon the movement of a limb or the utterance of a syllable, I could have neither stirred nor spoken. The beast, whatever it was, retained his position without attempting any immediate violence, while I lay in an utterly helpless, and, I fancied, a dying condition beneath him. I felt that my powers of body and mind were fast leaving me – in a word, that I was perishing, and perishing of sheer fright. My brain swam – I grew deadly sick – my vision failed – even the glaring eyeballs above me grew dim. Making a last strong effort, I at length breathed a faint ejaculation to God, and resigned myself to die. The sound of my voice seemed to arouse all the latent fury of the animal. He precipitated himself at full length upon my body, but what was my astonishment when, with a long and low whine, he commenced licking my face and hands with the greatest eagerness, and with the most extravagant demonstrations of affection and joy! I was bewildered, utterly lost in amazement – but I could not forget the peculiar whine of my Newfoundland dog Tiger, and the odd manner of his caresses I well knew. It was he. I experienced a sudden rush of blood to my temples – a giddy and overpowering sense of deliverance and reanimation. I rose hurriedly from the mattress upon which I had been lying, and, throwing myself upon the neck of my faithful follower and friend, relieved the long oppression of my bosom in a flood of the most passionate tears.

As upon a former occasion, my conceptions were in a state of the greatest indistinctness and confusion after leaving the mattress. For a long time I found it nearly impossible to connect any ideas, but, by very slow degrees, my thinking faculties returned, and I again called to memory the several incidents of my condition. For the presence of Tiger I tried in vain to account, and, after busying myself with a thousand different conjectures respecting him, was forced to content myself with rejoicing that he was with me to share my dreary solitude, and render me comfort by his caresses. Most people love their dogs – but for Tiger I had an affection far more

ardent than common, and never, certainly, did any creature more truly deserve it. For seven years he had been my inseparable companion, and in a multitude of instances had given evidence of all the noble qualities for which we value the animal. I had rescued him, when a puppy, from the clutches of a malignant little villain in Nantucket, who was leading him, with a rope around his neck, to the water, and the grown dog repaid the obligation, about three years afterwards, by saving me from the bludgeon of a street robber.

Getting now hold of the watch, I found, upon applying it to my ear, that it had again run down, but at this I was not at all surprised, being convinced, from the peculiar state of my feelings, that I had slept, as before, for a very long period of time – how long, it was of course impossible to say. I was burning up with fever, and my thirst was almost intolerable. I felt about the box for my little remaining supply of water, for I had no light, the taper having burnt to the socket of the lantern, and the phosphorus box not coming readily to hand. Upon finding the jug, however, I discovered it to be empty – Tiger, no doubt, having been tempted to drink it, as well as to devour the remnant of mutton, the bone of which lay, well picked, by the opening of the box. The spoilt meat I could well spare, but my heart sank as I thought of the water. I was feeble in the extreme – so much so that I shook all over, as with an ague, at the slightest movement or exertion. To add to my troubles, the brig was pitching and rolling with great violence, and the oil casks which lay upon my box were in momentary danger of falling down, so as to block up the only way of ingress or egress. I felt, also, terrible sufferings from seasickness. These considerations determined me to make my way, at all hazards, to the trap, and obtain immediate relief, before I should be incapacitated from doing so altogether. Having come to this resolve, I again felt about for the phosphorus box and tapers. The former I found after some little trouble, but, not discovering the tapers as soon as I had expected (for I remembered very nearly the spot in which I had placed them), I gave up the search for the present and, bidding Tiger lie quiet, began at once my journey towards the trap.

In this attempt my great feebleness became more than ever apparent. It was with the utmost difficulty I could crawl along at all, and very frequently my limbs sank suddenly from beneath me, when, falling prostrate on my face, I would remain for some minutes in a state bordering on insensibility. Still I struggled forward by slow degrees, dreading every moment that I should swoon amid the narrow and intricate windings of the lumber, in which event I had nothing but death to expect as the result. At length,

upon making a push forward with all the energy I could command, I struck my forehead violently against the sharp corner of an iron-bound crate. The accident only stunned me for a few moments, but I found, to my inexpressible grief, that the quick and violent roll of the vessel had thrown the crate entirely across my path, so as effectually to block up the passage. With my utmost exertions I could not move it a single inch from its position, it being closely wedged in among the surrounding boxes and ship furniture. It became necessary, therefore, enfeebled as I was, either to leave the guidance of the whipcord and seek out a new passage, or to climb over the obstacle, and resume the path on the other side. The former alternative presented too many difficulties and dangers to be thought of without a shudder. In my present weak state of both mind and body, I should infallibly lose my way if I attempted it, and perish miserably amid the dismal and disgusting labyrinths of the hold. I proceeded, therefore, without hesitation, to summon up all my remaining strength and fortitude, and endeavour, as I best might, to clamber over the crate.

Upon standing erect, with this end in view, I found the undertaking even a more serious task than my fears had led me to imagine. On each side of the narrow passage arose a complete wall of various heavy lumber, which the least blunder on my part might be the means of bringing down upon my head, or, if this accident did not occur, the path might be effectually blocked up against my return by the descending mass, as it was in front by the obstacle there. The crate itself was a long and unwieldy box, upon which no foothold could be obtained. In vain I attempted, by every means in my power, to reach the top, with the hope of being thus enabled to draw myself up. Had I succeeded in reaching it, it is certain that my strength would have proved utterly inadequate to the task of getting over, and it was better in every respect that I failed. At length, in a desperate effort to force the crate from its ground, I felt a strong vibration in the side next me. I thrust my hand eagerly to the edge of the planks, and found that a very large one was loose. With my pocket knife, which, luckily, I had with me, I succeeded, after great labour, in prying it entirely off, and, getting through the aperture, discovered, to my exceeding joy, that there were no boards on the opposite side – in other words, that the top was wanting, it being the bottom through which I had forced my way. I now met with no important difficulty in proceeding along the line until I finally reached the nail. With a beating heart I stood erect, and with a gentle touch pressed against the cover of the trap. It did not rise as soon as I had expected, and I pressed it with somewhat more determination, still dreading lest some other person

than Augustus might be in his stateroom. The door, however, to my aston-
ishment, remained steady, and I became somewhat uneasy, for I knew that
it had formerly required little or no effort to remove it. I pushed it strongly
– it was nevertheless firm; with all my strength – it still did not give way;
with rage, with fury, with despair – it set at defiance my utmost efforts, and
it was evident, from the unyielding nature of the resistance, that the hole
had either been discovered and effectually nailed up, or that some immense
weight had been placed upon it which it was useless to think of removing.

My sensations were those of extreme horror and dismay. In vain I
attempted to reason on the probable cause of my being thus entombed.
I could summon up no connected chain of reflection, and, sinking on the
floor, gave way, unresistingly, to the most gloomy imaginings, in which
the dreadful deaths of thirst, famine, suffocation and premature inter-
ment crowded upon me as the prominent disasters to be encountered. At
length there returned to me some portion of presence of mind. I arose,
and felt with my fingers for the seams or cracks of the aperture. Having
found them, I examined them closely to ascertain if they emitted any light
from the stateroom, but none was visible. I then forced the blade of my
penknife* through them, until I met with some hard obstacle. Scraping
against it, I discovered it to be a solid mass of iron, which, from its peculiar
wavy feel as I passed the blade along it, I concluded to be a chain-cable.
The only course now left me was to retrace my way to the box, and there
either yield to my sad fate, or try so to tranquillize my mind as to admit
of my arranging some plan of escape. I immediately set about the attempt,
and succeeded, after innumerable difficulties, in getting back. As I sank,
utterly exhausted, upon the mattress, Tiger threw himself at full length
by my side, and seemed as if desirous, by his caresses, of consoling me in
my troubles, and urging me to bear them with fortitude.

The singularity of his behaviour at length forcibly arrested my attention.
After licking my face and hands for some minutes, he would suddenly
cease doing so, and utter a low whine. Upon reaching out my hand towards
him, I then invariably found him lying on his back, with his paws uplifted.
This conduct, so frequently repeated, appeared strange, and I could in no
manner account for it. As the dog seemed distressed, I concluded that he
had received some injury, and, taking his paws in my hands, I examined
them one by one, but found no sign of any hurt. I then supposed him
hungry, and gave him a large piece of ham, which he devoured with avid-
ity – afterwards, however, resuming his extraordinary manoeuvres. I now
imagined that he was suffering, like myself, the torments of thirst, and was

about adopting this conclusion as the true one, when the idea occurred to me that I had as yet only examined his paws, and that there might possibly be a wound upon some portion of his body or head. The latter I felt carefully over, but found nothing. On passing my hand, however, along his back, I perceived a slight erection of the hair extending completely across it. Probing this with my finger, I discovered a string, and, tracing it up, found that it encircled the whole body. Upon a closer scrutiny, I came across a small slip of what had the feeling of letter paper, through which the string had been fastened in such a manner as to bring it immediately beneath the left shoulder of the animal.

CHAPTER III

The thought instantly occurred to me that the paper was a note from Augustus, and that, some unaccountable accident having happened to prevent his relieving me from my dungeon, he had devised this method of acquainting me with the true state of affairs. Trembling with eagerness, I now commenced another search for my phosphorus matches and tapers. I had a confused recollection of having put them carefully away just before falling asleep, and, indeed, previously to my last journey to the trap, I had been able to remember the exact spot where I had deposited them. But now I endeavoured in vain to call it to mind, and busied myself for a full hour in a fruitless and vexatious search for the missing articles – never, surely, was there a more tantalizing state of anxiety and suspense. At length, while groping about, with my head close to the ballast, near the opening of the box, and outside of it, I perceived a faint glimmering of light in the direction of the steerage. Greatly surprised, I endeavoured to make my way towards it, as it appeared to be but a few feet from my position. Scarcely had I moved with this intention when I lost sight of the glimmer entirely, and, before I could bring it into view again, was obliged to feel along by the box until I had exactly resumed my original situation. Now, moving my head with caution to and fro, I found that, by proceeding slowly, with great care, in an opposite direction to that in which I had at first started, I was enabled to draw near the light, still keeping it in view. Presently I came directly upon it (having squeezed my way through innumerable narrow windings), and found that it proceeded from some fragments of my matches lying in an empty barrel turned upon its side. I was wondering how they came in such a place when my hand fell upon

two or three pieces of taper wax, which had been evidently mumbled* by the dog. I concluded at once that he had devoured the whole of my supply of candles, and I felt hopeless of being ever able to read the note of Augustus. The small remnants of the wax were so mashed up among other rubbish in the barrel that I despaired of deriving any service from them, and left them as they were. The phosphorus, of which there was only a speck or two, I gathered up as well as I could, and returned with it, after much difficulty, to my box, where Tiger had all the while remained.

What to do next I could not tell. The hold was so intensely dark that I could not see my hand, however close I would hold it to my face. The white slip of paper could barely be discerned, and not even that when I looked at it directly; by turning the exterior portions of the retina towards it – that is to say, by surveying it slightly askance – I found that it became in some measure perceptible. Thus the gloom of my prison may be imagined, and the note of my friend, if indeed it were a note from him, seemed only likely to throw me into further trouble, by disquieting to no purpose my already enfeebled and agitated mind. In vain I revolved in my brain a multitude of absurd expedients for procuring light – such expedients precisely as a man in the perturbed sleep occasioned by opium would be apt to fall upon for a similar purpose – each and all of which appear by turns to the dreamer the most reasonable and the most preposterous of conceptions, just as the reasoning or imaginative faculties flicker, alternately, one above the other. At last an idea occurred to me which seemed rational, and which gave me cause to wonder, very justly, that I had not entertained it before. I placed the slip of paper on the back of a book, and, collecting the fragments of the phosphorus matches which I had brought from the barrel, laid them together upon the paper. I then, with the palm of my hand, rubbed the whole over quickly, yet steadily. A clear light diffused itself immediately throughout the whole surface, and had there been any writing upon it, I should not have experienced the least difficulty, I am sure, in reading it. Not a syllable was there, however – nothing but a dreary and unsatisfactory blank; the illumination died away in a few seconds, and my heart died away within me as it went.

I have before stated more than once that my intellect, for some period prior to this, had been in a condition nearly bordering on idiocy. There were, to be sure, momentary intervals of perfect sanity, and, now and then, even of energy, but these were few. It must be remembered that I had been, for many days certainly, inhaling the almost pestilential atmosphere of a close hold in a whaling vessel, and a long portion of that time but

scantily supplied with water. For the last fourteen or fifteen hours I had none – nor had I slept during that time. Salt provisions of the most exciting kind had been my chief, and, indeed, since the loss of the mutton, my only supply of food, with the exception of the sea biscuit, and these latter were utterly useless to me, as they were too dry and hard to be swallowed in the swollen and parched condition of my throat. I was now in a high state of fever, and in every respect exceedingly ill. This will account for the fact that many miserable hours of despondency elapsed after my last adventure with the phosphorus, before the thought suggested itself that I had examined only one side of the paper. I shall not attempt to describe my feelings of rage (for I believe I was more angry than anything else) when the egregious oversight I had committed flashed suddenly upon my perception. The blunder itself would have been unimportant had not my own folly and impetuosity rendered it otherwise – in my disappointment at not finding some words upon the slip, I had childishly torn it in pieces and thrown it away, it was impossible to say where.

From the worst part of this dilemma I was relieved by the sagacity of Tiger. Having got, after a long search, a small piece of the note, I put it to the dog's nose, and endeavoured to make him understand that he must bring me the rest of it. To my astonishment (for I had taught him none of the usual tricks for which his breed are famous), he seemed to enter at once into my meaning, and, rummaging about for a few moments, soon found another considerable portion. Bringing me this, he paused awhile, and, rubbing his nose against my hand, appeared to be waiting for my approval of what he had done. I patted him on the head, when he immediately made off again. It was now some minutes before he came back – but when he did come, he brought with him a large slip, which proved to be all the paper missing – it having been torn, it seems, only into three pieces. Luckily, I had no trouble in finding what few fragments of the phosphorus were left – being guided by the indistinct glow one or two of the particles still emitted. My difficulties had taught me the necessity of caution, and I now took time to reflect upon what I was about to do. It was very probable, I considered, that some words were written upon that side of the paper which had not been examined – but which side was that? Fitting the pieces together gave me no clue in this respect, although it assured me that the words (if there were any) would be found all on one side, and connected in a proper manner, as written. There was the greater necessity of ascertaining the point in question beyond a doubt, as the phosphorus remaining would be altogether insufficient for a third attempt, should I fail in the one I was

now about to make. I placed the paper on a book as before, and sat for some minutes thoughtfully revolving the matter over in my mind. At last I thought it barely possible that the written side might have some unevenness on its surface, which a delicate sense of feeling might enable me to detect. I determined to make the experiment and passed my finger very carefully over the side which first presented itself – nothing, however, was perceptible, and I turned the paper, adjusting it on the book. I now again carried my forefinger cautiously along, when I was aware of an exceedingly slight, but still discernible glow, which followed as it proceeded. This, I knew, must arise from some very minute remaining particles of the phosphorus with which I had covered the paper in my previous attempt. The other, or underside, then, was that on which lay the writing, if writing there should finally prove to be. Again I turned the note, and went to work as I had previously done. Having rubbed in the phosphorus, a brilliancy ensued as before – but this time several lines of MS in a large hand, and apparently in red ink, became distinctly visible. The glimmer, although sufficiently bright, was but momentary. Still, had I not been too greatly excited, there would have been ample time enough for me to peruse the whole three sentences before me – for I saw there were three. In my anxiety, however, to read all at once, I succeeded only in reading the seven concluding words, which thus appeared: *"blood – your life depends upon lying close."*

Had I been able to ascertain the entire contents of the note – the full meaning of the admonition which my friend had thus attempted to convey – that admonition, even although it should have revealed a story of disaster the most unspeakable, could not, I am firmly convinced, have imbued my mind with one tithe of the harrowing and yet indefinable horror with which I was inspired by the fragmentary warning thus received. And "blood", too, that word of all words – so rife at all times with mystery, and suffering, and terror – how trebly full of import did it now appear, how chillily and heavily (disjointed, as it thus was, from any foregoing words to qualify or render it distinct) did its vague syllables fall, amid the deep gloom of my prison, into the innermost recesses of my soul!

Augustus had, undoubtedly, good reasons for wishing me to remain concealed, and I formed a thousand surmises as to what they could be – but I could think of nothing affording a satisfactory solution of the mystery. Just after returning from my last journey to the trap, and before my attention had been otherwise directed by the singular conduct of Tiger, I had come to the resolution of making myself heard at all events by those on board, or, if I could not succeed in this directly, of trying to cut my way

through the orlop deck.* The half-certainty which I felt of being able to accomplish one of these two purposes in the last emergency had given me courage (which I should not otherwise have had) to endure the evils of my situation. The few words I had been able to read, however, had cut me off from these final resources, and I now, for the first time, felt all the misery of my fate. In a paroxysm of despair I threw myself again upon the mattress, where, for about the period of a day and night, I lay in a kind of stupor, relieved only by momentary intervals of reason and recollection.

At length I once more arose, and busied myself in reflection upon the horrors which encompassed me. For another twenty-four hours it was barely possible that I might exist without water – for a longer time I could not do so. During the first portion of my imprisonment I had made free use of the cordials with which Augustus had supplied me, but they only served to excite fever, without in the least degree assuaging thirst. I had now only about a gill* left, and this was of a species of strong peach liqueur at which my stomach revolted. The sausages were entirely consumed; of the ham nothing remained but a small piece of the skin; and all the biscuit, except a few fragments of one, had been eaten by Tiger. To add to my troubles, I found that my headache was increasing momentarily, and with it the species of delirium which had distressed me more or less since my first falling asleep. For some hours past it had been with the greatest difficulty I could breathe at all, and now each attempt at so doing was attended with the most distressing spasmodic action of the chest. But there was still another and very different source of disquietude, and one, indeed, whose harassing terrors had been the chief means of arousing me to exertion from my stupor on the mattress. It arose from the demeanour of the dog.

I first observed an alteration in his conduct while rubbing in the phosphorus on the paper in my last attempt. As I rubbed, he ran his nose against my hand with a slight snarl, but I was too greatly excited at the time to pay much attention to the circumstance. Soon afterwards, it will be remembered, I threw myself on the mattress, and fell into a species of lethargy. Presently I became aware of a singular hissing sound close at my ears, and discovered it to proceed from Tiger, who was panting and wheezing in a state of the greatest apparent excitement, his eyeballs flashing fiercely through the gloom. I spoke to him, when he replied with a low growl, and then remained quiet. Presently I relapsed into my stupor, from which I was again awakened in a similar manner. This was repeated three or four times, until finally his behaviour inspired me with so great a degree of fear that I became fully aroused. He was now lying close by the door of the box,

snarling fearfully, although in a kind of undertone, and grinding his teeth as if strongly convulsed. I had no doubt whatever that the want of water or the confined atmosphere of the hold had driven him mad, and I was at a loss what course to pursue. I could not endure the thought of killing him, yet it seemed absolutely necessary for my own safety. I could distinctly perceive his eyes fastened upon me with an expression of the most deadly animosity, and I expected every instant that he would attack me. At last I could endure my terrible situation no longer, and determined to make my way from the box at all hazards, and dispatch him, if his opposition should render it necessary for me to do so. To get out, I had to pass directly over his body, and he already seemed to anticipate my design – raising himself upon his forelegs (as I perceived by the altered position of his eyes) – and displaying the whole of his white fangs, which were easily discernible. I took the remains of the ham skin, and the bottle containing the liqueur, and secured them about my person, together with a large carving knife which Augustus had left me – then, folding my cloak as closely around me as possible, I made a movement towards the mouth of the box. No sooner did I do this than the dog sprang with a loud growl towards my throat. The whole weight of his body struck me on the right shoulder, and I fell violently to the left, while the enraged animal passed entirely over me. I had fallen upon my knees, with my head buried among the blankets, and these protected me from a second furious assault, during which I felt the sharp teeth pressing vigorously upon the woollen which enveloped my neck – yet, luckily, without being able to penetrate all the folds. I was now beneath the dog, and a few moments would place me completely in his power. Despair gave me strength, and I rose bodily up, shaking him from me by main force, and dragging with me the blankets from the mattress. These I now threw over him, and before he could extricate himself, I had got through the door and closed it effectually against his pursuit. In this struggle, however, I had been forced to drop the morsel of ham skin, and I now found my whole stock of provisions reduced to a single gill of liqueur. As this reflection crossed my mind, I felt myself actuated by one of those fits of perverseness which might be supposed to influence a spoilt child in similar circumstances, and, raising the bottle to my lips, I drained it to the last drop, and dashed it furiously upon the floor.

Scarcely had the echo of the crash died away when I heard my name pronounced in an eager but subdued voice, issuing from the direction of the steerage. So unexpected was anything of the kind, and so intense was the emotion excited within me by the sound, that I endeavoured in vain to

reply. My powers of speech totally failed, and, in an agony of terror lest my friend should conclude me dead, and return without attempting to reach me, I stood up between the crates near the door of the box, trembling convulsively, and gasping and struggling for utterance. Had a thousand worlds depended upon a syllable, I could not have spoken it. There was a slight movement now audible among the lumber somewhere forward of my station. The sound presently grew less distinct, then again less so, and still less. Shall I ever forget my feelings at this moment? He was going – my friend – my companion, from whom I had a right to expect so much – he was going – he would abandon me – he was gone! He would leave me to perish miserably, to expire in the most horrible and loathsome of dungeons – and one word, one little syllable, would save me – yet that single syllable I could not utter! I felt, I am sure, more than ten thousand times the agonies of death itself. My brain reeled, and I fell, deadly sick, against the end of the box.

As I fell the carving knife was shaken out from the waistband of my pantaloons, and dropped with a rattling sound to the floor. Never did any strain of the richest melody come so sweetly to my ears! With the intensest anxiety I listened to ascertain the effect of the noise upon Augustus – for I knew that the person who called my name could be no one but himself. All was silent for some moments. At length I again heard the word "*Arthur!*" repeated in a low tone, and one full of hesitation. Reviving hope loosened at once my powers of speech, and I now screamed at the top of my voice, "*Augustus! Oh, Augustus!*" "Hush! For God's sake be silent!" he replied in a voice trembling with agitation. "I will be with you immediately – as soon as I can make my way through the hold." For a long time I heard him moving among the lumber, and every moment seemed to me an age. At length I felt his hand upon my shoulder, and he placed, at the same moment, a bottle of water to my lips. Those only who have been suddenly redeemed from the jaws of the tomb, or who have known the insufferable torments of thirst under circumstances as aggravated as those which encompassed me in my dreary prison, can form any idea of the unutterable transports which that one long draught of the richest of all physical luxuries afforded.

When I had in some degree satisfied my thirst, Augustus produced from his pocket three or four boiled potatoes, which I devoured with the greatest avidity. He had brought with him a light in a dark lantern, and the grateful rays afforded me scarcely less comfort than the food and drink. But I was impatient to learn the cause of his protracted absence, and he proceeded to recount what had happened on board during my incarceration.

CHAPTER IV

The brig put to sea, as I had supposed, in about an hour after he had left the watch. This was on 20th June. It will be remembered that I had then been in the hold for three days, and, during this period, there was so constant a bustle on board, and so much running to and fro, especially in the cabin and staterooms, that he had had no chance of visiting me without the risk of having the secret of the trap discovered. When at length he did come, I had assured him that I was doing as well as possible, and, therefore, for the two next days he felt but little uneasiness on my account – still, however, watching an opportunity of going down. It was not *until the fourth day* that he found one. Several times during this interval he had made up his mind to let his father know of the adventure, and have me come up at once, but we were still within reaching distance of Nantucket, and it was doubtful, from some expressions which had escaped Captain Barnard, whether he would not immediately put back if he discovered me to be on board. Besides, upon thinking the matter over, Augustus, so he told me, could not imagine that I was in immediate want, or that I would hesitate, in such case, to make myself heard at the trap. When, therefore, he considered everything, he concluded to. let me stay until he could meet with an opportunity of visiting me unobserved. This, as I said before, did not occur until the fourth day after his bringing me the watch, and the seventh since I had first entered the hold. He then went down without taking with him any water or provisions, intending in the first place merely to call my attention, and get me to come from the box to the trap – when he would go up to the stateroom and thence hand me down a supply. When he descended for this purpose he found that I was asleep, for it seems that I was snoring very loudly. From all the calculations I can make on the subject, this must have been the slumber into which I fell just after my return from the trap with the watch, and which, consequently, must have lasted *for more than three entire days and nights* at the very least. Latterly, I have had reason, both from my own experience and the assurance of others, to be acquainted with the strong soporific effects of the stench arising from old fish oil when closely confined, and when I think of the condition of the hold in which I was imprisoned, and the long period during which the brig had been used as a whaling vessel, I am more inclined to wonder that I awoke at all, after once falling asleep, than that I should have slept uninterruptedly for the period specified above.

Augustus called to me at first in a low voice and without closing the trap – but I made him no reply. He then shut the trap, and spoke to me in a louder, and finally in a very loud tone – still I continued to snore. He was now at a loss what to do. It would take him some time to make his way through the lumber to my box, and in the meanwhile his absence would be noticed by Captain Barnard, who had occasion for his services every minute, in arranging and copying papers connected with the business of the voyage. He determined, therefore, upon reflection, to ascend, and await another opportunity of visiting me. He was the more easily induced to this resolve as my slumber appeared to be of the most tranquil nature, and he could not suppose that I had undergone any inconvenience from my incarceration. He had just made up his mind on these points when his attention was arrested by an unusual bustle, the sound of which proceeded apparently from the cabin. He sprang through the trap as quickly as possible, closed it and threw open the door of his stateroom. No sooner had he put his foot over the threshold than a pistol flashed in his face, and he was knocked down, at the same moment, by a blow from a handspike.*

A strong hand held him on the cabin floor, with a tight grasp upon his throat; still he was able to see what was going on around him. His father was tied hand and foot, and lying along the steps of the companionway,* with his head down, and a deep wound in the forehead, from which the blood was flowing in a continued stream. He spoke not a word, and was apparently dying. Over him stood the first mate, eyeing him with an expression of fiendish derision, and deliberately searching his pockets, from which he presently drew forth a large wallet and a chronometer.* Seven of the crew (among whom was the cook, a Negro) were rummaging the staterooms on the larboard for arms, where they soon equipped themselves with muskets and ammunition. Besides Augustus and Captain Barnard, there were nine men altogether in the cabin, and these among the most ruffianly of the brig's company. The villains now went upon deck, taking my friend with them, after having secured his arms behind his back. They proceeded straight to the forecastle, which was fastened down – two of the mutineers standing by it with axes – two also at the main hatch. The mate called out in a loud voice: "Do you hear there below? Tumble up with you, one by one – now, mark that – and no grumbling!" It was some minutes before anyone appeared – at last an Englishman, who had shipped as a raw hand, came up, weeping piteously, and entreating the mate, in the most humble manner, to spare his life. The only reply was a blow on the forehead from an axe. The poor fellow fell to the deck without a groan,

and the black cook lifted him up in his arms as he would a child, and tossed him deliberately into the sea. Hearing the blow and the plunge of the body, the men below could now be induced to venture on deck neither by threats nor promises, until a proposition was made to smoke them out. A general rush then ensued, and for a moment it seemed possible that the brig might be retaken. The mutineers, however, succeeded at last in closing the forecastle effectually before more than six of their opponents could get up. These six, finding themselves so greatly outnumbered and without arms, submitted after a brief struggle. The mate gave them fair words – no doubt with a view of inducing those below to yield, for they had no difficulty in hearing all that was said on deck. The result proved his sagacity, no less than his diabolical villainy. All in the forecastle presently signified their intention of submitting, and, ascending one by one, were pinioned and thrown on their backs, together with the first six – there being, in all of the crew who were not concerned in the mutiny, twenty-seven.*

A scene of the most horrible butchery ensued. The bound seamen were dragged to the gangway. Here the cook stood with an axe, striking each victim on the head as he was forced over the side of the vessel by the other mutineers. In this manner twenty-two perished, and Augustus had given himself up for lost, expecting every moment his own turn to come next. But it seemed that the villains were now either weary or in some measure disgusted with their bloody labour, for the four remaining prisoners, together with my friend, who had been thrown on the deck with the rest, were respited while the mate sent below for rum, and the whole murderous party held a drunken carouse, which lasted until sunset. They now fell to disputing in regard to the fate of the survivors, who lay not more than four paces off, and could distinguish every word said. Upon some of the mutineers the liquor appeared to have a softening effect, for several voices were heard in favour of releasing the captives altogether, on condition of joining the mutiny and sharing the profits. The black cook, however (who in all respects was a perfect demon, and who seemed to exert as much influence, if not more, than the mate himself), would listen to no proposition of the kind, and rose repeatedly for the purpose of resuming his work at the gangway. Fortunately he was so far overcome by intoxication as to be easily restrained by the less bloodthirsty of the party, among whom was a line manager,* who went by the name of Dirk Peters.* This man was the son of an Indian squaw of the tribe of Upsarokas, who live among the fastnesses of the Black Hills,* near the source of the Missouri. His father was a fur-trader, I believe, or at least connected in some manner with the

Indian trading posts on Lewis River.* Peters himself was one of the most ferocious-looking men I ever beheld. He was short in stature, not more than four feet eight inches high, but his limbs were of Herculean mould. His hands, especially, were so enormously thick and broad as hardly to retain a human shape. His arms, as well as legs, were *bowed* in the most singular manner, and appeared to possess no flexibility whatever. His head was equally deformed, being of immense size, with an indentation on the crown (like that on the head of most Negroes), and entirely bald. To conceal this latter deficiency, which did not proceed from old age, he usually wore a wig formed of any hair-like material which presented itself – occasionally the skin of a Spanish dog or American grizzly bear. At the time spoken of he had on a portion of one of these bearskins, and it added no little to the natural ferocity of his countenance, which betook of the Upsaroka character. The mouth extended nearly from ear to ear; the lips were thin, and seemed, like some other portions of his frame, to be devoid of natural pliancy, so that the ruling expression never varied under the influence of any emotion whatever. This ruling expression may be conceived when it is considered that the teeth were exceedingly long and protruding, and never even partially covered, in any instance, by the lips. To pass this man with a casual glance, one might imagine him to be convulsed with laughter, but a second look would induce a shuddering acknowledgement that if such an expression were indicative of merriment, the merriment must be that of a demon. Of this singular being many anecdotes were prevalent among the seafaring men of Nantucket. These anecdotes went to prove his prodigious strength when under excitement, and some of them had given rise to a doubt of his sanity. But on board the *Grampus*, it seems, he was regarded, at the time of the mutiny, with feelings more of derision than of anything else. I have been thus particular in speaking of Dirk Peters, because, ferocious as he appeared, he proved the main instrument in preserving the life of Augustus, and because I shall have frequent occasion to mention him hereafter in the course of my narrative – a narrative, let me here say, which, in its latter portions, will be found to include incidents of a nature so entirely out of the range of human experience, and for this reason so far beyond the limits of human credulity, that I proceed in utter hopelessness of obtaining credence for all that I shall tell, yet confidently trusting in time and progressing science to verify some of the most important and most improbable of my statements.

After much indecision and two or three violent quarrels, it was determined at last that all the prisoners (with the exception of Augustus, whom

Peters insisted in a jocular manner upon keeping as his clerk) should be set adrift in one of the smallest whaleboats. The mate went down into the cabin to see if Captain Barnard was still living – for, it will be remembered, he was left below when the mutineers came up. Presently the two made their appearance, the captain pale as death, but somewhat recovered from the effects of his wound. He spoke to the men in a voice hardly articulate, entreated them not to set him adrift, but to return to their duty, and promising to land them wherever they chose, and to take no steps for bringing them to justice. He might as well have spoken to the winds. Two of the ruffians seized him by the arms and hurled him over the brig's side into the boat, which had been lowered while the mate went below. The four men who were lying on the deck were then untied and ordered to follow, which they did without attempting any resistance – Augustus being still left in his painful position, although he struggled and prayed only for the poor satisfaction of being permitted to bid his father farewell. A handful of sea biscuit and a jug of water were now handed down, but neither mast, sail, oar nor compass. The boat was towed astern for a few minutes, during which the mutineers held another consultation – it was then finally cut adrift. By this time night had come on – there were neither moon nor stars visible – and a short and ugly sea was running, although there was no great deal of wind. The boat was instantly out of sight, and little hope could be entertained for the unfortunate sufferers who were in it. This event happened, however, in latitude 35° 30′ north, longitude 61° 20′ west, and consequently at no very great distance from the Bermuda Islands. Augustus therefore endeavoured to console himself with the idea that the boat might either succeed in reaching the land or come sufficiently near to be fallen in with by vessels off the coast.

All sail was now put upon the brig, and she continued her original course to the south-west – the mutineers being bent upon some piratical expedition, in which, from all that could be understood, a ship was to be intercepted on her way from the Cape Verd Islands to Porto Rico. No attention was paid to Augustus, who was untied and suffered to go about anywhere forward of the cabin companionway. Dirk Peters treated him with some degree of kindness, and on one occasion saved him from the brutality of the cook. His situation was still one of the most precarious, as the men were continually intoxicated, and there was no relying upon their continued good humour or carelessness in regard to himself. His anxiety on my account he represented, however, as the most distressing result of his condition, and, indeed, I had never reason to doubt the

sincerity of his friendship. More than once he had resolved to acquaint the mutineers with the secret of my being on board, but was restrained from so doing, partly through recollection of the atrocities he had already beheld, and partly through a hope of being able soon to bring me relief. For the latter purpose he was constantly on the watch, but, in spite of the most constant vigilance, three days elapsed after the boat was cut adrift before any chance occurred. At length, on the night of the third day, there came on a heavy blow from the eastward, and all hands were called up to take in sail. During the confusion which ensued, he made his way below unobserved, and into the stateroom. What was his grief and horror in discovering that the latter had been rendered a place of deposit for a variety of sea-stores and ship furniture, and that several fathoms of old chain-cable, which had been stowed away beneath the companion ladder, had been dragged thence to make room for a chest, and were now lying immediately upon the trap! To remove it without discovery was impossible, and he returned on deck as quickly as he could. As he came up, the mate seized him by the throat, and, demanding what he had been doing in the cabin, was about flinging him over the larboard bulwark, when his life was again preserved through the interference of Dirk Peters. Augustus was now put in handcuffs (of which there were several pairs on board), and his feet lashed tightly together. He was then taken into the steerage, and thrown into a lower berth next to the forecastle bulkheads, with the assurance that he should never put his foot on deck again "until the brig was no longer a brig". This was the expression of the cook, who threw him into the berth – it is hardly possible to say what precise meaning was intended by the phrase. The whole affair, however, proved the ultimate means of my relief, as will presently appear.

CHAPTER V

For some minutes after the cook had left the forecastle, Augustus abandoned himself to despair, never hoping to leave the berth alive. He now came to the resolution of acquainting the first of the men who should come down with my situation, thinking it better to let me take my chance with the mutineers than perish of thirst in the hold – for it had been ten days since I was first imprisoned, and my jug of water was not a plentiful supply even for four. As he was thinking on this subject, the idea came all at once into his head that it might be possible to communicate with me

by way of the main hold. In any other circumstances, the difficulty and hazard of the undertaking would have prevented him from attempting it, but now he had, at all events, little prospect of life, and consequently little to lose – he bent his whole mind, therefore, upon the task.

His handcuffs were the first consideration. At first he saw no method of removing them, and feared that he should thus be baffled in the very outset, but upon a closer scrutiny he discovered that the irons could be slipped off and on at pleasure, with very little effort or inconvenience, merely by squeezing his hands through them – this species of manacle being altogether ineffectual in confining young persons, in whom the smaller bones readily yield to pressure. He now untied his feet, and, leaving the cord in such a manner that it could easily be readjusted in the event of any person's coming down, proceeded to examine the bulkhead where it joined the berth. The partition here was of soft pine board, an inch thick, and he saw that he should have little trouble in cutting his way through. A voice was now heard at the forecastle companionway, and he had just time to put his right hand into its handcuff (the left had not been removed) and to draw the rope in a slip knot around his ankle, when Dirk Peters came below, followed by Tiger, who immediately leapt into the berth and lay down. The dog had been brought on board by Augustus, who knew my attachment to the animal, and thought it would give me pleasure to have him with me during the voyage. He went up to our house for him immediately after first taking me into the hold, but did not think of mentioning the circumstance upon his bringing the watch. Since the mutiny, Augustus had not seen him before his appearance with Dirk Peters, and had given him up for lost, supposing him to have been thrown overboard by some of the malignant villains belonging to the mate's gang. It appeared afterwards that he had crawled into a hole beneath a whaleboat, from which, not having room to turn round, he could not extricate himself. Peters at last let him out, and, with a species of good feeling which my friend knew well how to appreciate, had now brought him to him in the forecastle as a companion, leaving at the same time some salt junk* and potatoes, with a can of water; he then went on deck, promising to come down with something more to eat on the next day.

When he had gone, Augustus freed both hands from the manacles and unfastened his feet. He then turned down the head of the mattress on which he had been lying, and with his penknife (for the ruffians had not thought it worthwhile to search him) commenced cutting vigorously across one of the partition planks, as closely as possible to the floor of the berth. He

chose to cut here because, if suddenly interrupted, he would be able to conceal what had been done by letting the head of the mattress fall into its proper position. For the remainder of the day, however, no disturbance occurred, and by night he had completely divided the plank. It should here be observed that none of the crew occupied the forecastle as a sleeping place, living altogether in the cabin since the mutiny, drinking the wines and feasting on the sea-stores of Captain Barnard, and giving no more heed than was absolutely necessary to the navigation of the brig. These circumstances proved fortunate both for myself and Augustus, for, had matters been otherwise, he would have found it impossible to reach me. As it was, he proceeded with confidence in his design. It was near daybreak, however, before he completed the second division of the board (which was about a foot above the first cut), thus making an aperture quite large enough to admit his passage through with facility to the main orlop deck. Having got here, he made his way with but little trouble to the lower main hatch, although in so doing he had to scramble over tiers of oil casks piled nearly as high as the upper deck, there being barely room enough left for his body. Upon reaching the hatch, he found that Tiger had followed him below, squeezing between two rows of the casks. It was now too late, however, to attempt getting to me before dawn, as the chief difficulty lay in passing through the close stowage in the lower hold. He therefore resolved to return, and wait till the next night. With this design, he proceeded to loosen the hatch, so that he might have as little detention as possible when he should come again. No sooner had he loosened it than Tiger sprang eagerly to the small opening produced, snuffed for a moment, and then uttered a long whine, scratching at the same time, as if anxious to remove the covering with his paws. There could be no doubt, from his behaviour, that he was aware of my being in the hold, and Augustus thought it possible that he would be able to get to me if he put him down. He now hit upon the expedient of sending the note, as it was especially desirable that I should make no attempt at forcing my way out, at least under existing circumstances, and there could be no certainty of his getting to me himself on the morrow as he intended. After events proved how fortunate it was that the idea occurred to him as it did, for, had it not been for the receipt of the note, I should undoubtedly have fallen upon some plan, however desperate, of alarming the crew, and both our lives would most probably have been sacrificed in consequence.

Having concluded to write, the difficulty was now to procure the materials for so doing. An old toothpick was soon made into a pen, and this by

means of feeling altogether, for the between decks were as dark as pitch. Paper enough was obtained from the back of a letter – a duplicate of the forged letter from Mr Ross.* This had been the original draft, but the handwriting not being sufficiently well imitated, Augustus had written another, thrusting the first, by good fortune, into his coat pocket, where it was now most opportunely discovered. Ink alone was thus wanting, and a substitute was immediately found for this by means of a slight incision with the penknife on the back of a finger just above the nail – a copious flow of blood ensuing, as usual, from wounds in that vicinity. The note was now written, as well as it could be in the dark and under the circumstances. It briefly explained that a mutiny had taken place; that Captain Barnard was set adrift; and that I might expect immediate relief as far as provisions were concerned, but must not venture upon making any disturbance. It concluded with these words: "I have scrawled this with blood – your life depends upon lying close."

The slip of paper being tied upon the dog, he was now put down the hatchway, and Augustus made the best of his way back to the forecastle, where he found no reason to believe that any of the crew had been in his absence. To conceal the hole in the partition, he drove his knife in just above it, and hung up a pea jacket* which he found in the berth. His handcuffs were then replaced, and also the rope around his ankles.

These arrangements were scarcely completed when Dirk Peters came below, very drunk, but in excellent humour, and bringing with him my friend's allowance of provision for the day. This consisted of a dozen large Irish potatoes roasted, and a pitcher of water. He sat for some time on a chest by the berth, and talked freely about the mate and the general concerns of the brig. His demeanour was exceedingly capricious, and even grotesque. At one time Augustus was much alarmed by his odd conduct. At last, however, he went on deck, muttering a promise to bring his prisoner a good dinner on the morrow. During the day two of the crew (harpooners) came down, accompanied by the cook, all three in nearly the last stage of intoxication. Like Peters, they made no scruple of talking unreservedly about their plans. It appeared that they were much divided among themselves as to their ultimate course, agreeing in no point, except the attack on the ship from the Cape Verd Islands, with which they were in hourly expectation of meeting. As far as could be ascertained, the mutiny had not been brought about altogether for the sake of booty – a private pique of the chief mate's against Captain Barnard having been the main instigation. There now seemed to be two principal factions among the

crew – one headed by the mate, the other by the cook. The former party were for seizing the first suitable vessel which should present itself, and equipping it at some of the West India Islands for a piratical cruise. The latter division, however, which was the stronger, and included Dirk Peters among its partisans, were bent upon pursuing the course originally laid out for the brig into the South Pacific, there either to take whale or act otherwise, as circumstances should suggest. The representations of Peters, who had frequently visited these regions, had great weight, apparently, with the mutineers, wavering, as they were, between half-engendered notions of profit and pleasure. He dwelt on the world of novelty and amusement to be found among the innumerable islands of the Pacific, on the perfect security and freedom from all restraint to be enjoyed, but, more particularly, on the deliciousness of the climate, on the abundant means of good living and on the voluptuous beauty of the women. As yet, nothing had been absolutely determined upon, but the pictures of the hybrid line manager were taking strong hold upon the ardent imaginations of the seamen, and there was every probability that his intentions would be finally carried into effect.

The three men went away in about an hour, and no one else entered the forecastle all day. Augustus lay quiet until nearly night. He then freed himself from the rope and irons, and prepared for his attempt. A bottle was found in one of the berths, and this he filled with water from the pitcher left by Peters, storing his pockets at the same time with cold potatoes. To his great joy he also came across a lantern, with a small piece of tallow candle in it. This he could light at any moment, as he had in his possession a box of phosphorus matches. When it was quite dark, he got through the hole in the bulkhead, having taken the precaution to arrange the bed-clothes in the berth so as to convey the idea of a person covered up. When through, he hung up the pea jacket on his knife, as before, to conceal the aperture – this manoeuvre being easily effected as he did not readjust the piece of plank taken out until afterwards. He was now on the main orlop deck, and proceeded to make his way, as before, between the upper deck and the oil casks to the main hatchway.* Having reached this, he lit the piece of candle, and descended, groping with extreme difficulty among the compact stowage of the hold. In a few moments he became alarmed at the insufferable stench and the closeness of the atmosphere. He could not think it possible that I had survived my confinement for so long a period breathing so oppressive an air. He called my name repeatedly, but I made him no reply, and his apprehensions seemed thus to be confirmed. The brig was rolling violently, and there was so much noise in consequence that it

was useless to listen for any weak sound, such as those of my breathing or snoring. He threw open the lantern, and held it as high as possible, whenever an opportunity occurred, in order that, by observing the light, I might, if alive, be aware that succour was approaching. Still nothing was heard from me, and the supposition of my death began to assume the character of certainty. He determined, nevertheless, to force a passage, if possible, to the box, and at least ascertain beyond a doubt the truth of his surmises. He pushed on for some time in a most pitiable state of anxiety, until, at length, he found the pathway utterly blocked up, and that there was no possibility of making any farther way by the course in which he had set out. Overcome now by his feelings, he threw himself among the lumber in despair, and wept like a child. It was at this period that he heard the crash occasioned by the bottle which I had thrown down. Fortunate, indeed, was it that the incident occurred – for, upon this incident, trivial as it appears, the thread of my destiny depended. Many years elapsed, however, before I was aware of this fact.* A natural shame and regret for his weakness and indecision prevented Augustus from confiding to me at once what a more intimate and unreserved communion afterwards induced him to reveal. Upon finding his further progress in the hold impeded by obstacles which he could not overcome, he had resolved to abandon his attempt at reaching me, and return at once to the forecastle. Before condemning him entirely on this head, the harassing circumstances which embarrassed him should be taken into consideration. The night was fast wearing away, and his absence from the forecastle might be discovered, and, indeed, would necessarily be so, if he should fail to get back to the berth by daybreak. His candle was expiring in the socket, and there would be the greatest difficulty in retracing his way to the hatchway in the dark. It must be allowed, too, that he had every good reason to believe me dead, in which event no benefit could result to me from his reaching the box, and a world of danger would be encountered to no purpose by himself. He had repeatedly called, and I had made him no answer. I had been now eleven days and nights with no more water than that contained in the jug which he had left with me – a supply which it was not at all probable I had hoarded in the beginning of my confinement, as I had had every cause to expect a speedy release. The atmosphere of the hold, too, must have appeared to him, coming from the comparatively open air of the steerage, of a nature absolutely poisonous, and by far more intolerable than it had seemed to me upon my first taking up my quarters in the box – the hatchways at that time having been constantly open for many months previous. Add to

these considerations that of the scene of bloodshed and terror so lately witnessed by my friend, his confinement, privations and narrow escapes from death, together with the frail and equivocal tenure by which he still existed – circumstances all so well calculated to prostrate every energy of mind – and the reader will be easily brought, as I have been, to regard his apparent falling off in friendship and in faith with sentiments rather of sorrow than of anger.

The crash of the bottle was distinctly heard, yet Augustus was not sure that it proceeded from the hold. The doubt, however, was sufficient inducement to persevere. He clambered up nearly to the orlop deck by means of the stowage, and then, watching for a lull in the pitchings of the vessel, he called out to me in as loud a tone as he could command, regardless, for the moment, of the danger of being overheard by the crew. It will be remembered that on this occasion the voice reached me, but I was so entirely overcome by violent agitation as to be incapable of reply. Confident, now, that his worst apprehensions were well founded, he descended, with a view of getting back to the forecastle without loss of time. In his haste some small boxes were thrown down, the noise occasioned by which I heard, as will be recollected. He had made considerable progress on his return when the fall of the knife again caused him to hesitate. He retraced his steps immediately, and, clambering up the stowage a second time, called out my name, loudly as before, having watched for a lull. This time I found voice to answer. Overjoyed at discovering me to be still alive, he now resolved to brave every difficulty and danger in reaching me. Having extricated himself as quickly as possible from the labyrinth of lumber by which he was hemmed in, he at length struck into an opening which promised better, and finally, after a series of struggles, arrived at the box in a state of utter exhaustion.

CHAPTER VI

The leading particulars of this narration were all that Augustus communicated to me while we remained near the box. It was not until afterwards that he entered fully into all the details. He was apprehensive of being missed, and I was wild with impatience to leave my detested place of confinement. We resolved to make our way at once to the hole in the bulkhead, near which I was to remain for the present, while he went through to reconnoitre. To leave Tiger in the box was what neither of us

could endure to think of, yet how to act otherwise was the question. He now seemed to be perfectly quiet, and we could not even distinguish the sound of his breathing upon applying our ears closely to the box. I was convinced that he was dead, and determined to open the door. We found him lying at full length, apparently in a deep stupor, yet still alive. No time was to be lost, yet I could not bring myself to abandon an animal who had now been twice instrumental in saving my life without some attempt at preserving him. We therefore dragged him along with us as well as we could, although with the greatest difficulty and fatigue, Augustus, during part of the time, being forced to clamber over the impediments in our way with the huge dog in his arms – a feat to which the feebleness of my frame rendered me totally inadequate. At length we succeeded in reaching the hole, when Augustus got through, and Tiger was pushed in afterwards. All was found to be safe, and we did not fail to return sincere thanks to God for our deliverance from the imminent danger we had escaped. For the present, it was agreed that I should remain near the opening, through which my companion could readily supply me with a part of his daily provision, and where I could have the advantages of breathing an atmosphere comparatively pure.

In explanation of some portions of this narrative, wherein I have spoken of the stowage of the brig, and which may appear ambiguous to some of my readers who may have seen a proper or regular stowage, I must here state that the manner in which this most important duty had been performed on board the *Grampus* was a most shameful piece of neglect on the part of Captain Barnard, who was by no means as careful or as experienced a seaman as the hazardous nature of the service on which he was employed would seem necessarily to demand. A proper stowage cannot be accomplished in a careless manner, and many most disastrous accidents, even within the limits of my own experience, have arisen from neglect or ignorance in this particular. Coasting vessels, in the frequent hurry and bustle attendant upon taking in or discharging cargo, are the most liable to mishap from the want of a proper attention to stowage. The great point is to allow no possibility of the cargo or ballast's shifting position even in the most violent rollings of the vessel. With this end, great attention must be paid not only to the bulk taken in, but to the nature of the bulk, and whether there be a full or only a partial cargo. In most kinds of freight the stowage is accomplished by means of a screw. Thus, in a load of tobacco or flour, the whole is screwed so tightly into the hold of the vessel that the barrels or hogsheads, upon discharging,

are found to be completely flattened, and take some time to regain their original shape. This screwing, however, is resorted to principally with a view of obtaining more room in the hold, for in a *full* load of any such commodities as flour or tobacco there can be no danger of any shifting whatever, at least none from which inconvenience can result. There have been instances, indeed, where this method of screwing has resulted in the most lamentable consequences, arising from a cause altogether distinct from the danger attendant upon a shifting of cargo. A load of cotton, for example, tightly screwed while in certain conditions, has been known, through the expansion of its bulk, to rend a vessel asunder at sea. There can be no doubt, either, that the same result would ensue in the case of tobacco, while undergoing its usual course of fermentation, were it not for the interstices consequent upon the rotundity of the hogsheads.

It is when a partial cargo is received that danger is chiefly to be apprehended from shifting, and that precautions should be always taken to guard against such misfortune. Only those who have encountered a violent gale of wind, or rather who have experienced the rolling of a vessel in a sudden calm after the gale, can form an idea of the tremendous force of the plunges, and of the consequent terrible impetus given to all loose articles in the vessel. It is then that the necessity of a cautious stowage, when there is a partial cargo, becomes obvious. When lying to (especially with a small headsail), a vessel which is not properly modelled in the bows is frequently thrown upon her beam ends* – this occurring even every fifteen or twenty minutes upon an average, yet without any serious consequences resulting, *provided there be a proper stowage*. If this, however, has not been strictly attended to, in the first of these heavy lurches the whole of the cargo tumbles over to the side of the vessel which lies upon the water, and, being thus prevented from regaining her equilibrium, as she would otherwise necessarily do, she is certain to fill in a few seconds and go down. It is not too much to say that at least one half of the instances in which vessels have foundered in heavy gales at sea may be attributed to a shifting of cargo or of ballast.

When a partial cargo of any kind is taken on board, the whole, after being first stowed as compactly as may be, should be covered with a layer of stout shifting boards, extending completely across the vessel. Upon these boards strong temporary stanchions should be erected, reaching to the timbers above, and thus securing everything in its place. In cargoes consisting of grain, or any similar matter, additional precautions are requisite. A hold filled entirely with grain upon leaving port will be found not more than

three fourths full upon reaching its destination – this, too, although the freight, when measured bushel by bushel by the consignee, will overrun by a vast deal (on account of the swelling of the grain) the quantity consigned. This result is occasioned by *settling* during the voyage, and is the more perceptible in proportion to the roughness of the weather experienced. If grain loosely thrown in a vessel, then, is ever so well secured by shifting boards and stanchions, it will be liable to shift in a long passage so greatly as to bring about the most distressing calamities. To prevent these, every method should be employed before leaving port to *settle* the cargo as much as possible, and for this there are many contrivances, among which may be mentioned the driving of wedges into the grain. Even after all this is done, and unusual pains taken to secure the shifting boards, no seaman who knows what he is about will feel altogether secure in a gale of any violence with a cargo of grain on board, and, least of all, with a partial cargo. Yet there are hundreds of our coasting vessels, and, it is likely, many more from the ports of Europe, which sail daily with partial cargoes, even of the most dangerous species, and without any precautions whatever. The wonder is that no more accidents occur than do actually happen. A lamentable instance of this heedlessness occurred to my knowledge in the case of Captain Joel Rice of the schooner* *Firefly*, which sailed from Richmond, Virginia, to Madeira, with a cargo of corn, in the year 1825. The captain had gone many voyages without serious accident, although he was in the habit of paying no attention whatever to his stowage, more than to secure it in the ordinary manner. He had never before sailed with a cargo of grain, and on this occasion had the corn thrown on board loosely, when it did not much more than half fill the vessel. For the first portion of the voyage he met with nothing more than light breezes, but when within a day's sail of Madeira there came on a strong gale from the NNE which forced him to lie to. He brought the schooner to the wind under a double-reefed foresail* alone, when she rode as well as any vessel could be expected to do, and shipped not a drop of water. Towards night the gale somewhat abated, and she rolled with more unsteadiness than before, but still did very well, until a heavy lurch threw her upon her beam ends to starboard. The corn was then heard to shift bodily, the force of the movement bursting open the main hatchway. The vessel went down like a shot. This happened within hail of a small sloop from Madeira, which picked up one of the crew (the only person saved), and which rode out the gale in perfect security, as indeed a jolly-boat might have done under proper management.

The stowage on board the *Grampus* was most clumsily done, if stowage that could be called which was little better than a promiscuous huddling together of oil casks* and ship furniture. I have already spoken of the condition of articles in the hold. On the orlop deck there was space enough for my body (as I have stated) between the oil casks and the upper deck; a space was left open around the main hatchway, and several other large spaces were left in the stowage. Near the hole cut through the bulkhead by Augustus there was room enough for an entire cask, and in this space I found myself comfortably situated for the present.

By the time my friend had got safely into the berth, and readjusted his handcuffs and the rope, it was broad daylight. We had made a narrow escape indeed, for scarcely had he arranged all matters when the mate came below with Dirk Peters and the cook. They talked for some time about the vessel from the Cape Verds, and seemed to be excessively anxious for her appearance. At length the cook came to the berth in which Augustus was lying, and seated himself in it near the head. I could see and hear every-thing from my hiding place, for the piece cut out had not been put back, and I was in momentary expectation that the Negro would fall against the pea jacket, which was hung up to conceal the aperture, in which case all would have been discovered, and our lives would, no doubt, have been instantly sacrificed. Our good fortune prevailed, however, and although he frequently touched it as the vessel rolled, he never pressed against it sufficiently to bring about a discovery. The bottom of the jacket had been carefully fastened to the bulkhead, so that the hole might not be seen by its swinging to one side. All this time Tiger was lying in the foot of the berth, and appeared to have recovered in some measure his faculties, for I could see him occasionally open his eyes and draw a long breath.

After a few minutes the mate and cook went above, leaving Dirk Peters behind, who, as soon as they were gone, came and sat himself down in the place just occupied by the mate. He began to talk very sociably with Augustus, and we could now see that the greater part of his apparent intoxication, while the two others were with him, was a feint. He answered all my companion's questions with perfect freedom; told him that he had no doubt of his father's having been picked up, as there were no less than five sail* in sight just before sundown on the day he was cut adrift, and used other language of a consolatory nature, which occasioned me no less surprise than pleasure. Indeed, I began to entertain hopes that through the instrumentality of Peters we might be finally enabled to regain possession of the brig, and this idea I mentioned to Augustus as soon as I found an

opportunity. He thought the matter possible, but urged the necessity of the greatest caution in making the attempt, as the conduct of the hybrid appeared to be instigated by the most arbitrary caprice alone, and, indeed, it was difficult to say if he was at any moment of sound mind. Peters went upon deck in about an hour, and did not return again until noon, when he brought Augustus a plentiful supply of junk beef and pudding. Of this, when we were left alone, I partook heartily, without returning through the hole. No one else came down into the forecastle during the day, and at night I got into Augustus's berth, where I slept soundly and sweetly until nearly daybreak, when he awakened me upon hearing a stir upon deck, and I regained my hiding place as quickly as possible. When the day was fully broke, we found that Tiger had recovered his strength almost entirely, and gave no indications of hydrophobia, drinking a little water that was offered him with great apparent eagerness. During the day he regained all his former vigour and appetite. His strange conduct had been brought on, no doubt, by the deleterious quality of the air of the hold, and had no connection with canine madness. I could not sufficiently rejoice that I had persisted in bringing him with me from the box. This day was 30th June, and the thirteenth since the *Grampus* made sail from Nantucket.

On 2nd July the mate came below, drunk as usual, and in an excessively good humour. He came to Augustus's berth, and, giving him a slap on the back, asked him if he thought he could behave himself if he let him loose, and whether he would promise not to be going into the cabin again. To this, of course, my friend answered in the affirmative, when the ruffian set him at liberty, after making him drink from a flask of rum which he drew from his coat pocket. Both now went on deck, and I did not see Augustus for about three hours. He then came below with the good news that he had obtained permission to go about the brig as he pleased anywhere forward of the mainmast, and that he had been ordered to sleep, as usual, in the forecastle. He brought me, too, a good dinner, and a plentiful supply of water. The brig was still cruising for the vessel from the Cape Verds, and a sail was now in sight, which was thought to be the one in question. As the events of the ensuing eight days were of little importance, and had no direct bearing upon the main incidents of my narrative, I will here throw them into the form of a journal, as I do not wish to omit them altogether.

3rd July – Augustus furnished me with three blankets, with which I contrived a comfortable bed in my hiding place. No one came below, except my companion, during the day. Tiger took his station in the berth just by the aperture, and slept heavily, as if not yet entirely recovered

from the effects of his sickness. Towards night a flaw of wind* struck the brig before sail could be taken in, and very nearly capsized her. The puff died away immediately, however, and no damage was done beyond the splitting of the foretopsail.* Dirk Peters treated Augustus all this day with great kindness, and entered into a long conversation with him respecting the Pacific Ocean, and the islands he had visited in that region. He asked him whether he would not like to go with the mutineers on a kind of exploring and pleasure voyage in those quarters, and said that the men were gradually coming over to the mate's views. To this Augustus thought it best to reply that he would be glad to go on such an adventure, since nothing better could be done, and that anything was preferable to a piratical life.

4th July – The vessel in sight proved to be a small brig from Liverpool, and was allowed to pass unmolested. Augustus spent most of his time on deck, with a view of obtaining all the information in his power respecting the intentions of the mutineers. They had frequent and violent quarrels among themselves, in one of which a harpooner, Jim Bonner, was thrown overboard. The party of the mate was gaining ground. Jim Bonner belonged to the cook's gang, of which Peters was a partisan.

5th July – About daybreak there came on a stiff breeze from the west, which at noon freshened into a gale, so that the brig could carry nothing more than her trysail* and foresail. In taking in the foretopsail, Simms,* one of the common hands, and belonging also to the cook's gang, fell overboard, being very much in liquor, and was drowned – no attempt being made to save him. The whole number of persons on board was now thirteen, to wit: Dirk Peters, Seymour, the black cook, —— Jones, —— Greely,* Hartman Rogers and William Allen, of the cook's party; the mate, whose name I never learnt, Absalom Hicks, —— Wilson, John Hunt and Richard Parker, of the mate's party – besides Augustus and myself.

6th July – The gale lasted all this day, blowing in heavy squalls, accompanied with rain. The brig took in a good deal of water through her seams, and one of the pumps was kept continually going, Augustus being forced to take his turn. Just at twilight a large ship passed close by us, without having been discovered until within hail. This ship was supposed to be the one for which the mutineers were on the lookout. The mate hailed her, but the reply was drowned in the roaring of the gale. At eleven, a sea was shipped amidships, which tore away a great portion of the larboard bulwarks, and did some other slight damage. Towards morning the weather moderated, and at sunrise there was very little wind.

7th July – There was a heavy swell running all this day, during which the brig, being light, rolled excessively, and many articles broke loose in the hold, as I could hear distinctly from my hiding place. I suffered a great deal from seasickness. Peters had a long conversation this day with Augustus, and told him that two of his gang, Greely and Allen, had gone over to the mate, and were resolved to turn pirates. He put several questions to Augustus which he did not then exactly understand. During a part of this evening the leak gained upon the vessel, and little could be done to remedy it, as it was occasioned by the brig's straining, and taking in the water through her seams. A sail was thrummed, and got under the bows,* which aided us in some measure, so that we began to gain upon the leak.

8th July – A light breeze sprang up at sunrise from the eastward, when the mate headed the brig to the south-west, with the intention of making some of the West India Islands, in pursuance of his piratical designs. No opposition was made by Peters or the cook – at least none in the hearing of Augustus. All idea of taking the vessel from the Cape Verds was abandoned. The leak was now easily kept under by one pump going every three quarters of an hour. The sail was drawn from beneath the bows. Spoke two small schooners* during the day.

9th July – Fine weather. All hands employed in repairing bulwarks. Peters had again a long conversation with Augustus, and spoke more plainly than he had done heretofore. He said nothing should induce him to come into the mate's views, and even hinted his intention of taking the brig out of his hands. He asked my friend if he could depend upon his aid in such case, to which Augustus said, "Yes," without hesitation. Peters then said he would sound the others of his party upon the subject, and went away. During the remainder of the day Augustus had no opportunity of speaking with him privately.

CHAPTER VII

10th July – Spoke a brig from Rio, bound to Norfolk.* Weather hazy, with a light baffling wind from the eastward. Today Hartman Rogers died, having been attacked on the eighth with spasms after drinking a glass of grog. This man was of the cook's party, and one upon whom Peters placed his main reliance. He told Augustus that he believed the mate had poisoned him, and that he expected, if he did not be on the lookout, his own turn would come shortly. There were now only himself, Jones and the

cook belonging to his own gang – on the other side there were five.* He had spoken to Jones about taking the command from the mate, but the project having been coolly received, he had been deterred from pressing the matter any further, or from saying anything to the cook. It was well, as it happened, that he was so prudent, for in the afternoon the cook expressed his determination of siding with the mate, and went over formally to that party, while Jones took an opportunity of quarrelling with Peters, and hinted that he would let the mate know of the plan in agitation. There was now, evidently, no time to be lost, and Peters expressed his determination of attempting to take the vessel at all hazards, provided Augustus would lend him his aid. My friend at once assured him of his willingness to enter into any plan for that purpose, and, thinking the opportunity a favourable one, made known the fact of my being on board. At this the hybrid was not more astonished than delighted, as he had no reliance whatever upon Jones, whom he already considered as belonging to the party of the mate. They went below immediately, when Augustus called to me by name, and Peters and myself were soon made acquainted. It was agreed that we should attempt to retake the vessel upon the first good opportunity, leaving Jones altogether out of our councils. In the event of success, we were to run the brig into the first port that offered, and deliver her up. The desertion of his party had frustrated Peters's design of going into the Pacific – an adventure which could not be accomplished without a crew, and he depended upon either getting acquitted upon trial, on the score of insanity (which he solemnly averred had actuated him in lending his aid to the mutiny), or upon obtaining a pardon, if found guilty, through the representations of Augustus and myself. Our deliberations were interrupted for the present by the cry of "All hands take in sail", and Peters and Augustus ran up on deck.

As usual, the crew were nearly all drunk, and, before sail could be properly taken in, a violent squall laid the brig on her beam ends. By keeping her away, however, she righted, having shipped a good deal of water. Scarcely was everything secure when another squall took the vessel, and immediately afterwards another – no damage being done. There was every appearance of a gale of wind, which, indeed, shortly came on, with great fury, from the northward and westward. All was made as snug as possible, and we laid to, as usual, under a close-reefed foresail. As night drew on, the wind increased in violence, with a remarkably heavy sea. Peters now came into the forecastle with Augustus, and we resumed our deliberations.

We agreed that no opportunity could be more favourable than the present for carrying our design into effect, as an attempt at such a moment would

never be anticipated. As the brig was snugly laid to, there would be no necessity of manoeuvring her until good weather, when, if we succeeded in our attempt, we might liberate one, or perhaps two, of the men, to aid us in taking her into port. The main difficulty was the great disproportion in our forces. There were only three of us, and in the cabin there were nine. All the arms on board, too, were in their possession, with the exception of a pair of small pistols which Peters had concealed about his person, and the large seaman's knife which he always wore in the waistband of his pantaloons. From certain indications, too – such, for example, as there being no such thing as an axe or a handspike lying in their customary places – we began to fear that the mate had his suspicions, at least in regard to Peters, and that he would let slip no opportunity of getting rid of him. It was clear, indeed, that what we should determine to do could not be done too soon. Still the odds were too much against us to allow of our proceeding without the greatest caution.

Peters proposed that he should go up on deck, and enter into conversation with the watch (Allen), when he would be able to throw him into the sea without trouble, and without making any disturbance, by seizing a good opportunity; that Augustus and myself should then come up, and endeavour to provide ourselves with some kind of weapons from the deck; and that we should then make a rush together, and secure the companionway before any opposition could be offered. I objected to this, because I could not believe that the mate (who was a cunning fellow in all matters which did not affect his superstitious prejudices) would suffer himself to be so easily entrapped. The very fact of there being a watch on deck at all was sufficient proof that he was upon the alert – it not being usual, except in vessels where discipline is most rigidly enforced, to station a watch on deck when a vessel is lying to in a gale of wind. As I address myself principally, if not altogether, to persons who have never been to sea, it may be as well to state the exact condition of a vessel under such circumstances. Lying to, or, in sea parlance, "laying to", is a measure resorted to for various purposes, and effected in various manners. In moderate weather it is frequently done with a view of merely bringing the vessel to a standstill, to wait for another vessel, or any similar object. If the vessel which lies to is under full sail, the manoeuvre is usually accomplished by throwing round some portion of her sails, so as to let the wind take them aback,* when she becomes stationary. But we are now speaking of lying to in a gale of wind. This is done when the wind is ahead,* and too violent to admit of carrying sail without danger of capsizing, and sometimes even when

the wind is fair, but the sea too heavy for the vessel to be put before it. If a vessel be suffered to scud* before the wind in a very heavy sea, much damage is usually done her by the shipping of water over her stern, and sometimes by the violent plunges she makes forward. This manoeuvre, then, is seldom resorted to in such case, unless through necessity. When the vessel is in a leaky condition she is often put before the wind even in the heaviest seas, for, when lying to, her seams are sure to be greatly opened by her violent straining, and it is not so much the case when scudding. Often, too, it becomes necessary to scud a vessel, either when the blast is so exceedingly furious as to tear in pieces the sail which is employed with a view of bringing her head to the wind, or when, through the false modelling of the frame or other causes, this main object cannot be effected.

Vessels in a gale of wind are laid to in different manners, according to their peculiar construction. Some lie to best under a foresail, and this, I believe, is the sail most usually employed. Large square-rigged vessels have sails for the express purpose, called storm-staysails. But the jib is occasionally employed by itself – sometimes the jib and foresail, or a double-reefed foresail, and not unfrequently the after-sails, are made use of. Foretopsails are very often found to answer the purpose better than any other species of sail. The *Grampus* was generally laid to under a close-reefed foresail.

When a vessel is to be laid to, her head is brought up to the wind just so nearly as to fill the sail under which she lies when hauled flat aft – that is, when brought diagonally across the vessel.* This being done, the bows point within a few degrees of the direction from which the wind issues, and the windward bow of course receives the shock of the waves. In this situation a good vessel will ride out a very heavy gale of wind without shipping a drop of water, and without any further attention being requisite on the part of the crew. The helm is usually lashed down, but this is altogether unnecessary (except on account of the noise it makes when loose), for the rudder has no effect upon the vessel when lying to. Indeed, the helm had far better be left loose than lashed very fast, for the rudder is apt to be torn off by heavy seas if there be no room for the helm to play. As long as the sail holds, a well-modelled vessel will maintain her situation, and ride every sea, as if instinct with life and reason. If the violence of the wind, however, should tear the sail into pieces (a feat which it requires a perfect hurricane to accomplish under ordinary circumstances), there is then imminent danger. The vessel falls off from the wind, and, coming broadside to the sea, is completely at its mercy; the only resource in this case is to put her quickly before the wind, letting her scud until some other

sail can be set. Some vessels will lie to under no sail whatever, but such are not to be trusted at sea.

But to return from this digression. It had never been customary with the mate to have any watch on deck when lying to in a gale of wind, and the fact that he had now one, coupled with the circumstance of the missing axes and handspikes, fully convinced us that the crew were too well on the watch to be taken by surprise in the manner Peters had suggested. Something, however, was to be done, and that with as little delay as practicable, for there could be no doubt that a suspicion having been once entertained against Peters, he would be sacrificed upon the earliest occasion, and one would certainly be either found or made upon the breaking of the gale.

Augustus now suggested that if Peters could contrive to remove, under any pretext, the piece of chain-cable which lay over the trap in the state-room, we might possibly be able to come upon them unawares by means of the hold, but a little reflection convinced us that the vessel rolled and pitched too violently for any attempt of that nature.

By good fortune I at length hit upon the idea of working upon the super-stitious terrors and guilty conscience of the mate. It will be remembered that one of the crew, Hartman Rogers, had died during the morning, having been attacked two days before with spasms after drinking some spirits and water. Peters had expressed to us his opinion that this man had been poisoned by the mate, and for this belief he had reasons, so he said, which were incontrovertible, but which he could not be prevailed upon to explain to us – this wayward refusal being only in keeping with other points of his singular character. But whether or not he had any better grounds for suspecting the mate than we had ourselves, we were easily led to fall in with his suspicion, and determined to act accordingly.

Rogers had died about eleven in the forenoon, in violent convulsions, and the corpse presented in a few minutes after death one of the most horrid and loathsome spectacles I ever remember to have seen. The stomach was swollen immensely, like that of a man who has been drowned and lain underwater for many weeks. The hands were in the same condition, while the face was shrunken, shrivelled and of a chalky whiteness, except where relieved by two or three glaring red splotches, like those occasioned by the erysipelas;* one of these splotches extended diagonally across the face, completely covering up an eye as if with a band of red velvet. In this disgusting condition the body had been brought up from the cabin at noon to be thrown overboard, when the mate, getting a glimpse of it (for he now saw it for the first time), and being either touched with remorse for

55

his crime or struck with terror at so horrible a sight, ordered the men to sew the body up in its hammock, and allow it the usual rites of sea burial. Having given these directions, he went below, as if to avoid any further sight of his victim. While preparations were making to obey his orders, the gale came on with great fury, and the design was abandoned for the present. The corpse, left to itself, was washed into the larboard scuppers,* where it still lay at the time of which I speak, floundering about with the furious lurches of the brig.

Having arranged our plan, we set about putting it in execution as speedily as possible. Peters went upon deck, and, as he had anticipated, was immediately accosted by Allen, who appeared to be stationed more as a watch upon the forecastle than for any other purpose. The fate of this villain, however, was speedily and silently decided, for Peters, approaching him in a careless manner, as if about to address him, seized him by the throat, and, before he could utter a single cry, tossed him over the bulwarks. He then called to us, and we came up. Our first precaution was to look about for something with which to arm ourselves, and in doing this we had to proceed with great care, for it was impossible to stand on deck an instant without holding fast, and violent seas broke over the vessel at every plunge forward. It was indispensable, too, that we should be quick in our operations, for every minute we expected the mate to be up to set the pumps going, as it was evident the brig must be taking in water very fast. After searching about for some time, we could find nothing more fit for our purpose than the two pump handles, one of which Augustus took, and I the other. Having secured these, we stripped off the shirt of the corpse and dropped the body overboard. Peters and myself then went below, leaving Augustus to watch upon deck, where he took his station just where Allen had been placed, and with his back to the cabin companionway, so that, if any of the mate's gang should come up, he might suppose it was the watch.

As soon as I got below I commenced disguising myself so as to represent the corpse of Rogers. The shirt which we had taken from the body aided us very much, for it was of singular form and character, and easily recognizable – a kind of smock, which the deceased wore over his other clothing. It was a blue stockinet,* with large white stripes running across. Having put this on, I proceeded to equip myself with a false stomach, in imitation of the horrible deformity of the swollen corpse. This was soon effected by means of stuffing with some bedclothes. I then gave the same appearance to my hands by drawing on a pair of white woollen mittens,

and filling them in with any kind of rags that offered themselves. Peters then arranged my face, first rubbing it well over with white chalk, and afterwards splotching it with blood, which he took from a cut in his finger. The streak across the eye was not forgotten and presented a most shocking appearance.

CHAPTER VIII

As I viewed myself in a fragment of looking glass which hung up in the cabin, and by the dim light of a kind of battle lantern, I was so impressed with a sense of vague awe at my appearance, and at the recollection of the terrific reality which I was thus representing, that I was seized with a violent tremor, and could scarcely summon resolution to go on with my part. It was necessary, however, to act with decision, and Peters and myself went upon deck.

We there found everything safe, and, keeping close to the bulwarks, the three of us crept to the cabin companionway. It was only partially closed, precautions having been taken to prevent its being suddenly pushed to from without by means of placing billets of wood on the upper step so as to interfere with the shutting. We found no difficulty in getting a full view of the interior of the cabin through the cracks where the hinges were placed. It now proved to have been very fortunate for us that we had not attempted to take them by surprise, for they were evidently on the alert. Only one was asleep, and he lying just at the foot of the companion ladder, with a musket by his side. The rest were seated on several mattresses, which had been taken from the berths and thrown on the floor. They were engaged in earnest conversation, and although they had been carousing, as appeared from two empty jugs, with some tin tumblers which lay about, they were not as much intoxicated as usual. All had knives, one or two of them pistols, and a great many muskets were lying in a berth close at hand.

We listened to their conversation for some time before we could make up our minds how to act, having as yet resolved on nothing determinate, except that we would attempt to paralyse their exertions, when we should attack them, by means of the apparition of Rogers. They were discussing their piratical plans, in which all we could hear distinctly was that they would unite with the crew of a schooner *Hornet*, and, if possible, get the schooner herself into their possession preparatory to some attempt on a large scale, the particulars of which could not be made out by either of us.

One of the men spoke of Peters, when the mate replied to him in a low voice which could not be distinguished, and afterwards added more loudly, that he could not understand his being so much forward with the captain's brat in the forecastle, and he thought the sooner both of them were overboard the better. To this no answer was made, but we could easily perceive that the hint was well received by the whole party, and more particularly by Jones. At this period I was excessively agitated, the more so as I could see that neither Augustus nor Peters could determine how to act. I made up my mind, however, to sell my life as dearly as possible, and not to suffer myself to be overcome by any feelings of trepidation.

The tremendous noise made by the roaring of the wind in the rigging, and the washing of the sea over the deck, prevented us from hearing what was said, except during momentary lulls. In one of these, we all distinctly heard the mate tell one of the men to "go forward, and order the d—d lubbers to come into the cabin", where he could have an eye upon them, for he wanted no such secret doings on board the brig. It was well for us that the pitching of the vessel at this moment was so violent as to prevent this order from being carried into instant execution. The cook got up from his mattress to go for us, when a tremendous lurch, which I thought would carry away the masts, threw him headlong against one of the larboard stateroom doors, bursting it open, and creating a good deal of other confusion. Luckily, neither of our party was thrown from his position, and we had time to make a precipitate retreat to the forecastle, and arrange a hurried plan of action before the messenger made his appearance, or rather before he put his head out of the companion hatch, for he did not come on deck. From this station he could not notice the absence of Allen, and he accordingly bawled out, as if to him, repeating the orders of the mate. Peters cried out, "Ay, ay," in a disguised voice, and the cook immediately went below, without entertaining a suspicion that all was not right.

My two companions now proceeded boldly aft and down into the cabin, Peters closing the door after him in the same manner he had found it. The mate received them with feigned cordiality, and told Augustus that, since he had behaved himself so well of late, he might take up his quarters in the cabin and be one of them for the future. He then poured him out a tumbler half full of rum, and made him drink it. All this I saw and heard, for I followed my friends to the cabin as soon as the door was shut, and took up my old point of observation. I had brought with me the two pump handles, one of which I secured near the companionway, to be ready for use when required.

I now steadied myself as well as possible so as to have a good view of all that was passing within, and endeavoured to nerve myself to the task of descending among the mutineers when Peters should make a signal to me, as agreed upon. Presently he contrived to turn the conversation upon the bloody deeds of the mutiny, and by degrees led the men to talk of the thousand superstitions which are so universally current among seamen. I could not make out all that was said, but I could plainly see the effects of the conversation in the countenances of those present. The mate was evidently much agitated, and presently, when someone mentioned the terrific appearance of Rogers's corpse, I thought he was upon the point of swooning. Peters now asked him if he did not think it would be better to have the body thrown overboard at once as it was too horrible a sight to see it floundering about in the scuppers. At this the villain absolutely gasped for breath, and turned his head slowly round upon his companions, as if imploring someone to go up and perform the task. No one, however, stirred, and it was quite evident that the whole party were wound up to the highest pitch of nervous excitement. Peters now made me the signal. I immediately threw open the door of the companionway, and, descending, without uttering a syllable, stood erect in the midst of the party.

The intense effect produced by this sudden apparition is not at all to be wondered at when the various circumstances are taken into consideration. Usually, in cases of a similar nature, there is left in the mind of the spectator some glimmering of doubt as to the reality of the vision before his eyes: a degree of hope, however feeble, that he is the victim of chicanery, and that the apparition is not actually a visitant from the world of shadows. It is not too much to say that such remnants of doubt have been at the bottom of almost every such visitation, and that the appalling horror which has sometimes been brought about is to be attributed, even in the cases most in point, and where most suffering has been experienced, more to a kind of anticipative horror, lest the apparition *might possibly be* real, than to an unwavering belief in its reality. But, in the present instance, it will be seen immediately that in the minds of the mutineers there was not even the shadow of a basis upon which to rest a doubt that the apparition of Rogers was indeed a revivification of his disgusting corpse, or at least its spiritual image. The isolated situation of the brig, with its entire inaccessibility on account of the gale, confined the apparently possible means of deception within such narrow and definite limits that they must have thought themselves enabled to survey them all at a glance. They had now been at sea twenty-four days, without holding more than a speaking

communication with any vessel whatever. The whole of the crew, too –
at least all whom they had the most remote reason for suspecting to be
on board – were assembled in the cabin, with the exception of Allen, the
watch, and his gigantic stature (he was six feet six inches high) was too
familiar in their eyes to permit the notion that he was the apparition before
them to enter their minds even for an instant. Add to these considerations
the awe-inspiring nature of the tempest, and that of the conversation
brought about by Peters; the deep impression which the loathsomeness of
the actual corpse had made in the morning upon the imaginations of the
men; the excellence of the imitation in my person, and the uncertain and
wavering light in which they beheld me, as the glare of the cabin lantern,
swinging violently to and fro, fell dubiously and fitfully upon my figure,
and there will be no reason to wonder that the deception had even more
than the entire effect which we had anticipated. The mate sprang up from
the mattress on which he was lying, and, without uttering a syllable, fell
back, stone dead, upon the cabin floor, and was hurled to the leeward like
a log by a heavy roll of the brig. Of the remaining seven, there were but
three who had at first any degree of presence of mind. The four others sat
for some time rooted apparently to the floor – the most pitiable objects of
horror and utter despair my eyes ever encountered. The only opposition
we experienced at all was from the cook, John Hunt and Richard Parker,
but they made but a feeble and irresolute defence. The two former were
shot instantly by Peters, and I felled Parker with a blow on the head
from the pump handle which I had brought with me. In the mean time,
Augustus seized one of the muskets lying on the floor and shot another
mutineer (—— Wilson) through the breast. There were now but three
remaining, but by this time they had become aroused from their lethargy,
and perhaps began to see that a deception had been practised upon them,
for they fought with great resolution and fury, and, but for the immense
muscular strength of Peters, might have ultimately got the better of us.
These three men were —— Jones, —— Greely and Absalom Hicks. Jones
had thrown Augustus on the floor, stabbed him in several places along the
right arm, and would no doubt have soon dispatched him (as neither Peters
nor myself could immediately get rid of our own antagonists) had it not
been for the timely aid of a friend, upon whose assistance we, surely, had
never depended. This friend was no other than Tiger.* With a low growl
he bounded into the cabin, at a most critical moment for Augustus, and,
throwing himself upon Jones, pinned him to the floor in an instant. My
friend, however, was now too much injured to render us any aid whatever,

and I was so encumbered with my disguise that I could do but little. The dog would not leave his hold upon the throat of Jones – Peters, nevertheless, was far more than a match for the two men who remained, and would, no doubt, have dispatched them sooner had it not been for the narrow space in which he had to act, and the tremendous lurches of the vessel. Presently he was enabled to get hold of a heavy stool, several of which lay about the floor. With this he beat out the brains of Greely as he was in the act of discharging a musket at me, and immediately afterwards a roll of the brig throwing him in contact with Hicks, he seized him by the throat, and, by dint of sheer strength, strangled him instantaneously. Thus, in far less time than I have taken to tell it, we found ourselves masters of the brig.

The only person of our opponents who was left alive was Richard Parker. This man, it will be remembered, I had knocked down with a blow from the pump handle at the commencement of the attack. He now lay motionless by the door of the shattered stateroom, but, upon Peters touching him with his foot, he spoke, and entreated for mercy. His head was only slightly cut, and otherwise he had received no injury, having been merely stunned by the blow. He now got up, and, for the present, we secured his hands behind his back. The dog was still growling over Jones, but, upon examination, we found him completely dead, the blood issuing in a stream from a deep wound in the throat, inflicted, no doubt, by the sharp teeth of the animal.

It was now about one o'clock in the morning, and the wind was still blowing tremendously. The brig evidently laboured much more than usual, and it became absolutely necessary that something should be done with a view of easing her in some measure. At almost every roll to leeward she shipped a sea,* several of which came partially down into the cabin during our scuffle, the hatchway having been left open by myself when I descended. The entire range of bulwarks to larboard had been swept away, as well as the caboose,* together with the jolly-boat from the counter. The creaking and working of the mainmast, too, gave indication that it was nearly sprung.* To make room for more stowage in the after-hold, the heel of this mast had been stepped between decks* (a very reprehensible practice, occasionally resorted to by ignorant shipbuilders), so that it was in imminent danger of working from its step. But, to crown all our difficulties, we plumbed the well, and found no less than seven feet water.

Leaving the bodies of the crew lying in the cabin, we got to work immediately at the pumps – Parker, of course, being set at liberty to assist

us in the labour. Augustus's arm was bound up as well as we could effect it, and he did what he could, but that was not much. However, we found that we could just manage to keep the leak from gaining upon us by having one pump constantly going. As there were only four of us, this was severe labour, but we endeavoured to keep up our spirits, and looked anxiously for daybreak, when we hoped to lighten the brig by cutting away the mainmast.

In this manner we passed a night of terrible anxiety and fatigue, and, when the day at length broke, the gale had neither abated in the least, nor were there any signs of its abating. We now dragged the bodies on deck and threw them overboard. Our next care was to get rid of the mainmast. The necessary preparations having been made, Peters cut away at the mast (having found axes in the cabin), while the rest of us stood by the stays and lanyards. As the brig gave a tremendous lee-lurch, the word was given to cut away the weather lanyards,* which being done, the whole mass of wood and rigging plunged into the sea, clear of the brig, and without doing any material injury. We now found that the vessel did not labour quite as much as before, but our situation was still exceedingly precarious, and in spite of the utmost exertions, we could not gain upon the leak without the aid of both pumps.* The little assistance which Augustus could render us was not really of any importance. To add to our distress, a heavy sea, striking the brig to windward, threw her off several points from the wind, and, before she could regain her position, another broke completely over her, and hurled her full upon her beam ends. The ballast now shifted in a mass to leeward (the stowage had been knocking about perfectly at random for some time), and for a few moments we thought nothing could save us from capsizing. Presently, however, we partially righted, but the ballast still retaining its place to larboard, we lay so much along that it was useless to think of working the pumps, which indeed we could not have done much longer in any case, as our hands were entirely raw with the excessive labour we had undergone, and were bleeding in the most horrible manner.

Contrary to Parker's advice, we now proceeded to cut away the foremast, and at length accomplished it after much difficulty, owing to the position in which we lay. In going overboard the wreck took with it the bowsprit,* and left us a complete hulk.

So far we had had reason to rejoice in the escape of our longboat, which had received no damage from any of the huge seas which had come on board. But we had not long to congratulate ourselves, for the foremast having gone, and, of course, the foresail with it, by which the brig had been steadied, every sea now made a complete breach over us, and in five

minutes our deck was swept from stem to stern, the longboat and star-board bulwarks torn off, and even the windlass* shattered into fragments. It was, indeed, hardly possible for us to be in a more pitiable condition.

At noon there seemed to be some slight appearance of the gale's abating, but in this we were sadly disappointed, for it only lulled for a few minutes to blow with redoubled fury. About four in the afternoon it was utterly impossible to stand up against the violence of the blast, and, as the night closed in upon us, I had not a shadow of hope that the vessel would hold together until morning.

By midnight we had settled very deep in the water, which was now up to the orlop deck. The rudder went soon afterwards, the sea which tore it away lifting the after portion of the brig entirely from the water, against which she thumped in her descent with such a concussion as would be occasioned by going ashore. We had all calculated that the rudder would hold its own to the last, as it was unusually strong, being rigged as I have never seen one rigged either before or since. Down its main timber there ran a succession of stout iron hooks, and others in the same manner down the sternpost.* Through these hooks there extended a very thick wrought-iron rod, the rudder being thus held to the sternpost and swinging freely on the rod. The tremendous force of the sea which tore it off may be estimated by the fact that the hooks in the sternpost, which ran entirely through it, being clinched on the inside, were drawn every one of them completely out of the solid wood.

We had scarcely time to draw breath after the violence of this shock when one of the most tremendous waves I had then ever known broke right on board of us, sweeping the companionway clear off, bursting in the hatchways, and filling every inch of the vessel with water.

CHAPTER IX

Luckily, just before night, all four of us had lashed ourselves firmly to the fragments of the windlass, lying in this manner as flat upon the deck as possible. This precaution alone saved us from destruction. As it was, we were all more or less stunned by the immense weight of water which tumbled upon us, and which did not roll from above us until we were nearly exhausted. As soon as I could recover breath, I called aloud to my companions. Augustus alone replied, saying: "It is all over with us, and may God have mercy upon our souls!" By and by both the others were

enabled to speak, when they exhorted us to take courage, as there was still hope – it being impossible, from the nature of the cargo, that the brig could go down, and there being every chance that the gale would blow over by the morning. These words inspired me with new life, for, strange as it may seem, although it was obvious that a vessel with a cargo of empty oil casks would not sink, I had been hitherto so confused in mind as to have overlooked this consideration altogether, and the danger which I had for some time regarded as the most imminent was that of foundering. As hope revived within me, I made use of every opportunity to strengthen the lashings which held me to the remains of the windlass, and in this occupation I soon discovered that my companions were also busy. The night was as dark as it could possibly be, and the horrible shrieking din and confusion which surrounded us it is useless to attempt describing. Our deck lay level with the sea, or rather we were encircled with a towering ridge of foam, a portion of which swept over us every instant. It is not too much to say that our heads were not fairly out of water more than one second in three. Although we lay close together, no one of us could see the other, or, indeed, any portion of the brig itself, upon which we were so tempestuously hurled about. At intervals we called one to the other, thus endeavouring to keep alive hope, and render consolation and encouragement to such of us as stood most in need of it. The feeble condition of Augustus made him an object of solicitude with us all, and as, from the lacerated condition of his right arm, it must have been impossible for him to secure his lashings with any degree of firmness, we were in momentary expectation of finding that he had gone overboard – yet to render him aid was a thing altogether out of the question. Fortunately, his station was more secure than that of any of the rest of us, for the upper part of his body lying just beneath a portion of the shattered windlass, the seas, as they tumbled in upon him, were greatly broken in their violence. In any other situation than this (into which he had been accidentally thrown after having lashed himself in a very exposed spot) he must inevitably have perished before morning. Owing to the brig's lying so much along, we were all less liable to be washed off than otherwise would have been the case. The heel, as I have before stated, was to larboard, about one half of the deck being constantly underwater. The seas, therefore, which struck us to starboard were much broken by the vessel's side, only reaching us in fragments as we lay flat on our faces, while those which came from larboard, being what are called back-water seas, and obtaining little hold upon us on account of our posture, had not sufficient force to drag us from our fastenings.

In this frightful situation we lay until the day broke so as to show us more fully the horrors which surrounded us. The brig was a mere log, rolling about at the mercy of every wave; the gale was upon the increase, if anything, blowing indeed a complete hurricane, and there appeared to us no earthly prospect of deliverance. For several hours we held on in silence, expecting every moment that our lashings would either give way, that the remains of the windlass would go by the board, or that some of the huge seas, which roared in every direction around us and above us, would drive the hulk so far beneath the water that we should be drowned before it could regain the surface. By the mercy of God, however, we were preserved from these imminent dangers, and about midday were cheered by the light of the blessed sun. Shortly afterwards we could perceive a sensible diminution in the force of the wind, when, now for the first time since the latter part of the evening before, Augustus spoke, asking Peters, who lay closest to him, if he thought there was any possibility of our being saved. As no reply was at first made to this question, we all concluded that the hybrid had been drowned where he lay, but presently, to our great joy, he spoke, although very feebly, saying that he was in great pain, being so cut by the tightness of his lashings across the stomach that he must either find means of loosening them or perish, as it was impossible that he could endure his misery much longer. This occasioned us great distress, as it was altogether useless to think of aiding him in any manner while the sea continued washing over us as it did. We exhorted him to bear his sufferings with fortitude, and promised to seize the first opportunity which should offer itself to relieve him. He replied that it would soon be too late, that it would be all over with him before we could help him, and then, after moaning for some minutes, lay silent, when we concluded that he had perished.

As the evening drew on, the sea had fallen so much that scarcely more than one wave broke over the hulk from windward in the course of five minutes, and the wind had abated a great deal, although still blowing a severe gale. I had not heard any of my companions speak for hours, and now called to Augustus. He replied, although very feebly, so that I could not distinguish what he said. I then spoke to Peters and to Parker, neither of whom returned any answer.

Shortly after this period I fell into a state of partial insensibility, during which the most pleasing images floated in my imagination: such as green trees, waving meadows of ripe grain, processions of dancing girls, troops of cavalry and other fantasies. I now remember that, in all which passed before my mind's eye, *motion* was a predominant idea. Thus, I never

fancied any stationary object, such as a house, a mountain or anything of that kind, but windmills, ships, large birds, balloons, people on horseback, carriages driving furiously and similar moving objects presented themselves in endless succession. When I recovered from this state, the sun was, as near as I could guess, an hour high.* I had the greatest difficulty in bringing to recollection the various circumstances connected with my situation, and for some time remained firmly convinced that I was still in the hold of the brig, near the box, and that the body of Parker was that of Tiger.

When I at length completely came to my senses, I found that the wind blew no more than a moderate breeze, and that the sea was comparatively calm – so much so that it only washed over the brig amidships. My left arm had broken loose from its lashings, and was much cut about the elbow; my right was entirely benumbed, and the hand and wrist swollen prodigiously by the pressure of the rope, which had worked from the shoulder downwards. I was also in great pain from another rope which went about my waist, and had been drawn to an insufferable degree of tightness. Looking round upon my companions, I saw that Peters still lived, although a thick line was pulled so forcibly around his loins as to give him the appearance of being cut nearly in two; as I stirred, he made a feeble motion to me with his hand, pointing to the rope. Augustus gave no indication of life whatever, and was bent nearly double across a splinter of the windlass. Parker spoke to me when he saw me moving, and asked me if I had not sufficient strength to release him from his situation, saying that if I would summon up what spirits I could, and contrive to untie him, we might yet save our lives, but that otherwise we must all perish. I told him to take courage, and I would endeavour to free him. Feeling in my pantaloons' pocket, I got hold of my penknife, and, after several ineffectual attempts, at length succeeded in opening it. I then, with my left hand, managed to free my right from its fastenings, and afterwards cut the other ropes which held me. Upon attempting, however, to move from my position, I found that my legs failed me altogether, and that I could not get up – neither could I move my right arm in any direction. Upon mentioning this to Parker, he advised me to lie quiet for a few minutes, holding on to the windlass with my left hand, so as to allow time for the blood to circulate. Doing this, the numbness presently began to die away so that I could move first one of my legs, and then the other, and, shortly afterwards, I regained the partial use of my right arm. I now crawled with great caution towards Parker, without getting on my legs, and soon cut loose all the lashings

about him, when, after a short delay, he also recovered the partial use of his limbs. We now lost no time in getting loose the rope from Peters. It had cut a deep gash through the waistband of his woollen pantaloons, and through two shirts, and made its way into his groin, from which the blood flowed out copiously as we removed the cordage. No sooner had we removed it, however, than he spoke, and seemed to experience instant relief, being able to move with much greater ease than either Parker or myself – this was no doubt owing to the discharge of blood.

We had little hope that Augustus would recover, as he evinced no signs of life, but, upon getting to him, we discovered that he had merely swooned from loss of blood, the bandages we had placed around his wounded arm having been torn off by the water – none of the ropes which held him to the windlass were drawn sufficiently tight to occasion his death. Having relieved him from the fastenings, and got him clear of the broken wood about the windlass, we secured him in a dry place to windward, with his head somewhat lower than his body, and all three of us busied ourselves in chafing his limbs. In about half an hour he came to himself, although it was not until the next morning that he gave signs of recognizing any of us, or had sufficient strength to speak. By the time we had thus got clear of our lashings it was quite dark, and it began to cloud up, so that we were again in the greatest agony lest it should come on to blow hard, in which event nothing could have saved us from perishing, exhausted as we were. By good fortune it continued very moderate during the night, the sea subsiding every minute, which gave us great hopes of ultimate preservation. A gentle breeze still blew from the NW, but the weather was not at all cold. Augustus was lashed carefully to windward in such a manner as to prevent him from slipping overboard with the rolls of the vessel, as he was still too weak to hold on at all. For ourselves there was no such necessity. We sat close together, supporting each other with the aid of the broken ropes about the windlass, and devising methods of escape from our frightful situation. We derived much comfort from taking off our clothes and wringing the water from them. When we put them on after this, they felt remarkably warm and pleasant, and served to invigorate us in no little degree. We helped Augustus off with his, and wrung them for him, when he experienced the same comfort.

Our chief sufferings were now those of hunger and thirst, and when we looked forward to the means of relief in this respect, our hearts sank within us, and we were induced to regret that we had escaped the less dreadful perils of the sea. We endeavoured, however, to console ourselves

with the hope of being speedily picked up by some vessel and encouraged each other to bear with fortitude the evils that might happen.

The morning of the fourteenth at length dawned, and the weather still continued clear and pleasant, with a steady but very light breeze from the NW. The sea was now quite smooth, and as, from some cause which we could not determine, the brig did not lie so much along as she had done before, the deck was comparatively dry, and we could move about with freedom. We had now been better than three entire days and nights without either food or drink, and it became absolutely necessary that we should make an attempt to get up something from below. As the brig was completely full of water, we went to this work despondingly, and with but little expectation of being able to obtain anything. We made a kind of drag by driving some nails which we broke out from the remains of the companion hatch into two pieces of wood. Tying these across each other, and fastening them to the end of a rope, we threw them into the cabin, and dragged them to and fro, in the faint hope of being thus able to entangle some article which might be of use to us for food, or which might at least render us assistance in getting it. We spent the greater part of the morning in this labour without effect, fishing up nothing more than a few bedclothes, which were readily caught by the nails. Indeed, our contrivance was so very clumsy that any greater success was hardly to be anticipated.

We now tried the forecastle, but equally in vain, and were upon the brink of despair when Peters proposed that we should fasten a rope to his body, and let him make an attempt to get up something by diving into the cabin. This proposition we hailed with all the delight which reviving hope could inspire. He proceeded immediately to strip off his clothes with the exception of his pantaloons, and a strong rope was then carefully fastened around his middle, being brought up over his shoulders in such a manner that there was no possibility of its slipping. The undertaking was one of great difficulty and danger, for, as we could hardly expect to find much, if any, provision in the cabin itself, it was necessary that the diver, after letting himself down, should make a turn to the right, and proceed underwater a distance of ten or twelve feet, in a narrow passage, to the storeroom, and return, without drawing breath.

Everything being ready, Peters now descended into the cabin, going down the companion ladder until the water reached his chin. He then plunged in, head first, turning to the right as he plunged, and endeavouring to make his way to the storeroom. In this first attempt, however, he was altogether unsuccessful. In less than half a minute after his going down we felt the

rope jerked violently (the signal we had agreed upon when he desired to be drawn up). We accordingly drew him up instantly, but so incautiously as to bruise him badly against the ladder. He had brought nothing with him, and had been unable to penetrate more than a very little way into the passage, owing to the constant exertions he found it necessary to make in order to keep himself from floating up against the deck. Upon getting out he was very much exhausted, and had to rest full fifteen minutes before he could again venture to descend.

The second attempt met with even worse success, for he remained so long underwater without giving the signal that, becoming alarmed for his safety, we drew him out without it, and found that he was almost at the last gasp, having, as he said, repeatedly jerked at the rope without our feeling it. This was probably owing to a portion of it having become entangled in the balustrade at the foot of the ladder. This balustrade was, indeed, so much in the way that we determined to remove it, if possible, before proceeding with our design. As we had no means of getting it away except by main force, we all descended into the water as far as we could on the ladder, and, giving a pull against it with our united strength, succeeded in breaking it down.

The third attempt was equally unsuccessful with the two first, and it now became evident that nothing could be done in this manner without the aid of some weight with which the diver might steady himself, and keep to the floor of the cabin while making his search. For a long time we looked about in vain for something which might answer this purpose, but at length, to our great joy, we discovered one of the weather forechains* so loose that we had not the least difficulty in wrenching it off. Having fastened this securely to one of his ankles, Peters now made his fourth descent into the cabin, and this time succeeded in making his way to the door of the steward's room. To his inexpressible grief, however, he found it locked, and was obliged to return without effecting an entrance, as, with the greatest exertion, he could remain underwater not more, at the utmost extent, than a single minute. Our affairs now looked gloomy indeed, and neither Augustus nor myself could refrain from bursting into tears, as we thought of the host of difficulties which encompassed us, and the slight probability which existed of our finally making an escape. But this weakness was not of long duration. Throwing ourselves on our knees to God, we implored his aid in the many dangers which beset us, and arose with renewed hope and vigour to think what could yet be done by mortal means towards accomplishing our deliverance.

CHAPTER X

Shortly afterwards an incident occurred which I am induced to look upon as more intensely productive of emotion, as far more replete with the extremes first of delight and then of horror, than even any of the thousand chances which afterwards befell me in nine long years,* crowded with events of the most startling and, in many cases, of the most unconceived and unconceivable character. We were lying on the deck near the companionway, and debating the possibility of yet making our way into the storeroom, when, looking towards Augustus, who lay fronting myself, I perceived that he had become all at once deadly pale, and that his lips were quivering in the most singular and unaccountable manner. Greatly alarmed, I spoke to him, but he made me no reply, and I was beginning to think that he was suddenly taken ill when I took notice of his eyes, which were glaring apparently at some object behind me. I turned my head, and shall never forget the ecstatic joy which thrilled through every particle of my frame when I perceived a large brig bearing down upon us, and not more than a couple of miles off. I sprang to my feet as if a musket bullet had suddenly struck me to the heart, and, stretching out my arms in the direction of the vessel, stood in this manner, motionless, and unable to articulate a syllable. Peters and Parker were equally affected, although in different ways. The former danced about the deck like a madman, uttering the most extravagant rodomontades, intermingled with howls and imprecations, while the latter burst into tears, and continued for many minutes weeping like a child.

The vessel in sight was a large hermaphrodite brig,* of a Dutch build, and painted black, with a tawdry gilt figurehead. She had evidently seen a good deal of rough weather, and, we supposed, had suffered much in the gale which had proved so disastrous to ourselves, for her foretopmast* was gone, and some of her starboard bulwarks. When we first saw her, she was, as I have already said, about two miles off and to windward, bearing down upon us. The breeze was very gentle, and what astonished us chiefly was that she had no other sails set than her foresail and mainsail, with a flying jib – of course she came down but slowly, and our impatience amounted nearly to frenzy. The awkward manner in which she steered, too, was remarked by all of us, even excited as we were. She yawed about so considerably that once or twice we thought it impossible she could see us, or imagined that, having seen us, and discovered no person on board, she was about to tack and make off in another direction. Upon each of

these occasions we screamed and shouted at the top of our voices, when the stranger would appear to change for a moment her intention, and again hold on towards us – this singular conduct being repeated two or three times, so that at last we could think of no other manner of accounting for it than by supposing the helmsman to be in liquor.

No person was seen upon her decks* until she arrived within about a quarter of a mile of us. We then saw three seamen, whom by their dress we took to be Hollanders. Two of these were lying on some old sails near the forecastle, and the third, who appeared to be looking at us with great curiosity, was leaning over the starboard bow near the bowsprit. This last was a stout and tall man, with a very dark skin. He seemed by his manner to be encouraging us to have patience, nodding to us in a cheerful although rather odd way, and smiling constantly, so as to display a set of the most brilliantly white teeth. As his vessel drew nearer, we saw a red flannel cap which he had on fall from his head into the water, but of this he took little or no notice, continuing his odd smiles and gesticulations. I relate these things and circumstances minutely, and I relate them, it must be understood, precisely as they *appeared* to us.

The brig came on slowly, and now more steadily than before, and – I cannot speak calmly of this event – our hearts leapt up wildly within us, and we poured out our whole souls in shouts and thanksgiving to God for the complete, unexpected and glorious deliverance that was so palpably at hand. Of a sudden, and all at once, there came wafted over the ocean from the strange vessel (which was now close upon us) a smell, a stench, such as the whole world has no name for – no conception of – hellish – utterly suffocating – insufferable, inconceivable. I gasped for breath, and, turning to my companions, perceived that they were paler than marble. But we had now no time left for question or surmise – the brig was within fifty feet of us, and it seemed to be her intention to run under our counter, that we might board her without putting out a boat. We rushed aft, when, suddenly, a wide yaw* threw her off full five or six points from the course she had been running and, as she passed under our stern at the distance of about twenty feet, we had a full view of her decks. Shall I ever forget the triple horror of that spectacle? Twenty-five or thirty human bodies, among whom were several females, lay scattered about between the counter and the galley in the last and most loathsome state of putrefaction! We plainly saw that not a soul lived in that fated vessel! Yet we could not help shouting to the dead for help! Yes, long and loudly did we beg, in the agony of the moment, that those silent and disgusting images would stay for us,

would not abandon us to become like them, would receive us among their goodly company! We were raving with horror and despair – thoroughly mad through the anguish of our grievous disappointment.

As our first loud yell of terror broke forth, it was replied to by something, from near the bowsprit of the stranger, so closely resembling the scream of a human voice that the nicest* ear might have been startled and deceived. At this instant another sudden yaw brought the region of the forecastle for a moment into view, and we beheld at once the origin of the sound. We saw the tall stout figure still leaning on the bulwark, and still nodding his head to and fro, but his face was now turned from us so that we could not behold it. His arms were extended over the rail, and the palms of his hands fell outward. His knees were lodged upon a stout rope, tightly stretched, and reaching from the heel of the bowsprit to a cathead.* On his back, from which a portion of the shirt had been torn, leaving it bare, there sat a huge seagull, busily gorging itself with the horrible flesh, its bill and talons deep buried, and its white plumage spattered all over with blood. As the brig moved farther round so as to bring us close in view, the bird, with much apparent difficulty, drew out its crimsoned head, and, after eyeing us for a moment as if stupefied, arose lazily from the body upon which it had been feasting, and, flying directly above our deck, hovered there a while with a portion of clotted and liver-like substance in its beak. The horrid morsel dropped at length with a sullen splash immediately at the feet of Parker. May God forgive me, but now, for the first time, there flashed through my mind a thought, a thought which I will not mention, and I felt myself making a step towards the ensanguined spot. I looked upwards, and the eyes of Augustus met my own with a degree of intense and eager meaning which immediately brought me to my senses. I sprang forward quickly, and, with a deep shudder, threw the frightful thing into the sea.

The body from which it had been taken, resting as it did upon the rope, had been easily swayed to and fro by the exertions of the carnivorous bird, and it was this motion which had at first impressed us with the belief of its being alive. As the gull relieved it of its weight, it swung round and fell partially over, so that the face was fully discovered. Never, surely, was any object so terribly full of awe! The eyes were gone, and the whole flesh around the mouth, leaving the teeth utterly naked. This, then, was the smile which had cheered us on to hope! This the... But I forbear. The brig, as I have already told, passed under our stern, and made its way slowly but steadily to leeward. With her and with her terrible crew went all our gay visions of deliverance and joy. Deliberately as she went by, we might

possibly have found means of boarding her, had not our sudden disappoint-
ment and the appalling nature of the discovery which accompanied it laid
entirely prostrate every active faculty of mind and body. We had seen and
felt, but we could neither think nor act, until – alas! – too late. How much
our intellects had been weakened by this incident may be estimated by the
fact that when the vessel had proceeded so far that we could perceive no
more than the half of her hull, the proposition was seriously entertained
of attempting to overtake her by swimming!

I have, since this period, vainly endeavoured to obtain some clue to the
hideous uncertainty which enveloped the fate of the stranger. Her build and
general appearance, as I have before stated, led us to the belief that she was
a Dutch trader, and the dresses of the crew also sustained this opinion. We
might have easily seen the name upon her stern, and, indeed, taken other
observations, which would have guided us in making out her character,
but the intense excitement of the moment blinded us to everything of that
nature. From the saffron-like hue of such of the corpses as were not entirely
decayed, we concluded that the whole of her company had perished by the
yellow fever,* or some other virulent disease of the same fearful kind. If
such were the case (and I know not what else to imagine), death, to judge
from the positions of the bodies, must have come upon them in a manner
awfully sudden and overwhelming – in a way totally distinct from that
which generally characterizes even the most deadly pestilences with which
mankind are acquainted. It is possible, indeed, that poison, accidentally
introduced into some of their sea-stores, may have brought about the dis-
aster, or that the eating some unknown venomous species of fish, or other
marine animal, or oceanic bird, might have induced it – but it is utterly
useless to form conjectures where all is involved, and will, no doubt, remain
for ever involved, in the most appalling and unfathomable mystery.

CHAPTER XI

We spent the remainder of the day in a condition of stupid lethargy, gazing
after the retreating vessel until the darkness, hiding her from our sight,
recalled us in some measure to our senses. The pangs of hunger and thirst
then returned, absorbing all other cares and considerations. Nothing,
however, could be done until the morning, and, securing ourselves as well
as possible, we endeavoured to snatch a little repose. In this I succeeded
beyond my expectation, sleeping until my companions, who had not been

so fortunate, aroused me at daybreak to renew our attempts at getting up provision from the hull.

It was now a dead calm, with the sea as smooth as I have ever known it – the weather warm and pleasant. The brig was out of sight. We commenced our operations by wrenching off, with some trouble, another of the forechains, and having fastened both to Peters's feet, he again made an endeavour to reach the door of the storeroom, thinking it possible that he might be able to force it open, provided he could get at it in sufficient time, and this he hoped to do, as the hulk lay much more steadily than before.

He succeeded very quickly in reaching the door, when, loosening one of the chains from his ankle, he made every exertion to force a passage with it, but in vain, the framework of the room being far stronger than was anticipated. He was quite exhausted with his long stay underwater, and it became absolutely necessary that some other one of us should take his place. For this service Parker immediately volunteered, but, after making three ineffectual efforts, found that he could never even succeed in getting near the door. The condition of Augustus's wounded arm rendered it useless for him to attempt going down, as he would be unable to force the room open should he reach it, and it accordingly now devolved upon me to exert myself for our common deliverance.

Peters had left one of the chains in the passage, and I found, upon plunging in, that I had not sufficient ballast to keep me firmly down. I determined, therefore, to attempt no more, in my first effort, than merely to recover the other chain. In groping along the floor of the passage for this, I felt a hard substance, which I immediately grasped, not having time to ascertain what it was, but returning and ascending instantly to the surface. The prize proved to be a bottle, and our joy may be conceived when I say that it was found to be full of port wine. Giving thanks to God for this timely and cheering assistance, we immediately drew the cork with my penknife, and, each taking a moderate sup, felt the most indescribable comfort from the warmth, strength and spirits with which it inspired us. We then carefully recorked the bottle, and, by means of a handkerchief, swung it in such a manner that there was no possibility of its getting broken.

Having rested a while after this fortunate discovery, I again descended, and now recovered the chain, with which I instantly came up. I then fastened it on and went down for the third time, when I became fully satisfied that no exertions whatever, in that situation, would enable me to force open the door of the storeroom. I therefore returned in despair.

There seemed now to be no longer any room for hope, and I could perceive in the countenances of my companions that they had made up their minds to perish. The wine had evidently produced in them a species of delirium, which, perhaps, I had been prevented from feeling by the immersion I had undergone since drinking it. They talked incoherently, and about matters unconnected with our condition, Peters repeatedly asking me questions about Nantucket. Augustus, too, I remember, approached me with a serious air, and requested me to lend him a pocket comb, as his hair was full of fish scales, and he wished to get them out before going on shore. Parker appeared somewhat less affected, and urged me to dive at random into the cabin, and bring up any article which might come to hand. To this I consented, and, in the first attempt, after staying under a full minute, brought up a small leather trunk belonging to Captain Barnard. This was immediately opened in the faint hope that it might contain something to eat or drink. We found nothing, however, except a box of razors and two linen shirts. I now went down again, and returned without any success. As my head came above water I heard a crash on deck, and, upon getting up, saw that my companions had ungratefully taken advantage of my absence to drink the remainder of the wine, having let the bottle fall in the endeavour to replace it before I saw them. I remonstrated with them on the heartlessness of their conduct, when Augustus burst into tears. The other two endeavoured to laugh the matter off as a joke, but I hope never again to behold laughter of such a species: the distortion of countenance was absolutely frightful. Indeed, it was apparent that the stimulus, in the empty state of their stomachs, had taken instant and violent effect, and that they were all exceedingly intoxicated. With great difficulty I prevailed upon them to lie down, when they fell very soon into a heavy slumber, accompanied with loud stertorous breathing.

I now found myself, as it were, alone in the brig, and my reflections, to be sure, were of the most fearful and gloomy nature. No prospect offered itself to my view but a lingering death by famine, or, at the best, by being overwhelmed in the first gale which should spring up, for in our present exhausted condition we could have no hope of living through another.

The gnawing hunger which I now experienced was nearly insupportable, and I felt myself capable of going to any lengths in order to appease it. With my knife I cut off a small portion of the leather trunk, and endeavoured to eat it, but found it utterly impossible to swallow a single morsel, although I fancied that some little alleviation of my suffering was obtained by chewing small pieces of it and spitting them out. Towards

night my companions awoke, one by one, each in an indescribable state of weakness and horror, brought on by the wine, whose fumes had now evaporated. They shook as if with a violent ague, and uttered the most lamentable cries for water. Their condition affected me in the most lively degree, at the same time causing me to rejoice in the fortunate train of circumstances which had prevented me from indulging in the wine, and consequently from sharing their melancholy and most distressing sensations. Their conduct, however, gave me great uneasiness and alarm, for it was evident that, unless some favourable change took place, they could afford me no assistance in providing for our common safety. I had not yet abandoned all idea of being able to get up something from below, but the attempt could not possibly be resumed until some one of them was sufficiently master of himself to aid me by holding the end of the rope while I went down. Parker appeared to be somewhat more in possession of his senses than the others, and I endeavoured, by every means in my power, to arouse him. Thinking that a plunge in the sea water might have a beneficial effect, I contrived to fasten the end of a rope around his body, and then, leading him to the companionway (he remaining quite passive all the while), pushed him in, and immediately drew him out. I had good reason to congratulate myself upon having made this experiment, for he appeared much revived and invigorated, and, upon getting out, asked me, in a rational manner, why I had so served him. Having explained my object, he expressed himself indebted to me, and said that he felt greatly better from the immersion, afterwards conversing sensibly upon our situation. We then resolved to treat Augustus and Peters in the same way, which we immediately did, when they both experienced much benefit from the shock. This idea of sudden immersion had been suggested to me by reading in some medical work the good effect of the shower bath in a case where the patient was suffering from *mania a potu.**

Finding that I could now trust my companions to hold the end of the rope, I again made three or four plunges into the cabin, although it was now quite dark, and a gentle but long swell from the northward rendered the hulk somewhat unsteady. In the course of these attempts I succeeded in bringing up two case knives, a three-gallon jug – empty – and a blanket, but nothing which could serve us for food. I continued my efforts, after getting these articles, until I was completely exhausted, but brought up nothing else. During the night Parker and Peters occupied themselves by turns in the same manner, but, nothing coming to hand, we now gave up this attempt in despair, concluding that we were exhausting ourselves in vain.

We passed the remainder of this night in a state of the most intense mental and bodily anguish that can possibly be imagined. The morning of the sixteenth at length dawned, and we looked eagerly around the horizon for relief, but to no purpose. The sea was still smooth, with only a long swell from the northward, as on yesterday. This was the sixth day since we had tasted either food or drink, with the exception of the bottle of port wine, and it was clear that we could hold out but a very little while longer unless something could be obtained. I never saw before, nor wish to see again, human beings so utterly emaciated as Peters and Augustus. Had I met them on shore in their present condition I should not have had the slightest suspicion that I had ever beheld them. Their countenances were totally changed in character, so that I could not bring myself to believe them really the same individuals with whom I had been in company but a few days before. Parker, although sadly reduced, and so feeble that he could not raise his head from his bosom, was not so far gone as the other two. He suffered with great patience, making no complaint, and endeavouring to inspire us with hope in every manner he could devise. For myself, although at the commencement of the voyage I had been in bad health, and was at all times of a delicate constitution, I suffered less than any of us, being much less reduced in frame, and retaining my powers of mind in a surprising degree, while the rest were completely prostrated in intellect, and seemed to be brought to a species of second childhood, generally simpering in their expressions, with idiotic smiles, and uttering the most absurd platitudes. At intervals, however, they would appear to revive suddenly, as if inspired all at once with a consciousness of their condition, when they would spring upon their feet in a momentary flash of vigour, and speak, for a short period, of their prospects, in a manner altogether rational, although full of the most intense despair. It is possible, however, that my companions may have entertained the same opinion of their own condition as I did of mine, and that I may have unwittingly been guilty of the same extravagances and imbecilities as themselves – this is a matter which cannot be determined.

About noon Parker declared that he saw land off the larboard quarter, and it was with the utmost difficulty I could restrain him from plunging into the sea with the view of swimming towards it. Peters and Augustus took little notice of what he said, being apparently wrapped up in moody contemplation. Upon looking in the direction pointed out, I could not perceive the faintest appearance of the shore – indeed, I was too well aware that we were far from any land to indulge in a hope of that nature. It was

a long time, nevertheless, before I could convince Parker of his mistake. He then burst into a flood of tears, weeping like a child, with loud cries and sobs, for two or three hours, when, becoming exhausted, he fell asleep.

Peters and Augustus now made several ineffectual efforts to swallow portions of the leather. I advised them to chew it and spit it out, but they were too excessively debilitated to be able to follow my advice. I continued to chew pieces of it at intervals, and found some relief from so doing; my chief distress was for water, and I was only prevented from taking a draught from the sea by remembering the horrible consequences which thus have resulted to others who were similarly situated with ourselves.

The day wore on in this manner, when I suddenly discovered a sail to the eastward, and on our larboard bow. She appeared to be a large ship, and was coming nearly athwart us, being probably twelve or fifteen miles distant. None of my companions had as yet discovered her, and I forbore to tell them of her for the present, lest we might again be disappointed of relief. At length, upon her getting nearer, I saw distinctly that she was heading immediately for us, with her light sails filled. I could now contain myself no longer, and pointed her out to my fellow sufferers. They immediately sprang to their feet, again indulging in the most extravagant demonstrations of joy, weeping, laughing in an idiotic manner, jumping, stamping upon the deck, tearing their hair, and praying and cursing by turns. I was so affected by their conduct, as well as by what I now considered a sure prospect of deliverance, that I could not refrain from joining in with their madness, and gave way to the impulses of my gratitude and ecstasy by lying and rolling on the deck, clapping my hands, shouting, and other similar acts, until I was suddenly called to my recollection, and once more to the extreme human misery and despair, by perceiving the ship all at once with her stern fully presented towards us, and steering in a direction nearly opposite to that in which I had at first perceived her.

It was some time before I could induce my poor companions to believe that this sad reverse in our prospects had actually taken place. They replied to all my assertions with a stare and a gesture implying that they were not to be deceived by such misrepresentations. The conduct of Augustus most sensibly affected me. In spite of all I could say or do to the contrary, he persisted in saying that the ship was rapidly nearing us, and in making preparations to go on board of her. Some seaweed floating by the brig, he maintained that it was the ship's boat, and endeavoured to throw himself upon it, howling and shrieking in the most heart-rending manner, when I forcibly restrained him from thus casting himself into the sea.

Having become in some degree pacified, we continued to watch the ship until we finally lost sight of her, the weather becoming hazy, with a light breeze springing up. As soon as she was entirely gone, Parker turned suddenly towards me with an expression of countenance which made me shudder. There was about him an air of self-possession which I had not noticed in him until now, and before he opened his lips my heart told me what he would say. He proposed, in a few words, that one of us should die to preserve the existence of the others.

CHAPTER XII

I had, for some time past, dwelt upon the prospect of our being reduced to this last horrible extremity, and had secretly made up my mind to suffer death in any shape or under any circumstances rather than resort to such a course. Nor was this resolution in any degree weakened by the present intensity of hunger under which I laboured. The proposition had not been heard by either Peters or Augustus. I therefore took Parker aside, and, mentally praying to God for power to dissuade him from the horrible purpose he entertained, I expostulated with him for a long time, and in the most supplicating manner, begging him in the name of everything which he held sacred, and urging him by every species of argument which the extremity of the case suggested, to abandon the idea, and not to mention it to either of the other two.

He heard all I said without attempting to controvert any of my arguments, and I had begun to hope that he would be prevailed upon to do as I desired. But when I had ceased speaking, he said that he knew very well all I had said was true, and that to resort to such a course was the most horrible alternative which could enter into the mind of man, but that he had now held out as long as human nature could be sustained; that it was unnecessary for all to perish, when, by the death of one, it was possible, and even probable, that the rest might be finally preserved, adding that I might save myself the trouble of trying to turn him from his purpose, his mind having been thoroughly made up on the subject even before the appearance of the ship, and that only her heaving in sight had prevented him from mentioning his intention at an earlier period.

I now begged him, if he would not be prevailed upon to abandon his design, at least to defer it for another day, when some vessel might come to our relief, again reiterating every argument I could devise, and which

I thought likely to have influence with one of his rough nature. He said, in reply, that he had not spoken until the very last possible moment, that he could exist no longer without sustenance of some kind, and that therefore in another day his suggestion would be too late, as regarded himself at least.

Finding that he was not to be moved by anything I could say in a mild tone, I now assumed a different demeanour, and told him that he must be aware I had suffered less than any of us from our calamities; that my health and strength, consequently, were at that moment far better than his own, or than that either of Peters or Augustus; in short, that I was in a condition to have my own way by force if I found it necessary, and that if he attempted in any manner to acquaint the others with his bloody and cannibal designs, I would not hesitate to throw him into the sea. Upon this he immediately seized me by the throat, and drawing a knife, made several ineffectual efforts to stab me in the stomach – an atrocity which his excessive debility alone prevented him from accomplishing. In the mean time, being roused to a high pitch of anger, I forced him to the vessel's side, with the full intention of throwing him overboard. He was saved from this fate, however, by the interference of Peters, who now approached and separated us, asking the cause of the disturbance. This Parker told before I could find means in any manner to prevent him.

The effect of his words was even more terrible than what I had antici-pated. Both Augustus and Peters, who, it seems, had long secretly enter-tained the same fearful idea which Parker had been merely the first to broach, joined with him in his design, and insisted upon its being imme-diately carried into effect. I had calculated that one at least of the two former would be found still possessed of sufficient strength of mind to side with myself in resisting any attempt to execute so dreadful a purpose, and, with the aid of either one of them, I had no fear of being able to prevent its accomplishment. Being disappointed in this expectation, it became absolutely necessary that I should attend to my own safety, as a further resistance on my part might possibly be considered by men in their frightful condition a sufficient excuse for refusing me fair play in the tragedy that I knew would speedily be enacted.

I now told them I was willing to submit to the proposal, merely request-ing a delay of about one hour, in order that the fog which had gathered around us might have an opportunity of lifting, when it was possible that the ship we had seen might be again in sight. After great difficulty I obtained from them a promise to wait thus long, and, as I had anticipated

(a breeze rapidly coming in), the fog lifted before the hour had expired, when, no vessel appearing in sight, we prepared to draw lots.

It is with extreme reluctance that I dwell upon the appalling scene which ensued; a scene which, with its minutest details, no after events have been able to efface in the slightest degree from my memory, and whose stern recollection will embitter every future moment of my existence. Let me run over this portion of my narrative with as much haste as the nature of the events to be spoken of will permit. The only method we could devise for the terrific lottery, in which we were to take each a chance, was that of drawing straws. Small splinters of wood were made to answer our purpose, and it was agreed that I should be the holder. I retired to one end of the hulk, while my poor companions silently took up their station in the other with their backs turned towards me. The bitterest anxiety which I endured at any period of this fearful drama was while I occupied myself in the arrangement of the lots. There are few conditions into which man can possibly fall where he will not feel a deep interest in the preservation of his existence, an interest momentarily increasing with the frailness of the tenure by which that existence may be held. But now that the silent, definite and stern nature of the business in which I was engaged (so different from the tumultuous dangers of the storm or the gradually approaching horrors of famine) allowed me to reflect on the few chances I had of escaping the most appalling of deaths – a death for the most appalling of purposes – every particle of that energy which had so long buoyed me up departed like feathers before the wind, leaving me a helpless prey to the most abject and pitiable terror. I could not, at first, even summon up sufficient strength to tear and fit together the small splinters of wood, my fingers absolutely refusing their office, and my knees knocking violently against each other. My mind ran over rapidly a thousand absurd projects by which to avoid becoming a partner in the awful speculation. I thought of falling on my knees to my companions, and entreating them to let me escape this necessity; of suddenly rushing upon them, and, by putting one of them to death, of rendering the decision by lot useless – in short, of everything but of going through with the matter I had in hand. At last, after wasting a long time in this imbecile conduct, I was recalled to my senses by the voice of Parker, who urged me to relieve them at once from the terrible anxiety they were enduring. Even then I could not bring myself to arrange the splinters upon the spot, but thought over every species of finesse by which I could trick some one of my fellow sufferers to draw the short straw, as it had been agreed that whoever drew the shortest of four

splinters from my hand was to die for the preservation of the rest. Before anyone condemn me for this apparent heartlessness, let him be placed in a situation precisely similar to my own.

At length delay was no longer possible, and, with a heart almost bursting from my bosom, I advanced to the region of the forecastle, where my companions were awaiting me. I held out my hand with the splinters, and Peters immediately drew. He was free – *his*, at least, was not the shortest, and there was now another chance against my escape. I summoned up all my strength, and passed the lots to Augustus. He also drew immediately, and he also was free – and now, whether I should live or die, the chances were no more than precisely even. At this moment all the fierceness of the tiger possessed my bosom, and I felt towards my poor fellow creature, Parker, the most intense, the most diabolical hatred. But the feeling did not last, and, at length, with a convulsive shudder and closed eyes, I held out the two remaining splinters towards him. It was full five minutes before he could summon resolution to draw, during which period of heart-rending suspense I never once opened my eyes. Presently one of the two lots was quickly drawn from my hand. The decision was then over, yet I knew not whether it was for me or against me. No one spoke, and still I dared not satisfy myself by looking at the splinter I held. Peters at length took me by the hand, and I forced myself to look up, when I immediately saw by the countenance of Parker that I was safe, and that he it was who had been doomed to suffer. Gasping for breath, I fell senseless to the deck.

I recovered from my swoon in time to behold the consummation of the tragedy in the death of him who had been chiefly instrumental in bringing it about. He made no resistance whatever, and was stabbed in the back by Peters, when he fell instantly dead. I must not dwell upon the fearful repast which immediately ensued. Such things may be imagined, but words have no power to impress the mind with the exquisite horror of their reality. Let it suffice to say that, having in some measure appeased the raging thirst which consumed us by the blood of the victim, and having by common consent taken off the hands, feet and head, throwing them, together with the entrails, into the sea, we devoured the rest of the body, piecemeal, during the four ever-memorable days of the seventeenth, eighteenth, nineteenth and twentieth of the month.

On the nineteenth, there coming on a smart shower which lasted fifteen or twenty minutes, we contrived to catch some water by means of a sheet which had been fished up from the cabin by our drag just after the gale.

The quantity we took in all did not amount to more than half a gallon, but even this scanty allowance supplied us with comparative strength and hope.

On the twenty-first we were again reduced to the last necessity. The weather still remained warm and pleasant, with occasional fogs and light breezes, most usually from N. to W.

On the twenty-second, as we were sitting close huddled together, gloomily revolving over our lamentable condition, there flashed through my mind all at once an idea which inspired me with a bright gleam of hope. I remembered that, when the foremast had been cut away, Peters, being in the windward chains, passed one of the axes into my hand, requesting me to put it, if possible, in a place of security, and that a few minutes before the last heavy sea struck the brig and filled her I had taken this axe into the forecastle, and laid it in one of the larboard berths. I now thought it possible that, by getting at this axe, we might cut through the deck over the storeroom, and thus readily supply ourselves with provisions.

When I communicated this project to my companions, they uttered a feeble shout of joy, and we all proceeded forthwith to the forecastle. The difficulty of descending here was greater than that of going down in the cabin, the opening being much smaller, for it will be remembered that the whole framework about the cabin companion hatch had been carried away, whereas the forecastle-way, being a simple hatch of only about three feet square, had remained uninjured. I did not hesitate, however, to attempt the descent, and, a rope being fastened round my body as before, I plunged boldly in, feet foremost, made my way quickly to the berth, and at the very first attempt brought up the axe. It was hailed with the most ecstatic joy and triumph, and the ease with which it had been obtained was regarded as an omen of our ultimate preservation.

We now commenced cutting at the deck with all the energy of rekindled hope, Peters and myself taking the axe by turns, Augustus's wounded arm not permitting him to aid us in any degree. As we were still so feeble as to be scarcely able to stand unsupported, and could consequently work but a minute or two without resting, it soon became evident that many long hours would be requisite to accomplish our task – that is, to cut an opening sufficiently large to admit of a free access to the storeroom. This consideration, however, did not discourage us, and, working all night by the light of the moon, we succeeded in effecting our purpose by daybreak on the morning of the twenty-third.

Peters now volunteered to go down, and, having made all arrangements as before, he descended, and soon returned, bringing up with him

a small jar, which, to our great joy, proved to be full of olives. Having shared these among us, and devoured them with the greatest avidity, we proceeded to let him down again. This time he succeeded beyond our utmost expectations, returning instantly with a large ham and a bottle of Madeira wine. Of the latter we each took a moderate sup, having learnt by experience the pernicious consequences of indulging too freely. The ham, except about two pounds near the bone, was not in a condition to be eaten, having been entirely spoilt by the salt water. The sound part was divided among us. Peters and Augustus, not being able to restrain their appetite, swallowed theirs upon the instant, but I was more cautious, and ate but a small portion of mine, dreading the thirst which I knew would ensue. We now rested a while from our labours, which had been intolerably severe.

By noon, feeling somewhat strengthened and refreshed, we again renewed our attempt at getting up provision, Peters and myself going down alternately, and always with more or less success, until sundown. During this interval we had the good fortune to bring up, altogether, four more small jars of olives, another ham, a carboy containing nearly three gallons of excellent Cape Madeira wine, and, what gave us still more delight, a small tortoise of the Gallipago* breed, several of which had been taken on board by Captain Barnard, as the *Grampus* was leaving port, from the schooner *Mary Pitts*, just returned from a sealing voyage in the Pacific.

In a subsequent portion of this narrative I shall have frequent occasion to mention this species of tortoise.* It is found principally, as most of my readers may know, in the group of islands called the Gallipagos, which, indeed, derive their name from the animal – the Spanish word *galápago* meaning a freshwater terrapin. From the peculiarity of their shape and action they have been sometimes called the elephant tortoise. They are frequently found of an enormous size. I have myself seen several which would weigh from twelve to fifteen hundred pounds, although I do not remember that any navigator speaks of having seen them weighing more than eight hundred. Their appearance is singular, and even disgusting. Their steps are very slow, measured and heavy, their bodies being carried about a foot from the ground. Their neck is long, and exceedingly slender; from eighteen inches to two feet is a very common length, and I killed one where the distance from the shoulder to the extremity of the head was no less than three feet ten inches. The head has a striking resemblance to that of a serpent. They can exist without food for an almost incredible length of time, instances having been known where they have been thrown into

the hold of a vessel and lain two years without nourishment of any kind – being as fat and, in every respect, in as good order at the expiration of the time as when they were first put in. In one particular these extraordinary animals bear a resemblance to the dromedary, or camel of the desert. In a bag at the root of the neck they carry with them a constant supply of water.* In some instances, upon killing them after a full year's deprivation of all nourishment, as much as three gallons of perfectly sweet and fresh water have been found in their bags. Their food is chiefly wild parsley and celery, with purslane, sea kelp and prickly pears, upon which latter vegetable they thrive wonderfully, a great quantity of it being usually found on the hillsides near the shore wherever the animal itself is discovered. They are excellent and highly nutritious food, and have, no doubt, been the means of preserving the lives of thousands of seamen employed in the whale fishery and other pursuits in the Pacific.

The one which we had the good fortune to bring up from the storeroom was not of a large size, weighing probably sixty-five or seventy pounds. It was a female, and in excellent condition, being exceedingly fat, and having more than a quart of limpid and sweet water in its bag. This was indeed a treasure, and, falling on our knees with one accord, we returned fervent thanks to God for so seasonable a relief.

We had great difficulty in getting the animal up through the opening, as its struggles were fierce and its strength prodigious. It was upon the point of making its escape from Peters's grasp, and slipping back into the water, when Augustus, throwing a rope with a slip knot around its throat, held it up in this manner until I jumped into the hole by the side of Peters, and assisted him in lifting it out.

The water we drew carefully from the bag into the jug, which, it will be remembered, had been brought up before from the cabin. Having done this, we broke off the neck of a bottle so as to form, with the cork, a kind of glass, holding not quite half a gill. We then each drank one of these measures full, and resolved to limit ourselves to this quantity per day as long as it should hold out.

During the last two or three days, the weather having been dry and pleasant, the bedding we had obtained from the cabin, as well as our clothing, had become thoroughly dry, so that we passed this night (that of the twenty-third) in comparative comfort, enjoying a tranquil repose, after having supped plentifully on olives and ham, with a small allowance of the wine. Being afraid of losing some of our stores overboard during the night, in the event of a breeze springing up, we secured them as well

as possible with cordage to the fragments of the windlass. Our tortoise, which we were anxious to preserve alive as long as we could, we threw on his back, and otherwise carefully fastened.

CHAPTER XIII

24th July – This morning saw us wonderfully recruited* in spirits and strength. Notwithstanding the perilous situation in which we were still placed, ignorant of our position, although certainly at a great distance from land, without more food than would last us for a fortnight even with great care, almost entirely without water, and floating about at the mercy of every wind and wave on the merest wreck in the world, still the infinitely more terrible distresses and dangers from which we had so lately and so providentially been delivered caused us to regard what we now endured as but little more than an ordinary evil – so strictly comparative is either good or ill.

At sunrise we were preparing to renew our attempts at getting up something from the storeroom when, a smart shower coming on, with some lightning, we turned our attention to the catching of water by means of the sheet we had used before for this purpose. We had no other means of collecting the rain than by holding the sheet spread out with one of the forechain plates in the middle of it. The water, thus conducted to the centre, was drained through into our jug. We had nearly filled it in this manner when a heavy squall coming on from the northward obliged us to desist, as the hulk began once more to roll so violently that we could no longer keep our feet. We now went forward, and, lashing ourselves securely to the remnant of the windlass as before, awaited the event with far more calmness than could have been anticipated, or would have been imagined possible under the circumstances. At noon the wind had freshened into a two-reef breeze, and by night into a stiff gale, accompanied with a tremendously heavy swell. Experience having taught us, however, the best method of arranging our lashings, we weathered this dreary night in tolerable security, although thoroughly drenched at almost every instant by the sea, and in momentary dread of being washed off. Fortunately, the weather was so warm as to render the water rather grateful* than otherwise.

25th July – This morning the gale had diminished to a mere ten-knot breeze, and the sea had gone down with it so considerably that we were able to keep ourselves dry upon the deck. To our great grief, however, we

found that two jars of our olives, as well as the whole of our ham, had been washed overboard, in spite of the careful manner in which they had been fastened. We determined not to kill the tortoise as yet, and contented ourselves for the present with a breakfast on a few of the olives, and a measure of water each, which latter we mixed, half and half, with wine, finding great relief and strength from the mixture, without the distressing intoxication which had ensued upon drinking the port. The sea was still far too rough for the renewal of our efforts at getting up provision from the storeroom. Several articles, of no importance to us in our present situation, floated up through the opening during the day, and were immediately washed overboard. We also now observed that the hulk lay more along than ever, so that we could not stand an instant without lashing ourselves. On this account we passed a gloomy and uncomfortable day. At noon the sun appeared to be nearly vertical, and we had no doubt that we had been driven down by the long succession of northward* and north-westerly winds into the near vicinity of the equator. Towards evening saw several sharks, and were somewhat alarmed by the audacious manner in which an enormously large one approached us. At one time, a lurch throwing the deck very far beneath the water, the monster actually swam in upon us, floundering for some moments just over the companion hatch, and striking Peters violently with his tail. A heavy sea at length hurled him overboard, much to our relief. In moderate weather we might have easily captured him.

26th July – This morning, the wind having greatly abated, and the sea not being very rough, we determined to renew our exertions in the storeroom. After a great deal of hard labour during the whole day, we found that nothing further was to be expected from this quarter, the partitions of the room having been stove during the night, and its contents swept into the hold. This discovery, as may be supposed, filled us with despair.

27th July – The sea nearly smooth, with a light wind, and still from the northward and westward. The sun coming out hotly in the afternoon, we occupied ourselves in drying our clothes. Found great relief from thirst, and much comfort otherwise, by bathing in the sea – in this, however, we were forced to use great caution, being afraid of sharks, several of which were seen swimming around the brig during the day.

28th July – Good weather still. The brig now began to lie along* so alarmingly that we feared she would eventually roll bottom up. Prepared ourselves as well as we could for this emergency, lashing our tortoise, water jug and two remaining jars of olives as far as possible over to the

windward, placing them outside the hull, below the main-chains. The sea very smooth all day, with little or no wind.

29th July – A continuance of the same weather. Augustus's wounded arm began to evince symptoms of mortification. He complained of drowsiness and excessive thirst, but no acute pain. Nothing could be done for his relief beyond rubbing his wounds with a little of the vinegar from the olives, and from this no benefit seemed to be experienced. We did everything in our power for his comfort, and trebled his allowance of water.

30th July – An excessively hot day, with no wind. An enormous shark kept close by the hulk during the whole of the forenoon. We made several unsuccessful attempts to capture him by means of a noose. Augustus much worse, and evidently sinking as much from want of proper nourishment as from the effect of his wounds. He constantly prayed to be released from his sufferings, wishing for nothing but death. This evening we ate the last of our olives, and found the water in our jug so putrid that we could not swallow it at all without the addition of wine. Determined to kill our tortoise in the morning.

31st July – After a night of excessive anxiety and fatigue, owing to the position of the hulk, we set about killing and cutting up our tortoise. He proved to be much smaller than we had supposed,* although in good condition – the whole meat about him not amounting to more than ten pounds. With a view of preserving a portion of this as long as possible, we cut it into fine pieces, and filled with them our three remaining olive jars and the wine bottle (all of which had been kept), pouring in afterwards the vinegar from the olives. In this manner we put away about three pounds of the tortoise, intending not to touch it until we had consumed the rest. We concluded to restrict ourselves to about four ounces of the meat per day – the whole would thus last us thirteen days. A brisk shower, with severe thunder and lightning, came on about dusk, but lasted so short a time that we only succeeded in catching about half a pint of water. The whole of this, by common consent, was given to Augustus, who now appeared to be in the last extremity. He drank the water from the sheet as we caught it (we holding it above him as he lay so as to let it run into his mouth), for we had now nothing left capable of holding water, unless we had chosen to empty out our wine from the carboy, or the stale water from the jug. Either of these expedients would have been resorted to had the shower lasted.

The sufferer seemed to derive but little benefit from the draught. His arm was completely black from the wrist to the shoulder, and his feet were like ice. We expected every moment to see him breathe his last. He was

frightfully emaciated – so much so that, although he weighed a hundred and twenty-seven pounds upon his leaving Nantucket, he now did not weigh more than *forty or fifty at the farthest*. His eyes were sunk far in his head, being scarcely perceptible, and the skin of his cheeks hung so loosely as to prevent his masticating any food, or even swallowing any liquid, without great difficulty.

1st August – A continuance of the same calm weather, with an oppressively hot sun. Suffered exceedingly from thirst, the water in the jug being absolutely putrid and swarming with vermin. We contrived, nevertheless, to swallow a portion of it by mixing it with wine; our thirst, however, was but little abated. We found more relief by bathing in the sea, but could not avail ourselves of this expedient except at long intervals, on account of the continual presence of sharks. We now saw clearly that Augustus could not be saved – that he was evidently dying. We could do nothing to relieve his sufferings, which appeared to be great. About twelve o'clock he expired in strong convulsions, and without having spoken for several hours. His death filled us with the most gloomy forebodings, and had so great an effect upon our spirits that we sat motionless by the corpse during the whole day, and never addressed each other except in a whisper. It was not until some time after dark that we took courage to get up and throw the body overboard. It was then loathsome beyond expression, and so far decayed that, as Peters attempted to lift it, an entire leg came off in his grasp. As the mass of putrefaction slipped over the vessel's side into the water, the glare of phosphoric light with which it was surrounded plainly discovered to us seven or eight large sharks, the clashing of whose horrible teeth, as their prey was torn to pieces among them, might have been heard at the distance of a mile. We shrank within ourselves in the extremity of horror at the sound.

2nd August – The same fearfully calm and hot weather. The dawn found us in a state of pitiable dejection as well as bodily exhaustion. The water in the jug was now absolutely useless, being a thick gelatinous mass – nothing but frightful-looking worms mingled with slime. We threw it out, and washed the jug well in the sea, afterwards pouring a little vinegar in it from our bottles of pickled tortoise. Our thirst could now scarcely be endured, and we tried in vain to relieve it by wine, which seemed only to add fuel to the flame, and excited us to a high degree of intoxication. We afterwards endeavoured to relieve our sufferings by mixing the wine with sea water, but this instantly brought about the most violent retchings, so that we never again attempted it. During the whole day we anxiously sought an

opportunity of bathing, but to no purpose, for the hulk was now entirely besieged on all sides with sharks – no doubt the identical monsters who had devoured our poor companion on the evening before, and who were in momentary expectation of another similar feast. This circumstance occasioned us the most bitter regret and filled us with the most depressing and melancholy forebodings. We had experienced indescribable relief in bathing, and to have this resource cut off in so frightful a manner was more than we could bear. Nor, indeed, were we altogether free from the apprehension of immediate danger, for the least slip or false movement would have thrown us at once within reach of these voracious fish, who frequently thrust themselves directly upon us, swimming up to leeward. No shouts or exertions on our part seemed to alarm them. Even when one of the largest was struck with an axe by Peters and much wounded, he persisted in his attempts to push in where we were. A cloud came up at dusk, but, to our extreme anguish, passed over without discharging itself. It is quite impossible to conceive our sufferings from thirst at this period. We passed a sleepless night, both on this account and through dread of the sharks.

3rd August – No prospect of relief, and the brig lying still more and more along, so that now we could not maintain a footing upon deck at all. Busied ourselves in securing our wine and tortoise meat, so that we might not lose them in the event of our rolling over. Got out two stout spikes from the forechains, and, by means of the axe, drove them into the hull to windward within a couple of feet of the water, this not being very far from the keel, as we were nearly upon our beam ends. To these spikes we now lashed our provisions, as being more secure than their former position beneath the chains. Suffered great agony from thirst during the whole day – no chance of bathing on account of the sharks, which never left us for a moment. Found it impossible to sleep.

4th August – A little before daybreak we perceived that the hulk was heeling over, and aroused ourselves to prevent being thrown off by the movement. At first the roll was slow and gradual, and we contrived to clamber over to windward very well, having taken the precaution to leave ropes hanging from the spikes we had driven in for the provision. But we had not calculated sufficiently upon the acceleration of the impetus, for presently the heel became too violent to allow of our keeping pace with it, and, before either of us knew what was to happen, we found ourselves hurled furiously into the sea, and struggling several fathoms beneath the surface, with the huge hull immediately above us.

In going under the water I had been obliged to let go my hold upon the rope, and finding that I was completely beneath the vessel, and my strength utterly exhausted, I scarcely made a struggle for life, and resigned myself, in a few seconds, to die. But here again I was deceived, not having taken into consideration the natural rebound of the hull to windward. The whirl of the water upwards, which the vessel occasioned in rolling partially back, brought me to the surface still more violently than I had been plunged beneath. Upon coming up I found myself about twenty yards from the hulk, as near as I could judge. She was lying keel up, rocking furiously from side to side, and the sea in all directions around was much agitated, and full of strong whirlpools. I could see nothing of Peters. An oil cask was floating within a few feet of me, and various other articles from the brig were scattered about.

My principal terror was now on account of the sharks, which I knew to be in my vicinity. In order to deter these, if possible, from approaching me, I splashed the water vigorously with both hands and feet as I swam towards the hulk, creating a body of foam. I have no doubt that to this expedient, simple as it was, I was indebted for my preservation, for the sea all around the brig, just before her rolling over, was so crowded with these monsters that I must have been, and really was, in actual contact with some of them during my progress. By great good fortune, however, I reached the side of the vessel in safety, although so utterly weakened by the violent exertion I had used that I should never have been able to get upon it but for the timely assistance of Peters, who, now, to my great joy, made his appearance (having scrambled up to the keel from the opposite side of the hull), and threw me the end of a rope – one of those which had been attached to the spikes.

Having barely escaped this danger, our attention was now directed to the dreadful imminency of another – that of absolute starvation. Our whole stock of provision had been swept overboard in spite of all our care in securing it, and, seeing no longer the remotest possibility of obtaining more, we gave way both of us to despair, weeping aloud like children, and neither of us attempting to offer consolation to the other. Such weakness can scarcely be conceived, and to those who have never been similarly situated will, no doubt, appear unnatural, but it must be remembered that our intellects were so entirely disordered by the long course of privation and terror to which we had been subjected that we could not justly be considered, at that period, in the light of rational beings. In subsequent perils, nearly as great, if not greater, I bore up with fortitude against all the evils

of my situation, and Peters, it will be seen, evinced a stoical philosophy nearly as incredible as his present childlike supineness and imbecility – the mental condition made the difference.

The overturning of the brig, even with the consequent loss of the wine and turtle, would not, in fact, have rendered our situation more deplorable than before, except for the disappearance of the bedclothes by which we had been hitherto enabled to catch rainwater, and of the jug in which we had kept it when caught, for we found the whole bottom, from within two or three feet of the bends as far as the keel, together with the keel itself, *thickly covered with large barnacles, which proved to be excellent and highly nutritious food.** Thus, in two important respects, the accident we had so greatly dreaded proved a benefit rather than an injury: it had opened to us a supply of provisions which we could not have exhausted, using it moderately, in a month, and it had greatly contributed to our comfort as regards position, we being much more at ease, and in infinitely less danger, than before.

The difficulty, however, of now obtaining water blinded us to all the benefits of the change in our condition. That we might be ready to avail ourselves, as far as possible, of any shower which might fall, we took off our shirts, to make use of them as we had of the sheets – not hoping, of course, to get more in this way, even under the most favourable circumstances, than half a gill at a time. No signs of a cloud appeared during the day, and the agonies of our thirst were nearly intolerable. At night, Peters obtained about an hour's disturbed sleep, but my intense sufferings would not permit me to close my eyes for a single moment.

5th August – Today, a gentle breeze springing up carried us through a vast quantity of seaweed, among which we were so fortunate as to find eleven small crabs, which afforded us several delicious meals. Their shells being quite soft, we ate them entire, and found that they irritated our thirst far less than the barnacles. Seeing no trace of sharks among the seaweed, we also ventured to bathe, and remained in the water for four or five hours, during which we experienced a very sensible diminution of our thirst. Were greatly refreshed, and spent the night somewhat more comfortably than before, both of us snatching a little sleep.

6th August – This day we were blessed by a brisk and continual rain, lasting from about noon until after dark. Bitterly did we now regret the loss of our jug and carboy, for, in spite of the little means we had of catching the water, we might have filled one, if not both of them. As it was, we contrived to satisfy the cravings of thirst by suffering the shirts to become

saturated, and then wringing them so as to let the grateful fluid trickle into our mouths. In this occupation we passed the entire day.

7th August – Just at daybreak we both at the same instant descried a sail to the eastward, and *evidently coming towards us*! We hailed the glorious sight with a long, although feeble shout of rapture, and began instantly to make every signal in our power, by flaring the shirts in the air, leaping as high as our weak condition would permit, and even by hallooing with all the strength of our lungs, although the vessel could not have been less than fifteen miles distant. However, she still continued to near our hulk, and we felt that, if she but held her present course, she must eventually come so close as to perceive us. In about an hour after we first discovered her, we could clearly see the people on her decks. She was a long, low and rakish-looking* topsail schooner, with a black ball in her foretopsail, and had, apparently, a full crew. We now became alarmed, for we could hardly imagine it possible that she did not observe us, and were apprehensive that she meant to leave us to perish as we were – an act of fiendish barbarity, which, however incredible it may appear, has been repeatedly perpetrated at sea, under circumstances very nearly similar, and by beings who were regarded as belonging to the human species.* In this instance, however, by the mercy of God, we were destined to be most happily deceived, for presently we were aware of a sudden commotion on the deck of the stranger, who immediately afterwards ran up a British flag, and, hauling her wind,* bore up directly upon us. In half an hour more we found ourselves in her cabin. She proved to be the *Jane Guy*, of Liverpool, Captain Guy, bound on a sealing and trading voyage to the South Seas and Pacific.

CHAPTER XIV*

The *Jane Guy* was a fine-looking topsail schooner of a hundred and eighty tons burden. She was unusually sharp in the bows, and on a wind, in moderate weather, the fastest sailer I have ever seen. Her qualities, however, as a rough sea boat, were not so good, and her draught of water was by far too great for the trade to which she was destined.* For this peculiar service, a larger vessel, and one of a light proportionate draught, is desirable – say a vessel of from three to three hundred and fifty tons. She should be barque-rigged,* and in other respects of a different construction from the usual South Sea ships. It is absolutely necessary that she should be well armed. She should have, say, ten or twelve twelve-pound carronades,

and two or three long twelves,* with brass blunderbusses, and watertight arm-chests for each top. Her anchors and cables should be of far greater strength than is required for any other species of trade, and, above all, her crew should be numerous and efficient – not less, for such a vessel as I have described, than fifty or sixty able-bodied men. The *Jane Guy* had a crew of thirty-five, all able seamen, besides the captain and mate, but she was not altogether as well armed or otherwise equipped as a navigator acquainted with the difficulties and dangers of the trade could have desired.

Captain Guy was a gentleman of great urbanity of manner, and of considerable experience in the southern traffic, to which he had devoted a great portion of his life. He was deficient, however, in energy, and, consequently, in that spirit of enterprise which is here so absolutely requisite. He was part owner of the vessel in which he sailed, and was invested with discretionary powers to cruise in the South Seas for any cargo which might come most readily to hand. He had on board, as usual in such voyages, beads, looking glasses, tinder-works, axes, hatchets, saws, adzes, planes, chisels, gouges, gimlets, files, spokeshaves, rasps, hammers, nails, knives, scissors, razors, needles, thread, crockery ware, calico, trinkets and other similar articles.

The schooner sailed from Liverpool on 10th July, crossed the Tropic of Cancer on the 25th, in longitude twenty degrees west, and reached Sal, one of the Cape Verd Islands, on the 29th, where she took in salt and other necessaries for the voyage. On 3rd August, she left the Cape Verds and steered south-west, stretching over towards the coast of Brazil, so as to cross the equator between the meridians of twenty-eight and thirty degrees west longitude. This is the course usually taken by vessels bound from Europe to the Cape of Good Hope, or by that route to the East Indies. By proceeding thus they avoid the calms and strong contrary currents which continually prevail on the coast of Guinea, while, in the end, it is found to be the shortest track, as westerly winds are never wanting afterwards by which to reach the Cape. It was Captain Guy's intention to make his first stoppage at Kerguelen's Land* – I hardly know for what reason. On the day we were picked up the schooner was off Cape St Roque,* in longitude 31° W. – so that, when found, we had drifted probably, from north to south, *not less than five-and-twenty degrees.*

On board the *Jane Guy* we were treated with all the kindness our distressed situation demanded. In about a fortnight, during which time we continued steering to the south-east, with gentle breezes and fine weather, both Peters and myself recovered entirely from the effects of our

late privation and dreadful suffering, and we began to remember what had passed rather as a frightful dream from which we had been happily awakened than as events which had taken place in sober and naked reality. I have since found that this species of partial oblivion is usually brought about by sudden transition, whether from joy to sorrow or from sorrow to joy – the degree of forgetfulness being proportioned to the degree of difference in the exchange. Thus, in my own case, I now feel it impossible to realize the full extent of the misery which I endured during the days spent upon the hulk. The incidents are remembered, but not the feelings which the incidents elicited at the time of their occurrence. I only know that when they did occur, I *then* thought human nature could sustain nothing more of agony.

We continued our voyage for some weeks without any incidents of greater moment than the occasional meeting with whaling ships, and more frequently with the black or right whale, so called in contradistinction to the spermaceti.* These, however, were chiefly found south of the twenty-fifth parallel. On 16th September, being in the vicinity of the Cape of Good Hope, the schooner encountered her first gale of any violence since leaving Liverpool. In this neighbourhood, but more frequently to the south and east of the promontory (we were to the westward), navigators have often to contend with storms from the northward, which rage with great fury. They always bring with them a heavy sea, and one of their most dangerous features is the instantaneous chopping round of the wind, an occurrence almost certain to take place during the greatest force of the gale. A perfect hurricane will be blowing at one moment from the northward or north-east, and in the next not a breath of wind will be felt in that direction, while from the south-west it will come out all at once with a violence almost inconceivable. A bright spot to the southward is the sure forerunner of the change, and vessels are thus enabled to take the proper precautions.

It was about six in the morning when the blow came on with a white squall, and, as usual, from the northward. By eight it had increased very much, and brought down upon us one of the most tremendous seas I had then ever beheld. Everything had been made as snug as possible, but the schooner laboured excessively, and gave evidence of her bad qualities as a sea boat, pitching her forecastle under at every plunge, and with the greatest difficulty struggling up from one wave before she was buried in another. Just before sunset the bright spot for which we had been on the lookout made its appearance in the south-west, and in an hour afterwards

we perceived the little headsail we carried flapping listlessly against the mast. In two minutes more, in spite of every preparation, we were hurled on our beam ends, as if by magic, and a perfect wilderness of foam made a clear breach over us as we lay. The blow from the south-west, however, luckily proved to be nothing more than a squall, and we had the good fortune to right the vessel without the loss of a spar. A heavy cross sea gave us great trouble for a few hours after this, but towards morning we found ourselves in nearly as good condition as before the gale. Captain Guy considered that he had made an escape little less than miraculous.

On 13th October we came in sight of Prince Edward's Island, in latitude 46° 53′ S., longitude 37° 46′ E. Two days afterwards we found ourselves near Possession Island, and presently passed the islands of Crozet, in latitude 42° 59′ S., longitude 48° E.* On the 18th we made Kerguelen's or Desolation Island, in the southern Indian Ocean, and came to anchor in Christmas Harbour,* having four fathoms of water.

This island, or rather group of islands, bears south-east from the Cape of Good Hope, and is distant therefrom nearly eight hundred leagues. It was first discovered in 1772, by the Baron de Kergulen, or Kerguelen, a Frenchman, who, thinking the land to form a portion of an extensive southern continent, carried home information to that effect, which produced much excitement at the time. The government, taking the matter up, sent the baron back in the following year for the purpose of giving his new discovery a critical examination, when the mistake was discovered. In 1777, Captain Cook fell in with the same group, and gave to the principal one the name of Desolation Island, a title which it certainly well deserves. Upon approaching the land, however, the navigator might be induced to suppose otherwise, as the sides of most of the hills, from September to March, are clothed with very brilliant verdure. This deceitful appearance is caused by a small plant resembling saxifrage, which is abundant, growing in large patches on a species of crumbling moss. Besides this plant there is scarcely a sign of vegetation on the island, if we except some coarse rank grass near the harbour, some lichen and a shrub which bears resemblance to a cabbage shooting into seed, and which has a bitter and acrid taste.

The face of the country is hilly, although none of the hills can be called lofty. Their tops are perpetually covered with snow. There are several harbours, of which Christmas Harbour is the most convenient. It is the first to be met with on the north-east side of the island after passing Cape François, which forms the northern shore, and, by its peculiar shape, serves

to distinguish the harbour. Its projecting point terminates in a high rock, through which is a large hole, forming a natural arch. The entrance is in latitude 48° 40′ S., longitude 69° 6′ E. Passing in here, good anchorage may be found under the shelter of several small islands, which form a sufficient protection from all easterly winds. Proceeding on eastwardly from this anchorage you come to Wasp Bay, at the head of the harbour. This is a small basin, completely landlocked, into which you can go with four fathoms, and find anchorage in from ten to three,* hard clay bottom. A ship might lie here with her best bower ahead* all the year round without risk. To the westward, at the head of Wasp Bay, is a small stream of excellent water, easily procured.

Some seal of the fur and hair species are still to be found on Kerguelen Island, and sea elephants* abound. The feathered tribes are discovered in great numbers. Penguins are very plenty, and of these there are four different kinds. The royal penguin,* so called from its size and beautiful plumage, is the largest. The upper part of the body is usually grey, sometimes of a lilac tint, the under portion of the purest white imaginable. The head is of a glossy and most brilliant black, the feet also. The chief beauty of the plumage, however, consists in two broad stripes of a gold colour, which pass along from the head to the breast. The bill is long, and either pink or bright scarlet. These birds walk erect, with a stately carriage. They carry their heads high with their wings drooping like two arms, and, as their tails project from their body in a line with the legs, the resemblance to a human figure is very striking, and would be apt to deceive the spectator at a casual glance or in the gloom of the evening. The royal penguins which we met with on Kerguelen's Land were rather larger than a goose. The other kinds are the macaroni, the jackass and the rookery penguin. These are much smaller, less beautiful in plumage and different in other respects.

Besides the penguin many other birds are here to be found, among which may be mentioned sea hens, blue petrels, teal, ducks, Port Egmont hens, shags, Cape pigeons, the nelly, sea swallows, terns, seagulls, Mother Carey's chickens, Mother Carey's geese, or the great petrel, and, lastly, the albatross.*

The great petrel is as large as the common albatross, and is carnivorous. It is frequently called the "break-bones", or osprey petrel. They are not at all shy, and, when properly cooked, are palatable food. In flying they sometimes sail very close to the surface of the water, with the wings expanded, without appearing to move them in the least degree, or make any exertion with them whatever.

The albatross is one of the largest and fiercest of the South Sea birds.* It is of the gull species, and takes its prey on the wing, never coming on land except for the purpose of breeding. Between this bird and the penguin the most singular friendship exists. Their nests are constructed with great uniformity, upon a plan concerted between the two species – that of the albatross being placed in the centre of a little square formed by the nests of four penguins. Navigators have agreed in calling an assemblage of such encampments a *rookery*. These rookeries have been often described, but as my readers may not all have seen these descriptions, and as I shall have occasion hereafter to speak of the penguin and albatross, it will not be amiss to say something here of their mode of building and living.

When the season for incubation arrives, the birds assemble in vast numbers, and for some days appear to be deliberating upon the proper course to be pursued. At length they proceed to action. A level piece of ground is selected, of suitable extent, usually comprising three or four acres, and situated as near the sea as possible, being still beyond its reach. The spot is chosen with reference to its evenness of surface, and that is preferred which is the least encumbered with stones. This matter being arranged, the birds proceed, with one accord, and actuated apparently by one mind, to trace out, with mathematical accuracy, either a square or other parallelogram, as may best suit the nature of the ground, and of just sufficient size to accommodate easily all the birds assembled, and no more – in this particular seeming determined upon preventing the access of future stragglers who have not participated in the labour of the encampment. One side of the place thus marked out runs parallel with the water's edge, and is left open for ingress or egress.

Having defined the limits of the rookery, the colony now begin to clear it of every species of rubbish, picking up stone by stone, and carrying them outside of the lines, and close by them, so as to form a wall on the three inland sides. Just within this wall a perfectly level and smooth walk is formed, from six to eight feet wide, and extending around the encampment – thus serving the purpose of a general promenade.

The next process is to partition out the whole area into small squares exactly equal in size. This is done by forming narrow paths, very smooth, and crossing each other at right angles throughout the entire extent of the rookery. At each intersection of these paths the nest of an albatross is constructed, and a penguin's nest in the centre of each square – thus every penguin is surrounded by four albatrosses, and each albatross by a like number of penguins. The penguin's nest consists of a hole in the earth,

very shallow, being only just of sufficient depth to keep her single egg from rolling. The albatross is somewhat less simple in her arrangements, erecting a hillock about a foot high and two in diameter. This is made of earth, seaweed and shells. On its summit she builds her nest.

The birds take especial care never to leave their nests unoccupied for an instant during the period of incubation, or, indeed, until the young progeny are sufficiently strong to take care of themselves. While the male is absent at sea in search of food, the female remains on duty, and it is only upon the return of her partner that she ventures abroad. The eggs are never left uncovered at all – while one bird leaves the nest, the other nestling in by its side. This precaution is rendered necessary by the thievish propensities prevalent in the rookery, the inhabitants making no scruple to purloin each other's eggs at every good opportunity.

Although there are some rookeries in which the penguin and albatross are the sole population, yet in most of them a variety of oceanic birds are to be met with, enjoying all the privileges of citizenship, and scattering their nests here and there, wherever they can find room, never interfering, however, with the stations of the larger species. The appearance of such encampments, when seen from a distance, is exceedingly singular. The whole atmosphere just above the settlement is darkened with the immense number of the albatross (mingled with the smaller tribes) which are continually hovering over it, either going to the ocean or returning home. At the same time a crowd of penguins are to be observed, some passing to and fro in the narrow alleys, and some marching, with the military strut so peculiar to them, around the general promenade ground which encircles the rookery. In short, survey it as we will, nothing can be more astonishing than the spirit of reflection evinced by these feathered beings, and nothing surely can be better calculated to elicit reflection in every well-regulated human intellect.

On the morning after our arrival in Christmas Harbour the chief mate, Mr Patterson, took the boats, and (although it was somewhat early in the season) went in search of seal, leaving the captain and a young relation of his on a point of barren land to the westward, they having some business, whose nature I could not ascertain, to transact in the interior of the island. Captain Guy took with him a bottle, in which was a sealed letter, and made his way from the point on which he was set on shore towards one of the highest peaks in the place. It is probable that his design was to leave the letter on that height for some vessel which he expected to come after him. As soon as we lost sight of him we proceeded (Peters and

myself being in the mate's boat) on our cruise around the coast, looking for seal. In this business we were occupied about three weeks, examining with great care every nook and corner, not only of Kerguelen's Land, but of the several small islands in the vicinity. Our labours, however, were not crowned with any important success. We saw a great many fur seal, but they were exceedingly shy, and with the greatest exertions we could only procure three hundred and fifty skins in all. Sea elephants were abundant, especially on the western coast of the main island, but of these we killed only twenty, and this with great difficulty. On the smaller islands we discovered a good many of the hair seal, but did not molest them. We returned to the schooner on the 11th, where we found Captain Guy and his nephew, who gave a very bad account of the interior, representing it as one of the most dreary and utterly barren countries in the world. They had remained two nights on the island, owing to some misunderstanding, on the part of the second mate, in regard to the sending a jolly-boat from the schooner to take them off.

CHAPTER XV*

On the 12th we made sail from Christmas Harbour, retracing our way to the westward, and leaving Marion's Island, one of Crozet's group,* on the larboard. We afterwards passed Prince Edward's Island, leaving it also on our left, then, steering more to the northward, made, in fifteen days, the islands of Tristan da Cunha,* in latitude 37° 8′ S., longitude 12° 8′ W.

This group, now so well known, and which consists of three circular islands, was first discovered by the Portuguese, and was visited afterwards by the Dutch in 1643, and by the French in 1767.* The three islands together form a triangle, and are distant from each other about ten miles, there being fine open passages between. The land in all of them is very high, especially in Tristan da Cunha, properly so called. This is the largest of the group, being fifteen miles in circumference, and so elevated that it can be seen in clear weather at the distance of eighty or ninety miles. A part of the land towards the north rises more than a thousand feet perpendicularly from the sea. A tableland at this height extends back nearly to the centre of the island, and from this tableland arises a lofty cone like that of Tenerife. The lower half of this cone is clothed with trees of good size, but the upper region is barren rock, usually hidden among the clouds, and covered with snow during the greater part of the year. There are no shoals

or other dangers about the island, the shores being remarkably bold and the water deep. On the north-western coast is a bay, with a beach of black sand, where a landing with boats can be easily effected, provided there be a southerly wind. Plenty of excellent water may here be readily procured; also cod, and other fish, may be taken with hook and line.

The next island in point of size, and the most westwardly of the group, is that called the Inaccessible. Its precise situation is 37° 17′ S. latitude, longitude 12° 24′ W. It is seven or eight miles in circumference, and on all sides presents a forbidding and precipitous aspect. Its top is perfectly flat, and the whole region is sterile, nothing growing upon it except a few stunted shrubs.

Nightingale Island, the smallest and most southerly, is in latitude 37° 26′ S., longitude 12° 12′ W. Off its southern extremity is a high ledge of rocky islets; a few also of a similar appearance are seen to the north-east. The ground is irregular and sterile, and a deep valley partially separates it.

The shores of these islands abound, in the proper season, with sea lions, sea elephants, the hair and fur seal, together with a great variety of oceanic birds. Whales are also plenty in their vicinity. Owing to the ease with which these various animals were here formerly taken, the group has been much visited since its discovery. The Dutch and French frequented it at a very early period. In 1790, Captain Patten, of the ship *Industry*, of Philadelphia, made Tristan da Cunha, where he remained seven months (from August 1790 to April 1791) for the purpose of collecting sealskins. In this time he gathered no less than five thousand, six hundred, and says that he would have had no difficulty in loading a large ship with oil in three weeks. Upon his arrival he found no quadrupeds, with the exception of a few wild goats; the island now abounds with all our most valuable domestic animals, which have been introduced by subsequent navigators.

I believe it was not long after Captain Patten's visit that Captain Colquhoun, of the American brig *Betsey*, touched at the largest of the islands for the purpose of refreshment. He planted onions, potatoes, cabbages and a great many other vegetables, an abundance of all which are now to be met with.

In 1811, a Captain Heywood, in the *Nereus*, visited Tristan. He found there three Americans, who were residing upon the island to prepare sealskins and oil. One of these men was named Jonathan Lambert, and he called himself the sovereign of the country. He had cleared and cultivated about sixty acres of land, and turned his attention to raising the coffee plant and sugar cane, with which he had been furnished by the American

minister at Rio Janeiro. This settlement, however, was finally abandoned, and in 1817 the islands were taken possession of by the British government,* who sent a detachment for that purpose from the Cape of Good Hope. They did not, however, retain them long, but, upon the evacuation of the country as a British possession, two or three English families took up their residence there independently of the government. On 25th March 1824, the *Berwick*, Captain Jeffrey, from London to Van Diemen's Land,* arrived at the place, where they found an Englishman of the name of Glass,* formerly a corporal in the British artillery. He claimed to be supreme governor of the islands, and had under his control twenty-one men and three women. He gave a very favourable account of the salubrity of the climate and of the productiveness of the soil. The population occupied themselves chiefly in collecting sealskins and sea-elephant oil, with which they traded to the Cape of Good Hope, Glass owning a small schooner. At the period of our arrival the governor was still a resident, but his little community had multiplied, there being fifty-six persons upon Tristan, besides a smaller settlement of seven on Nightingale Island. We had no difficulty in procuring almost every kind of refreshment which we required – sheep, hogs, bullocks, rabbits, poultry, goats, fish in great variety, and vegetables were abundant. Having come to anchor close in with the large island, in eighteen fathoms, we took all we wanted on board very conveniently. Captain Guy also purchased of Glass five hundred sealskins and some ivory. We remained here a week, during which the prevailing winds were from the northward and westward, and the weather somewhat hazy. On 5th November* we made sail to the southward and westward, with the intention of having a thorough search for a group of islands called the Auroras,* respecting whose existence a great diversity of opinion has existed.

These islands are said to have been discovered as early as 1762, by the commander of the ship *Aurora*. In 1790, Captain Manuel de Oyarvido, in the ship *Princess*, belonging to the Royal Philippine Company, sailed, as he asserts, directly among them. In 1794, the Spanish corvette *Atrevida** went with the determination of ascertaining their precise situation, and, in a paper published by the Royal Hydrographical Society of Madrid in the year 1809, the following language is used respecting this expedition: "The corvette *Atrevida* practised, in their immediate vicinity, from 21st to 27th January, all the necessary observations, and measured by chronometers the difference of longitude between these islands and the port of Soledad in the Malninas.* The islands are three; they are very nearly in the same meridian; the centre one is rather low, and the other two may

be seen at nine leagues' distance." The observations made on board the *Atrevida* give the following results as the precise situation of each island. The most northern is in latitude 52° 37′ 24″ S., longitude 47° 43′ 15″ W.; the middle one in latitude 53° 2′ 40″ S., longitude 47° 55′ 15″ W.; and the most southern in latitude 53° 15′ 22″ S., longitude 47° 57′ 15″ W.

On 27th January 1820, Captain James Weddell,* of the British navy, sailed from Staten Land* also in search of the Auroras. He reports that, having made the most diligent search and passed not only immediately over the spots indicated by the commander of the *Atrevida*, but in every direction throughout the vicinity of these spots, he could discover no indication of land. These conflicting statements have induced other navigators to look out for the islands, and, strange to say, while some have sailed through every inch of sea where they are supposed to lie without finding them, there have been not a few who declare positively that they have seen them, and even been close in with their shores. It was Captain Guy's intention to make every exertion within his power to settle the question so oddly in dispute.*

We kept on our course, between the south and west, with variable weather, until the 20th of the month, when we found ourselves on the debated ground, being in latitude 53° 15′ S., longitude 47° 58′ W. – that is to say, very nearly upon the spot indicated as the situation of the most southern of the group. Not perceiving any sign of land, we continued to the westward in the parallel of fifty-three degrees south, as far as the meridian of fifty degrees west. We then stood to the north as far as the parallel of fifty-two degrees south, when we turned to the eastward, and kept our parallel by double altitudes, morning and evening, and meridian altitudes of the planets and moon. Having thus gone eastwardly to the meridian of the western coast of Georgia,* we kept that meridian until we were in the latitude from which we set out. We then took diagonal courses throughout the entire extent of sea circumscribed, keeping a lookout constantly at the masthead, and repeating our examination with the greatest care for a period of three weeks, during which the weather was remarkably pleasant and fair, with no haze whatsoever. Of course we were thoroughly satisfied that, whatever islands might have existed in this vicinity at any former period, no vestige of them remained at the present day. Since my return home I find that the same ground was traced over, with equal care, in 1822, by Captain Johnson, of the American schooner *Henry*, and by Captain Morrell, in the American schooner *Wasp** – in both cases with the same result as in our own.

CHAPTER XVI*

It had been Captain Guy's original intention, after satisfying himself about the Auroras, to proceed through the Strait of Magellan,* and up along the western coast of Patagonia, but information received at Tristan da Cunha induced him to steer to the southward, in the hope of falling in with some small islands said to lie about the parallel of 60° S., longitude 41° 20′ W. In the event of his not discovering these lands, he designed, should the season prove favourable, to push on towards the pole. Accordingly, on 12th December, we made sail in that direction. On the 18th we found ourselves about the station indicated by Glass, and cruised for three days in that neighbourhood without finding any traces of the islands he had mentioned. On the 21st, the weather being unusually pleasant, we again made sail to the southward, with the resolution of penetrating in that course as far as possible. Before entering upon this portion of my narrative, it may be as well, for the information of those readers who have paid little attention to the progress of discovery in these regions, to give some brief account of the very few attempts at reaching the southern pole which have hitherto been made.

That of Captain Cook was the first of which we have any distinct account. In 1772 he sailed to the south in the *Resolution*, accompanied by Lieutenant Furneaux in the *Adventure*.* In December he found himself as far as the fifty-eighth parallel of south latitude, and in longitude 26° 57′ E. Here he met with narrow fields of ice, about eight or ten inches thick, and running north-west and south-east. This ice was in large cakes, and usually it was packed so closely that the vessels had great difficulty in forcing a passage. At this period Captain Cook supposed, from the vast number of birds to be seen, and from other indications, that he was in the near vicinity of land. He kept on to the southward, the weather being exceedingly cold, until he reached the sixty-fourth parallel, in longitude 38° 14′ E. Here he had mild weather, with gentle breezes, for five days, the thermometer being at thirty-six. In January 1773, the vessels crossed the Antarctic Circle, but did not succeed in penetrating much farther, for, upon reaching latitude 67° 15′, they found all farther progress impeded by an immense body of ice, extending all along the southern horizon as far as the eye could reach. This ice was of every variety – and some large floes of it, miles in extent, formed a compact mass, rising eighteen or twenty feet above the water. It being late in the season, and no hope entertained of rounding these obstructions, Captain Cook now reluctantly turned to the northward.

In the November following he renewed his search in the Antarctic. In latitude 59° 40′ he met with a strong current setting to the southward. In December, when the vessels were in latitude 67° 31′, longitude 142° 54′ W., the cold was excessive, with heavy gales and fog. Here also birds were abundant: the albatross, the penguin and the petrel especially. In latitude 70° 23′ some large islands of ice were encountered, and shortly afterwards the clouds to the southward were observed to be of a snowy whiteness, indicating the vicinity of field ice. In latitude 71° 10′, longitude 106° 54′ W., the navigators were stopped, as before, by an immense frozen expanse, which filled the whole area of the southern horizon. The northern edge of this expanse was ragged and broken, so firmly wedged together as to be utterly impassable, and extending about a mile to the southward. Behind it the frozen surface was comparatively smooth for some distance, until terminated in the extreme background by gigantic ranges of ice mountains, the one towering above the other. Captain Cook concluded that this vast field reached the southern pole or was joined to a continent. Mr J.N. Reynolds, whose great exertions and perseverance have at length succeeded in getting set on foot a national expedition, partly for the purpose of exploring these regions, thus speaks of the attempt of the *Resolution*.

We are not surprised that Captain Cook was unable to go beyond 71° 10′, but we are astonished that he did attain that point on the meridian of 106° 54′ west longitude. Palmer's Land lies south of the Shetland,* latitude sixty-four degrees, and tends to the southward and westward farther than any navigator has yet penetrated. Cook was standing for this land when his progress was arrested by the ice, which, we apprehend, must always be the case in that point, and so early in the season as 6th January – and we should not be surprised if a portion of the icy mountains described was attached to the main body of Palmer's Land, or to some other portions of land lying farther to the southward and westward.

In 1803, Captains Kreutzenstern and Lisiausky were dispatched by Alexander of Russia for the purpose of circumnavigating the globe.* In endeavouring to get south, they made no farther than 59° 58′, in longitude 70° 15′ W. They here met with strong currents setting eastwardly. Whales were abundant, but they saw no ice. In regard to this voyage, Mr Reynolds observes that if Kreutzenstern had arrived where he did earlier in the season, he must have encountered ice – it was March when he reached the latitude specified. The winds, prevailing, as they do, from the southward

and westward, had carried the floes, aided by currents, into that icy region bounded on the north by Georgia, east by Sandwich Land and the South Orkneys,* and west by the South Shetland Islands.

In 1822, Captain James Weddell, of the British navy, with two very small vessels, penetrated farther to the south than any previous navigator, and this, too, without encountering extraordinary difficulties. He states that although he was frequently hemmed in by ice *before* reaching the seventy-second parallel, yet, upon attaining it, not a particle was to be discovered, and that, upon arriving at the latitude of 74° 15', no fields, and only three islands of ice were visible. It is somewhat remarkable that, although vast flocks of birds were seen, and other usual indications of land, and although, south of the Shetlands, unknown coasts were observed from the masthead tending southwardly, Weddell discourages the idea of land existing in the polar regions of the south.

On 11th January 1823, Captain Benjamin Morrell, of the American schooner *Wasp*, sailed from Kerguelen's Land with a view of penetrating as far south as possible.* On the first of February he found himself in latitude 64° 52' S., longitude 118° 27' E. The following passage is extracted from his journal of that date.

The wind soon freshened to an eleven-knot breeze, and we embraced this opportunity of making to the west; being however convinced that the farther we went south beyond latitude sixty-four degrees, the less ice was to be apprehended, we steered a little to the southward, until we crossed the Antarctic Circle, and were in latitude 69° 15' E. In this latitude there was *no field ice*, and very few ice islands in sight.

Under the date of 14th March I find also this entry.

The sea was now entirely free of field ice, and there were not more than a dozen ice islands in sight. At the same time the temperature of the air and water was at least thirteen degrees higher (more mild) than we had ever found it between the parallels of sixty and sixty-two south. We were now in latitude 70° 14' S., and the temperature of the air was forty-seven, and that of the water forty-four. In this situation I found the variation to be 14° 27' easterly, per azimuth…* I have several times passed within the Antarctic Circle, on different meridians, and have uniformly found the temperature, both of the air and the water, to become more and more mild the farther I advanced beyond the sixty-fifth degree of

south latitude, and that the variation decreases in the same proportion. While north of this latitude, say between sixty and sixty-five south, we frequently had great difficulty in finding a passage for the vessel between the immense and almost innumerable ice islands, some of which were from one to two miles in circumference, and more than five hundred feet above the surface of the water.

Being nearly destitute of fuel and water, and without proper instruments, it being also late in the season, Captain Morrell was now obliged to put back, without attempting any farther progress to the southward, although an entirely open sea lay before him. He expresses the opinion that, had not these overruling considerations obliged him to retreat, he could have penetrated, if not to the pole itself, at least to the eighty-fifth parallel. I have given his ideas respecting these matters somewhat at length, that the reader may have an opportunity of seeing how far they were borne out by my own subsequent experience.

In 1831, Captain Briscoe, in the employ of the Messieurs Enderby, whale-ship owners of London, sailed in the brig *Lively* for the South Seas, accompanied by the cutter *Tula*.* On 28th February, being in latitude 66° 30′ S., longitude 47° 31′ E., he descried land, and "clearly discovered through the snow the black peaks of a range of mountains running ESE". He remained in this neighbourhood during the whole of the following month, but was unable to approach the coast nearer than within ten leagues, owing to the boisterous state of the weather. Finding it impossible to make farther discovery during this season, he returned northward to winter in Van Diemen's Land.

In the beginning of 1832 he again proceeded southwardly, and on 4th February was seen to the south-east in latitude 67° 15′, longitude 69° 29′ W. This was soon found to be an island near the headland of the country he had first discovered. On the 21st of the month he succeeded in landing on the latter, and took possession of it in the name of William IV, calling it Adelaide's Island, in honour of the English queen. These particulars being made known to the Royal Geographical Society of London, the conclusion was drawn by that body "that there is a continuous tract of land extending from 47° 30′ E. to 69° 29′ W. longitude, running the parallel of from sixty-six to sixty-seven degrees south latitude". In respect to this conclusion Mr Reynolds observes: "In the correctness of it we by no means concur; nor do the discoveries of Briscoe warrant any such inference. It was within these limits that Weddell proceeded south on a meridian to

the east of Georgia, Sandwich Land, and the South Orkney and Shetland islands." My own experience will be found to testify most directly to the falsity of the conclusion arrived at by the society.

These are the principal attempts which have been made at penetrating to a high southern latitude, and it will now be seen that there remained, previous to the voyage of the *Jane*, nearly three hundred degrees of longitude in which the Antarctic Circle had not been crossed at all. Of course a wide field lay before us for discovery, and it was with feelings of most intense interest that I heard Captain Guy express his resolution of pushing boldly to the southward.

CHAPTER XVII*

We kept our course southwardly for four days after giving up the search for Glass's islands, without meeting with any ice at all. On the 26th, at noon, we were in latitude 63° 23′ S., longitude 41° 25′ W. We now saw several large ice islands, and a floe of field ice, not, however, of any great extent. The winds generally blew from the south-east, or the north-east, but were very light. Whenever we had a westerly wind, which was seldom, it was invariably attended with a rain squall. Every day we had more or less snow. The thermometer, on the 27th, stood at thirty-five.

1st January 1828 – This day we found ourselves completely hemmed in by the ice, and our prospects looked cheerless indeed. A strong gale blew, during the whole forenoon, from the north-east, and drove large cakes of the drift against the rudder and counter with such violence that we all trembled for the consequences. Towards evening, the gale still blowing with fury, a large field in front separated, and we were enabled, by carrying a press of sail,* to force a passage through the smaller flakes into some open water beyond. As we approached this space we took in sail by degrees, and having at length got clear, lay to under a single reefed foresail.

2nd January – We had now tolerably pleasant weather. At noon we found ourselves in latitude 69° 10′ S., longitude 42° 20′ W., having crossed the Antarctic Circle. Very little ice was to be seen to the southward, although large fields of it lay behind us. This day we rigged some sounding gear, using a large iron pot capable of holding twenty gallons, and a line of two hundred fathoms. We found the current setting to the north, about a quarter of a mile per hour. The temperature of the air was now about thirty-three. Here we found the variation to be 14° 28′ easterly, per azimuth.*

5th January – We had still held on to the southward without any very great impediments. On this morning, however, being in latitude 73° 15′ E., longitude 42° 10′ W., we were again brought to a stand by an immense expanse of firm ice. We saw, nevertheless, much open water to the southward, and felt no doubt of being able to reach it eventually. Standing to the eastward along the edge of the floe, we at length came to a passage of about a mile in width, through which we warped our way* by sundown. The sea in which we now were was thickly covered with ice islands, but had no field ice, and we pushed on boldly as before. The cold did not seem to increase, although we had snow very frequently, and now and then hail squalls of great violence. Immense flocks of the albatross flew over the schooner this day, going from south-east to north-west.

7th January – The sea still remained pretty well open, so that we had no difficulty in holding on our course. To the westward we saw some icebergs of incredible size, and in the afternoon passed very near one whose summit could not have been less than four hundred fathoms from the surface of the ocean. Its girth was probably, at the base, three quarters of a league, and several streams of water were running from crevices in its sides. We remained in sight of this island two days, and then only lost it in a fog.

10th January – Early this morning we had the misfortune to lose a man overboard. He was an American, named Peter Vredenburgh,* a native of New York, and was one of the most valuable hands on board the schooner. In going over the bows his foot slipped, and he fell between two cakes of ice, never rising again. At noon of this day we were in latitude 78° 30′, longitude 40° 15′ W. The cold was now excessive, and we had hail squalls continually from the northward and eastward. In this direction also we saw several more immense icebergs, and the whole horizon to the eastward appeared to be blocked up with field ice, rising in tiers, one mass above the other. Some driftwood floated by during the evening, and a great quantity of birds flew over, among which were nellies, petrels, albatrosses and a large bird of a brilliant blue plumage. The variation here, per azimuth, was less than it had been previously to our passing the Antarctic Circle.

12th January – Our passage to the south again looked doubtful, as nothing was to be seen in the direction of the pole but one apparently limitless floe, backed by absolute mountains of ragged ice, one precipice of which arose frowningly above the other. We stood to the westward until the 14th, in the hope of finding an entrance.

14th January – This morning we reached the western extremity of the field which had impeded us, and, weathering it, came to an open sea,

without a particle of ice. Upon sounding with two hundred fathoms, we here found a current setting southwardly at the rate of half a mile per hour. The temperature of the air was forty-seven, that of the water thirty-four. We now sailed to the southward without meeting any interruption of moment until the 16th, when, at noon, we were in latitude 81° 21', longitude 42° W. We here again sounded, and found a current setting still southwardly, and at the rate of three quarters of a mile per hour. The variation per azimuth had diminished, and the temperature of the air was mild and pleasant, the thermometer being as high as fifty-one. At this period not a particle of ice was to be discovered. All hands on board now felt certain of attaining the pole.

17th January – This day was full of incident. Innumerable flights of birds flew over us from the southward, and several were shot from the deck; one of them, a species of pelican, proved to be excellent eating. About midday a small floe of ice was seen from the masthead off the larboard bow, and upon it there appeared to be some large animal. As the weather was good and nearly calm, Captain Guy ordered out two of the boats to see what it was. Dirk Peters and myself accompanied the mate in the larger boat. Upon coming up with the floe, we perceived that it was in the possession of a gigantic creature of the race of the Arctic bear, but far exceeding in size the largest of these animals. Being well armed, we made no scruple of attacking it at once. Several shots were fired in quick succession, the most of which took effect, apparently, in the head and body. Nothing discouraged, however, the monster threw himself from the ice, and swam, with open jaws, to the boat in which were Peters and myself. Owing to the confusion which ensued among us at this unexpected turn of the adventure, no person was ready immediately with a second shot, and the bear had actually succeeded in getting half his vast bulk across our gunwale,* and seizing one of the men by the small of his back, before any efficient means were taken to repel him. In this extremity nothing but the promptness and agility of Peters saved us from destruction. Leaping upon the back of the huge beast, he plunged the blade of a knife behind the neck, reaching the spinal marrow at a blow. The brute tumbled into the sea lifeless, and without a struggle, rolling over Peters as he fell. The latter soon recovered himself, and a rope being thrown him, he secured the carcass before entering the boat. We then returned in triumph to the schooner, towing our trophy behind us. This bear, upon admeasurement, proved to be full fifteen feet in his greatest length. His wool was perfectly white, and very coarse, curling tightly. The eyes were of a blood red, and

larger than those of the Arctic bear; the snout also more rounded, rather resembling the snout of the bulldog. The meat was tender, but excessively rank and fishy, although the men devoured it with avidity, and declared it excellent eating.

Scarcely had we got our prize alongside when the man at the masthead gave the joyful shout of "*Land on the starboard bow!*" All hands were now upon the alert, and, a breeze springing up very opportunely from the northward and eastward, we were soon close in with the coast. It proved to be a low rocky islet, of about a league in circumference, and altogether destitute of vegetation, if we except a species of prickly pear. In approaching it from the northward, a singular ledge of rock is seen projecting into the sea, and bearing a strong resemblance to corded bales of cotton. Around this ledge to the westward is a small bay, at the bottom of which our boats effected a convenient landing.

It did not take us long to explore every portion of the island, but, with one exception, we found nothing worthy of observation. In the southern extremity, we picked up near the shore, half buried in a pile of loose stones, a piece of wood, which seemed to have formed the prow of a canoe. There had been evidently some attempt at carving upon it, and Captain Guy fancied that he made out the figure of a tortoise, but the resemblance did not strike me very forcibly. Besides this prow, if such it were, we found no other token that any living creature had ever been here before. Around the coast we discovered occasional small floes of ice – but these were very few. The exact situation of this islet (to which Captain Guy gave the name of Bennet's Islet, in honour of his partner in the ownership of the schooner) is 82° 50′ S. latitude, 42° 20′ W. longitude.

We had now advanced to the southward more than eight degrees farther than any previous navigators, and the sea still lay perfectly open before us. We found, too, that the variation uniformly decreased as we proceeded, and, what was still more surprising, that the temperature of the air, and latterly of the water, became milder. The weather might even be called pleasant, and we had a steady but very gentle breeze always from some northern point of the compass. The sky was usually clear, with now and then a slight appearance of thin vapour in the southern horizon – this, however, was invariably of brief duration. Two difficulties alone presented themselves to our view: we were getting short of fuel, and symptoms of scurvy had occurred among several of the crew. These considerations began to impress upon Captain Guy the necessity of returning, and he spoke of it frequently. For my own part, confident as I was of soon arriving at land

of some description upon the course we were pursuing, and having every reason to believe, from present appearances, that we should not find it the sterile soil met with in the higher Arctic latitudes, I warmly pressed upon him the expediency of persevering, at least for a few days longer, in the direction we were now holding. So tempting an opportunity of solving the great problem in regard to an Antarctic continent had never yet been afforded to man, and I confess that I felt myself bursting with indignation at the timid and ill-timed suggestions of our commander. I believe, indeed, that what I could not refrain from saying to him on this head had the effect of inducing him to push on. While, therefore, I cannot but lament the most unfortunate and bloody events which immediately arose from my advice, I must still be allowed to feel some degree of gratification at having been instrumental, however remotely, in opening to the eye of science one of the most intensely exciting secrets which has ever engrossed its attention.

CHAPTER XVIII

18th January – This morning* we continued to the southward, with the same pleasant weather as before. The sea was entirely smooth, the air tolerably warm and from the north-east, the temperature of the water fifty-three. We now again got our sounding gear in order, and, with a hundred and fifty fathoms of line, found the current setting towards the pole at the rate of a mile an hour. This constant tendency to the southward, both in the wind and current, caused some degree of speculation, and even of alarm, in different quarters of the schooner, and I saw distinctly that no little impression had been made upon the mind of Captain Guy. He was exceedingly sensitive to ridicule, however, and I finally succeeded in laughing him out of his apprehensions. The variation was now very trivial. In the course of the day we saw several large whales of the right species, and innumerable flights of the albatross passed over the vessel. We also picked up a bush, full of red berries, like those of the hawthorn, and the carcass of a singular-looking land animal. It was three feet in length, and but six inches in height, with four very short legs, the feet armed with long claws of a brilliant scarlet, and resembling coral in substance. The body was covered with a straight silky hair, perfectly white. The tail was peaked like that of a rat, and about a foot and a half long. The head resembled a cat's, with the exception of the ears – these were flapped like the ears of a dog. The *teeth* were of the same brilliant scarlet as the claws.

19th January – Today, being in latitude 83° 20′, longitude 43° 5′ W. (the sea being of an extraordinarily dark colour), we again saw land from the masthead, and, upon a closer scrutiny, found it to be one of a group of very large islands.* The shore was precipitous, and the interior seemed to be well wooded, a circumstance which occasioned us great joy. In about four hours from our first discovering the land we came to anchor in ten fathoms, sandy bottom, a league from the coast, as a high surf, with strong ripples here and there, rendered a nearer approach of doubtful expediency. The two largest boats were now ordered out, and a party, well armed (among whom were Peters and myself), proceeded to look for an opening in the reef which appeared to encircle the island. After searching about for some time, we discovered an inlet, which we were entering when we saw four large canoes put off from the shore, filled with men who seemed to be well armed. We waited for them to come up, and, as they moved with great rapidity, they were soon within hail. Captain Guy now held up a white handkerchief on the blade of an oar, when the strangers made a full stop, and commenced a loud jabbering all at once, intermingled with occasional shouts, in which we could distinguish the words *Anamoo-moo!* and *Lama-Lama!* They continued this for at least half an hour, during which we had a good opportunity of observing their appearance.

In the four canoes, which might have been fifty feet long and five broad, there were a hundred and ten savages in all. They were about the ordinary stature of Europeans, but of a more muscular and brawny frame. Their complexion a jet black, with thick and long woolly hair.* They were clothed in skins of an unknown black animal, shaggy and silky, and made to fit the body with some degree of skill, the hair being inside, except where turned out about the neck, wrists and ankles. Their arms consisted principally of clubs, of a dark, and apparently very heavy wood. Some spears, however, were observed among them, headed with flint, and a few slings. The bottoms of the canoes were full of black stones about the size of a large egg.

When they had concluded their harangue (for it was clear they intended their jabbering for such), one of them who seemed to be the chief stood up in the prow of his canoe, and made signs for us to bring our boats alongside of him. This hint we pretended not to understand, thinking it the wiser plan to maintain, if possible, the interval between us, as their number more than quadrupled our own. Finding this to be the case, the chief ordered the three other canoes to hold back, while he advanced towards us with his own. As soon as he came up with us he leapt on board the largest of our boats, and seated himself by the side of Captain Guy, pointing at the

same time to the schooner, and repeating the words *Anamoo-moo!* and *Lama-Lama!* We now put back to the vessel, the four canoes following at a little distance.

Upon getting alongside, the chief evinced symptoms of extreme surprise and delight, clapping his hands, slapping his thighs and breast and laughing obstreperously. His followers behind joined in his merriment, and for some minutes the din was so excessive as to be absolutely deafening. Quiet being at length restored, Captain Guy ordered the boats to be hoisted up, as a necessary precaution, and gave the chief (whose name we soon found to be "Too-wit") to understand that we could admit no more than twenty of his men on deck at one time. With this arrangement he appeared perfectly satisfied, and gave some directions to the canoes, when one of them approached, the rest remaining about fifty yards off. Twenty of the savages now got on board, and proceeded to ramble over every part of the deck, and scramble about among the rigging, making themselves much at home, and examining every article with great inquisitiveness.

It was quite evident that they had never before seen any of the white race – from whose complexion, indeed, they appeared to recoil. They believed the *Jane* to be a living creature, and seemed to be afraid of hurting it with the points of their spears, carefully turning them up. Our crew were much amused with the conduct of Too-wit in one instance. The cook was splitting some wood near the galley, and, by accident, struck his axe into the deck, making a gash of considerable depth. The chief immediately ran up, and, pushing the cook on one side rather roughly, commenced a half whine, half howl, strongly indicative of sympathy in what he considered the sufferings of the schooner, patting and smoothing the gash with his hand, and washing it from a bucket of sea water which stood by. This was a degree of ignorance for which we were not prepared, and for my part I could not help thinking some of it affected.

When the visitors had satisfied, as well as they could, their curiosity in regard to our upper works, they were admitted below, when their amazement exceeded all bounds. Their astonishment now appeared to be far too deep for words, for they roamed about in silence, broken only by low ejaculations. The arms afforded them much food for speculation, and they were suffered to handle and examine them at leisure. I do not believe that they had the least suspicion of their actual use, but rather took them for idols, seeing the care we had of them, and the attention with which we watched their movements while handling them. At the great guns their wonder was redoubled. They approached them with every mark of the

profoundest reverence and awe, but forbore to examine them minutely. There were two large mirrors in the cabin, and here was the acme of their amazement. Too-wit was the first to approach them, and he had got in the middle of the cabin, with his face to one and his back to the other, before he fairly perceived them. Upon raising his eyes and seeing his reflected self in the glass, I thought the savage would go mad, but, upon turning short round to make a retreat, and beholding himself a second time in the opposite direction, I was afraid he would expire upon the spot. No persuasions could prevail upon him to take another look, but, throwing himself upon the floor, with his face buried in his hands, he remained thus until we were obliged to drag him upon deck.

The whole of the savages were admitted on board in this manner, twenty at a time, Too-wit being suffered to remain during the entire period. We saw no disposition to thievery among them, nor did we miss a single article after their departure. Throughout the whole of their visit they evinced the most friendly manner. There were, however, some points in their demeanour which we found it impossible to understand: for example, we could not get them to approach several very harmless objects – such as the schooner's sails, an egg, an open book or a pan of flour. We endeavoured to ascertain if they had among them any articles which might be turned to account in the way of traffic, but found great difficulty in being comprehended. We made out, nevertheless, what greatly astonished us, that the islands abounded in the large tortoise of the Gallipagos, one of which we saw in the canoe of Too-wit. We saw also some *biche de mer** in the hands of one of the savages, who was greedily devouring it in its natural state. These anomalies – for they were such when considered in regard to the latitude – induced Captain Guy to wish for a thorough investigation of the country, in the hope of making a profitable speculation in his discovery. For my own part, anxious as I was to know something more of these islands, I was still more earnestly bent on prosecuting the voyage to the southward without delay. We had now fine weather, but there was no telling how long it would last, and, being already in the eighty-fourth parallel, with an open sea before us, a current setting strongly to the southward and the wind fair, I could not listen with any patience to a proposition of stopping longer than was absolutely necessary for the health of the crew and the taking on board a proper supply of fuel and fresh provisions. I represented to the captain that we might easily make this group on our return, and winter here in the event of being blocked up by the ice. He at length came into my views (for in some way, hardly known to myself, I had

acquired much influence over him), and it was finally resolved that, even in the event of our finding *biche de mer*, we should only stay here a week to recruit, and then push on to the southward while we might. Accordingly we made every necessary preparation, and, under the guidance of Too-wit, got the *Jane* through the reef in safety, coming to anchor about a mile from the shore, in an excellent bay, completely landlocked, on the south-eastern coast of the main island, and in ten fathoms of water, black sandy bottom. At the head of this bay there were three fine springs (we were told) of good water, and we saw abundance of wood in the vicinity. The four canoes followed us in, keeping, however, at a respectful distance. Too-wit himself remained on board, and, upon our dropping anchor, invited us to accompany him on shore, and visit his village in the interior. To this Captain Guy consented, and, ten savages being left on board as hostages, a party of us, twelve in all, got in readiness to attend the chief. We took care to be well armed, yet without evincing any distrust. The schooner had her guns run out, her boarding nettings up, and every other proper precaution was taken to guard against surprise. Directions were left with the chief mate to admit no person on board during our absence, and, in the event of our not appearing in twelve hours, to send the cutter, with a swivel,* round the island in search of us.

At every step we took inland the conviction forced itself upon us that we were in a country differing essentially from any hitherto visited by civilized men. We saw nothing with which we had been formerly conver-sant. The trees resembled no growth of either the torrid, the temperate or the northern frigid zones, and were altogether unlike those of the lower southern latitudes we had already traversed. The very rocks were novel in their mass, their colour and their stratification, and the streams themselves, utterly incredible as it may appear, had so little in common with those of other climates that we were scrupulous of tasting them, and, indeed, had difficulty in bringing ourselves to believe that their qualities were purely those of nature. At a small brook which crossed our path (the first we had reached) Too-wit and his attendants halted to drink. On account of the singular character of the water, we refused to taste it, supposing it to be polluted, and it was not until some time afterwards we came to under-stand that such was the appearance of the streams throughout the whole group. I am at a loss to give a distinct idea of the nature of this liquid, and cannot do so without many words. Although it flowed with rapidity in all declivities where common water would do so, yet never, except when falling in a cascade, had it the customary appearance of *limpidity*. It was,

nevertheless, in point of fact, as perfectly limpid as any limestone water in existence, the difference being only in appearance. At first sight, and especially in cases where little declivity was found, it bore resemblance, as regards consistency, to a thick infusion of gum arabic* in common water. But this was only the least remarkable of its extraordinary qualities. It was *not* colourless, nor was it of any one uniform colour – presenting to the eye, as it flowed, every possible shade of purple, like the hues of a changeable silk. This variation in shade was produced in a manner which excited as profound astonishment in the minds of our party as the mirror had done in the case of Too-wit. Upon collecting a basinful, and allowing it to settle thoroughly, we perceived that the whole mass of liquid was made up of a number of distinct veins, each of a distinct hue, that these veins did not commingle, and that their cohesion was perfect in regard to their own particles among themselves, and imperfect in regard to neighbouring veins. Upon passing the blade of a knife athwart the veins, the water closed over it immediately, as with us, and also, in withdrawing it, all traces of the passage of the knife were instantly obliterated. If, however, the blade was passed down accurately between two veins, a perfect separation was effected, which the power of cohesion did not immediately rectify. The phenomena of this water formed the first definite link in that vast chain of apparent miracles with which I was destined to be at length encircled.

CHAPTER XIX

We were nearly three hours in reaching the village, it being more than nine miles in the interior, and the path lying through a rugged country. As we passed along, the party of Too-wit (the whole hundred and ten savages of the canoes)* was momentarily strengthened by smaller detachments, of from two to six or seven, which joined us, as if by accident, at different turns in the road. There appeared so much of system in this that I could not help feeling distrust, and I spoke to Captain Guy of my apprehensions. It was now too late, however, to recede, and we concluded that our best security lay in evincing a perfect confidence in the good faith of Too-wit. We accordingly went on, keeping a wary eye upon the manoeuvres of the savages, and not permitting them to divide our numbers by pushing in between. In this way, passing through a precipitous ravine, we at length reached what we were told was the only collection of habitations upon the island. As we came in sight of them, the chief set up a shout, and

frequently repeated the word *Klock-Klock*, which we supposed to be the name of the village, or perhaps the generic name for villages.

The dwellings were of the most miserable description imaginable, and, unlike those of even the lowest of the savage races with which mankind are acquainted, were of no uniform plan. Some of them (and these we found belonged to the *Wampoos* or *Yampoos*, the great men of the land) consisted of a tree cut down at about four feet from the root, with a large black skin thrown over it, and hanging in loose folds upon the ground. Under this the savage nestled. Others were formed by means of rough limbs of trees, with the withered foliage upon them, made to recline, at an angle of forty-five degrees, against a bank of clay, heaped up, without regular form, to the height of five or six feet. Others, again, were mere holes dug in the earth perpendicularly, and covered over with similar branches, these being removed when the tenant was about to enter, and pulled on again when he had entered. A few were built among the forked limbs of trees as they stood, the upper limbs being partially cut through, so as to bend over upon the lower, thus forming thicker shelter from the weather. The greater number, however, consisted of small shallow caverns, apparently scratched in the face of a precipitous ledge of dark stone, resembling fuller's earth, with which three sides of the village was bounded. At the door of each of these primitive caverns was a small rock, which the tenant carefully placed before the entrance upon leaving his residence, for what purpose I could not ascertain, as the stone itself was never of sufficient size to close up more than a third of the opening.

This village, if it were worthy of the name, lay in a valley of some depth, and could only be approached from the southward, the precipitous ledge of which I have already spoken cutting off all access in other directions. Through the middle of the valley ran a brawling stream of the same magical-looking water which has been described. We saw several strange animals about the dwellings, all appearing to be thoroughly domesticated. The largest of these creatures resembled our common hog in the structure of the body and snout; the tail, however, was bushy, and the legs slender as those of the antelope. Its motion was exceedingly awkward and indecisive, and we never saw it attempt to run. We noticed also several animals very similar in appearance, but of a greater length of body, and covered with a black wool. There were a great variety of tame fowls running about, and these seemed to constitute the chief food of the natives. To our astonishment we saw black albatross among these birds in a state of entire domestication, going to sea periodically for food, but always returning

to the village as a home, and using the southern shore in the vicinity as a place of incubation. There they were joined by their friends the pelicans* as usual, but these latter never followed them to the dwellings of the savages. Among the other kinds of tame fowls were ducks, differing very little from the canvas-back* of our own country, black gannets and a large bird not unlike the buzzard in appearance, but not carnivorous. Of fish there seemed to be a great abundance. We saw, during our visit, a quantity of dried salmon, rock cod, blue dolphins, mackerel, blackfish, skate, conger eels, elephant fish, mullets, soles, parrotfish, leatherjackets, gurnards, hake, flounders, paracutas* and innumerable other varieties. We noticed, too, that most of them were similar to the fish about the group of the Lord Auckland Islands,* in a latitude as low as fifty-one degrees south. The Gallipago tortoise was also very plentiful. We saw but few wild animals, and none of a large size, or of a species with which we were familiar. One or two serpents of a formidable aspect crossed our path, but the natives paid them little attention, and we concluded that they were not venomous.

As we approached the village with Too-wit and his party, a vast crowd of the people rushed out to meet us, with loud shouts, among which we could only distinguish the everlasting *Anamoo-moo!* and *Lama-Lama!* We were much surprised at perceiving that, with one or two exceptions, these newcomers were entirely naked, the skins being used only by the men of the canoes. All the weapons of the country seemed also to be in the possession of the latter, for there was no appearance of any among the villagers. There were a great many women and children, the former not altogether wanting in what might be termed personal beauty. They were straight, tall and well formed, with a grace and freedom of carriage not to be found in civilized society. Their lips, however, like those of the men, were thick and clumsy, so that, even when laughing, the teeth were never disclosed. Their hair was of a finer texture than that of the males. Among these naked villagers there might have been ten or twelve who were clothed, like the party of Too-wit, in dresses of black skin, and armed with lances and heavy clubs. These appeared to have great influence among the rest, and were always addressed by the title *Wampoo*. These, too, were the tenants of the black skin palaces. That of Too-wit was situated in the centre of the village, and was much larger and somewhat better constructed than others of its kind. The tree which formed its support was cut off at a distance of twelve feet or thereabout from the root, and there were several branches left just below the cut, these serving to extend the covering, and in this way prevent its flapping about the trunk. The covering, too, which

consisted of four very large skins fastened together with wooden skewers, was secured at the bottom with pegs driven through it and into the ground. The floor was strewed with a quantity of dry leaves by way of carpet.

To this hut we were conducted with great solemnity, and as many of the natives crowded in after us as possible. Too-wit seated himself on the leaves, and made signs that we should follow his example. This we did, and presently found ourselves in a situation peculiarly uncomfortable, if not indeed critical. We were on the ground, twelve in number, with the savages, as many as forty, sitting on their hams so closely around us that, if any disturbance had arisen, we should have found it impossible to make use of our arms, or indeed to have risen on our feet. The pressure was not only inside the tent, but outside, where probably was every individual on the whole island, the crowd being prevented from trampling us to death only by the incessant exertions and vociferations of Too-wit. Our chief security lay, however, in the presence of Too-wit himself among us, and we resolved to stick by him closely, as the best chance of extricating ourselves from the dilemma, sacrificing him immediately upon the first appearance of hostile design.

After some trouble a certain degree of quiet was restored, when the chief addressed us in a speech of great length, and very nearly resembling the one delivered in the canoes, with the exception that the *Anamoo-moos!* were now somewhat more strenuously insisted upon than the *Lama-Lamas!* We listened in profound silence until the conclusion of his harangue, when Captain Guy replied by assuring the chief of his eternal friendship and goodwill, concluding what he had to say by a present of several strings of blue beads and a knife. At the former the monarch, much to our surprise, turned up his nose with some expression of contempt, but the knife gave him the most unlimited satisfaction, and he immediately ordered dinner. This was handed into the tent over the heads of the attendants, and consisted of the palpitating entrails of a species of unknown animal, probably one of the slim-legged hogs which we had observed in our approach to the village. Seeing us at a loss how to proceed, he began, by way of setting us an example, to devour yard after yard of the enticing food, until we could positively stand it no longer, and evinced such manifest symptoms of rebellion of stomach as inspired His Majesty with a degree of astonishment only inferior to that brought about by the looking glasses. We declined, however, partaking of the delicacies before us, and endeavoured to make him understand that we had no appetite whatever, having just finished a hearty *déjeuner.*

When the monarch had made an end of his meal, we commenced a series of cross-questioning in every ingenious manner we could devise, with a view of discovering what were the chief productions of the country, and whether any of them might be turned to profit. At length he seemed to have some idea of our meaning, and offered to accompany us to a part of the coast where he assured us the *biche de mer* (pointing to a specimen of that animal) was to be found in great abundance. We were glad at this early opportunity of escaping from the oppression of the crowd, and signified our eagerness to proceed. We now left the tent, and, accompanied by the whole population of the village, followed the chief to the southeastern extremity of the island, not far from the bay where our vessel lay at anchor. We waited here for about an hour, until the four canoes were brought round by some of the savages to our station. The whole of our party then getting into one of them, we were paddled along the edge of the reef before mentioned, and of another still farther out, where we saw a far greater quantity of *biche de mer* than the oldest seaman among us had ever seen in those groups of the lower latitudes most celebrated for this article of commerce. We stayed near these reefs only long enough to satisfy ourselves that we could easily load a dozen vessels with the animal if necessary, when we were taken alongside the schooner, and parted with Too-wit, after obtaining from him a promise that he would bring us, in the course of twenty-four hours, as many of the canvas-back ducks and Gallipago tortoises as his canoes would hold. In the whole of this adventure we saw nothing in the demeanour of the natives calculated to create suspicion, with the single exception of the systematic manner in which their party was strengthened during our route from the schooner to the village.

CHAPTER XX

The chief was as good as his word, and we were soon plentifully supplied with fresh provision. We found the tortoises as fine as we had ever seen, and the ducks surpassed our best species of wildfowl, being exceedingly tender, juicy and well flavoured. Besides these, the savages brought us, upon our making them comprehend our wishes, a vast quantity of brown celery and scurvy grass,* with a canoe-load of fresh fish and some dried. The celery was a treat indeed, and the scurvy grass proved of incalculable benefit in restoring those of our men who had shown symptoms of disease. In a very short time we had not a single person on the sick list. We had

also plenty of other kinds of fresh provision, among which may be mentioned a species of shellfish resembling the mussel in shape, but with the taste of an oyster. Shrimps, too, and prawns were abundant, and albatross and other birds' eggs with dark shells. We took in, too, a plentiful stock of the flesh of the hog which I have mentioned before. Most of the men found it a palatable food, but I thought it fishy and otherwise disagreeable. In return for these good things we presented the natives with blue beads, brass trinkets, nails, knives and pieces of red cloth, they being fully delighted in the exchange. We established a regular market on shore, just under the guns of the schooner, where our barterings were carried on with every appearance of good faith, and a degree of order which their conduct at the village of Klock-Klock had not led us to expect from the savages.

Matters went on thus very amicably for several days, during which parties of the natives were frequently on board the schooner, and parties of our men frequently on shore, making long excursions into the interior, and receiving no molestation whatever. Finding the ease with which the vessel might be loaded with *biche de mer*, owing to the friendly disposition of the islanders, and the readiness with which they would render us assistance in collecting it, Captain Guy resolved to enter into negotiation with Too-wit for the erection of suitable houses in which to cure the article, and for the services of himself and tribe in gathering as much as possible, while he himself took advantage of the fine weather to prosecute his voyage to the southward. Upon mentioning this project to the chief he seemed very willing to enter into an agreement. A bargain was accordingly struck, perfectly satisfactory to both parties, by which it was arranged that, after making the necessary preparations, such as laying off the proper grounds, erecting a portion of the buildings, and doing some other work in which the whole of our crew would be required, the schooner should proceed on her route, leaving three of her men on the island to superintend the fulfilment of the project, and instruct the natives in drying the *biche de mer*. In regard to terms, these were made to depend upon the exertions of the savages in our absence. They were to receive a stipulated quantity of blue beads, knives, red cloth and so forth, for every certain number of piculs* of the *biche de mer* which should be ready on our return.

A description of the nature of this important article of commerce, and the method of preparing it, may prove of some interest to my readers, and I can find no more suitable place than this for introducing an account of it. The following comprehensive notice of the substance is taken from a modern history of a voyage to the South Seas:*

It is that *mollusca* from the Indian Seas which is known in commerce by the French name *bouche de mer* (a nice morsel from the sea).* If I am not much mistaken, the celebrated Cuvier calls it *Gasteropeda pulmonifera*.* It is abundantly gathered in the coasts of the Pacific islands, and gathered especially for the Chinese market, where it commands a great price, perhaps as much as their much-talked-of edible birds' nests, which are probably made up of the gelatinous matter picked up by a species of swallow from the body of these *molluscæ*. They have no shell, no legs, nor any prominent part, except an *absorbing* and an *excretory*, opposite organs, but, by their elastic wings, like caterpillars or worms, they creep in shallow waters, in which, when low, they can be seen by a kind of swallow, the sharp bill of which, inserted in the soft animal, draws a gummy and filamentous substance, which, by drying, can be wrought into the solid walls of their nest. Hence the name of *Gasteropeda pulmonifera*.

This mollusca is oblong, and of different sizes, from three to eighteen inches in length, and I have seen a few that were not less than two feet long. They are nearly round, a little flattish on one side, which lies next the bottom of the sea, and they are from one to eight inches thick. They crawl up into shallow water at particular seasons of the year, probably for the purpose of gendering,* as we often find them in pairs. It is when the sun has the most power on the water, rendering it tepid, that they approach the shore, and they often go up into places so shallow that, on the tide's receding, they are left dry, exposed to the heat of the sun. But they do not bring forth their young in shallow water, as we never see any of their progeny, and the full-grown ones are always observed coming in from deep water. They feed principally on that class of zoophytes* which produce the coral.

The *biche de mer* is generally taken in three or four feet water, after which they are brought on shore, and split at one end with a knife, the incision being one inch or more, according to the size of the mollusca. Through this opening the entrails are forced out by pressure, and they are much like those of any other small tenant of the deep. The article is then washed, and afterwards boiled to a certain degree, which must not be too much or too little. They are then buried in the ground for four hours, then boiled again for a short time, after which they are dried, either by the fire or the sun. Those cured by the sun are worth the most, but where one picul (133 ⅓ lbs) can be cured that way, I can cure thirty piculs by the fire. When once properly cured, they can be kept in

a dry place for two or three years without any risk, but they should be examined once in every few months, say four times a year, to see if any dampness is likely to affect them.

The Chinese, as before stated, consider *biche de mer* a very great luxury, believing that it wonderfully strengthens and nourishes the system, and renews the exhausted system of the immoderate voluptuary. The first quality commands a high price in Canton, being worth ninety dollars a picul; the second quality, seventy-five dollars; the third, fifty dollars; the fourth, thirty dollars; the fifth, twenty dollars; the sixth, twelve dollars; the seventh, eight dollars; and the eighth, four dollars; small cargoes, however, will often bring more in Manila, Singapore and Batavia.*

An agreement having been thus entered into, we proceeded immediately to land everything necessary for preparing the buildings and clearing the ground. A large flat space near the eastern shore of the bay was selected, where there was plenty both of wood and water, and within a convenient distance of the principal reefs on which the *biche de mer* was to be procured. We now all set to work in good earnest, and soon, to the great astonishment of the savages, had felled a sufficient number of trees for our purpose, getting them quickly in order for the framework of the houses, which in two or three days were so far under way that we could safely trust the rest of the work to the three men whom we intended to leave behind. These were John Carson, Alfred Harris and —— Peterson* (all natives of London, I believe), who volunteered their services in this respect.

By the last of the month we had everything in readiness for departure. We had agreed, however, to pay a formal visit of leave-taking to the village, and Too-wit insisted so pertinaciously upon our keeping the promise that we did not think it advisable to run the risk of offending him by a final refusal. I believe that not one of us had at this time the slightest suspicion of the good faith of the savages. They had uniformly behaved with the greatest decorum, aiding us with alacrity in our work, offering us their commodities, frequently without price, and never, in any instance, pilfering a single article, although the high value they set upon the goods we had with us was evident by the extravagant demonstrations of joy always manifested upon our making them a present. The women especially were most obliging in every respect, and, upon the whole, we should have been the most suspicious of human beings had we entertained a single thought

of perfidy on the part of a people who treated us so well. A very short while sufficed to prove that this apparent kindness of disposition was only the result of a deeply laid plan for our destruction, and that the islanders for whom we entertained such inordinate feelings of esteem were among the most barbarous, subtle and bloodthirsty wretches that ever contaminated the face of the globe.

It was on the first of February that we went on shore for the purpose of visiting the village. Although, as said before, we entertained not the slightest suspicion, still no proper precaution was neglected. Six men were left in the schooner, with instructions to permit none of the savages to approach the vessel during our absence, under any pretence whatever, and to remain constantly on deck. The boarding nettings were up, the guns double-shotted with grape and canister,* and the swivels loaded with canisters of musket balls. She lay, with her anchor apeak,* about a mile from the shore, and no canoe could approach her in any direction without being distinctly seen and exposed to the full fire of our swivels immediately.

The six men being left on board, our shore party consisted of thirty-two persons in all. We were armed to the teeth, having with us muskets, pistols and cutlasses; besides, each a long kind of seaman's knife, somewhat resembling the bowie knife now so much used throughout our western and southern country.* A hundred of the black-skin warriors met us at the landing for the purpose of accompanying us on our way. We noticed, however, with some surprise, that they were now entirely without arms, and, upon questioning Too-wit in relation to this circumstance, he merely answered that "*Mattee non we pa pa si*" – meaning that there was no need of arms where all were brothers. We took this in good part, and proceeded.

We had passed the spring and rivulet of which I before spoke, and were now entering upon a narrow gorge leading through the chain of soapstone hills among which the village was situated. This gorge was very rocky and uneven, so much so that it was with no little difficulty we scrambled through it on our first visit to Klock-Klock. The whole length of the ravine might have been a mile and a half, or probably two miles. It wound in every possible direction through the hills (having apparently formed, at some remote period, the bed of a torrent), in no instance proceeding more than twenty yards without an abrupt turn. The sides of this dell would have averaged, I am sure, seventy or eighty feet in perpendicular altitude throughout the whole of their extent, and in some portions they arose to an astonishing height, overshadowing the pass so completely that but

little of the light of day could penetrate. The general width was about forty feet, and occasionally it diminished so as not to allow the passage of more than five or six persons abreast. In short, there could be no place in the world better adapted for the consummation of an ambuscade, and it was no more than natural that we should look carefully to our arms as we entered upon it. When I now think of our egregious folly, the chief subject of astonishment seems to be that we should have ever ventured, under any circumstances, so completely into the power of unknown savages as to permit them to march both before and behind us in our progress through this ravine. Yet such was the order we blindly took up, trusting foolishly to the force of our party, the unarmed condition of Too-wit and his men, the certain efficacy of our firearms (whose effect was yet a secret to the natives), and, more than all, to the long-sustained pretension of friendship kept up by these infamous wretches. Five or six of them went on before, as if to lead the way, ostentatiously busying themselves in removing the larger stones and rubbish from the path. Next came our own party. We walked closely together, taking care only to prevent separation. Behind followed the main body of the savages, observing unusual order and decorum.

Dirk Peters, a man named Wilson Allen and myself were on the right of our companions, examining, as we went along, the singular stratification of the precipice which overhung us. A fissure in the soft rock attracted our attention. It was about wide enough for one person to enter without squeezing, and extended back into the hill some eighteen or twenty feet in a straight course, sloping afterwards to the left. The height of the opening, as far as we could see into it from the main gorge, was perhaps sixty or seventy feet. There were one or two stunted shrubs growing from the crevices, bearing a species of filbert,* which I felt some curiosity to examine, and pushed in briskly for that purpose, gathering five or six of the nuts at a grasp, and then hastily retreating. As I turned, I found that Peters and Allen had followed me. I desired them to go back, as there was not room for two persons to pass, saying they should have some of my nuts. They accordingly turned, and were scrambling back, Allen being close to the mouth of the fissure, when I was suddenly aware of a concussion resembling nothing I had ever before experienced, and which impressed me with a vague conception, if indeed I then thought of anything, that the whole foundations of the solid globe were suddenly rent asunder, and that the day of universal dissolution was at hand.

CHAPTER XXI

As soon as I could collect my scattered senses, I found myself nearly suffocated, and grovelling in utter darkness among a quantity of loose earth, which was also falling upon me heavily in every direction, threatening to bury me entirely. Horribly alarmed at this idea, I struggled to gain my feet, and at length succeeded. I then remained motionless for some moments, endeavouring to conceive what had happened to me, and where I was. Presently I heard a deep groan just at my ear, and afterwards the smothered voice of Peters calling to me for aid in the name of God. I scrambled one or two paces forward, when I fell directly over the head and shoulders of my companion, who, I soon discovered, was buried in a loose mass of earth as far as his middle, and struggling desperately to free himself from the pressure. I tore the dirt from around him with all the energy I could command, and at length succeeded in getting him out.

As soon as we sufficiently recovered from our fright and surprise to be capable of conversing rationally, we both came to the conclusion that the walls of the fissure in which we had ventured had, by some convulsion of nature, or probably from their own weight, caved in overhead, and that we were consequently lost for ever, being thus entombed alive. For a long time we gave up supinely to the most intense agony and despair, such as cannot be adequately imagined by those who have never been in a similar situation. I firmly believe that no incident ever occurring in the course of human events is more adapted to inspire the supremeness of mental and bodily distress than a case like our own, of living inhumation. The blackness of darkness* which envelops the victim, the terrific oppression of lungs, the stifling fumes from the damp earth, unite with the ghastly considerations that we are beyond the remotest confines of hope, and that such is the allotted portion of *the dead*, to carry into the human heart a degree of appalling awe and horror not to be tolerated – never to be conceived.

At length Peters proposed that we should endeavour to ascertain precisely the extent of our calamity, and grope about our prison, it being barely possible, he observed, that some opening might be yet left us for escape. I caught eagerly at this hope, and, arousing myself to exertion, attempted to force my way through the loose earth. Hardly had I advanced a single step before a glimmer of light became perceptible, enough to convince me that, at all events, we should not immediately perish for want of air. We now took some degree of heart, and encouraged each other to hope for the best. Having scrambled over a bank of rubbish which impeded our farther

progress in the direction of the light, we found less difficulty in advancing, and also experienced some relief from the excessive oppression of lungs which had tormented us. Presently we were enabled to obtain a glimpse of the objects around, and discovered that we were near the extremity of the straight portion of the fissure, where it made a turn to the left. A few struggles more, and we reached the bend, when, to our inexpressible joy, there appeared a long seam or crack extending upwards a vast distance, generally at an angle of about forty-five degrees, although sometimes much more precipitous. We could not see through the whole extent of this opening, but, as a good deal of light came down it, we had little doubt of finding at the top of it (if we could by any means reach the top) a clear passage into the open air.

I now called to mind that three of us had entered the fissure from the main gorge, and that our companion, Allen, was still missing; we determined at once to retrace our steps and look for him. After a long search, and much danger from the further caving-in of the earth above us, Peters at length cried out to me that he had hold of our companion's foot, and that his whole body was deeply buried beneath the rubbish, beyond a possibility of extricating him. I soon found that what he said was too true, and that, of course, life had been long extinct. With sorrowful hearts, therefore, we left the corpse to its fate, and again made our way to the bend.

The breadth of the seam was barely sufficient to admit us, and, after one or two ineffectual efforts at getting up, we began once more to despair. I have before said that the chain of hills through which ran the main gorge was composed of a species of soft rock resembling soapstone. The sides of the cleft we were now attempting to ascend were of the same material, and so excessively slippery, being wet, that we could get but little foothold upon them even in their least precipitous parts; in some places, where the ascent was nearly perpendicular, the difficulty was, of course, much aggravated, and, indeed, for some time we thought insurmountable. We took courage, however, from despair, and, by dint of cutting steps in the soft stone with our bowie knives, and swinging at the risk of our lives, to small projecting points of a harder species of slaty rock which now and then protruded from the general mass, we at length reached a natural platform, from which was perceptible a patch of blue sky, at the extremity of a thickly wooded ravine.* Looking back now, with somewhat more leisure, at the passage through which we had thus far proceeded, we clearly saw, from the appearance of its sides, that it was of late formation, and we concluded that the concussion, whatever it was, which had so unexpectedly

overwhelmed us, had also, at the same moment, laid open this path for escape. Being quite exhausted with exertion, and, indeed, so weak that we were scarcely able to stand or articulate, Peters now proposed that we should endeavour to bring our companions to the rescue by firing the pistols which still remained in our girdles – the muskets as well as cutlasses had been lost among the loose earth at the bottom of the chasm. Subsequent events proved that, had we fired, we should have sorely repented it, but, luckily, a half-suspicion of foul play had by this time arisen in my mind, and we forbore to let the savages know of our whereabouts.

After having reposed for about an hour, we pushed on slowly up the ravine, and had gone no great way before we heard a succession of tremendous yells. At length we reached what might be called the surface of the ground, for our path hitherto, since leaving the platform, had lain beneath an archway of high rock and foliage, at a vast distance overhead. With great caution we stole to a narrow opening, through which we had a clear sight of the surrounding country, when the whole dreadful secret of the concussion broke upon us in one moment and at one view.

The spot from which we looked was not far from the summit of the highest peak in the range of the soapstone hills. The gorge in which our party of thirty-two had entered ran within fifty feet to the left of us. But, for at least one hundred yards, the channel or bed of this gorge was entirely filled up with the chaotic ruins of more than a million tons of earth and stone that had been artificially tumbled within it. The means* by which the vast mass had been precipitated were not more simple than evident, for sure traces of the murderous work were yet remaining. In several spots along the top of the eastern side of the gorge (we were now on the western) might be seen stakes of wood driven into the earth. In these spots the earth had not given way, but throughout the whole extent of the face of the precipice from which the mass *had* fallen, it was clear, from marks left in the soil resembling those made by the drill of the rock-blaster, that stakes similar to those we saw standing had been inserted, at not more than a yard apart, for the length of perhaps three hundred feet, and ranging at about ten feet back from the edge of the gulf. Strong cords of grapevine were attached to the stakes still remaining on the hill, and it was evident that such cords had also been attached to each of the other stakes. I have already spoken of the singular stratification of these soapstone hills, and the description just given of the narrow and deep fissure through which we effected our escape from inhumation will afford a further conception of its nature. This was such that almost every natural convulsion would be sure to split the

soil into perpendicular layers or ridges running parallel with one another, and a very moderate exertion of art would be sufficient for effecting the same purpose. Of this stratification the savages had availed themselves to accomplish their treacherous ends. There can be no doubt that, by the continuous line of stakes, a partial rupture of the soil had been brought about, probably to the depth of one or two feet, when, by means of a savage pulling at the end of each of the cords (these cords being attached to the tops of the stakes, and extending back from the edge of the cliff), a vast leverage power was obtained, capable of hurling the whole face of the hill, upon a given signal, into the bosom of the abyss below. The fate of our poor companions was no longer a matter of uncertainty. We alone had escaped from the tempest of that overwhelming destruction. We were the only living white men upon the island.*

CHAPTER XXII

Our situation, as it now appeared, was scarcely less dreadful than when we had conceived ourselves entombed for ever. We saw before us no prospect but that of being put to death by the savages, or of dragging out a miserable existence in captivity among them. We might, to be sure, conceal ourselves for a time from their observation among the fastnesses of the hills, and, as a final resort, in the chasm from which we had just issued, but we must either perish in the long polar winter through cold and famine, or be ultimately discovered in our efforts to obtain relief.

The whole country around us seemed to be swarming with savages, crowds of whom, we now perceived, had come over from the islands to the southward on flat rafts, doubtless with a view of lending their aid in the capture and plunder of the *Jane*. The vessel still lay calmly at anchor in the bay, those on board being apparently quite unconscious of any danger awaiting them. How we longed at that moment to be with them, either to aid in effecting their escape, or to perish with them in attempting a defence! We saw no chance even of warning them of their danger without bringing immediate destruction upon our own heads, with but a remote hope of benefit to them. A pistol fired might suffice to apprise them that something wrong had occurred, but the report could not possibly inform them that their only prospect of safety lay in getting out of the harbour forthwith – it could not tell them that no principles of honour now bound them to remain, that their companions were no longer among the living.

Upon hearing the discharge they could not be more thoroughly prepared to meet the foe, who were now getting ready to attack, than they already were, and always had been. No good, therefore, and infinite harm, would result from our firing, and, after mature deliberation, we forbore.

Our next thought was to attempt a rush towards the vessel, to seize one of the four canoes which lay at the head of the bay, and endeavour to force a passage on board. But the utter impossibility of succeeding in this desperate task soon became evident. The country, as I said before, was literally swarming with the natives, skulking among the bushes and recesses of the hills, so as not to be observed from the schooner. In our immediate vicinity especially, and blockading the sole path by which we could hope to attain the shore in the proper point, were stationed the whole party of the black-skin warriors, with Too-wit at their head, and apparently only waiting for some reinforcement to commence his onset upon the *Jane*. The canoes, too, which lay at the head of the bay, were manned with savages, unarmed, it is true, but who undoubtedly had arms within reach. We were forced, therefore, however unwillingly, to remain in our place of conceal-ment, mere spectators of the conflict which presently ensued.

In about half an hour we saw some sixty or seventy rafts, or flatboats, with outriggers, filled with savages, and coming round the southern bight* of the harbour. They appeared to have no arms except short clubs, and stones which lay in the bottom of the rafts. Immediately afterwards another detachment, still larger, approached in an opposite direction, and with similar weapons. The four canoes, too, were now quickly filled with natives, starting up from the bushes at the head of the bay, and put off swiftly to join the other parties. Thus, in less time than I have taken to tell it, and as if by magic, the *Jane* saw herself surrounded by an immense multitude of desperadoes evidently bent upon capturing her at all hazards.

That they would succeed in so doing could not be doubted for an instant.* The six men left in the vessel, however resolutely they might engage in her defence, were altogether unequal to the proper management of the guns, or in any manner to sustain a contest at such odds. I could hardly imagine that they would make resistance at all, but in this was deceived, for presently I saw them get springs upon the cable,* and bring the vessel's starboard broadside to bear upon the canoes, which by this time were within pistol range, the rafts being nearly a quarter of a mile to windward. Owing to some cause unknown, but most probably to the agitation of our poor friends at seeing themselves in so hopeless a situa-tion, the discharge was an entire failure. Not a canoe was hit or a single

savage injured, the shots striking short and ricocheting over their heads. The only effect produced upon them was astonishment at the unexpected report and smoke, which was so excessive that for some moments I almost thought they would abandon their design entirely, and return to the shore. And this they would most likely have done had our men followed up their broadside by a discharge of small arms, in which, as the canoes were now so near at hand, they could not have failed in doing some execution, sufficient, at least, to deter this party from a farther advance, until they could have given the rafts also a broadside. But, in place of this, they left the canoe party to recover from their panic, and, by looking about them, to see that no injury had been sustained, while they flew to the larboard to get ready for the rafts.

The discharge to larboard produced the most terrible effect. The star and double-headed shot* of the large guns cut seven or eight of the rafts completely asunder, and killed, perhaps, thirty or forty of the savages outright, while a hundred of them, at least, were thrown into the water, the most of them dreadfully wounded. The remainder, frightened out of their senses, commenced at once a precipitate retreat, not even waiting to pick up their maimed companions, who were swimming about in every direction, screaming and yelling for aid. This great success, however, came too late for the salvation of our devoted people. The canoe party were already on board the schooner to the number of more than a hundred and fifty, the most of them having succeeded in scrambling up the chains and over the boarding nettings even before the matches had been applied to the larboard guns. Nothing could now withstand their brute rage. Our men were borne down at once, overwhelmed, trodden under foot and absolutely torn to pieces in an instant.

Seeing this, the savages on the rafts got the better of their fears, and came up in shoals to the plunder. In five minutes the *Jane* was a pitiable scene indeed of havoc and tumultuous outrage. The decks were split open and ripped up; the cordage, sails and everything movable on deck demolished as if by magic; while, by dint of pushing at the stern, towing with the canoes and hauling at the sides, as they swam in thousands around the vessel, the wretches finally forced her on shore (the cable having been slipped), and delivered her over to the good offices of Too-wit, who, during the whole of the engagement, had maintained, like a skilful general, his post of security and reconnaissance among the hills, but, now that the victory was completed to his satisfaction, condescended to scamper down with his warriors of the black skin, and become a partaker in the spoils.

Too-wit's descent left us at liberty to quit our hiding place and recon-
noitre the hill in the vicinity of the chasm. At about fifty yards from the
mouth of it we saw a small spring of water, at which we slaked the burning
thirst that now consumed us. Not far from the spring we discovered several
of the filbert bushes which I mentioned before. Upon tasting the nuts we
found them palatable, and very nearly resembling in flavour the common
English filbert. We collected our hats full immediately, deposited them
within the ravine, and returned for more. While we were busily employed
in gathering these, a rustling in the bushes alarmed us, and we were upon
the point of stealing back to our covert when a large black bird of the
bittern species strugglingly and slowly arose above the shrubs. I was so
much startled that I could do nothing, but Peters had sufficient presence
of mind to run up to it before it could make its escape, and seize it by the
neck. Its struggles and screams were tremendous, and we had thoughts of
letting it go, lest the noise should alarm some of the savages who might
be still lurking in the neighbourhood. A stab with a bowie knife, however,
at length brought it to the ground, and we dragged it into the ravine, con-
gratulating ourselves that, at all events, we had thus obtained a supply of
food enough to last us for a week.

We now went out again to look about us, and ventured a considerable
distance down the southern declivity of the hill, but met with nothing else
which could serve us for food. We therefore collected a quantity of dry
wood and returned, seeing one or two large parties of the natives on their
way to the village, laden with the plunder of the vessel, and who, we were
apprehensive, might discover us in passing beneath the hill.

Our next care was to render our place of concealment as secure as
possible, and, with this object, we arranged some brushwood over the
aperture which I have before spoken of as the one through which we saw
the patch of blue sky, on reaching the platform from the interior of the
chasm. We left only a very small opening, just wide enough to admit of
our seeing the bay, without the risk of being discovered from below. Having
done this, we congratulated ourselves upon the security of the position,
for we were now completely excluded from observation, as long as we
chose to remain within the ravine itself, and not venture out upon the hill.
We could perceive no traces of the savages having ever been within this
hollow, but, indeed, when we came to reflect upon the probability that the
fissure through which we attained it had been only just now created by
the fall of the cliff opposite, and that no other way of attaining it could
be perceived, we were not so much rejoiced at the thought of being secure

from molestation as fearful lest there should be absolutely no means left us for descent. We resolved to explore the summit of the hill thoroughly, when a good opportunity should offer. In the mean time we watched the motions of the savages through our loophole.

They had already made a complete wreck of the vessel,* and were now preparing to set her on fire. In a little while we saw the smoke ascending in huge volumes from her main hatchway, and, shortly afterwards, a dense mass of flame burst up from the forecastle. The rigging, masts and what remained of the sails caught immediately, and the fire spread rapidly along the decks. Still a great many of the savages retained their stations about her, hammering with large stones, axes and cannonballs at the bolts and other copper and iron work. On the beach, and in canoes and rafts, there were not less, altogether, in the immediate vicinity of the schooner, than ten thousand natives, besides the shoals of them who, laden with booty, were making their way inland and over to the neighbouring islands. We now anticipated a catastrophe, and were not disappointed. First of all there came a smart shock (which we felt distinctly where we were as if we had been slightly galvanized), but unattended with any visible signs of an explosion. The savages were evidently startled, and paused for an instant from their labours and yellings. They were upon the point of recommencing, when suddenly a mass of smoke puffed up from the decks, resembling a black and heavy thundercloud – then, as if from its bowels, arose a tall stream of vivid fire to the height, apparently, of a quarter of a mile – then there came a sudden circular expansion of the flame – then the whole atmosphere was magically crowded, in a single instant, with a wild chaos of wood, and metal, and human limbs – and, lastly, came the concussion in its fullest fury, which hurled us impetuously from our feet, while the hills echoed and re-echoed the tumult, and a dense shower of the minutest fragments of the ruins tumbled headlong in every direction around us.

The havoc among the savages far exceeded our utmost expectation, and they had now, indeed, reaped the full and perfect fruits of their treachery. Perhaps a thousand perished by the explosion, while at least an equal number were desperately mangled. The whole surface of the bay was literally strewn with the struggling and drowning wretches, and on shore matters were even worse. They seemed utterly appalled by the suddenness and completeness of their discomfiture, and made no efforts at assisting one another. At length we observed a total change in their demeanour. From absolute stupor, they appeared to be, all at once, aroused to the

highest pitch of excitement, and rushed wildly about, going to and from a certain point on the beach, with the strangest expressions of mingled horror, rage and intense curiosity depicted on their countenances, and shouting, at the top of their voices, "*Tekeli-li! Tekeli-li!*"

Presently we saw a large body go off into the hills, whence they returned in a short time, carrying stakes of wood. These they brought to the station where the crowd was the thickest, which now separated so as to afford us a view of the object of all this excitement. We perceived something white lying on the ground, but could not immediately make out what it was. At length we saw that it was the carcass of the strange animal with the scarlet teeth and claws which the schooner had picked up at sea on 18th January. Captain Guy had had the body preserved for the purpose of stuffing the skin and taking it to England. I remember he had given some directions about it just before our making the island, and it had been brought into the cabin and stowed away in one of the lockers. It had now been thrown on shore by the explosion, but why it had occasioned so much concern among the savages was more than we could comprehend. Although they crowded around the carcass at a little distance, none of them seemed willing to approach it closely. By and by the men with the stakes drove them in a circle around it, and no sooner was this arrangement completed than the whole of the vast assembly rushed into the interior of the island, with loud screams of "*Tekeli-li! Tekeli-li!*"

CHAPTER XXIII*

During the six or seven days immediately following we remained in our hiding place upon the hill, going out only occasionally, and then with the greatest precaution, for water and filberts. We had made a kind of penthouse on the platform, furnishing it with a bed of dry leaves, and placing in it three large flat stones, which served us for both fireplace and table. We kindled a fire without difficulty by rubbing two pieces of dry wood together, the one soft, the other hard. The bird we had taken in such good season proved excellent eating, although somewhat tough. It was not an oceanic fowl, but a species of bittern, with jet-black and grizzly plumage, and diminutive wings in proportion to its bulk. We afterwards saw three of the same kind in the vicinity of the ravine, apparently seeking for the one we had captured, but, as they never alighted, we had no opportunity of catching them.

As long as this fowl lasted we suffered nothing from our situation, but it was now entirely consumed, and it became absolutely necessary that we should look out for provision. The filberts would not satisfy the cravings of hunger, afflicting us, too, with severe gripings of the bowels, and, if freely indulged in, with violent headache. We had seen several large tortoises near the seashore to the eastward of the hill, and perceived they might be easily taken, if we could get at them without the observation of the natives. It was resolved, therefore, to make an attempt at descending.

We commenced by going down the southern declivity, which seemed to offer the fewest difficulties, but had not proceeded a hundred yards before (as we had anticipated from appearances on the hilltop) our progress was entirely arrested by a branch of the gorge in which our companions had perished. We now passed along the edge of this for about a quarter of a mile, when we were again stopped by a precipice of immense depth, and, not being able to make our way along the brink of it, we were forced to retrace our steps by the main ravine.

We now pushed over to the eastward, but with precisely similar fortune. After an hour's scramble, at the risk of breaking our necks, we discovered that we had merely descended into a vast pit of black granite, with fine dust at the bottom, and whence the only egress was by the rugged path in which we had come down. Toiling again up this path, we now tried the northern edge of the hill. Here we were obliged to use the greatest possible caution in our manoeuvres, as the least indiscretion would expose us to the full view of the savages in the village. We crawled along, therefore, on our hands and knees, and, occasionally, were even forced to throw ourselves at full length, dragging our bodies along by means of the shrubbery. In this careful manner we had proceeded but a little way, when we arrived at a chasm far deeper than any we had yet seen, and leading directly into the main gorge. Thus our fears were fully confirmed, and we found ourselves cut off entirely from access to the world below. Thoroughly exhausted by our exertions, we made the best of our way back to the platform, and, throwing ourselves upon the bed of leaves, slept sweetly and soundly for some hours.

For several days after this fruitless search we were occupied in exploring every part of the summit of the hill, in order to inform ourselves of its actual resources. We found that it would afford us no food, with the exception of the unwholesome filberts, and a rank species of scurvy grass, which grew in a little patch of not more than four rods square, and would be soon exhausted. On 15th February, as near as I can remember, there was

not a blade of this left, and the nuts were growing scarce – our situation, therefore, could hardly be more lamentable.* On the 16th we again went round the walls of our prison, in hope of finding some avenue of escape, but to no purpose. We also descended the chasm in which we had been overwhelmed, with the faint expectation of discovering, through this channel, some opening to the main ravine. Here, too, we were disappointed, although we found and brought up with us a musket.

On the 17th we set out with the determination of examining more thoroughly the chasm of black granite into which we had made our way in the first search. We remembered that one of the fissures in the sides of this pit had been but partially looked into, and we were anxious to explore it, although with no expectation of discovering here any opening.

We found no great difficulty in reaching the bottom of the hollow as before, and were now sufficiently calm to survey it with some attention. It was, indeed, one of the most singular-looking places imaginable, and we could scarcely bring ourselves to believe it altogether the work of nature. The pit, from its eastern to its western extremity, was about five hundred yards in length, when all its windings were threaded, the distance from east to west in a straight line not being more (I should suppose, having no means of accurate examination) than forty or fifty yards. Upon first descending into the chasm – that is to say, for a hundred feet downwards from the summit of the hill – the sides of the abyss bore little resemblance to each other, and, apparently, had at no time been connected, the one surface being of the soapstone, and the other of marl, granulated with some metallic matter. The average breadth or interval between the two cliffs was probably here sixty feet, but there seemed to be no regularity of formation. Passing down, however, beyond the limit spoken of, the interval rapidly contracted, and the sides began to run parallel, although, for some distance farther, they were still dissimilar in their material and form of surface. Upon arriving within fifty feet of the bottom, a perfect regularity commenced. The sides were now entirely uniform in substance, in colour and in lateral direction, the material being a very black and shining granite, and the distance between the two sides, at all points facing each other, exactly twenty yards. The precise formation of the chasm will be best understood by means of a delineation taken upon the spot, for I had luckily with me a pocketbook and pencil, which I preserved with great care through a long series of subsequent adventure, and to which I am indebted for memoranda of many subjects which would otherwise have been crowded from my remembrance.

Figure 1

This figure (see Figure 1) gives the general outlines of the chasm, without the minor cavities in the sides, of which there were several, each cavity having a corresponding protuberance opposite. The bottom of the gulf was covered to the depth of three or four inches with a powder almost impalpable, beneath which we found a continuation of the black granite. To the right, at the lower extremity, will be noticed the appearance of a small opening: this is the fissure alluded to above, and to examine which more minutely than before was the object of our second visit. We now pushed into it with vigour, cutting away a quantity of brambles which impeded us, and removing a vast heap of sharp flints somewhat resembling arrowheads in shape. We were encouraged to persevere, however, by perceiving some little light proceeding from the farther end. We at length squeezed our way for about thirty feet, and found that the aperture was a low and regularly formed arch, having a bottom of the same impalpable powder as that in the main chasm. A strong light now broke upon us, and, turning a short bend, we found ourselves in another lofty chamber, similar to the one we had left in every respect but longitudinal form. Its general figure is here given. (See Figure 2.)

Figure 2

The total length of this chasm, commencing at the opening *a* and proceeding round the curve *b* to the extremity *d*, is five hundred and fifty yards. At *c* we discovered a small aperture similar to the one through which we had issued from the other chasm, and this was choked up in the same manner with brambles and a quantity of the white arrowhead flints. We forced our way through it, finding it about forty feet long, and emerged into a third chasm. This, too, was precisely like the first, except in its longitudinal shape, which was thus. (See Figure 3.)

Figure 3 Figure 5

We found the entire length of the third chasm three hundred and twenty yards. At the point *a* was an opening about six feet wide, and extending fifteen feet into the rock, where it terminated in a bed of marl, there being no other chasm beyond, as we had expected. We were about leaving this fissure, into which very little light was admitted, when Peters called my attention to a range of singular-looking indentures* in the surface of the marl forming the termination of the cul-de-sac. With a very slight exertion of the imagination, the left, or most northerly, of these indentures might have been taken for the intentional, although rude, representation of a human figure standing erect, with outstretched arm. The rest of them bore also some little resemblance to alphabetical characters, and Peters was willing, at all events, to adopt the idle opinion that they were really such. I convinced him of his error, finally, by directing his attention to the floor of the fissure, where, among the powder, we picked up, piece by piece, several large flakes of the marl, which had evidently been broken off by some convulsion from the surface where the indentures were found, and which had projecting points exactly fitting the indentures, thus proving them to have been the work of nature. Figure 4 presents an accurate copy of the whole.

Figure 4

After satisfying ourselves that these singular caverns afforded us no means of escape from our prison, we made our way back, dejected and dispirited, to the summit of the hill. Nothing worth mentioning occurred during the next twenty-four hours, except that, in examining the ground to the eastward of the third chasm, we found two triangular holes of great depth, and also with black granite sides. Into these holes we did not think it worthwhile to attempt descending, as they had the appearance of mere natural wells, without outlet. They were each about twenty yards in circumference, and their shape, as well as relative position in regard to the third chasm, is shown in Figure 5 above.

CHAPTER XXIV

On the 20th of the month, finding it altogether impossible to subsist any longer upon the filberts, the use of which occasioned us the most excruciating torment, we resolved to make a desperate attempt at descending the southern declivity of the hill. The face of the precipice was here of the softest species of soapstone, although nearly perpendicular throughout its whole extent (a depth of a hundred and fifty feet at the least), and in many places even overarching. After a long search we discovered a narrow ledge about twenty feet below the brink of the gulf; upon this Peters contrived to leap, with what assistance I could render him by means of our pocket handkerchiefs tied together. With somewhat more difficulty I also got down, and we then saw the possibility of descending the whole way by the process in which we had clambered up from the chasm when we had been buried by the fall of the hill – that is, by cutting steps in the face of the soapstone with our knives. The extreme hazard of the attempt can scarcely be conceived, but, as there was no other resource, we determined to undertake it.

Upon the ledge where we stood there grew some filbert bushes, and to one of these we made fast an end of our rope of handkerchiefs. The other end being tied round Peters's waist, I lowered him down over the edge of the precipice until the handkerchiefs were stretched tight. He now proceeded to dig a deep hole in the soapstone (as far in as eight or ten inches), sloping away the rock above to the height of a foot, or thereabout, so as to allow of his driving, with the butt of a pistol, a tolerably strong peg into the levelled surface. I then drew him up for about four feet, when he made a hole similar to the one below, driving in a peg as before, and having thus a resting place for both feet and hands. I now unfastened the handkerchiefs from the bush, throwing him the end, which he tied to the peg in the uppermost hole, letting himself down gently to a station about three feet lower than he had yet been – that is, to the full extent of the handkerchiefs. Here he dug another hole, and drove another peg. He then drew himself up, so as to rest his feet in the hole just cut, taking hold with his hands upon the peg in the one above. It was now necessary to untie the handkerchiefs from the topmost peg, with the view of fastening them to the second, and here he found that an error had been committed in cutting the holes at so great a distance apart. However, after one or two unsuccessful and dangerous attempts at reaching the knot (having to hold on with his left hand while he laboured to undo the fastening with

his right), he at length cut the string, leaving six inches of it affixed to the peg. Tying the handkerchiefs now to the second peg, he descended to a station below the third, taking care not to go too far down. By these means (means which I should never have conceived of myself, and for which we were indebted altogether to Peters's ingenuity and resolution) my companion finally succeeded, with the occasional aid of projections in the cliff, in reaching the bottom without accident.

It was some time before I could summon sufficient resolution to follow him, but I did at length attempt it. Peters had taken off his shirt before descending, and this, with my own, formed the rope necessary for the adventure. After throwing down the musket found in the chasm, I fastened this rope to the bushes, and let myself down rapidly, striving, by the vigour of my movements, to banish the trepidation which I could overcome in no other manner. This answered sufficiently well for the first four or five steps, but presently I found my imagination growing terribly excited by thoughts of the vast depth yet to be descended, and the precarious nature of the pegs and soapstone holes which were my only support. It was in vain I endeavoured to banish these reflections, and to keep my eyes steadily bent upon the flat surface of the cliff before me. The more earnestly I struggled *not to think*, the more intensely vivid became my conceptions, and the more horribly distinct. At length arrived that crisis of fancy, so fearful in all similar cases, the crisis in which we begin to anticipate the feelings with which we *shall* fall – to picture to ourselves the sickness, and dizziness, and the last struggle, and the half swoon, and the final bitterness of the rushing and headlong descent. And now I found these fancies creating their own realities, and all imagined horrors crowding upon me in fact. I felt my knees strike violently together, while my fingers were gradually yet certainly relaxing their grasp. There was a ringing in my ears, and I said, "This is my knell of death!" And now I was consumed with the irrepressible desire of looking below. I could not, I would not, confine my glances to the cliff, and, with a wild, indefinable emotion, half of horror, half of a relieved oppression, I threw my vision far down into the abyss. For one moment my fingers clutched convulsively upon their hold, while, with the movement, the faintest possible idea of ultimate escape wandered, like a shadow, through my mind – in the next my whole soul was pervaded with a *longing to fall*: a desire, a yearning, a passion utterly uncontrollable. I let go at once my grasp upon the peg, and, turning half round from the precipice, remained tottering for an instant against its naked face. But now there came a spinning of the brain; a shrill-sounding

and phantom voice screamed within my ears; a dusky, fiendish and filmy figure stood immediately beneath me – and, sighing, I sank down with a bursting heart, and plunged within its arms.

I had swooned, and Peters had caught me as I fell. He had observed my proceedings from his station at the bottom of the cliff, and perceiving my imminent danger, had endeavoured to inspire me with courage by every suggestion he could devise, although my confusion of mind had been so great as to prevent my hearing what he said, or being conscious that he had even spoken to me at all. At length, seeing me totter, he hastened to ascend to my rescue, and arrived just in time for my preservation. Had I fallen with my full weight, the rope of linen would inevitably have snapped, and I should have been precipitated into the abyss; as it was, he contrived to let me down gently, so as to remain suspended without danger until animation returned. This was in about fifteen minutes. On recovery, my trepidation had entirely vanished: I felt a new being, and, with some little further aid from my companion, reached the bottom also in safety.

We now found ourselves not far from the ravine which had proved the tomb of our friends, and to the southward of the spot where the hill had fallen. The place was one of singular wildness, and its aspect brought to my mind the descriptions given by travellers of those dreary regions marking the site of degraded Babylon.* Not to speak of the ruins of the disrup-tured cliff, which formed a chaotic barrier in the vista to the northward, the surface of the ground in every other direction was strewn with huge tumuli,* apparently the wreck of some gigantic structures of art – although, in detail, no semblance of art could be detected. Scoria* were abundant, and large shapeless blocks of the black granite, intermingled with others of marl,* and both granulated with metal. Of vegetation there were no traces whatsoever throughout the whole of the desolate area within sight. Several immense scorpions were seen, and various reptiles not elsewhere to be found in the high latitudes.

As food was our most immediate object, we resolved to make our way to the sea coast, distant not more than half a mile, with a view of catching turtle, several of which we had observed from our place of con-cealment on the hill. We had proceeded some hundred yards, threading our route cautiously between the huge rocks and tumuli, when, upon turning a corner, five savages sprang upon us from a small cavern, felling Peters to the ground with a blow from a club. As he fell the whole party rushed upon him to secure their victim, leaving me time to recover from my astonishment. I still had the musket, but the barrel had received so

much injury in being thrown from the precipice that I cast it aside as useless, preferring to trust my pistols, which had been carefully preserved in order. With these I advanced upon the assailants, firing one after the other in quick succession. Two savages fell, and one, who was in the act of thrusting a spear into Peters, sprang to his feet without accomplishing his purpose. My companion being thus released, we had no further difficulty. He had his pistols also, but prudently declined using them, confiding in his great personal strength, which far exceeded that of any person I have ever known. Seizing a club from one of the savages who had fallen, he dashed out the brains of the three who remained, killing each instantaneously with a single blow of the weapon, and leaving us completely masters of the field.

So rapidly had these events passed that we could scarcely believe in their reality, and were standing over the bodies of the dead in a species of stupid contemplation when we were brought to recollection by the sound of shouts in the distance. It was clear that the savages had been alarmed by the firing, and that we had little chance of avoiding discovery. To regain the cliff, it would be necessary to proceed in the direction of the shouts, and even should we succeed in arriving at its base, we should never be able to ascend it without being seen. Our situation was one of the greatest peril, and we were hesitating in which path to commence a flight when one of the savages whom I had shot, and supposed dead, sprang briskly to his feet, and attempted to make his escape. We overtook him, however, before he had advanced many paces, and were about to put him to death when Peters suggested that we might derive some benefit from forcing him to accompany us in our attempt at escape. We therefore dragged him with us, making him understand that we would shoot him if he offered resistance. In a few minutes he was perfectly submissive, and ran by our sides as we pushed in among the rocks, making for the seashore.

So far, the irregularities of the ground we had been traversing hid the sea, except at intervals, from our sight, and, when we first had it fairly in view, it was, perhaps, two hundred yards distant. As we emerged into the open beach we saw, to our great dismay, an immense crowd of the natives pouring from the village, and from all visible quarters of the island, making towards us with gesticulations of extreme fury, and howling like wild beasts. We were upon the point of turning upon our steps, and trying to secure a retreat among the fastnesses of the rougher ground, when I discovered the bows of two canoes projecting from behind a large rock which ran out into the water. Towards these we now ran with all speed, and, reaching them,

found them unguarded, and without any other freight than three of the large Gallipago turtles and the usual supply of paddles for sixty rowers. We instantly took possession of one of them, and, forcing our captive on board, pushed out to sea with all the strength we could command.

We had not made, however, more than fifty yards from the shore before we became sufficiently calm to perceive the great oversight of which we had been guilty in leaving the other canoe in the power of the savages, who, by this time, were not more than twice as far from the beach as ourselves, and were rapidly advancing to the pursuit. No time was now to be lost. Our hope was, at best, a forlorn one, but we had none other. It was very doubtful whether, with the utmost exertion, we could get back in time to anticipate them in taking possession of the canoe, but yet there was a chance that we could. We might save ourselves if we succeeded, while not to make the attempt was to resign ourselves to inevitable butchery.

The canoe was modelled with the bow and stern alike, and, in place of turning it round, we merely changed our position in paddling. As soon as the savages perceived this they redoubled their yells, as well as their speed, and approached with inconceivable rapidity. We pulled, however, with all the energy of desperation, and arrived at the contested point before more than one of the natives had attained it. This man paid dearly for his superior agility, Peters shooting him through the head with a pistol as he approached the shore. The foremost among the rest of his party were probably some twenty or thirty paces distant as we seized upon the canoe. We at first endeavoured to pull her into the deep water, beyond the reach of the savages, but, finding her too firmly aground, and there being no time to spare, Peters, with one or two heavy strokes from the butt of the musket, succeeded in dashing out a large portion of the bow and of one side. We then pushed off. Two of the natives by this time had got hold of our boat, obstinately refusing to let go, until we were forced to dispatch them with our knives. We were now clear off, and making great way out to sea. The main body of the savages, upon reaching the broken canoe, set up the most tremendous yell of rage and disappointment conceivable. In truth, from everything I could see of these wretches, they appeared to be the most wicked, hypocritical, vindictive, bloodthirsty and altogether fiendish race of men upon the face of the globe. It is clear we should have had no mercy had we fallen into their hands. They made a mad attempt at following us in the fractured canoe, but, finding it useless, again vented their rage in a series of hideous vociferations, and rushed up into the hills.

We were thus relieved from immediate danger, but our situation was still sufficiently gloomy. We knew that four canoes of the kind we had were at one time in the possession of the savages, and were not aware of the fact (afterwards ascertained from our captive) that two of these had been blown to pieces in the explosion of the *Jane Guy*. We calculated, therefore, upon being yet pursued, as soon as our enemies could get round to the bay (distant about three miles) where the boats were usually laid up. Fearing this, we made every exertion to leave the island behind us, and went rapidly through the water, forcing the prisoner to take a paddle. In about half an hour, when we had gained, probably, five or six miles to the southward, a large fleet of the flat-bottomed canoes or rafts was seen to emerge from the bay evidently with the design of pursuit. Presently they put back, despairing to overtake us.

CHAPTER XXV

We now found ourselves in the wide and desolate Antarctic Ocean, in a latitude exceeding eighty-four degrees, in a frail canoe, and with no provision but the three turtles. The long polar winter, too, could not be considered as far distant, and it became necessary that we should deliberate well upon the course to be pursued. There were six or seven islands in sight belonging to the same group, and distant from each other about five or six leagues, but upon neither of these had we any intention to venture. In coming from the northward in the *Jane Guy* we had been gradually leaving behind us the severest regions of ice – this, however little it may be in accordance with the generally received notions respecting the Antarctic, was a fact experience would not permit us to deny. To attempt, therefore, getting back would be folly – especially at so late a period of the season. Only one course seemed to be left open for hope. We resolved to steer boldly to the southward, where there was at least a probability of discovering other lands, and more than a probability of finding a still milder climate.

So far we had found the Antarctic, like the Arctic Ocean, peculiarly free from violent storms or immoderately rough water, but our canoe was, at best, of frail structure, although large, and we set busily to work with a view of rendering her as safe as the limited means in our possession would admit. The body of the boat was of no better material than bark – the bark of a tree unknown. The ribs were of a tough osier,* well adapted to the purpose for which it was used. We had fifty feet room from stem

to stern, from four to six in breadth, and in depth throughout four feet and a half – the boats thus differing vastly in shape from those of any other inhabitants of the Southern Ocean with whom civilized nations are acquainted. We never did believe them the workmanship of the ignorant islanders who owned them, and some days after this period discovered, by questioning our captive, that they were in fact made by the natives of a group to the south-west of the country where we found them, having fallen accidentally into the hands of our barbarians. What we could do for the security of our boat was very little indeed. Several wide rents were discovered near both ends, and these we contrived to patch up with pieces of woollen jacket. With the help of the superfluous paddles, of which there were a great many, we erected a kind of framework about the bow, so as to break the force of any seas which might threaten to fill us in that quarter. We also set up two paddle blades for masts, placing them opposite each other, one by each gunwale, thus saving the necessity of a yard. To these masts we attached a sail made of our shirts – doing this with some difficulty, as here we could get no assistance from our prisoner whatever, although he had been willing enough to labour in all the other operations. The sight of the linen seemed to affect him in a very singular manner. He could not be prevailed upon to touch it or go near it, shuddering when we attempted to force him, and shrieking out, "*Tekeli-li!*"

Having completed our arrangements in regard to the security of the canoe, we now set sail to the south-south-east for the present, with the view of weathering the most southerly of the group in sight. This being done, we turned the bow full to the southward. The weather could by no means be considered disagreeable. We had a prevailing and very gentle wind from the northward, a smooth sea and continual daylight. No ice whatever was to be seen – *nor did I ever see one particle of this after leaving the parallel of Bennet's Islet*. Indeed, the temperature of the water was here far too warm for its existence in any quantity. Having killed the largest of our tortoises, and obtained from him not only food but a copious supply of water, we continued on our course, without any incident of moment, for perhaps seven or eight days, during which period we must have proceeded a vast distance to the southward, as the wind blew constantly with us, and a very strong current set continually in the direction we were pursuing.

*1st March** – Many unusual phenomena now indicated that we were entering upon a region of novelty and wonder. A high range of light-grey vapour appeared constantly in the southern horizon, flaring up occasionally in lofty streaks, now darting from east to west, now from west to

east, and again presenting a level and uniform summit – in short, having all the wild variations of the aurora borealis. The average height of this vapour, as apparent from our station, was about twenty-five degrees. The temperature of the sea seemed to be increasing momentarily, and there was a very perceptible alteration in its colour.

2nd March – Today, by repeated questioning of our captive, we came to the knowledge of many particulars in regard to the island of the massacre, its inhabitants and customs – but with these how can I *now* detain the reader? I may say, however, that we learnt there were eight islands in the group; that they were governed by a common king, named "Tsalemon" or "Psalemoun", who resided in one of the smallest of the islands; that the black skins forming the dress of the warriors came from an animal of huge size to be found only in a valley near the court of the king; that the inhabitants of the group fabricated no other boats than the flat-bottomed rafts, the four canoes being all of the kind in their possession, and these having been obtained, by mere accident, from some large island to the south-west; that his own name was Nu-Nu; that he had no knowledge of Bennet's Islet; and that the appellation of the island we had left was "Tsalal". The commencement of the words "Tsalemon" and "Tsalal" was given with a prolonged hissing sound, which we found it impossible to imitate, even after repeated endeavours, and which was precisely the same with the note of the black bittern we had eaten upon the summit of the hill.

3rd March – The heat of the water was now truly remarkable, and its colour was undergoing a rapid change, being no longer transparent, but of a milky consistency and hue. In our immediate vicinity it was usually smooth, never so rough as to endanger the canoe – but we were frequently surprised at perceiving, to our right and left, at different distances, sudden and extensive agitations of the surface – these, we at length noticed, were always preceded by wild flickerings in the region of the vapour to the southward.

4th March – Today, with the view of widening our sail, the breeze from the northward dying away perceptibly, I took from my coat pocket a white handkerchief. Nu-Nu was seated at my elbow, and the linen accidentally flaring in his face, he became violently affected with convulsions. These were succeeded by drowsiness and stupor, and low murmurings of "*Tekeli-li! Tekeli-li!*"

5th March – The wind had entirely ceased, but it was evident that we were still hurrying on to the southward, under the influence of a powerful current. And now, indeed, it would seem reasonable that we should

experience some alarm at the turn events were taking – but we felt none. The countenance of Peters indicated nothing of this nature, although it wore at times an expression I could not fathom. The polar winter appeared to be coming on – but coming without its terrors. I felt a *numbness* of body and mind – a dreaminess of sensation – but this was all.

6th March – The grey vapour had now arisen many more degrees above the horizon, and was gradually losing its greyness of tint. The heat of the water was extreme, even unpleasant to the touch, and its milky hue was more evident than ever. Today a violent agitation of the water occurred very close to the canoe. It was attended, as usual, with a wild flaring up of the vapour at its summit, and a momentary division at its base. A fine white powder, resembling ashes – but certainly not such – fell over the canoe and over a large surface of the water, as the flickering died away among the vapour and the commotion subsided in the sea. Nu-Nu now threw himself on his face in the bottom of the boat, and no persuasions could induce him to arise.

7th March – This day we questioned Nu-Nu concerning the motives of his countrymen in destroying our companions, but he appeared to be too utterly overcome by terror to afford us any rational reply. He still obstinately lay in the bottom of the boat, and, upon our reiterating the questions as to the motive, made use only of idiotic gesticulations, such as raising with his forefinger the upper lip, and displaying the teeth which lay beneath it. These were black. We had never before seen the teeth of an inhabitant of Tsalal.

8th March – Today there floated by us one of the white animals whose appearance upon the beach at Tsalal had occasioned so wild a commotion among the savages. I would have picked it up, but there came over me a sudden listlessness, and I forbore. The heat of the water still increased, and the hand could no longer be endured within it. Peters spoke little, and I knew not what to think of his apathy. Nu-Nu breathed, and no more.

9th March – The white ashy material fell now continually around us, and in vast quantities. The range of vapour to the southward had arisen prodigiously in the horizon, and began to assume more distinctness of form. I can liken it to nothing but a limitless cataract, rolling silently into the sea from some immense and far-distant rampart in the heaven. The gigantic curtain ranged along the whole extent of the southern horizon. It emitted no sound.

21st March – A sullen darkness now hovered above us – but from out the milky depths of the ocean a luminous glare arose, and stole up along

the bulwarks of the boat. We were nearly overwhelmed by the white ashy shower which settled upon us and upon the canoe, but melted into the water as it fell. The summit of the cataract was utterly lost in the dimness and the distance. Yet we were evidently approaching it with a hideous velocity. At intervals there were visible in it wide, yawning, but momentary rents, and from out these rents, within which was a chaos of flitting and indistinct images, there came rushing and mighty, but soundless winds, tearing up the enkindled ocean in their course.

22nd March – The darkness had materially increased, relieved only by the glare of the water thrown back from the white curtain before us. Many gigantic and pallidly white birds flew continuously now from beyond the veil, and their scream was the eternal "*Tekeli-li!*" as they retreated from our vision. Hereupon Nu-Nu stirred in the bottom of the boat, but, upon touching him, we found his spirit departed. And now we rushed into the embraces of the cataract, where a chasm threw itself open to receive us. But there arose in our pathway a shrouded human figure, very far larger in its proportions than any dweller among men. And the hue of the skin of the figure was of the perfect whiteness of the snow.

NOTE

The circumstances connected with the late sudden and distressing death of Mr Pym are already well known to the public through the medium of the daily press. It is feared that the few remaining chapters which were to have completed his narrative, and which were retained by him, while the above were in type, for the purpose of revision, have been irrecoverably lost through the accident by which he perished himself. This, however, may prove not to be the case, and the papers, if ultimately found, will be given to the public.

No means have been left untried to remedy the deficiency. The gentleman whose name is mentioned in the preface, and who, from the statement there made, might be supposed able to fill the vacuum, has declined the task – this for satisfactory reasons connected with the general inaccuracy of the details afforded him, and his disbelief in the entire truth of the latter portions of the narration. Peters, from whom some information might be expected, is still alive, and a resident of Illinois, but cannot be met with at present. He may hereafter be found, and will, no doubt, afford material for a conclusion of Mr Pym's account.

The loss of the two or three final chapters (for there were but two or three) is the more deeply to be regretted as, it cannot be doubted, they contained matter relative to the pole itself, or at least to regions in its very near proximity – and as, too, the statements of the author in relation to these regions may shortly be verified or contradicted by means of the governmental expedition now preparing for the Southern Ocean.*

On one point in the narrative some remarks may be well offered, and it would afford the writer of this appendix much pleasure if what he may here observe should have a tendency to throw credit, in any degree, upon the very singular pages now published. We allude to the chasms found in the island of Tsalal, and to the whole of the figures upon pages 138–39.

Mr Pym has given the figures of the chasms without comment, and speaks decidedly of the "indentures" found at the extremity of the most

easterly of these chasms as having but a fanciful resemblance to alphabetical characters, and, in short, as being positively *not such*. This assertion is made in a manner so simple, and sustained by a species of demonstration so conclusive (viz. the fitting of the projections of the fragments found among the dust into the indentures upon the wall), that we are forced to believe the writer in earnest, and no reasonable reader should suppose otherwise. But as the facts in relation to *all* the figures are most singular (especially when taken in connection with statements made in the body of the narrative), it may be as well to say a word or two concerning them all* – this, too, the more especially as the facts in question have, beyond doubt, escaped the attention of Mr Poe.

Figure 1, then, Figure 2, Figure 3 and Figure 5, when conjoined with one another in the precise order which the chasms themselves presented, and when deprived of the small lateral branches or arches (which, it will be remembered, served only as means of communication between the main chambers, and were of totally distinct character), constitute an Ethiopian* verbal root – the root 𐤀𐤍𐤏 , "to be shady" – whence all the inflections of shadow or darkness.

In regard to the "left or most northwardly" of the indentures in Figure 4, it is more than probable that the opinion of Peters was correct, and that the hieroglyphical appearance was really the work of art, and intended as the representation of a human form. The delineation is before the reader, and he may, or may not, perceive the resemblance suggested, but the rest of the indentures afford strong confirmation of Peters's idea. The upper range is evidently the Arabic verbal root 𐤀𐤋𐤁 , "to be white", whence all the inflections of brilliancy and whiteness. The lower range is not so immediately perspicuous. The characters are somewhat broken and disjointed; nevertheless, it cannot be doubted that, in their perfect state, they formed the full Egyptian word Π ⲀⲨⲨⲢ ΗϹ , "the region of the south". It should be observed that these interpretations confirm the opinion of Peters in regard to the "most northwardly" of the figures. The arm is outstretched towards the south.

Conclusions such as these open a wide field for speculation and exciting conjecture. They should be regarded, perhaps, in connection with some of the most faintly detailed incidents of the narrative – although in no visible manner is this chain of connection complete. *Tekeli-li!* was the cry of the affrighted natives of Tsalal upon discovering the carcass of the *white* animal picked up at sea. This also was the shuddering exclamation of the captive Tsalalian upon encountering the *white* materials in possession of Mr Pym.

This also was the shriek of the swift-flying, *white* and gigantic birds which issued from the vapoury *white* curtain of the south. Nothing *white* was to be found at Tsalal, and nothing otherwise in the subsequent voyage to the region beyond. It is not impossible that "Tsalal", the appellation of the island of the chasms, may be found, upon minute philological scrutiny, to betray either some alliance with the chasms themselves, or some reference to the Ethiopian characters so mysteriously written in their windings.

"*I have graven it within the hills, and my vengeance upon the dust within the rock.*"*

LOSS OF BREATH*

A TALE NEITHER IN NOR OUT
OF *BLACKWOOD**

O breathe not, etc.

— MOORE'S MELODIES*

The most notorious ill fortune must, in the end, yield to the untiring courage of philosophy – as the most stubborn city to the ceaseless vigilance of an enemy. Salmanezer, as we have it in holy writings, lay three years before Samaria; yet it fell. Sardanapalus – see Diodorus – maintained himself seven in Nineveh; but to no purpose. Troy expired at the close of the second lustrum; and Azoth, as Aristaeus declares upon his honour as a gentleman, opened at last her gates to Psammitticus, after having barred them for the fifth part of a century.*

*

"Thou wretch! Thou vixen! Thou shrew!" said I to my wife on the morning after our wedding. "Thou witch! Thou hag! Thou whippersnapper!* Thou sink of iniquity! Thou fiery-faced quintessence of all that is abominable! Thou – thou…" Here standing upon tiptoe, seizing her by the throat, and placing my mouth close to her ear, I was preparing to launch forth a new and more decided epithet of opprobrium, which should not fail, if ejaculated, to convince her of her insignificance, when, to my extreme horror and astonishment, I discovered that I *had lost my breath.*

The phrases "I am out of breath", "I have lost my breath", etc., are often enough repeated in common conversation, but it had never occurred to me that the terrible accident of which I speak could bona fide and actually happen! Imagine – that is if you have a fanciful turn – imagine, I say, my wonder – my consternation – my despair!

There is a good genius, however, which has never entirely deserted me. In my most ungovernable moods I still retain a sense of propriety, "*et le chemin des passions me conduit*" – as Lord Édouard in the *Julie* says it did him – "*à la philosophie véritable.*"*

Although I could not at first precisely ascertain to what degree the occurrence had affected me, I determined at all events to conceal the matter from my wife, until further experience should discover to me the extent of this my unheard-of calamity. Altering my countenance, therefore, in

a moment, from its bepuffed and distorted appearance, to an expression of arch and coquettish benignity, I gave my lady a pat on the one cheek, and a kiss on the other, and without saying one syllable (Furies! I could not), left her astonished at my drollery, as I pirouetted out of the room in a *pas de Zephyr.**

Behold me then safely ensconced in my private boudoir, a fearful instance of the ill consequences attending upon irascibility – alive, with the qualifications of the dead – dead, with the propensities of the living – an anomaly on the face of the earth – being very calm, yet breathless.

Yes! Breathless. I am serious in asserting that my breath was entirely gone. I could not have stirred with it a feather if my life had been at issue, or sullied even the delicacy of a mirror. Hard fate! Yet there was some alleviation to the first overwhelming paroxysm of my sorrow. I found, upon trial, that the powers of utterance which, upon my inability to proceed in the conversation with my wife, I then concluded to be totally destroyed, were in fact only partially impeded, and I discovered that had I, at that interesting crisis, dropped my voice to a singularly deep guttural, I might still have continued to her the communication of my sentiments, this pitch of voice (the guttural) depending, I find, not upon the current of the breath, but upon a certain spasmodic action of the muscles of the throat.

Throwing myself upon a chair, I remained for some time absorbed in meditation. My reflections, be sure, were of no consolatory kind. A thousand vague and lachrymatory* fancies took possession of my soul – and even the idea of suicide flitted across my brain, but it is a trait in the perversity of human nature to reject the obvious and the ready, for the far distant and equivocal. Thus I shuddered at self-murder as the most decided of atrocities while the tabby cat purred strenuously upon the rug, and the very water dog* wheezed assiduously under the table, each taking to itself much merit for the strength of its lungs, and all obviously done in derision of my own pulmonary incapacity.

Oppressed with a tumult of vague hopes and fears, I at length heard the footsteps of my wife descending the staircase. Being now assured of her absence, I returned with a palpitating heart to the scene of my disaster.

Carefully locking the door on the inside, I commenced a vigorous search. It was possible, I thought, that, concealed in some obscure corner, or lurking in some closet or drawer, might be found the lost object of my enquiry. It might have a vapoury – it might even have a tangible form. Most philosophers, upon many points of philosophy, are still very un-philosophical. William Godwin, however, says in his *Mandeville*, that

"invisible things are the only realities",* and this, all will allow, is a case in point. I would have the judicious reader pause before accusing such asseverations of an undue quantum of absurdity. Anaxagoras, it will be remembered, maintained that snow is black,* and this I have since found to be the case.

Long and earnestly did I continue the investigation: but the contemptible reward of my industry and perseverance proved to be only a set of false teeth, two pair of hips, an eye and a bundle of billets-doux from Mr Windenough to my wife. I might as well here observe that this confirmation of my lady's partiality for Mr W. occasioned me little uneasiness. That Mrs Lackobreath should admire anything so dissimilar to myself was a natural and necessary evil. I am, it is well known, of a robust and corpulent appearance, and at the same time somewhat diminutive in stature. What wonder then that the lath-like tenuity of my acquaintance, and his altitude, which has grown into a proverb, should have met with all due estimation in the eyes of Mrs Lackobreath. But to return.

My exertions, as I have before said, proved fruitless. Closet after closet – drawer after drawer – corner after corner – were scrutinized to no purpose. At one time, however, I thought myself sure of my prize, having, in rummaging a dressing case, accidentally demolished a bottle of Grandjean's Oil of Archangels – which, as an agreeable perfume, I here take the liberty of recommending.

With a heavy heart I returned to my boudoir – there to ponder upon some method of eluding my wife's penetration, until I could make arrangements prior to my leaving the country, for to this I had already made up my mind. In a foreign climate, being unknown, I might, with some probability of success, endeavour to conceal my unhappy calamity – a calamity calculated, even more than beggary, to estrange the affections of the multitude, and to draw down upon the wretch the well-merited indignation of the virtuous and the happy. I was not long in hesitation. Being naturally quick, I committed to memory the entire tragedy of *Metamora*.* I had the good fortune to recollect that in the accentuation of this drama, or at least such portion of it as is allotted to the hero, the tones of voice in which I found myself deficient were altogether unnecessary, and the deep guttural was expected to reign monotonously throughout.

I practised for some time by the borders of a well-frequented marsh – herein, however, having no reference to a similar proceeding of Demosthenes,* but from a design peculiarly and conscientiously my own. Thus armed at all points, I determined to make my wife believe that

I was suddenly smitten with a passion for the stage. In this, I succeeded to a miracle, and to every question or suggestion found myself at liberty to reply in my most frog-like and sepulchral tones with some passage from the tragedy – any portion of which, as I soon took great pleasure in observing, would apply equally well to any particular subject. It is not to be supposed, however, that in the delivery of such passages I was found at all deficient in the looking asquint – the showing my teeth – the working my knees – the shuffling my feet – or in any of those unmentionable graces which are now justly considered the characteristics of a popular performer. To be sure they spoke of confining me in a straitjacket – but, good God! they never suspected me of having lost my breath.

Having at length put my affairs in order, I took my seat very early one morning in the mail stage for ——, giving it to be understood, among my acquaintances, that business of the last importance required my immediate personal attendance in that city.

The coach was crammed to repletion, but in the uncertain twilight the features of my companions could not be distinguished. Without making any effectual resistance, I suffered myself to be placed between two gentlemen of colossal dimensions, while a third, of a size larger, requesting pardon for the liberty he was about to take, threw himself upon my body at full length, and falling asleep in an instant, drowned all my guttural ejaculations for relief, in a snore which would have put to blush the roarings of the bull of Phalaris.* Happily the state of my respiratory faculties rendered suffocation an accident entirely out of the question.

As, however, the day broke more distinctly in our approach to the outskirts of the city, my tormentor, arising and adjusting his shirt collar, thanked me in a very friendly manner for my civility. Seeing that I remained motionless (all my limbs were dislocated and my head twisted on one side), his apprehensions began to be excited, and, arousing the rest of the passengers, he communicated, in a very decided manner, his opinion that a dead man had been palmed upon them during the night for a living and responsible fellow traveller, here giving me a thump on the right eye, by way of demonstrating the truth of his suggestion.

Hereupon all, one after another (there were nine in company), believed it their duty to pull me by the ear. A young practising physician, too, having applied a pocket mirror to my mouth, and found me without breath, the assertion of my persecutor was pronounced a true bill, and the whole party expressed a determination to endure tamely no such impositions for the future, and to proceed no farther with any such carcasses for the present.

I was here, accordingly, thrown out at the sign of the Crow (by which tavern the coach happened to be passing), without meeting with any further accident than the breaking of both my arms, under the left hind wheel of the vehicle. I must besides do the driver the justice to state that he did not forget to throw after me the largest of my trunks, which, unfortunately falling on my head, fractured my skull in a manner at once interesting and extraordinary.

The landlord of the Crow, who is a hospitable man, finding that my trunk contained sufficient to indemnify him for any little trouble he might take in my behalf, sent forthwith for a surgeon of his acquaintance, and delivered me to his care with a bill and receipt for ten dollars.

The purchaser took me to his apartments and commenced operations immediately. Having cut off my ears, however, he discovered signs of animation. He now rang the bell, and sent for a neighbouring apothecary with whom to consult in the emergency. In case of his suspicions with regard to my existence proving ultimately correct, he, in the mean time, made an incision in my stomach, and removed several of my viscera for private dissection.

The apothecary had an idea that I was actually dead. This idea I endeavoured to confute, kicking and plunging with all my might, and making the most furious contortions – for the operations of the surgeon had, in a measure, restored me to the possession of my faculties. All, however, was attributed to the effects of a new galvanic battery,* wherewith the apothecary, who is really a man of information, performed several curious experiments, in which, from my personal share in their fulfilment, I could not help feeling deeply interested. It was a source of mortification to me, nevertheless, that although I made several attempts at conversation, my powers of speech were so entirely in abeyance that I could not even open my mouth – much less, then, make reply to some ingenious but fanciful theories of which, under other circumstances, my minute acquaintance with the Hippocratian pathology* would have afforded me a ready confutation.

Not being able to arrive at a conclusion, the practitioners remanded me for further examination. I was taken up into a garret, and, the surgeon's lady having accommodated me with drawers and stockings, the surgeon himself fastened my hands, and tied up my jaws with a pocket handkerchief – then bolted the door on the outside as he hurried to his dinner, leaving me alone to silence and to meditation.

I now discovered to my extreme delight that I could have spoken had not my mouth been tied up by the pocket handkerchief. Consoling myself with this reflection, I was mentally repeating some passages of the *Omnipresence*

*of the Deity,** as is my custom before resigning myself to sleep, when two cats, of a greedy and vituperative turn, entering at a hole in the wall, leapt up with a flourish *à la* Catalani,* and, alighting opposite one another on my visage, betook themselves to indecorous contention for the paltry consideration of my nose.

But, as the loss of his ears proved the means of elevating to the throne of Cyrus the Magian or Mige-Gush of Persia, and as the cutting off his nose gave Zopyrus possession of Babylon,* so the loss of a few ounces of my countenance proved the salvation of my body. Aroused by the pain, and burning with indignation, I burst, at a single effort, the fastenings and the bandage. Stalking across the room I cast a glance of contempt at the belligerents, and, throwing open the sash to their extreme horror and disappointment, precipitated myself, very dexterously, from the window.

The mail-robber W——, to whom I bore a singular resemblance, was at this moment passing from the city jail to the scaffold erected for his execution in the suburbs.* His extreme infirmity and long-continued ill health had obtained him the privilege of remaining unmanacled, and habited in his gallows costume – one very similar to my own – he lay at full length in the bottom of the hangman's cart (which happened to be under the windows of the surgeon at the moment of my precipitation) without any other guard than the driver, who was asleep, and two recruits of the sixth infantry, who were drunk.

As ill luck would have it, I alit upon my feet within the vehicle. W——, who was an acute fellow, perceived his opportunity. Leaping up immediately, he bolted out behind, and, turning down an alley, was out of sight in the twinkling of an eye. The recruits, aroused by the bustle, could not exactly comprehend the merits of the transaction. Seeing, however, a man, the precise counterpart of the felon, standing upright in the cart before their eyes, they were of the opinion that the rascal (meaning W——) was after making his escape (so they expressed themselves), and, having communicated this opinion to one another, they took each a dram, and then knocked me down with the butt ends of their muskets.

It was not long ere we arrived at the place of destination. Of course nothing could be said in my defence. Hanging was my inevitable fate. I resigned myself thereto with a feeling half stupid, half acrimonious. Being little of a cynic, I had all the sentiments of a dog. The hangman, however, adjusted the noose about my neck. The drop fell.

I forbear to depict my sensations upon the gallows – although here, undoubtedly, I could speak to the point, and it is a topic upon which

nothing has been well said. In fact, to write upon such a theme it is necessary to have been hanged. Every author should confine himself to matters of experience. Thus Mark Antony composed a treatise upon getting drunk.*

I may just mention, however, that die I did not. My body *was*, but I had no breath *to be*, suspended, and but for the knot under my left ear (which had the feel of a military stock) I dare say that I should have experienced very little inconvenience. As for the jerk given to my neck upon the falling of the drop, it merely proved a corrective to the twist afforded me by the fat gentleman in the coach.

For good reasons, however, I did my best to give the crowd the worth of their trouble. My convulsions were said to be extraordinary. My spasms it would have been difficult to beat. The populace encored. Several gentlemen swooned, and a multitude of ladies were carried home in hysterics. Pinxit availed himself of the opportunity to retouch, from a sketch taken upon the spot, his admirable painting of the *Marsyas Flayed Alive*.*

When I had afforded sufficient amusement, it was thought proper to remove my body from the gallows – this the more especially as the real culprit had in the mean time been retaken and recognized, a fact which I was so unlucky as not to know.

Much sympathy was, of course, exercised in my behalf, and as no one made claim to my corpse, it was ordered that I should be interred in a public vault.

Here, after due interval, I was deposited. The sexton departed, and I was left alone. A line of Marston's *Malcontent* –

Death's a good fellow and keeps open house –*

struck me at that moment as a palpable lie.

I knocked off, however, the lid of my coffin, and stepped out. The place was dreadfully dreary and damp, and I became troubled with ennui. By way of amusement, I felt my way among the numerous coffins ranged in order around. I lifted them down, one by one, and, breaking open their lids, busied myself in speculations about the mortality within.

"This," I soliloquized, tumbling over a carcass, puffy, bloated and rotund, "this has been, no doubt, in every sense of the word, an unhappy – an unfortunate man. It has been his terrible lot not to walk but to waddle – to pass through life not like a human being, but like an elephant – not like a man, but like a rhinoceros.

"His attempts at getting on have been mere abortions, and his circum-gyratory proceedings a palpable failure. Taking a step forward, it has been his misfortune to take two towards the right, and three towards the left. His studies have been confined to the poetry of Crabbe.* He can have had no idea of the wonder of a pirouette. To him a *pas de papillon** has been an abstract conception. He has never ascended the summit of a hill. He has never viewed from any steeple the glories of a metropolis. Heat has been his mortal enemy. In the dog days his days have been the days of a dog. Therein, he has dreamt of flames and suffocation – of mountains upon mountains – of Pelion upon Ossa.* He was short of breath – to say all in a word, he was short of breath. He thought it extravagant to play upon wind instruments. He was the inventor of self-moving fans, wind sails and ventilators. He patronized Du Pont the bellows-maker, and he died miserably in attempting to smoke a cigar. His was a case in which I feel a deep interest – a lot in which I sincerely sympathize.

"But here," said I, "here" – and I dragged spitefully from its receptacle a gaunt, tall and peculiar-looking form, whose remarkable appearance struck me with a sense of unwelcome familiarity – "here is a wretch entitled to no earthly commiseration." Thus saying, in order to obtain a more distinct view of my subject, I applied my thumb and forefinger to its nose, and, causing it to assume a sitting position upon the ground, held it thus, at the length of my arm, while I continued my soliloquy.

"Entitled," I repeated, "to no earthly commiseration. Who indeed would think of compassioning a shadow? Besides, has he not had his full share of the blessings of mortality? He was the originator of tall monuments: shot towers* – lightning rods – Lombardy poplars.* His treatise upon *Shades and Shadows* has immortalized him. He edited with distinguished ability the last edition of *South on the Bones.** He went early to college and studied pneumatics. He then came home, talked eternally, and played upon the French horn. He patronized the bagpipes. Captain Barclay, who walked against Time,* would not walk against *him.* Windham and Allbreath were his favourite writers – his favourite artist, Phiz.* He died gloriously while inhaling gas – *levique flatu corrumpitur*, like the *fama pudicitiæ* in Hieronymus.* He was indubitably a—"

"How *can* you? How – can – you?" interrupted the object of my animad-versions, gasping for breath, and tearing off, with a desperate exertion, the bandage around its jaws. "How *can* you, Mr Lackobreath, be so infernally cruel as to pinch me in that manner by the nose? Did you not see how they had fastened up my mouth – and you *must* know – if you know anything

– how vast a superfluity of breath I have to dispose of! If you do *not* know, however, sit down and you shall see. In my situation it is really a great relief to be able to open one's mouth – to be able to expatiate – to be able to communicate with a person like yourself, who do not think yourself called upon at every period to interrupt the thread of a gentleman's discourse. Interruptions are annoying and should undoubtedly be abolished – don't you think so? No reply, I beg you – one person is enough to be speaking at a time. I shall be done by and by, and then you may begin. How the devil, sir, did you get into this place? Not a word I beseech you – been here some time myself – terrible accident! – heard of it, I suppose? – awful calamity! – walking under your windows – some short while ago – about the time you were stage-struck – horrible occurrence! – heard of 'catching one's breath', eh? Hold your tongue I tell you! I caught somebody else's! – had always too much of my own – met Blab at the corner of the street – wouldn't give me a chance for a word – couldn't get in a syllable edgeways – attacked, consequently, with epilepsis – Blab made his escape – damn all fools! – they took me up for dead, and put me in this place – pretty doings all of them! – heard all you said about me – every word a lie – horrible! – wonderful – outrageous! – hideous! – incomprehensible! – et cetera – et cetera – et cetera – et cetera…"

It is impossible to conceive my astonishment at so unexpected a discourse, or the joy with which I became gradually convinced that the breath so fortunately caught by the gentleman (whom I soon recognized as my neighbour Windenough) was, in fact, the identical expiration mislaid by myself in the conversation with my wife. Time, place and circumstances rendered it a matter beyond question. I did not, however, immediately release my hold upon Mr W.'s proboscis – not at least during the long period in which the inventor of Lombardy poplars continued to favour me with his explanations.

In this respect I was actuated by that habitual prudence which has ever been my predominating trait. I reflected that many difficulties might still lie in the path of my preservation which only extreme exertion on my part would be able to surmount. Many persons, I considered, are prone to estimate commodities in their possession – however valueless to the then proprietor – however troublesome, or distressing – in direct ratio with the advantages to be derived by others from their attainment, or by themselves from their abandonment. Might not this be the case with Mr Windenough? In displaying anxiety for the breath of which he was at present so willing to get rid, might I not lay myself open to the exactions

of his avarice? There are scoundrels in this world, I remembered with a sigh, who will not scruple to take unfair opportunities with even a next-door neighbour, and (this remark is from Epictetus) it is precisely at that time when men are most anxious to throw off the burden of their own calamities that they feel the least desirous of relieving them in others.*

Upon considerations similar to these, and still retaining my grasp upon the nose of Mr W., I accordingly thought proper to model my reply.

"Monster!" I began in a tone of the deepest indignation. "Monster and double-winded idiot! Dost *thou*, whom for thine iniquities it has pleased Heaven to accurse with a twofold respiration – dost *thou*, I say, presume to address me in the familiar language of an old acquaintance? 'I lie,' forsooth! And 'hold my tongue', to be sure! Pretty conversation, indeed, to a gentleman with a single breath! All this, too, when I have it in my power to relieve the calamity under which thou dost so justly suffer – to curtail the superfluities of thine unhappy respiration."

Like Brutus, I paused for a reply* – with which, like a tornado, Mr Windenough immediately overwhelmed me. Protestation followed upon protestation, and apology upon apology. There were no terms with which he was unwilling to comply, and there were none of which I failed to take the fullest advantage.

Preliminaries being at length arranged, my acquaintance delivered me the respiration, for which (having carefully examined it) I gave him afterwards a receipt.

I am aware that by many I shall be held to blame for speaking, in a manner so cursory, of a transaction so impalpable. It will be thought that I should have entered more minutely into the details of an occurrence by which – and this is very true – much new light might be thrown upon a highly interesting branch of physical philosophy.

To all this I am sorry that I cannot reply. A hint is the only answer which I am permitted to make. There were *circumstances* – but I think it much safer upon consideration to say as little as possible about an affair so delicate – *so delicate*, I repeat, and at the time involving the interests of a third party whose sulphurous resentment I have not the least desire, at this moment, of incurring.

We were not long after this necessary arrangement in effecting an escape from the dungeons of the sepulchre. The united strength of our resuscitated voices was soon sufficiently apparent. Scissors, the Whig editor, republished a treatise upon "the nature and origin of subterranean noises". A reply – rejoinder – confutation – and justification – followed in the columns of a

Democratic gazette. It was not until the opening of the vault to decide the controversy that the appearance of Mr Windenough and myself proved both parties to have been decidedly in the wrong.

I cannot conclude these details of some very singular passages in a life at all times sufficiently eventful without again recalling to the attention of the reader the merits of that indiscriminate philosophy which is a sure and ready shield against those shafts of calamity which can neither be seen, felt nor fully understood. It was in the spirit of this wisdom that, among the ancient Hebrews, it was believed the gates of heaven would be inevitably opened to that sinner, or saint, who, with good lungs and implicit confidence, should vociferate the word "*Amen!*"* It was in the spirit of this wisdom that, when a great plague raged at Athens, and every means had been in vain attempted for its removal, Epimenides, as Laertius relates, in his second book, of that philosopher, advised the erection of a shrine and temple "to the proper God".*

<div align="right">LITTLETON BARRY</div>

MYSTIFICATION*

'Slid, if these be your "passados" and
"montantes", I'll have none o' them.
— NED KNOWLES*

The Baron Ritzner von Jung was of a noble Hungarian family, every member of which (at least as far back into antiquity as any certain records extend) was more or less remarkable for talent of some description – the majority for that species of grotesquerie in conception of which Tieck, a scion of the house, has given some vivid, although by no means the most vivid exemplifications.* My acquaintance with Ritzner commenced at the magnificent Chateau Jung, into which a train of droll adventures, not to be made public, threw me during the summer months of the year 18—. Here it was that I obtained a place in his regard, and here, with somewhat more difficulty, a partial insight into his mental conformation. In later days this insight grew more clear, as the intimacy which had at first permitted it became more close, and when, after three years' separation, we met at G——n, I knew all that it was necessary to know of the character of the Baron Ritzner von Jung.

I remember the buzz of curiosity which his advent excited within the college precincts on the night of 25th June. I remember still more distinctly that while he was pronounced by all parties at first sight "the most remarkable man in the world", no person made any attempt at accounting for this opinion. That he was *unique* appeared so undeniable that it was deemed impertinent to enquire wherein the uniquity consisted. But, letting this matter pass for the present, I will merely observe that, from the first moment of his setting foot within the limits of the university, he began to exercise over the habits, manners, persons, purses and propensities of the whole community which surrounded him, an influence the most extensive and despotic, yet at the same time the most indefinitive and altogether unaccountable. Thus the brief period of his residence at the university forms an era in its annals, and is characterized by all classes of people appertaining to it or its dependencies as "that very extraordinary epoch forming the domination of the Baron Ritzner von Jung".

Upon his advent to G——n, he sought me out in my apartments. He was then of no particular age, by which I mean that it was impossible to

form a guess respecting his age by any data personally afforded. He might have been fifteen or fifty, and *was* twenty-one years and seven months. He was by no means a handsome man – perhaps the reverse. The contour of his face was somewhat angular and harsh. His forehead was lofty and very fair, his nose a snub, his eyes large, heavy, glassy and meaningless. About the mouth there was more to be observed. The lips were gently protruded, and rested the one upon the other, after such a fashion that it is impossible to conceive any, even the most complex, combination of human features conveying so entirely, and so singly, the idea of unmitigated gravity, solemnity and repose.

It will be perceived, no doubt, from what I have already said that the baron was one of those human anomalies now and then to be found who make the science of *mystification* the study and the business of their lives. For this science a peculiar turn of mind gave him instinctively the cue, while his physical appearance afforded him unusual facilities for carrying his projects into effect. I firmly believe that no student at G――n, during that renowned epoch so quaintly termed the domination of the Baron Ritzner von Jung, ever rightly entered into the mystery which overshadowed his character. I truly think that no person at the university, with the exception of myself, ever suspected him to be capable of a joke, verbal or practical – the old bulldog at the garden gate would sooner have been accused – the ghost of Heraclitus* – or the wig of the Emeritus Professor of Theology. This, too, when it was evident that the most egregious and unpardonable of all conceivable tricks, whimsicalities and buffooneries were brought about, if not directly by him, at least plainly through his intermediate agency or connivance. The beauty, if I may so call it, of his *art mystifique** lay in that consummate ability (resulting from an almost intuitive knowledge of human nature, and a most wonderful self-possession), by means of which he never failed to make it appear that the drolleries he was occupied in bringing to a point arose partly in spite, and partly in consequence of, the laudable efforts he was making for their prevention, and for the preservation of the good order and dignity of Alma Mater. The deep, the poignant, the overwhelming mortification, which upon each such failure of his praiseworthy endeavours would suffuse every lineament of his countenance, left not the slightest room for doubt of his sincerity in the bosoms of even his most sceptical companions. The adroitness, too, was no less worthy of observation by which he contrived to shift the sense of the grotesque from the creator to the created – from his own person to the absurdities to which he had given rise. In no instance before that of

which I speak have I known the habitual mystific escape the natural consequence of his manoeuvres – an attachment of the ludicrous to his own character and person. Continually enveloped in an atmosphere of whim, my friend appeared to live only for the severities of society, and not even his own household have for a moment associated other ideas than those of the rigid and august with the memory of the Baron Ritzner von Jung.

During the epoch of his residence at G——n it really appeared that the demon of the *dolce far niente** lay like an incubus upon the university. Nothing, at least, was done beyond eating and drinking and making merry. The apartments of the students were converted into so many pot-houses,* and there was no pot-house of them all more famous or more frequented than that of the baron. Our carousals here were many, and boisterous, and long, and never unfruitful of events.

Upon one occasion we had protracted our sitting until nearly daybreak, and an unusual quantity of wine had been drunk. The company consisted of seven or eight individuals besides the baron and myself. Most of these were young men of wealth, of high connection, of great family pride, and all alive with an exaggerated sense of honour. They abounded in the most ultra German opinions respecting the *duello*.* To these quixotic notions some recent Parisian publications, backed by three or four desperate and fatal *rencontres** at G——n, had given new vigour and impulse, and thus the conversation, during the greater part of the night, had run wild upon the all-engrossing topic of the times. The baron, who had been unusually silent and abstracted in the earlier portion of the evening, at length seemed to be aroused from his apathy, took a leading part in the discourse, and dwelt upon the benefits, and more especially upon the beauties, of the received code of etiquette in passages of arms with an ardour, an eloquence, an impressiveness and an affectionateness of manner which elicited the warmest enthusiasm from his hearers in general, and absolutely staggered even myself, who well knew him to be at heart a ridiculer of those very points for which he contended, and especially to hold the entire *fanfaronnade** of duelling etiquette in the sovereign contempt which it deserves.

Looking around me during a pause in the baron's discourse (of which my readers may gather some faint idea when I say that it bore resemblance to the fervid, chanting, monotonous, yet musical sermonic manner of Coleridge*), I perceived symptoms of even more than the general interest in the countenance of one of the party. This gentleman, whom I shall call Hermann, was an original in every respect – except, perhaps, in the single particular that he was a very great fool. He contrived to bear, however,

among a particular set at the university, a reputation for deep metaphysical thinking, and, I believe, for some logical talent. As a duellist he had acquired great renown, even at G——n. I forget the precise number of victims who had fallen at his hands, but they were many. He was a man of courage undoubtedly. But it was upon his minute acquaintance with the etiquette of the *duello*, and the *nicety* of his sense of honour, that he most especially prided himself. These things were a hobby which he rode to the death. To Ritzner, ever upon the lookout for the grotesque, his peculiarities had for a long time past afforded food for mystification. Of this, however, I was not aware, although, in the present instance, I saw clearly that something of a whimsical nature was upon the tapis* with my friend, and that Hermann was its especial object.

As the former proceeded in his discourse, or rather monologue, I perceived the excitement of the latter momently increasing. At length he spoke, offering some objection to a point insisted upon by R., and giving his reasons in detail. To these the baron replied at length (still maintaining his exaggerated tone of sentiment) and concluding, in what I thought very bad taste, with a sarcasm and a sneer. The hobby of Hermann now took the bit in his teeth. This I could discern by the studied hair-splitting farrago of his rejoinder. His last words I distinctly remember. "Your opinions, allow me to say, Baron von Jung, although in the main correct, are, in many nice points, discreditable to yourself and to the university of which you are a member. In a few respects they are even unworthy of serious refutation. I would say more than this, sir, were it not for the fear of giving you offence" (here the speaker smiled blandly), "I would say, sir, that your opinions are not the opinions to be expected from a gentleman."

As Hermann completed this equivocal sentence, all eyes were turned upon the baron. He became pale, then excessively red; then, dropping his pocket handkerchief, stooped to recover it, when I caught a glimpse of his countenance, while it could be seen by no one else at the table. It was radiant with the quizzical expression which was its natural character, but which I had never seen it assume except when we were alone together, and when he unbent himself freely. In an instant afterwards he stood erect, confronting Hermann, and so total an alteration of countenance in so short a period I certainly never saw before. For a moment I even fancied that I had misconceived him, and that he was in sober earnest. He appeared to be stifling with passion, and his face was cadaverously white. For a short time he remained silent, apparently striving to master his emotion. Having at length seemingly succeeded, he reached a decanter which stood

near him, saying, as he held it firmly clenched: "The language you have thought proper to employ, Mynheer Hermann, in addressing yourself to me, is objectionable in so many particulars, that I have neither temper nor time for specification. That my opinions, however, are not the opinions to be expected from a gentleman is an observation so directly offensive as to allow me but one line of conduct. Some courtesy, nevertheless, is due to the presence of this company, and to yourself, at this moment, as my guest. You will pardon me, therefore, if, upon this consideration, I deviate slightly from the general usage among gentlemen in similar cases of personal affront. You will forgive me for the moderate tax I shall make upon your imagination, and endeavour to consider, for an instant, the reflection of your person in yonder mirror as the living Mynheer Hermann himself. This being done, there will be no difficulty whatever. I shall discharge this decanter of wine at your image in yonder mirror, and thus fulfil all the spirit, if not the exact letter, of resentment for your insult, while the necessity of physical violence to your real person will be obviated."

With these words he hurled the decanter, full of wine, against the mirror which hung directly opposite Hermann, striking the reflection of his person with great precision, and of course shattering the glass into fragments. The whole company at once started to their feet, and, with the exception of myself and Ritzner, took their departure. As Hermann went out, the baron whispered me that I should follow him and make an offer of my services. To this I agreed, not knowing precisely what to make of so ridiculous a piece of business.

The duellist accepted my aid with his usual stiff and ultra recherché air, and, taking my arm, led me to his apartment. I could hardly forbear laughing in his face while he proceeded to discuss, with the profoundest gravity, what he termed "the refinedly peculiar character" of the insult he had received. After a tiresome harangue in his ordinary style, he took down from his bookshelves a number of musty volumes on the subject of the *duello*, and entertained me for a long time with their contents, reading aloud, and commenting earnestly as he read. I can just remember the titles of some of the works. There were the *Ordonnance of Philip le Bel on Single Combat*, the *Theatre of Honour*, by Favyn, and a treatise *On the Permission of Duels*, by Audiguier. He displayed, also, with much pomposity, Brantôme's *Memoirs of Duels*, published at Cologne, in 1666, in the types of Elzevir – a precious and unique vellum-paper volume, with a fine margin, and bound by Derome.* But he requested my attention particularly, and with an air of mysterious sagacity, to a thick octavo,

written in barbarous Latin by one Hedelin, a Frenchman, and having the quaint title *Duelli lex scripta, et non; aliterque.** From this he read me one of the drollest chapters in the world concerning "*Injuriæ per applicationem, per constructionem, et per se*",* about half of which, he averred, was strictly applicable to his own "refinedly peculiar" case, although not one syllable of the whole matter could I understand for the life of me. Having finished the chapter, he closed the book, and demanded what I thought necessary to be done. I replied that I had entire confidence in his superior delicacy of feeling, and would abide by what he proposed. With this answer he seemed flattered, and sat down to write a note to the baron. It ran thus:

SIR – My friend, Mr P——, will hand you this note. I find it incumbent upon me to request, at your earliest convenience, an explanation of this evening's occurrences at your chambers. In the event of your declining this request, Mr P. will be happy to arrange, with any friend whom you may appoint, the steps preliminary to a meeting.

With sentiments of perfect respect,

Your most humble servant,

JOHAN HERMANN

To the Baron Ritzner von Jung,
18th August 18—

Not knowing what better to do, I called upon Ritzner with this epistle. He bowed as I presented it; then, with a grave countenance, motioned me to a seat. Having perused the cartel,* he wrote the following reply, which I carried to Hermann.

SIR – Through our common friend, Mr P., I have received your note of this evening. Upon due reflection I frankly admit the propriety of the explanation you suggest. This being admitted, I still find great difficulty (owing to the *refinedly peculiar* nature of our disagreement, and of the personal affront offered on my part) in so wording what I have to say by way of apology, as to meet all the minute exigencies, and all the variable shadows, of the case. I have great reliance, however, on that extreme delicacy of discrimination, in matters appertaining to the rules of etiquette, for which you have been so long and so pre-eminently distinguished. With perfect certainty, therefore, of being comprehended,

I beg leave, in lieu of offering any sentiments of my own, to refer you to the opinions of the Sieur Hedelin, as set forth in the ninth paragraph of the chapter of *"Injuriæ per applicationem, per constructionem, et per se"*, in his *Duelli lex scripta, et non; aliterque*. The nicety of your discernment in all the matters here treated will be sufficient, I am assured, to convince you *that the mere circumstance of my referring you* to this admirable passage ought to satisfy your request, as a man of honour, for explanation.

With sentiments of profound respect,

Your most obedient servant,

VON JUNG

The Herr Johan Hermann,
18th August 18—

Hermann commenced the perusal of this epistle with a scowl, which, how-ever, was converted into a smile of the most ludicrous self-complacency as he came to the rigmarole about *Injuriæ per applicationem, per con-structionem, et per se*. Having finished reading, he begged me, with the blandest of all possible smiles, to be seated, while he made reference to the treatise in question. Turning to the passage specified, he read it with great care to himself, then closed the book, and desired me, in my character of confidential acquaintance, to express to the Baron von Jung his exalted sense of his chivalrous behaviour, and, in that of second, to assure him that the explanation offered was of the fullest, the most honourable, and the most unequivocally satisfactory nature.

Somewhat amazed at all this, I made my retreat to the baron. He seemed to receive Hermann's amicable letter as a matter of course, and, after a few words of general conversation, went to an inner room and brought out the everlasting treatise *Duelli lex scripta, et non; aliterque*. He handed me the volume and asked me to look over some portion of it. I did so, but to little purpose, not being able to gather the least particle of meaning. He then took the book himself, and read me a chapter aloud. To my surprise, what he read proved to be a most horribly absurd account of a duel between two baboons. He now explained the mystery, showing that the volume, as it appeared prima facie, was written upon the plan of the nonsense verses of Du Bartas* – that is to say, the language was ingeniously framed so as to present to the ear all the outward signs of intelligibility, and even of profundity, while in fact not a shadow of meaning existed. The key to the

whole was found in leaving out every second and third word alternately, when there appeared a series of ludicrous quizzes upon single combat as practised in modern times.

The baron afterwards informed me that he had purposely thrown the treatise in Hermann's way two or three weeks before the adventure, and that he was satisfied, from the general tenor of his conversation, that he had studied it with the deepest attention, and firmly believed it to be a work of unusual merit. Upon this hint he proceeded. Hermann would have died a thousand deaths rather than acknowledge his inability to understand anything and everything in the universe that had ever been written about the *duello*.

HOW TO WRITE
A *BLACKWOOD* ARTICLE*

In the name of the Prophet – figs!
– CRY OF THE TURKISH FIG-PEDLAR*

I presume everybody has heard of me. My name is the Signora Psyche Zenobia.* This I know to be a fact. Nobody but my enemies ever calls me Suky Snobbs. I have been assured that Suky is but a vulgar corruption of Psyche, which is good Greek, and means "the soul" (that's me, I'm *all* soul) and sometimes "a butterfly", which latter meaning undoubtedly alludes to my appearance in my new crimson satin dress, with the sky-blue Arabian *mantelet*, and the trimmings of green *agraffas*, and the seven flounces of orange-coloured *auriculas*.* As for Snobbs – any person who should look at me would be instantly aware that my name wasn't Snobbs. Miss Tabitha Turnip propagated that report through sheer envy. Tabitha Turnip indeed! Oh, the little wretch! But what can we expect from a turnip? Wonder if she remembers the old adage about "blood out of a turnip", etc. (Mem.: put her in mind of it the first opportunity.) (Mem. again: pull her nose.) Where was I? Ah! I have been assured that Snobbs is a mere corruption of Zenobia, and that Zenobia was a queen (so am I. Dr Moneypenny always calls me the Queen of the Hearts) and that Zenobia, as well as Psyche, is good Greek, and that my father was "a Greek",* and that consequently I have a right to our patronymic, which is Zenobia, and not by any means Snobbs. Nobody but Tabitha Turnip calls me Suky Snobbs. I am the Signora Psyche Zenobia.

As I said before, everybody has heard of me. I am that very Signora Psyche Zenobia so justly celebrated as corresponding secretary to the "Philadelphia, Regular, Exchange, Tea, Total, Young, Belles, Lettres, Universal, Experimental, Bibliographical, Association, To, Civilize, Humanity". Dr Moneypenny made the title for us, and says he chose it because it sounded big like an empty rum puncheon.* (A vulgar man that sometimes – but he's deep.) We all sign the initials of the society after our names, in the fashion of the RSA, Royal Society of Arts, the SDUK, Society for the Diffusion of Useful Knowledge,* etc., etc. Dr Moneypenny says that S stands for "stale", and that DUK spells "duck" (but it don't), and that SDUK stands for "Stale Duck" and not for Lord Brougham's society – but

then Dr Moneypenny is such a queer man that I am never sure when he is telling me the truth. At any rate we always add to our names the initials PRETTYBLUEBATCH – that is to say, Philadelphia, Regular, Exchange, Tea, Total, Young, Belles, Lettres, Universal, Experimental, Bibliographical, Association, To, Civilize, Humanity – one letter for each word, which is a decided improvement upon Lord Brougham. Dr Moneypenny will have it that our initials give our true character – but for my life I can't see what he means.

Notwithstanding the good offices of the doctor, and the strenuous exertions of the association to get itself into notice, it met with no very great success until I joined it. The truth is, the members indulged in too flippant a tone of discussion. The papers read every Saturday evening were characterized less by depth than buffoonery. They were all whipped syllabub. There was no investigation of first causes, first principles. There was no investigation of anything at all. There was no attention paid to that great point, the "fitness of things".* In short there was no fine writing like this. It was all low – very! No profundity, no reading, no metaphysics – nothing which the learned call spirituality, and which the unlearned choose to stigmatize as cant. (Dr M. says I ought to spell "cant" with a capital K* – but I know better.)

When I joined the society it was my endeavour to introduce a better style of thinking and writing, and all the world knows how well I have succeeded. We get up as good papers now in the PRETTYBLUEBATCH as any to be found even in *Blackwood*. I say *Blackwood* because I have been assured that the finest writing, upon every subject, is to be discovered in the pages of that justly celebrated magazine. We now take it for our model upon all themes, and are getting into rapid notice accordingly. And, after all, it's not so very difficult a matter to compose an article of the genuine *Blackwood* stamp, if one only goes properly about it. Of course I don't speak of the political articles. Everybody knows how *they* are managed, since Dr Moneypenny explained it. Mr Blackwood has a pair of tailor's shears, and three apprentices who stand by him for orders. One hands him the *Times*, another the *Examiner* and a third a *Gulley's New Compendium of Slang-Whang*.* Mr B. merely cuts out and intersperses. It is soon done: nothing but *Examiner*, *Slang-Whang* and *Times*; then *Times*, *Slang-Whang* and *Examiner*; and then *Times*, *Examiner* and *Slang-Whang*.

But the chief merit of the magazine lies in its miscellaneous articles, and the best of these come under the head of what Dr Moneypenny calls the "bizarreries" (whatever that may mean) and what everybody else calls the

"intensities". This is a species of writing which I have long known how to appreciate, although it is only since my late visit to Mr Blackwood (deputed by the society) that I have been made aware of the exact method of composition. This method is very simple, but not so much so as the politics. Upon my calling at Mr B.'s, and making known to him the wishes of the society, he received me with great civility, took me into his study and gave me a clear explanation of the whole process.

"My dear madam," said he, evidently struck with my majestic appearance, for I had on the crimson satin, with the green *agraffas*, and orange-coloured *auriculas*. "My *dear* madam," said he, "sit down. The matter stands thus: in the first place your writer of intensities must have very black ink, and a very big pen, with a very blunt nib. And, mark me, Miss Psyche Zenobia!" he continued, after a pause, with the most impressive energy and solemnity of manner. "Mark me! *That pen – must – never be mended!* Herein, madam, lies the secret, the soul, of intensity. I assume it upon myself to say that no individual, of however great genius, ever wrote with a good pen – understand me – a good article. You may take it for granted that when manuscript can be read it is never worth reading. This is a leading principle in our faith, to which if you cannot readily assent, our conference is at an end."

He paused. But, of course, as I had no wish to put an end to the conference, I assented to a proposition so very obvious, and one, too, of whose truth I had all along been sufficiently aware. He seemed pleased, and went on with his instructions.

"It may appear invidious in me, Miss Psyche Zenobia, to refer you to an article, or set of articles, in the way of model or study, yet perhaps I may as well call your attention to a few cases.* Let me see. There was 'The Dead Alive', a capital thing! The record of a gentleman's sensations when entombed before the breath was out of his body – full of taste, terror, sentiment, metaphysics and erudition. You would have sworn that the writer had been born and brought up in a coffin. Then we had the *Confessions of an Opium-Eater* – fine, very fine! – glorious imagination – deep philosophy – acute speculation – plenty of fire and fury, and a good spicing of the decidedly unintelligible. That was a nice bit of flummery, and went down the throats of the people delightfully. They would have it that Coleridge wrote the paper – but not so. It was composed by my pet baboon, Juniper, over a rummer of Hollands and water,* 'hot, without sugar'." (This I could scarcely have believed had it been anybody but Mr Blackwood, who assured me of it.) "Then there was 'The Involuntary

Experimentalist', all about a gentleman who got baked in an oven, and came out alive and well, although certainly done to a turn. And then there was 'The Diary of a Late Physician', where the merit lay in good rant, and indifferent Greek – both of them, taking things with the public. And then there was 'The Man in the Bell', a paper, by the by, Miss Zenobia, which I cannot sufficiently recommend to your attention. It is the history of a young person who goes to sleep under the clapper of a church bell, and is awakened by its tolling for a funeral. The sound drives him mad, and, accordingly, pulling out his tablets, he gives a record of his sensations. Sensations are the great things after all. Should you ever be drowned or hung, be sure and make a note of your sensations – they will be worth to you ten guineas a sheet. If you wish to write forcibly, Miss Zenobia, pay minute attention to the sensations."

"That I certainly will, Mr Blackwood," said I.

"Good!" he replied. "I see you are a pupil after my own heart. But I must put you au fait to the details necessary in composing what may be denominated a genuine *Blackwood* article of the sensation stamp – the kind which you will understand me to say I consider the best for all purposes.

"The first thing requisite is to get yourself into such a scrape as no one ever got into before. The oven, for instance – that was a good hit. But if you have no oven, or big bell, at hand, and if you cannot conveniently tumble out of a balloon, or be swallowed up in an earthquake, or get stuck fast in a chimney, you will have to be contented with simply imagining some similar misadventure. I should prefer, however, that you have the actual fact to bear you out. Nothing so well assists the fancy as an experimental knowledge of the matter in hand. 'Truth is strange,' you know, 'stranger than fiction'* – besides being more to the purpose."

Here I assured him I had an excellent pair of garters, and would go and hang myself forthwith.

"Good!" he replied. "Do so – although hanging is somewhat hackneyed. Perhaps you might do better. Take a dose of Brandreth's pills,* and then give us your sensations. However, my instructions will apply equally well to any variety of misadventure, and in your way home you may easily get knocked in the head, or run over by an omnibus, or bitten by a mad dog, or drowned in a gutter. But to proceed.

"Having determined upon your subject, you must next consider the tone, or manner, of your narration. There is the tone didactic, the tone enthu-siastic, the tone natural – all commonplace enough. But then there is the tone laconic, or curt, which has lately come much into use. It consists in

short sentences. Somehow thus: can't be too brief. Can't be too snappish. Always a full stop. And never a paragraph.

"Then there is the tone elevated, diffusive and interjectional. Some of our best novelists patronize this tone. The words must be all in a whirl, like a humming top, and make a noise very similar, which answers remarkably well instead of meaning. This is the best of all possible styles where the writer is in too great a hurry to think.

"The tone metaphysical is also a good one. If you know any big words this is your chance for them. Talk of the Ionic and Eleatic schools – of Archytas, Gorgias and Alcmaeon.* Say something about objectivity and subjectivity. Be sure and abuse a man named Locke.* Turn up your nose at things in general, and when you let slip anything a little *too* absurd, you need not be at the trouble of scratching it out, but just add a footnote and say that you are indebted for the above profound observation to the *Kritik der reinem Vernunft*, or to the *Metaphysische Anfangsgründe der Naturwissenschaft.** This would look erudite and – and – and frank.

"There are various other tones of equal celebrity, but I shall mention only two more – the tone transcendental and the tone heterogeneous. In the former the merit consists in seeing into the nature of affairs a very great deal farther than anybody else. This second sight is very efficient when properly managed. A little reading of the *Dial** will carry you a great way. Eschew, in this case, big words – get them as small as possible, and write them upside down. Look over Channing's poems and quote what he says about a 'fat little man with a delusive show of Can'.* Put in something about the Supernal Oneness. Don't say a syllable about the Infernal Twoness. Above all, study innuendo. Hint everything – assert nothing. If you feel inclined to say 'bread and butter', do not by any means say it outright. You may say anything and everything *approaching* to 'bread and butter'. You may hint at buckwheat cake, or you may even go so far as to insinuate oatmeal porridge, but if bread and butter be your real meaning, be cautious, my *dear* Miss Psyche, not on any account to say 'bread and butter'!"

I assured him that I should never say it again as long as I lived. He kissed me and continued:

"As for the tone heterogeneous, it is merely a judicious mixture, in equal proportions, of all the other tones in the world, and is consequently made up of everything deep, great, odd, piquant, pertinent and pretty.

"Let us suppose now you have determined upon your incidents and tone. The most important portion – in fact, the soul of the whole business – is yet to be attended to; I allude to *the filling up*. It is not to be supposed that

a lady, or gentleman either, has been leading the life of a bookworm. And yet above all things it is necessary that your article have an air of erudition, or at least afford evidence of extensive general reading. Now I'll put you in the way of accomplishing this point. See here!" (pulling down some three or four ordinary-looking volumes, and opening them at random). "By casting your eye down almost any page of any book in the world, you will be able to perceive at once a host of little scraps of either learning or *bel-esprit-ism*,* which are the very thing for the spicing of a *Blackwood* article. You might as well note down a few while I read them to you. I shall make two divisions: first, 'Piquant Facts for the Manufacture of Similes', and, second, 'Piquant Expressions to Be Introduced as Occasion May Require'. Write now!" – and I wrote as he dictated.

"PIQUANT FACTS FOR SIMILES. 'There were originally but three Muses: Melete, Mneme, Aoede – meditation, memory and singing.'* You may make a good deal of that little fact if properly worked. You see it is not generally known, and looks recherché. You must be careful and give the thing with a downright improviso air.

"Again. 'The river Alpheus passed beneath the sea, and emerged without injury to the purity of its waters.'* Rather stale that, to be sure, but, if properly dressed and dished up, will look quite as fresh as ever.

"Here is something better. 'The Persian Iris appears to some persons to possess a sweet and very powerful perfume, while to others it is perfectly scentless.' Fine that, and very delicate! Turn it about a little, and it will do wonders. We'll have something else in the botanical line. There's nothing goes down so well, especially with the help of a little Latin. Write!

"'The *Epidendrum flos aeris*,* of Java, bears a very beautiful flower, and will live when pulled up by the roots. The natives suspend it by a cord from the ceiling, and enjoy its fragrance for years.' That's capital! That will do for the similes. Now for the 'Piquant Expressions'.

"PIQUANT EXPRESSIONS. 'The venerable Chinese novel *Ju-Kiao-Li*'.* Good! By introducing these few words with dexterity you will evince your intimate acquaintance with the language and literature of the Chinese. With the aid of this you may either get along without either Arabic, or Sanscrit, or Chickasaw.* There is no passing muster, however, without Spanish, Italian, German, Latin and Greek. I must look you out a little specimen of each. Any scrap will answer, because you must depend upon your own ingenuity to make it fit into your article. Now write!

"'*Aussi tendre que Zaïre*' – as tender as Zaïre – French. Alludes to the frequent repetition of the phrase '*la tendre Zaïre*' in the French tragedy of

that name.* Properly introduced, will show not only your knowledge of the language but your general reading and wit. You can say, for instance, that the chicken you were eating (write an article about being choked to death by a chicken bone) was not altogether *aussi tendre que Zaïre*. Write!

Ven muerte tan escondida,
 Que no te sienta venir,
Porque el plazer del morir,
 No me torne a dar la vida.

That's Spanish – from Miguel de Cervantes.* 'Come quickly, O death! but be sure and don't let me see you coming, lest the pleasure I shall feel at your appearance should unfortunately bring me back again to life.' This you may slip in quite *à propos* when you are struggling in the last agonies with the chicken bone. Write!

 Il pover' uomo, che non se n'era accorto,
 Andava combattendo, ed era morto.

That's Italian, you perceive – from Ariosto.* It means that a great hero, in the heat of combat, not perceiving that he had been fairly killed, continued to fight valiantly, dead as he was. The application of this to your own case is obvious – for I trust, Miss Psyche, that you will not neglect to kick for at least an hour and a half after you have been choked to death by that chicken bone. Please to write!

 Und sterb' ich doch, so sterb' ich denn
 Durch sie – durch sie!

That's German – from Schiller.* 'And if I die, at least I die – for thee – for thee!' Here it is clear that you are apostrophizing the *cause* of your disaster, the chicken. Indeed, what gentleman (or lady either) of sense *wouldn't* die, I should like to know, for a well-fattened capon of the right Molucca* breed, stuffed with capers and mushrooms, and served up in a salad bowl, with orange jellies *en mosaïques*.* Write! (You can get them that way at Tortoni's.*) Write, if you please!

 "Here is a nice little Latin phrase, and rare too (one can't be too recherché or brief in one's Latin, it's getting so common): *ignoratio elenchi*.* He has committed an *ignoratio elenchi* – that is to say, he has understood the

words of your proposition, but not the ideas. The man was a fool, you see. Some poor fellow whom you addressed while choking with that chicken bone, and who therefore didn't precisely understand what you were talking about. Throw the *ignoratio elenchi* in his teeth, and, at once, you have him annihilated. If he dares to reply, you can tell him from Lucan (here it is) that speeches are mere *anemonæ verborum*, anemone words.* The anemone, with great brilliancy, has no smell. Or, if he begins to bluster, you may be down upon him with *insomnia Jovis*, reveries of Jupiter – a phrase which Silius Italicus (see here!) applies to thoughts pompous and inflated.* This will be sure and cut him to the heart. He can do nothing but roll over and die. Will you be kind enough to write?

"In Greek we must have something pretty – from Demosthenes, for example. Ανηρ ο φευγων και παλιν μαχησεται (*Aner o pheugon kai palin makesetai*). There is a tolerably good translation of it in *Hudibras*:

For he that flies may fight again,
Which he can never do that's slain.*

In a *Blackwood* article nothing makes so fine a show as your Greek. The very letters have an air of profundity about them. Only observe, madam, the astute look of that epsilon! That phi ought certainly to be a bishop! Was ever there a smarter fellow than that omicron? Just twig that tau! In short, there is nothing like Greek for a genuine sensation paper. In the present case your application is the most obvious thing in the world. Rap out the sentence, with a huge oath, and by way of ultimatum at the good-for-nothing dunderheaded villain who couldn't understand your plain English in relation to the chicken bone. He'll take the hint and be off, you may depend upon it."

These were all the instructions Mr B. could afford me upon the topic in question, but I felt they would be entirely sufficient. I was, at length, able to write a genuine *Blackwood* article, and determined to do it forthwith. In taking leave of me, Mr B. made a proposition for the purchase of the paper when written, but as he could offer me only fifty guineas a sheet, I thought it better to let our society have it than sacrifice it for so paltry a sum. Notwithstanding this niggardly spirit, however, the gentleman showed his consideration for me in all other respects, and indeed treated me with the greatest civility. His parting words made a deep impression upon my heart, and I hope I shall always remember them with gratitude.

"My dear Miss Zenobia," he said, while the tears stood in his eyes, "is there *any*thing else I can do to promote the success of your laudable undertaking? Let me reflect! It is just possible that you may not be able, so soon as convenient, to – to – get yourself drowned, or – choked with a chicken bone, or – or hung – or – bitten by a – but stay! Now I think me of it, there are a couple of very excellent bulldogs in the yard – fine fellows, I assure you – savage, and all that – indeed just the thing for your money – they'll have you eaten up, *auriculas* and all, in less than five minutes (here's my watch!) – and then only think of the sensations! Here! I say – Tom! – Peter! – Dick, you villain! – let out those" – but as I was really in a great hurry, and had not another moment to spare, I was reluctantly forced to expedite my departure, and accordingly took leave *at once* – somewhat more abruptly, I admit, than strict courtesy would have otherwise allowed.

It was my primary object, upon quitting Mr Blackwood, to get into some immediate difficulty, pursuant to his advice, and with this view I spent the greater part of the day in wandering about Edinburgh, seeking for desperate adventures – adventures adequate to the intensity of my feelings, and adapted to the vast character of the article I intended to write. In this excursion I was attended by my Negro servant, Pompey, and my little lapdog Diana, whom I had brought with me from Philadelphia. It was not, however, until late in the afternoon that I fully succeeded in my arduous undertaking. An important event then happened of which the following *Blackwood* article, in the tone heterogeneous, is the substance and result.

A PREDICAMENT*

What chance, good lady, hath
bereft you thus?

<div style="text-align: right">— COMUS*</div>

It was a quiet and still afternoon when I strolled forth in the goodly city of Edina.* The confusion and bustle in the streets were terrible. Men were talking. Women were screaming. Children were choking. Pigs were whistling. Carts they rattled. Bulls they bellowed. Cows they lowed. Horses they neighed. Cats they caterwauled. Dogs they danced. *Danced!* Could it then be possible? *Danced!* Alas, thought I, *my* dancing days are over! Thus it is ever. What a host of gloomy recollections will ever and anon be awakened in the mind of genius and imaginative contemplation, especially of a genius doomed to the everlasting and eternal, and continual, and, as one might say, the – *continued* – yes, the *continued and continuous*, bitter, harassing, disturbing, and, if I may be allowed the expression, the *very* disturbing influence of the serene, and godlike, and heavenly, and exalting, and elevated, and purifying effect of what may be rightly termed the most enviable, the most *truly* enviable – nay! – the most benignly beautiful, the most deliciously ethereal, and, as it were, the most *pretty* (if I may use so bold an expression) *thing* (pardon me, gentle reader!) in the world – but I am always led away by my feelings. In *such* a mind, I repeat, what a host of recollections are stirred up by a trifle! The dogs danced! I – I *could* not! They frisked – I wept. They capered – I sobbed aloud. Touching circumstances! which cannot fail to bring to the recollection of the classical reader that exquisite passage in relation to the fitness of things, which is to be found in the commencement of the third volume of that admirable and venerable Chinese novel the *Jo-Go-Slow*.*

In my solitary walk through the city I had two humble but faithful companions. Diana, my poodle! Sweetest of creatures! She had a quantity of hair over her one eye, and a blue riband tied fashionably around her neck. Diana was not more than five inches in height, but her head was somewhat bigger than her body, and her tail, being cut off exceedingly close, gave an air of injured innocence to the interesting animal which rendered her a favourite with all.

And Pompey, my Negro! Sweet Pompey! How shall I ever forget thee? I had taken Pompey's arm. He was three feet in height (I like to be particular) and about seventy, or perhaps eighty, years of age. He had bow legs and was corpulent. His mouth should not be called small, nor his ears short. His teeth, however, were like pearl, and his large full eyes were deliciously white. Nature had endowed him with no neck, and had placed his ankles (as usual with that race) in the middle of the upper portion of the feet. He was clad with a striking simplicity. His sole garments were a stock of nine inches in height, and a nearly new drab overcoat which had formerly been in the service of the tall, stately and illustrious Dr Moneypenny. It was a good overcoat. It was well cut. It was well made. The coat was nearly new. Pompey held it up out of the dirt with both hands.

There were three persons in our party, and two of them have already been the subject of remark. There was a third – that third person was myself. I am the Signora Psyche Zenobia. I am *not* Suky Snobbs. My appearance is commanding. On the memorable occasion of which I speak I was habited in a crimson satin dress, with a sky-blue Arabian *mantelet*. And the dress had trimmings of green *agraffas*, and seven graceful flounces of the orange-coloured *auricula*.* I thus formed the third of the party. There was the poodle. There was Pompey. There was myself. We were *three*. Thus it is said there were originally but three Furies – Melty, Nimmy and Hetty – Meditation, Memory and Fiddling.*

Leaning upon the arm of the gallant Pompey, and attended at a respectable distance by Diana, I proceeded down one of the populous and very pleasant streets of the now deserted Edina. On a sudden, there presented itself to view a church – a Gothic cathedral – vast, venerable and with a tall steeple, which towered into the sky. What madness now possessed me? Why did I rush upon my fate? I was seized with an uncontrollable desire to ascend the giddy pinnacle, and thence survey the immense extent of the city. The door of the cathedral stood invitingly open. My destiny prevailed. I entered the ominous archway. Where then was my guardian angel? If indeed such angels there be. *If!* Distressing monosyllable! What a world of mystery, and meaning, and doubt, and uncertainty is there involved in thy two letters! I entered the ominous archway! I entered, and, without injury to my orange-coloured *auriculas*, I passed beneath the portal, and emerged within the vestibule. Thus it is said the immense river Alfred passed, unscathed, and unwetted, beneath the sea.*

I thought the staircases would never have an end. *Round!* Yes, they went round and up, and round and up and round and up, until I could not

help surmising, with the sagacious Pompey, upon whose supporting arm I leant in all the confidence of early affection – I *could* not help surmising that the upper end of the continuous spiral ladder had been accidentally, or perhaps designedly, removed. I paused for breath, and, in the mean time, an incident occurred of too momentous a nature in a moral, and also in a metaphysical point of view, to be passed over without notice. It appeared to me – indeed I was quite confident of the fact – I could not be mistaken – no! I had, for some moments, carefully and anxiously observed the motions of my Diana – I say that *I could not be* mistaken – Diana *smelt a rat*! At once I called Pompey's attention to the subject, and he – he agreed with me. There was then no longer any reasonable room for doubt. The rat had been smelt – and by Diana. Heavens! Shall I ever forget the intense excitement of the moment? Alas! What is the boasted intellect of man? The rat! It was there – that is to say, it was somewhere. Diana smelt the rat. *I* – I *could* not! Thus it is said the Prussian Isis has, for some persons, a sweet and very powerful perfume, while to others it is perfectly scentless.*

The staircase had been surmounted, and there were now only three or four more upward steps intervening between us and the summit. We still ascended, and now only one step remained. One step! One little, little step! Upon one such little step in the great staircase of human life how vast a sum of human happiness or misery often depends! I thought of myself, then of Pompey, and then of the mysterious and inexplicable destiny which surrounded us. I thought of Pompey! Alas, I thought of love! I thought of the many false *steps* which have been taken, and may be taken again. I resolved to be more cautious, more reserved. I abandoned the arm of Pompey, and, without his assistance, surmounted the one remaining step, and gained the chamber of the belfry. I was followed immediately afterwards by my poodle. Pompey alone remained behind. I stood at the head of the staircase, and encouraged him to ascend. He stretched forth to me his hand, and unfortunately in so doing was forced to abandon his firm hold upon the overcoat. Will the gods never cease their persecution? The overcoat it dropped, and, with one of his feet, Pompey stepped upon the long and trailing skirt of the overcoat. He stumbled and fell – this consequence was inevitable. He fell forward, and, with his accursed head, striking me full in the – in the breast, precipitated me headlong, together with himself, upon the hard, filthy and detestable floor of the belfry. But my revenge was sure, sudden and complete. Seizing him furiously by the wool with both hands, I tore out a vast quantity of the black, and crisp,

and curling material, and tossed it from me with every manifestation of disdain. It fell among the ropes of the belfry and remained. Pompey arose, and said no word. But he regarded me piteously with his large eyes and – sighed. Ye gods – that sigh! It sank into my heart. And the hair – the wool! Could I have reached that wool I would have bathed it with my tears, in testimony of regret. But alas! It was now far beyond my grasp. As it dangled among the cordage of the bell, I fancied it still alive. I fancied that it stood on end with indignation. Thus the *happydandy flos aeris* of Java bears, it is said, a beautiful flower, which will live when pulled up by the roots.* The natives suspend it by a cord from the ceiling and enjoy its fragrance for years.

Our quarrel was now made up, and we looked about the room for an aperture through which to survey the city of Edina. Windows there were none. The sole light admitted into the gloomy chamber proceeded from a square opening, about a foot in diameter, at a height of about seven feet from the floor. Yet what will the energy of true genius not effect? I resolved to clamber up to this hole. A vast quantity of wheels, pinions and other cabbalistic-looking machinery stood opposite the hole, close to it, and through the hole there passed an iron rod from the machinery. Between the wheels and the wall where the hole lay there was barely room for my body – yet I was desperate, and determined to persevere. I called Pompey to my side.

"You perceive that aperture, Pompey. I wish to look through it. You will stand here just beneath the hole – so. Now, hold out one of your hands, Pompey, and let me step upon it – thus. Now, the other hand, Pompey, and with its aid I will get upon your shoulders."

He did everything I wished, and I found, upon getting up, that I could easily pass my head and neck through the aperture. The prospect was sublime. Nothing could be more magnificent. I merely paused a moment to bid Diana behave herself, and assure Pompey that I would be considerate and bear as lightly as possible upon his shoulders. I told him I would be tender of his feelings – *ossi tender que beefsteak*.* Having done this justice to my faithful friend, I gave myself up with great zest and enthusiasm to the enjoyment of the scene which so obligingly spread itself out before my eyes.

Upon this subject, however, I shall forbear to dilate. I will not describe the city of Edinburgh. Everyone has been to the city of Edinburgh. Everyone has been to Edinburgh – the classic Edina. I will confine myself to the momentous details of my own lamentable adventure. Having, in

some measure, satisfied my curiosity in regard to the extent, situation and general appearance of the city, I had leisure to survey the church in which I was, and the delicate architecture of the steeple. I observed that the aperture through which I had thrust my head was an opening in the dial plate of a gigantic clock, and must have appeared, from the street, as a large keyhole, such as we see in the face of the French watches. No doubt the true object was to admit the arm of an attendant, to adjust, when necessary, the hands of the clock from within. I observed also, with surprise, the immense size of these hands, the longest of which could not have been less than ten feet in length, and, where broadest, eight or nine inches in breadth. They were of solid steel apparently, and their edges appeared to be sharp. Having noticed these particulars, and some others, I again turned my eyes upon the glorious prospect below, and soon became absorbed in contemplation.

From this, after some minutes, I was aroused by the voice of Pompey, who declared that he could stand it no longer, and requested that I would be so kind as to come down. This was unreasonable, and I told him so in a speech of some length. He replied, but with an evident misunderstanding of my ideas upon the subject. I accordingly grew angry, and told him in plain words that he was a fool, that he had committed an *ignoramus e-clench-eye*, that his notions were mere *insommary Bovis*, and his words little better than *an enemy-werrybor'em*.* With this he appeared satisfied, and I resumed my contemplations.

It might have been half an hour after this altercation when, as I was deeply absorbed in the heavenly scenery beneath me, I was startled by something very cold which pressed with a gentle pressure on the back of my neck. It is needless to say that I felt inexpressibly alarmed. I knew that Pompey was beneath my feet, and that Diana was sitting, according to my explicit directions, upon her hind legs, in the farthest corner of the room. What could it be? Alas! I but too soon discovered. Turning my head gently to one side, I perceived, to my extreme horror, that the huge, glittering, scimitar-like minute hand of the clock had, in the course of its hourly revolution, *descended upon my neck*. There was, I knew, not a second to be lost. I pulled back at once – but it was too late. There was no chance of forcing my head through the mouth of that terrible trap in which it was so fairly caught, and which grew narrower and narrower with a rapidity too horrible to be conceived. The agony of that moment is not to be imagined. I threw up my hands and endeavoured, with all my strength, to force upwards the ponderous iron bar. I might

as well have tried to lift the cathedral itself. Down, down, down it came, closer and yet closer. I screamed to Pompey for aid, but he said that I had hurt his feelings by calling him "an ignorant old squint-eye". I yelled to Diana, but she only said "bow-wow-wow", and that I had told her "on no account to stir from the corner". Thus I had no relief to expect from my associates.

Meantime the ponderous and terrific *scythe of time** (for I now discovered the literal import of that classical phrase) had not stopped, nor was it likely to stop, in its career. Down and still down, it came. It had already buried its sharp edge a full inch in my flesh, and my sensations grew indistinct and confused. At one time I fancied myself in Philadelphia with the stately Dr Moneypenny, at another in the back parlour of Mr Blackwood receiving his invaluable instructions. And then again the sweet recollection of better and earlier times came over me, and I thought of that happy period when the world was not all a desert, and Pompey not altogether cruel.

The ticking of the machinery amused me. *Amused me*, I say, for my sensations now bordered upon perfect happiness, and the most trifling circumstances afforded me pleasure. The eternal *click-clack, click-clack, click-clack* of the clock was the most melodious of music in my ears, and occasionally even put me in mind of the grateful sermonic harangues of Dr Ollapod.* Then there were the great figures upon the dial plate – how intelligent, how intellectual, they all looked! And presently they took to dancing the mazurka, and I think it was the figure V. who performed the most to my satisfaction. She was evidently a lady of breeding. None of your swaggerers, and nothing at all indelicate in her motions. She did the pirouette to admiration – whirling round upon her apex. I made an endeavour to hand her a chair, for I saw that she appeared fatigued with her exertions – and it was not until then that I fully perceived my lamentable situation. Lamentable indeed! The bar had buried itself two inches in my neck. I was aroused to a sense of exquisite pain. I prayed for death, and, in the agony of the moment, could not help repeating those exquisite verses of the poet Miguel de Cervantes:

Vanny Buren, tan escondida
Query no te senty venny
Pork and pleasure, delly morry
*Nommy, torny, darry, widdy!**

But now a new horror presented itself, and one indeed sufficient to startle the strongest nerves. My eyes, from the cruel pressure of the machine, were absolutely starting from their sockets. While I was thinking how I should possibly manage without them, one actually tumbled out of my head, and, rolling down the steep side of the steeple, lodged in the rain gutter which ran along the eaves of the main building. The loss of the eye was not so much as the insolent air of independence and contempt with which it regarded me after it was out. There it lay in the gutter just under my nose, and the airs it gave itself would have been ridiculous had they not been disgusting. Such a winking and blinking were never before seen. This behaviour on the part of my eye in the gutter was not only irritating on account of its manifest insolence and shameful ingratitude, but was also exceedingly inconvenient on account of the sympathy which always exists between two eyes of the same head, however far apart. I was forced, in a manner, to wink and to blink, whether I would or not, in exact concert with the scoundrelly thing that lay just under my nose. I was presently relieved, however, by the dropping out of the other eye. In falling it took the same direction (possibly a concerted plot) as its fellow. Both rolled out of the gutter together, and in truth I was very glad to get rid of them.

The bar was now four inches and a half deep in my neck, and there was only a little bit of skin to cut through. My sensations were those of entire happiness, for I felt that in a few minutes, at furthest, I should be relieved from my disagreeable situation. And in this expectation I was not at all deceived. At twenty-five minutes past five in the afternoon, precisely, the huge minute hand had proceeded sufficiently far on its terrible revolution to sever the small remainder of my neck. I was not sorry to see the head which had occasioned me so much embarrassment at length make a final separation from my body. It first rolled down the side of the steeple, then lodged, for a few seconds, in the gutter, and then made its way, with a plunge, into the middle of the street.

I will candidly confess that my feelings were now of the most singular – nay, of the most mysterious, the most perplexing and incomprehensible character. My senses were here and there at one and the same moment. With my head I imagined, at one time, that I, the head, was the real Signora Psyche Zenobia – at another I felt convinced that myself, the body, was the proper identity. To clear my ideas on this topic I felt in my pocket for my snuffbox, but, upon getting it, and endeavouring to apply a pinch of its grateful contents in the ordinary manner, I became immediately aware of my peculiar deficiency, and threw the box at once down to my head. It took a pinch with great satisfaction, and smiled me an acknowledgement

in return. Shortly afterwards it made me a speech, which I could hear but indistinctly without ears. I gathered enough, however, to know that it was astonished at my wishing to remain alive under such circumstances. In the concluding sentences it quoted the noble words of Ariosto:

Il pover hommy che non sera corty
*And have a combat tenty erry morty,**

thus comparing me to the hero who, in the heat of the combat, not perceiving that he was dead, continued to contest the battle with inextinguishable valour. There was nothing now to prevent my getting down from my elevation, and I did so. What it was that Pompey saw so *very* peculiar in my appearance I have never yet been able to find out. The fellow opened his mouth from ear to ear, and shut his two eyes as if he were endeavouring to crack nuts between the lids. Finally, throwing off his overcoat, he made one spring for the staircase and disappeared. I hurled after the scoundrel those vehement words of Demosthenes:

Andrew O'Phlegethon, you really make haste to fly.*

and then turned to the darling of my heart, to the one-eyed! the shaggy-haired Diana. Alas! What horrible vision affronted my eyes? *Was* that a rat I saw skulking into his hole? *Are* these the picked bones of the little angel who has been cruelly devoured by the monster? Ye gods! And what *do* I behold – *is* that the departed spirit, the shade, the ghost, of my beloved puppy, which I perceive sitting with a grace so melancholy, in the corner? Hearken! For she speaks, and, heavens! it is in the German of Schiller:

Unt stubby duk, so stubby dun
*Duk she! duk she!**

Alas! And are not her words too true?

And if I died, at least I died
For thee – for thee.

Sweet creature! She *too* has sacrificed herself in my behalf. Dogless, nigger-less, headless, what *now* remains for the unhappy Signora Psyche Zenobia? Alas – *nothing!* I have done.

THE BALLOON HOAX*

Astounding News by Express, via Norfolk! – The Atlantic Crossed in Three Days! Signal Triumph of Mr Monck Mason's Flying Machine! – Arrival at Sullivan's Island, near Charlestown, SC,* of Mr Mason, Mr Robert Holland, Mr Henson, Mr Harrison Ainsworth* and four others, in the Steering Balloon *Victoria*, after a Passage of Seventy-five Hours from Land to Land! Full Particulars of the Voyage!

[The subjoined *jeu d'esprit* with the preceding heading in magnificent capitals, well interspersed with notes of admiration, was originally published, as matter of fact, in the *New York Sun*, a daily newspaper, and therein fully subserved the purpose of creating indigestible aliment for the quidnuncs* during the few hours intervening between a couple of the Charleston mails. The rush for the "sole paper which had the news" was something beyond even the prodigious, and, in fact, if (as some assert) the *Victoria did* not absolutely accomplish the voyage recorded, it will be difficult to assign a reason why she *should* not have accomplished it.]

The great problem is at length solved! The air, as well as the earth and the ocean, has been subdued by science, and will become a common and convenient highway for mankind. *The Atlantic has been actually crossed in a balloon!* And this too without difficulty – without any great apparent danger – with thorough control of the machine – and in the inconceivably brief period of seventy-five hours from shore to shore! By the energy of an agent at Charleston, SC, we are enabled to be the first to furnish the public with a detailed account of this most extraordinary voyage, which was performed between Saturday, the 6th instant, at 11 a.m., and 2 p.m., on Tuesday, the 9th instant, by Sir Everard Bringhurst; Mr Osborne, a nephew of Lord Bentinck's;* Mr Monck Mason and Mr

Robert Holland, the well-known aeronauts; Mr Harrison Ainsworth, author of *Jack Sheppard*, etc.; and Mr Henson, the projector of the late unsuccessful flying machine – with two seamen from Woolwich – in all, eight persons. The particulars furnished below may be relied on as authentic and accurate in every respect, as, with a slight exception, they are copied verbatim from the joint diaries of Mr Monck Mason and Mr Harrison Ainsworth, to whose politeness our agent is also indebted for much verbal information respecting the balloon itself, its construction and other matters of interest. The only alteration in the MS received has been made for the purpose of throwing the hurried account of our agent, Mr Forsyth, in a connected and intelligible form.

THE BALLOON

Two very decided failures, of late – those of Mr Henson and Sir George Cayley* – had much weakened the public interest in the subject of aerial navigation. Mr Henson's scheme (which at first was considered very feasible even by men of science) was founded upon the principle of an inclined plane, started from an eminence by an extrinsic force, applied and continued by the revolution of impinging vanes, in form and number resembling the vanes of a windmill. But, in all the experiments made with models at the Adelaide Gallery, it was found that the operation of these fans not only did not propel the machine, but actually impeded its flight. The only propelling force it ever exhibited was the mere impetus acquired from the descent of the inclined plane, and this impetus carried the machine farther when the vanes were at rest than when they were in motion – a fact which sufficiently demonstrates their inutility; and in the absence of the propelling, which was also the *sustaining*, power, the whole fabric would necessarily descend. This consideration led Sir George Cayley to think only of adapting a propeller to some machine having of itself an independent power of support – in a word, to a balloon; the idea, however, being novel, or original, with Sir George, only so far as regards the mode of its application to practice. He exhibited a model of his invention at the Polytechnic Institution. The propelling principle, or power, was here, also, applied to interrupted surfaces, or vanes, put in revolution. These vanes were four in number, but were found entirely ineffectual in moving the balloon, or in aiding its ascending power. The whole project was thus a complete failure.

It was at this juncture that Mr Monck Mason (whose voyage from Dover to Weilburg in the balloon *Nassau* occasioned so much excitement in 1837) conceived the idea of employing the principle of the Archimedean screw* for the purpose of propulsion through the air – rightly attributing the failure of Mr Henson's scheme, and of Sir George Cayley's, to the interruption of surface in the independent vanes. He made the first public experiment at Willis's Rooms,* but afterwards removed his model to the Adelaide Gallery.

Like Sir George Cayley's balloon, his own was an ellipsoid. Its length was thirteen feet six inches – height, six feet eight inches. It contained about three hundred and twenty cubic feet of gas, which, if pure hydrogen, would support twenty-one pounds upon its first inflation, before the gas has time to deteriorate or escape. The weight of the whole machine and apparatus was seventeen pounds – leaving about four pounds to spare. Beneath the centre of the balloon was a frame of light wood, about nine feet long, and rigged onto the balloon itself with a network in the customary manner. From this framework was suspended a wicker basket or car.

The screw consists of an axis of hollow brass tube, eighteen inches in length, through which, upon a semi-spiral inclined at fifteen degrees, pass a series of steel-wire radii, two feet long, and thus projecting a foot on either side. These radii are connected at the outer extremities by two bands of flattened wire – the whole in this manner forming the framework of the screw, which is completed by a covering of oiled silk cut into gores,* and tightened so as to present a tolerably uniform surface. At each end of its axis this screw is supported by pillars of hollow brass tube descending from the hoop. In the lower ends of these tubes are holes in which the pivots of the axis revolve. From the end of the axis which is next the car proceeds a shaft of steel, connecting the screw with the pinion of a piece of spring machinery fixed in the car. By the operation of this spring, the screw is made to revolve with great rapidity, communicating a progressive motion to the whole. By means of the rudder, the machine was readily turned in any direction. The spring was of great power, compared with its dimensions, being capable of raising forty-five pounds upon a barrel of four inches diameter, after the first turn, and gradually increasing as it was wound up. It weighed, altogether, eight pounds six ounces. The rudder was a light frame of cane covered with silk, shaped somewhat like a battledore,* and was about three feet long, and, at the widest, one foot. Its weight was about two ounces. It could be turned *flat*, and directed upwards or downwards, as well as to the right

or left, and thus enabled the aeronaut to transfer the resistance of the air, which in an inclined position it must generate in its passage, to any side upon which he might desire to act, thus determining the balloon in the opposite direction.

This model (which, through want of time, we have necessarily described in an imperfect manner) was put in action at the Adelaide Gallery, where it accomplished a velocity of five miles per hour, although, strange to say, it excited very little interest in comparison with the previous complex machine of Mr Henson – so resolute is the world to despise anything which carries with it an air of simplicity. To accomplish the great desideratum of aerial navigation, it was very generally supposed that some exceedingly complicated application must be made of some unusually profound principle in dynamics.

So well satisfied, however, was Mr Mason of the ultimate success of his invention that he determined to construct immediately, if possible, a balloon of sufficient capacity to test the question by a voyage of some extent – the original design being to cross the British Channel,* as before, in the *Nassau* balloon. To carry out his views, he solicited and obtained the patronage of Sir Everard Bringhurst and Mr Osborne, two gentlemen well known for scientific acquirement, and especially for the interest they have exhibited in the progress of aerostation.* The project, at the desire of Mr Osborne, was kept a profound secret from the public – the only persons entrusted with the design being those actually engaged in the construction of the machine, which was built (under the superintendence of Mr Mason, Mr Holland, Sir Everard Bringhurst and Mr Osborne) at the seat of the latter gentleman near Penstruthal, in Wales.* Mr Henson, accompanied by his friend Mr Ainsworth, was admitted to a private view of the balloon, on Saturday last – when the two gentlemen made final arrangements to be included in the adventure. We are not informed for what reason the two seamen were also included in the party – but, in the course of a day or two, we shall put our readers in possession of the minutest particulars respecting this extraordinary voyage.

The balloon is composed of silk, varnished with the liquid gum caoutchouc.* It is of vast dimensions, containing more than 40,000 cubic feet of gas, but as coal gas was employed in place of the more expensive and inconvenient hydrogen, the supporting power of the machine, when fully inflated, and immediately after inflation, is not more than about 2,500 pounds. The coal gas is not only much less costly, but is easily procured and managed.

For its introduction into common use for purposes of aerostation, we are indebted to Mr Charles Green.* Up to his discovery, the process of inflation was not only exceedingly expensive, but uncertain. Two and even three days have frequently been wasted in futile attempts to procure a sufficiency of hydrogen to fill a balloon, from which it had great tendency to escape, owing to its extreme subtlety, and its affinity for the surrounding atmosphere. In a balloon sufficiently perfect to retain its contents of coal gas unaltered, in quantity or amount, for six months, an equal quantity of hydrogen could not be maintained in equal purity for six weeks.

The supporting power being estimated at 2,500 pounds,* and the united weights of the party amounting only to about 1,200, there was left a surplus of 1,300, of which again 1,200 was exhausted by ballast, arranged in bags of different sizes, with their respective weights marked upon them – by cordage, barometers, telescopes, barrels containing provision for a fortnight, water casks, cloaks, carpetbags and various other indispensable matters, including a coffee-warmer, contrived for warming coffee by means of slack-lime,* so as to dispense altogether with fire, if it should be judged prudent to do so. All these articles, with the exception of the ballast, and a few trifles, were suspended from the hoop overhead. The car is much smaller and lighter, in proportion, than the one appended to the model. It is formed of a light wicker, and is wonderfully strong for so frail-looking a machine. Its rim is about four feet deep. The rudder is also very much larger, in proportion, than that of the model, and the screw is considerably smaller. The balloon is furnished besides with a grapnel and a guide rope, which latter is of the most indispensable importance. A few words, in explanation, will here be necessary for such of our readers as are not conversant with the details of aerostation.

As soon as the balloon quits the earth, it is subjected to the influence of many circumstances tending to create a difference in its weight, augmenting or diminishing its ascending power. For example, there may be a deposition of dew upon the silk, to the extent, even, of several hundred pounds; ballast has then to be thrown out, or the machine may descend. This ballast being discarded, and a clear sunshine evaporating the dew, and at the same time expanding the gas in the silk, the whole will again rapidly ascend. To check this ascent, the only resource is (or rather *was*, until Mr Green's invention of the guide rope) the permission of the escape of gas from the valve, but, in the loss of gas, is a proportionate general loss of ascending power, so that, in a comparatively brief period, the

best-constructed balloon must necessarily exhaust all its resources, and come to the earth. This was the great obstacle to voyages of length.

The guide rope remedies the difficulty in the simplest manner conceivable. It is merely a very long rope which is suffered to trail from the car, and the effect of which is to prevent the balloon from changing its level in any material degree. If, for example, there should be a deposition of moisture upon the silk, and the machine begins to descend in consequence, there will be no necessity for discharging ballast to remedy the increase of weight, for it is remedied, or counteracted, in an exactly just proportion, by the deposit on the ground of just so much of the end of the rope as is necessary. If, on the other hand, any circumstances should cause undue levity, and consequent ascent, this levity is immediately counteracted by the additional weight of rope upraised from the earth. Thus, the balloon can neither ascend or descend, except within very narrow limits, and its resources, either in gas or ballast, remain comparatively unimpaired. When passing over an expanse of water, it becomes necessary to employ small kegs of copper or wood, filled with liquid ballast of a lighter nature than water. These float, and serve all the purposes of a mere rope on land. Another most important office of the guide rope is to point out the *direction* of the balloon. The rope *drags*, either on land or sea, while the balloon is free; the latter, consequently, is always in advance, when any progress whatever is made: a comparison, therefore, by means of the compass, of the relative positions of the two objects, will always indicate the *course*. In the same way, the angle formed by the rope with the vertical axis of the machine, indicates the *velocity*. When there is *no* angle – in other words, when the rope hangs perpendicularly, the whole apparatus is stationary, but the larger the angle, that is to say, the farther the balloon precedes the end of the rope, the greater the velocity, and the converse.

As the original design was to cross the British Channel, and alight as near Paris as possible, the voyagers had taken the precaution to prepare themselves with passports directed to all parts of the Continent, specifying the nature of the expedition, as in the case of the *Nassau* voyage, and entitling the adventurers to exemption from the usual formalities of office; unexpected events, however, rendered these passports superfluous.

The inflation was commenced very quietly at daybreak, on Saturday morning, the 6th instant, in the courtyard of Weal-Vor House,* Mr Osborne's seat, about a mile from Penstruthal, in North Wales, and at seven minutes past eleven, everything being ready for departure, the balloon was set free, rising gently but steadily, in a direction nearly south, no use being

made, for the first half-hour, of either the screw or the rudder. We proceed now with the journal, as transcribed by Mr Forsyth from the joint MSS of Mr Monck Mason and Mr Ainsworth. The body of the journal, as given, is in the handwriting of Mr Mason, and a P.S. is appended, each day, by Mr Ainsworth, who has in preparation, and will shortly give the public a more minute, and, no doubt, a thrillingly interesting account of the voyage.

THE JOURNAL

Saturday 6th April. Every preparation likely to embarrass us having been made overnight, we commenced the inflation this morning at daybreak, but, owing to a thick fog, which encumbered the folds of the silk and rendered it unmanageable, we did not get through before nearly eleven o'clock. Cut loose, then, in high spirits, and rose gently but steadily, with a light breeze at north, which bore us in the direction of the Bristol Channel.* Found the ascending force greater than we had expected, and as we arose higher and so got clear of the cliffs, and more in the sun's rays, our ascent became very rapid. I did not wish, however, to lose gas at so early a period of the adventure, and so concluded to ascend for the present. We soon ran out our guide rope, but even when we had raised it clear of the earth, we still went up very rapidly. The balloon was unusually steady, and looked beautifully. In about ten minutes after starting, the barometer indicated an altitude of 15,000 feet. The weather was remarkably fine, and the view of the subjacent country – a most romantic one when seen from any point – was now especially sublime. The numerous deep gorges presented the appearance of lakes, on account of the dense vapours with which they were filled, and the pinnacles and crags to the south-east, piled in inextricable confusion, resembling nothing so much as the giant cities of Eastern fable. We were rapidly approaching the mountains in the south, but our elevation was more than sufficient to enable us to pass them in safety. In a few minutes we soared over them in fine style, and Mr Ainsworth, with the seamen, was surprised at their apparent want of altitude when viewed from the car, the tendency of great elevation in a balloon being to reduce inequalities of the surface below to nearly a dead level. At half-past eleven still proceeding nearly south, we obtained our first view of the Bristol Channel, and, in fifteen minutes afterwards, the line of breakers on the coast appeared immediately beneath us, and we were fairly out at sea. We now resolved to let off enough gas to bring our

guide rope, with the buoys affixed, into the water. This was immediately done, and we commenced a gradual descent. In about twenty minutes our first buoy dipped, and, at the touch of the second soon afterwards, we remained stationary as to elevation. We were all now anxious to test the efficiency of the rudder and screw, and we put them both into requisition forthwith, for the purpose of altering our direction more to the eastward, and in a line for Paris. By means of the rudder we instantly effected the necessary change of direction, and our course was brought nearly at right angles to that of the wind, when we set in motion the spring of the screw, and were rejoiced to find it propel us readily as desired. Upon this we gave nine hearty cheers, and dropped in the sea a bottle, enclosing a slip of parchment with a brief account of the principle of the invention. Hardly, however, had we done with our rejoicings when an unforeseen accident occurred which discouraged us in no little degree. The steel rod connecting the spring with the propeller was suddenly jerked out of place, at the car end (by a swaying of the car through some movement of one of the two seamen we had taken up), and in an instant hung dangling out of reach, from the pivot of the axis of the screw. While we were endeavouring to regain it, our attention being completely absorbed, we became involved in a strong current of wind from the east, which bore us, with rapidly increasing force, towards the Atlantic. We soon found ourselves driving out to sea at the rate of not less, certainly, than fifty or sixty miles an hour, so that we came up with Cape Clear,* at some forty miles to our north, before we had secured the rod, and had time to think what we were about. It was now that Mr Ainsworth made an extraordinary but, to my fancy, a by no means unreasonable or chimerical proposition, in which he was instantly seconded by Mr Holland – viz. that we should take advantage of the strong gale which bore us on, and, in place of beating back to Paris, make an attempt to reach the coast of North America. After slight reflection I gave a willing assent to this bold proposition, which (strange to say) met with objection from the two seamen only. As the stronger party, however, we overruled their fears, and kept resolutely upon our course. We steered due west, but as the trailing of the buoys materially impeded our progress, and we had the balloon abundantly at command, either for ascent or descent, we first threw out fifty pounds of ballast, and then wound up (by means of a windlass) so much of the rope as brought it quite clear of the sea. We perceived the effect of this manoeuvre immediately, in a vastly increased rate of progress, and, as the gale freshened, we flew with a velocity nearly inconceivable, the guide rope flying out behind the

car like a streamer from a vessel. It is needless to say that a very short time sufficed us to lose sight of the coast. We passed over innumerable vessels of all kinds, a few of which were endeavouring to beat up, but the most of them lying to.* We occasioned the greatest excitement on board all – an excitement greatly relished by ourselves, and especially by our two men, who, now under the influence of a dram of geneva,* seemed resolved to give all scruple, or fear, to the wind. Many of the vessels fired signal guns, and in all we were saluted with loud cheers (which we heard with surprising distinctness) and the waving of caps and handkerchiefs. We kept on in this manner throughout the day, with no material incident, and, as the shades of night closed around us, we made a rough estimate of the distance traversed. It could not have been less than five hundred miles, and was probably much more. The propeller was kept in constant operation, and, no doubt, aided our progress materially. As the sun went down, the gale freshened into an absolute hurricane, and the ocean beneath was clearly visible on account of its phosphorescence. The wind was from the east all night, and gave us the brightest omen of success. We suffered no little from cold, and the dampness of the atmosphere was most unpleasant, but the ample space in the car enabled us to lie down, and, by means of cloaks and a few blankets, we did sufficiently well.

P.S. [by Mr Ainsworth] The last nine hours have been unquestionably the most exciting of my life. I can conceive nothing more sublimating than the strange peril and novelty of an adventure such as this. May God grant that we succeed! I ask not success for mere safety to my insignificant person, but for the sake of human knowledge and – for the vastness of the triumph. And yet the feat is only so evidently feasible that the sole wonder is why men have scrupled to attempt it before. One single gale such as now befriends us – let such a tempest whirl forward a balloon for four or five days (these gales often last longer) and the voyager will be easily borne, in that period, from coast to coast. In view of such a gale the broad Atlantic becomes a mere lake. I am more struck, just now, with the supreme silence which reigns in the sea beneath us, notwithstanding its agitation, than with any other phenomenon presenting itself. The waters give up no voice to the heavens. The immense flaming ocean writhes and is tortured uncomplainingly. The mountainous surges suggest the idea of innumerable dumb gigantic fiends struggling in impotent agony. In a night such as is this to me, a man *lives* – lives a whole century of ordinary life – nor would I forgo this rapturous delight for that of a whole century of ordinary existence.

Sunday the 7th [Mr Mason's MS] – This morning the gale, by ten, had subsided to an eight- – or nine- – knot breeze (for a vessel at sea), and bears us, perhaps, thirty miles per hour, or more. It has veered, however, very considerably to the north, and now, at sundown, we are holding our course due west, principally by the screw and rudder, which answer their purposes to admiration. I regard the project as thoroughly successful, and the easy navigation of the air in any direction (not exactly in the teeth of a gale) as no longer problematical. We could not have made head against the strong wind of yesterday, but, by ascending, we might have got out of its influence, if requisite. Against a pretty stiff breeze, I feel convinced, we can make our way with the propeller. At noon, today, ascended to an elevation of nearly 25,000 feet, by discharging ballast. Did this to search for a more direct current, but found none so favourable as the one we are now in. We have an abundance of gas to take us across this small pond, even should the voyage last three weeks. I have not the slightest fear for the result. The difficulty has been strangely exaggerated and misapprehended. I can choose my current, and should I find *all* currents against me, I can make very tolerable headway with the propeller. We have had no incidents worth recording. The night promises fair.

P.S. [by Mr Ainsworth] I have little to record, except the fact (to me quite a surprising one) that, at an elevation equal to that of Cotopaxi,* I experienced neither very intense cold, nor headache, nor difficulty of breathing – neither, I find, did Mr Mason, nor Mr Holland, nor Sir Everard. Mr Osborne complained of constriction of the chest – but this soon wore off. We have flown at a great rate during the day, and we must be more than halfway across the Atlantic. We have passed over some twenty or thirty vessels of various kinds, and all seem to be delightfully astonished. Crossing the ocean in a balloon is not so difficult a feat after all. *Omne ignotum pro magnifico.** Mem.: at 25,000 feet elevation the sky appears nearly black, and the stars are distinctly visible, while the sea does not seem convex (as one might suppose) but absolutely and most unequivocally *concave.**

Monday the 8th [Mr Mason's MS] – This morning we had again some little trouble with the rod of the propeller, which must be entirely remodelled, for fear of serious accident – I mean the steel rod, not the vanes. The latter could not be improved. The wind has been blowing steadily and strongly from the north-east all day, and so far Fortune seems bent upon favouring us. Just before day, we were all somewhat alarmed at some odd noises and concussions in the balloon, accompanied with the apparent

rapid subsidence of the whole machine. These phenomena were occasioned by the expansion of the gas, through increase of heat in the atmosphere, and the consequent disruption of the minute particles of ice with which the network had become encrusted during the night. Threw down several bottles to the vessels below. Saw one of them picked up by a large ship – seemingly one of the New York-line packets.* Endeavoured to make out her name, but could not be sure of it. Mr Osborne's telescope made it out something like *Atalanta*. It is now twelve, at night, and we are still going nearly west, at a rapid pace. The sea is peculiarly phosphorescent.

P.S. [by Mr Ainsworth] It is now 2 a.m., and nearly calm, as well as I can judge – but it is very difficult to determine this point, since we move *with* the air so completely. I have not slept since quitting Weal-Vor, but can stand it no longer, and must take a nap. We cannot be far from the American coast.

Tuesday the 9th [Mr Ainsworth's MS] – *1 p.m. We are in full view of the low coast of South Carolina*. The great problem is accomplished. We have crossed the Atlantic – fairly and *easily* crossed it in a balloon! God be praised! Who shall say that anything is impossible hereafter?

*

The journal here ceases. Some particulars of the descent were communicated, however, by Mr Ainsworth to Mr Forsyth. It was nearly dead calm when the voyagers first came in view of the coast, which was immediately recognized by both the seamen, and by Mr Osborne. The latter gentleman having acquaintances at Fort Moultrie,* it was immediately resolved to descend in its vicinity. The balloon was brought over the beach (the tide being out and the sand hard, smooth and admirably adapted for a descent), and the grapnel let go, which took firm hold at once. The inhabitants of the island, and of the fort, thronged out, of course, to see the balloon, but it was with the greatest difficulty that anyone could be made to credit the actual voyage – *the crossing of the Atlantic*. The grapnel caught at 2 p.m. precisely, and thus the whole voyage was completed in seventy-five hours, or rather less, counting from shore to shore. No serious accident occurred. No real danger was at any time apprehended. The balloon was exhausted and secured without trouble, and when the MS from which this narrative is compiled was dispatched from Charleston, the party were still at Fort Moultrie. Their further intentions were not ascertained, but we can safely promise our readers some additional information either on Monday or in the course of the next day, at furthest.

This is unquestionably the most stupendous, the most interesting and the most important undertaking ever accomplished or even attempted by man. What magnificent events may ensue, it would be useless now to think of determining.

THE CASK OF AMONTILLADO*

The thousand injuries of Fortunato I had borne as I best could, but when he ventured upon insult, I vowed revenge. You, who so well know the nature of my soul, will not suppose, however, that I gave utterance to a threat. *At length* I would be avenged: this was a point definitively settled – but the very definitiveness with which it was resolved precluded the idea of risk. I must not only punish, but punish with impunity. A wrong is unredressed when retribution overtakes its redresser. It is equally unredressed when the avenger fails to make himself felt as such to him who has done the wrong.

It must be understood that neither by word nor deed had I given Fortunato cause to doubt my goodwill. I continued, as was my wont, to smile in his face, and he did not perceive that my smile *now* was at the thought of his immolation.

He had a weak point – this Fortunato – although in other regards he was a man to be respected and even feared. He prided himself upon his connoisseurship in wine. Few Italians have the true virtuoso spirit. For the most part their enthusiasm is adopted to suit the time and opportunity – to practise imposture upon the British and Austrian millionaires. In painting and gemmary Fortunato, like his countrymen, was a quack – but in the matter of old wines he was sincere. In this respect I did not differ from him materially: I was skilful in the Italian vintages myself, and bought largely whenever I could.

It was about dusk, one evening during the supreme madness of the carnival season,* that I encountered my friend. He accosted me with excessive warmth, for he had been drinking much. The man wore motley. He had on a tight-fitting parti-striped dress, and his head was surmounted by the conical cap and bells. I was so pleased to see him that I thought I should never have done wringing his hand.

I said to him: "My dear Fortunato, you are luckily met. How remarkably well you are looking today! But I have received a pipe* of what passes for amontillado, and I have my doubts."

"How?" said he. "Amontillado? A pipe? Impossible! And in the middle of the carnival!"

"I have my doubts," I replied, "and I was silly enough to pay the full amontillado price without consulting you in the matter. You were not to be found, and I was fearful of losing a bargain."

"Amontillado!"

"I have my doubts."

"Amontillado!"

"And I must satisfy them."

"Amontillado!"

"As you are engaged, I am on my way to Luchresi. If anyone has a critical turn, it is he. He will tell me—"

"Luchresi cannot tell amontillado from sherry."

"And yet some fools will have it that his taste is a match for your own."

"Come, let us go."

"Whither?"

"To your vaults."

"My friend, no – I will not impose upon your good nature. I perceive you have an engagement. Luchresi—"

"I have no engagement – come."

"My friend, no. It is not the engagement, but the severe cold with which I perceive you are afflicted. The vaults are insufferably damp. They are encrusted with nitre."*

"Let us go, nevertheless. The cold is merely nothing. Amontillado! You have been imposed upon. And as for Luchresi, he cannot distinguish sherry from amontillado."

Thus speaking, Fortunato possessed himself of my arm, and, putting on a mask of black silk, and drawing a roquelaire* closely about my person, I suffered him to hurry me to my palazzo.

There were no attendants at home: they had absconded to make merry in honour of the time. I had told them that I should not return until the morning, and had given them explicit orders not to stir from the house. These orders were sufficient, I well knew, to ensure their immediate disappearance, one and all, as soon as my back was turned.

I took from their sconces two flambeaux, and, giving one to Fortunato, bowed him through several suites of rooms to the archway that led into the vaults. I passed down a long and winding staircase, requesting him to be cautious as he followed. We came at length to the foot of the descent, and stood together upon the damp ground of the catacombs of the Montresors.

The gait of my friend was unsteady, and the bells upon his cap jingled as he strode.

"The pipe?" said he.

"It is farther on," said I, "but observe the white webwork which gleams from these cavern walls."

He turned towards me, and looked into my eyes with two filmy orbs that distilled the rheum of intoxication.

"Nitre?" he asked at length.

"Nitre," I replied. "How long have you had that cough?"

"Ugh! Ugh! Ugh!... Ugh! Ugh! Ugh!... Ugh! Ugh! Ugh!... Ugh! Ugh! Ugh!... Ugh! Ugh! Ugh!"

My poor friend found it impossible to reply for many minutes.

"It is nothing," he said at last.

"Come," I said with decision, "we will go back – your health is precious. You are rich, respected, admired, beloved – you are happy, as once I was. You are a man to be missed. For me it is no matter. We will go back – you will be ill, and I cannot be responsible. Besides, there is Luchresi—"

"Enough," he said. "The cough is a mere nothing – it will not kill me. I shall not die of a cough."

"True – true," I replied, "and, indeed, I had no intention of alarming you unnecessarily, but you should use all proper caution. A draught of this Médoc* will defend us from the damps."

Here I knocked off the neck of a bottle which I drew from a long row of its fellows that lay upon the mould.

"Drink," I said, presenting him the wine.

He raised it to his lips with a leer. He paused and nodded to me familiarly, while his bells jingled.

"I drink," he said, "to the buried that repose around us."

"And I to your long life."

He again took my arm, and we proceeded.

"These vaults," he said, "are extensive."

"The Montresors," I replied, "were a great and numerous family."

"I forget your arms."

"A huge human foot d'or, in a field azure; the foot crushes a serpent rampant whose fangs are embedded in the heel."*

"And the motto?"

"*Nemo me impune lacessit.*"*

"Good!" he said.

The wine sparkled in his eyes and the bells jingled. My own fancy grew warm with the Médoc. We had passed through long walls of piled skeletons, with casks and puncheons intermingling, into the inmost recesses of the

catacombs. I paused again, and this time I made bold to seize Fortunato by an arm above the elbow.

"The nitre!" I said. "See, it increases. It hangs like moss upon the vaults. We are below the river's bed. The drops of moisture trickle among the bones. Come, we will go back ere it is too late. Your cough—"

"It is nothing," he said. "Let us go on. But first, another draught of the Médoc."

I broke and reached him a flacon of De Grâve.* He emptied it at a breath. His eyes flashed with a fierce light. He laughed and threw the bottle upwards with a gesticulation I did not understand.

I looked at him in surprise. He repeated the movement – a grotesque one.

"You do not comprehend?" he said.

"Not I," I replied.

"Then you are not of the brotherhood."

"How?"

"You are not of the masons."*

"Yes, yes," I said. "Yes, yes."

"You? Impossible! A mason?"

"A mason," I replied.

"A sign," he said, "a sign."

"It is this," I answered, producing from beneath the folds of my roquelaire a trowel.

"You jest," he exclaimed, recoiling a few paces. "But let us proceed to the amontillado."

"Be it so," I said, replacing the tool beneath the cloak, and again offering him my arm. He leant upon it heavily. We continued our route in search of the amontillado. We passed through a range of low arches, descended, passed on and, descending again, arrived at a deep crypt, in which the foulness of the air caused our flambeaux rather to glow than flame.

At the most remote end of the crypt there appeared another less spacious. Its walls had been lined with human remains, piled to the vault overhead, in the fashion of the great catacombs of Paris. Three sides of this interior crypt were still ornamented in this manner. From the fourth side the bones had been thrown down, and lay promiscuously upon the earth, forming at one point a mound of some size. Within the wall thus exposed by the displacing of the bones we perceived a still interior crypt or recess, in depth about four feet, in width three, in height six or seven. It seemed to have been constructed for no especial use within itself, but formed merely the interval between two of the colossal supports of the

roof of the catacombs, and was backed by one of their circumscribing walls of solid granite.

It was in vain that Fortunato, uplifting his dull torch, endeavoured to pry into the depths of the recess. Its termination the feeble light did not enable us to see.

"Proceed," I said. "Herein is the amontillado. As for Luchresi—"

"He is an ignoramus," interrupted my friend as he stepped unsteadily forward, while I followed immediately at his heels. In an instant he had reached the extremity of the niche, and, finding his progress arrested by the rock, stood stupidly bewildered. A moment more and I had fettered him to the granite. In its surface were two iron staples, distant from each other about two feet, horizontally. From one of these depended a short chain, from the other a padlock. Throwing the links about his waist, it was but the work of a few seconds to secure it. He was too much astounded to resist. Withdrawing the key I stepped back from the recess.

"Pass your hand," I said, "over the wall: you cannot help feeling the nitre. Indeed it is *very* damp. Once more let me *implore* you to return. No? Then I will positively leave you. But I must first render you all the little attentions in my power."

"The amontillado!" ejaculated my friend, not yet recovered from his astonishment.

"True," I replied. "The amontillado."

As I said these words I busied myself among the pile of bones of which I have before spoken. Throwing them aside, I soon uncovered a quantity of building stone and mortar. With these materials and with the aid of my trowel, I began vigorously to wall up the entrance of the niche.

I had scarcely laid the first tier of my masonry when I discovered that the intoxication of Fortunato had in a great measure worn off. The earliest indication I had of this was a low moaning cry from the depth of the recess. It was *not* the cry of a drunken man. There was then a long and obstinate silence. I laid the second tier, and the third, and the fourth, and then I heard the furious vibration of the chain. The noise lasted for several minutes, during which, that I might hearken to it with the more satisfaction, I ceased my labours and sat down upon the bones. When at last the clanking subsided, I resumed the trowel, and finished without interruption the fifth, the sixth and the seventh tier. The wall was now nearly upon a level with my breast. I again paused, and holding the flambeaux over the mason-work, threw a few feeble rays upon the figure within.

A succession of loud and shrill screams, bursting suddenly from the throat of the chained form, seemed to thrust me violently back. For a brief moment I hesitated – I trembled. Unsheathing my rapier, I began to grope with it about the recess, but the thought of an instant reassured me. I placed my hand upon the solid fabric of the catacombs, and felt satisfied. I reapproached the wall. I replied to the yells of him who clamoured. I re-echoed – I aided – I surpassed them in volume and in strength. I did this, and the clamourer grew still.

It was now midnight, and my task was drawing to a close. I had completed the eighth, the ninth and the tenth tier. I had finished a portion of the last and the eleventh – there remained but a single stone to be fitted and plastered in. I struggled with its weight; I placed it partially in its destined position. But now there came from out the niche a low laugh that erected the hairs upon my head. It was succeeded by a sad voice, which I had difficulty in recognizing as that of the noble Fortunato. The voice said:

"Ha ha ha! He he he! A very good joke indeed – an excellent jest. We will have many a rich laugh about it at the palazzo – he he he! – over our wine – he he he!"

"The amontillado!" I said.

"He he he – he he he – yes, the amontillado. But is it not getting late? Will not they be awaiting us at the palazzo, the Lady Fortunato and the rest? Let us be gone."

"Yes," I said, "let us be gone."

"*For the love of God, Montresor!*"

"Yes," I said, "for the love of God!"

But to these words I hearkened in vain for a reply. I grew impatient. I called aloud:

"Fortunato!"

No answer. I called again:

"Fortunato!"

No answer still. I thrust a torch through the remaining aperture and let it fall within. There came forth in return only a jingling of the bells. My heart grew sick – it was the dampness of the catacombs that made it so. I hastened to make an end of my labour. I forced the last stone into its position; I plastered it up. Against the new masonry I re-erected the old rampart of bones. For the half of a century no mortal has disturbed them. *In pace requiescat!**

THE GOLD BUG*

What ho! What ho! This fellow is
dancing mad!
He hath been bitten by the tarantula.
— ALL IN THE WRONG*

Many years ago, I contracted an intimacy with a Mr William Legrand. He was of an ancient Huguenot family, and had once been wealthy, but a series of misfortunes had reduced him to want. To avoid the mortification consequent upon his disasters, he left New Orleans, the city of his forefathers, and took up his residence at Sullivan's Island, near Charleston, South Carolina.

This island is a very singular one. It consists of little else than the sea sand, and is about three miles long. Its breadth at no point exceeds a quarter of a mile. It is separated from the mainland by a scarcely perceptible creek, oozing its way through a wilderness of reeds and slime, a favourite resort of the marsh hen.* The vegetation, as might be supposed, is scant, or at least dwarfish. No trees of any magnitude are to be seen. Near the western extremity, where Fort Moultrie* stands, and where are some miserable frame buildings, tenanted, during summer, by the fugitives from Charleston dust and fever, may be found, indeed, the bristly palmetto, but the whole island, with the exception of this western point, and a line of hard, white beach on the sea coast, is covered with a dense undergrowth of the sweet myrtle so much prized by the horticulturists of England. The shrub here often attains the height of fifteen or twenty feet, and forms an almost impenetrable coppice, burthening the air with its fragrance.

In the inmost recesses of this coppice, not far from the eastern or more remote end of the island, Legrand had built himself a small hut, which he occupied when I first, by mere accident, made his acquaintance. This soon ripened into friendship – for there was much in the recluse to excite interest and esteem. I found him well educated, with unusual powers of mind, but infected with misanthropy, and subject to perverse moods of alternate enthusiasm and melancholy. He had with him many books, but rarely employed them. His chief amusements were gunning and fishing, or sauntering along the beach and through the myrtles, in quest of shells or entomological specimens – his collection of the latter might have been envied by a Swammerdam.* In these excursions he was usually

accompanied by an old Negro, called Jupiter, who had been manumitted*
before the reverses of the family, but who could be induced, neither
by threats nor by promises, to abandon what he considered his right
of attendance upon the footsteps of his young "Massa Will". It is not
improbable that the relatives of Legrand, conceiving him to be somewhat
unsettled in intellect, had contrived to instil this obstinacy into Jupiter,
with a view to the supervision and guardianship of the wanderer.

The winters in the latitude of Sullivan's Island are seldom very severe,
and in the fall of the year it is a rare event indeed when a fire is considered
necessary. About the middle of October, 18—, there occurred, however,
a day of remarkable chilliness. Just before sunset I scrambled my way
through the evergreens to the hut of my friend, whom I had not visited
for several weeks – my residence being, at that time, in Charleston, a
distance of nine miles from the island, while the facilities of passage and
repassage were very far behind those of the present day. Upon reaching
the hut I rapped, as was my custom, and, getting no reply, sought for the
key where I knew it was secreted, unlocked the door and went in. A fine
fire was blazing upon the hearth. It was a novelty, and by no means an
ungrateful one. I threw off an overcoat, took an armchair by the crackling
logs, and awaited patiently the arrival of my hosts.

Soon after dark they arrived, and gave me a most cordial welcome.
Jupiter, grinning from ear to ear, bustled about to prepare some marsh
hens for supper. Legrand was in one of his fits – how else shall I term
them? – of enthusiasm. He had found an unknown bivalve,* forming a
new genus, and, more than this, he had hunted down and secured, with
Jupiter's assistance, a *scarabæus** which he believed to be totally new, but
in respect to which he wished to have my opinion on the morrow.

"And why not tonight?" I asked, rubbing my hands over the blaze, and
wishing the whole tribe of *scarabæi* at the Devil.

"Ah, if I had only known you were here!" said Legrand. "But it's so long
since I saw you, and how could I foresee that you would pay me a visit this
very night of all others? As I was coming home I met Lieutenant G——,
from the fort, and, very foolishly, I lent him the bug, so it will be impos-
sible for you to see it until the morning. Stay here tonight, and I will send
Jup down for it at sunrise. It is the loveliest thing in creation!"

"What? Sunrise?"

"Nonsense! No! The bug. It is of a brilliant gold colour – about the size
of a large hickory nut – with two jet-black spots near one extremity of the
back, and another, somewhat longer, at the other. The antennae are—"

"Dey ain't *no* tin in him, Massa Will, I keep a-tellin on you," here interrupted Jupiter. "De bug is a goole bug, solid, ebery bit of him, inside and all, sep him wing – neber feel half so hebby a bug in my life."

"Well, suppose it is, Jup," replied Legrand, somewhat more earnestly, it seemed to me, than the case demanded, "is that any reason for your letting the birds burn? The colour" – here he turned to me – "is really almost enough to warrant Jupiter's idea. You never saw a more brilliant metallic lustre than the scales emit – but of this you cannot judge till tomorrow. In the mean time I can give you some idea of the shape." Saying this, he seated himself at a small table, on which were a pen and ink, but no paper. He looked for some in a drawer, but found none.

"Never mind," said he at length, "this will answer," and he drew from his waistcoat pocket a scrap of what I took to be very dirty foolscap, and made upon it a rough drawing with the pen. While he did this, I retained my seat by the fire, for I was still chilly. When the design was complete, he handed it to me without rising. As I received it, a loud growl was heard, succeeded by a scratching at the door. Jupiter opened it, and a large Newfoundland, belonging to Legrand, rushed in, leapt upon my shoulders and loaded me with caresses, for I had shown him much attention during previous visits. When his gambols were over, I looked at the paper, and, to speak the truth, found myself not a little puzzled at what my friend had depicted.

"Well!" I said, after contemplating it for some minutes. "This *is* a strange *scarabæus*, I must confess; new to me; never saw anything like it before – unless it was a skull, or a death's head, which it more nearly resembles than anything else that has come under *my* observation."

"A death's head!" echoed Legrand "Oh... yes... well, it has something of that appearance upon paper, no doubt. The two upper black spots look like eyes, eh? And the longer one at the bottom like a mouth – and then the shape of the whole is oval."

"Perhaps so," said I, "but, Legrand, I fear you are no artist. I must wait until I see the beetle itself, if I am to form any idea of its personal appearance."

"Well, I don't know," said he, a little nettled. "I draw tolerably – *should* do it at least – have had good masters, and flatter myself that I am not quite a blockhead."

"But, my dear fellow, you are joking then," said I. "This is a very passable *skull* – indeed, I may say that it is a very excellent skull, according to the vulgar notions about such specimens of physiology – and your *scarabæus* must be the queerest *scarabæus* in the world if it resembles

it. Why, we may get up a very thrilling bit of superstition upon this hint. I presume you will call the bug *scarabæus caput hominis*,* or something of that kind – there are many similar titles in the natural histories. But where are the antennae you spoke of?"

"The antennae!" said Legrand, who seemed to be getting unaccountably warm upon the subject. "I am sure you must see the antennae. I made them as distinct as they are in the original insect, and I presume that is sufficient."

"Well, well," I said, "perhaps you have – still I don't see them" – and I handed him the paper without additional remark, not wishing to ruffle his temper, but I was much surprised at the turn affairs had taken: his ill humour puzzled me – and, as for the drawing of the beetle, there were positively no antennae visible, and the whole *did* bear a very close resemblance to the ordinary cuts* of a death's head.

He received the paper very peevishly, and was about to crumple it, apparently to throw it in the fire, when a casual glance at the design seemed suddenly to rivet his attention. In an instant his face grew violently red – in another as excessively pale. For some minutes he continued to scrutinize the drawing minutely where he sat. At length he arose, took a candle from the table and proceeded to seat himself upon a sea chest in the farthest corner of the room. Here again he made an anxious examination of the paper, turning it in all directions. He said nothing, however, and his conduct greatly astonished me, yet I thought it prudent not to exacerbate the growing moodiness of his temper by any comment. Presently he took from his coat pocket a wallet, placed the paper carefully in it and deposited both in a writing desk, which he locked. He now grew more composed in his demeanour, but his original air of enthusiasm had quite disappeared. Yet he seemed not so much sulky as abstracted. As the evening wore away he became more and more absorbed in reverie, from which no sallies of mine could arouse him. It had been my intention to pass the night at the hut, as I had frequently done before, but, seeing my host in this mood, I deemed it proper to take leave. He did not press me to remain, but, as I departed, he shook my hand with even more than his usual cordiality.

It was about a month after this (and during the interval I had seen nothing of Legrand) when I received a visit, at Charleston, from his man, Jupiter. I had never seen the good old Negro look so dispirited, and I feared that some serious disaster had befallen my friend.

"Well, Jup," said I, "what is the matter now? How is your master?"

"Why, to speak de troof, massa, him not so berry well as mought be."

"Not well! I am truly sorry to hear it. What does he complain of?"

"Dar! Dat's it! Him neber plain of notin – but him berry sick for all dat."

"*Very* sick, Jupiter! Why didn't you say so at once? Is he confined to bed?"

"No, dat he ain't! He ain't find nowhar – dat's just whar de shoe pinch – my mind is got to be berry hebby bout poor Massa Will."

"Jupiter, I should like to understand what it is you are talking about. You say your master is sick. Hasn't he told you what ails him?"

"Why, massa, tain't worf while for to git mad bout de matter – Massa Will say noffin at all ain't de matter wid him – but den what make him go about looking dis here way, wid he head down and he soldiers up, and as white as a gose? And den he keep a syphon all de time—"

"Keeps a what, Jupiter?"

"Keeps a syphon wid de figgurs on de slate – de queerest figgurs I ebber did see. Ise gittin to be skeered, I tell you. Hab for to keep mighty tight eye pon him noovers. Todder day he gib me slip fore de sun up and was gone de whole ob de blessed day. I had a big stick ready cut for to gib him deuced good beating when he did come – but Ise sich a fool dat I hadn't de heart arter all – he look so berry poorly."

"Eh? What? Ah yes! Upon the whole I think you had better not be too severe with the poor fellow – don't flog him, Jupiter – he can't very well stand it – but can you form no idea of what has occasioned this illness, or rather this change of conduct? Has anything unpleasant happened since I saw you?"

"No, massa, dey ain't bin noffin unpleasant *since* den – 'twas *fore* den I'm feared – 'twas de berry day you was dare."

"How? What do you mean?"

"Why, massa, I mean de bug – dare now."

"The what?"

"De bug – I'm berry sartain dat Massa Will bin bit somewhere bout de head by dat goole bug."

"And what cause have you, Jupiter, for such a supposition?"

"Claws enuff, massa, and mouff too. I nebber did see sich a d—d bug – he kick and he bite ebery ting what cum near him. Massa Will cotch him fuss, but had for to let him go gin mighty quick, I tell you – den was de time he must ha got de bite. I didn't like de look ob de bug mouff, myself, nohow, so I wouldn't take hold ob him wid my finger, but I cotch him wid a piece ob paper dat I found. I rap him up in de paper and stuff a piece of it in he mouff – dat was de way."

"And you think, then, that your master was really bitten by the beetle, and that the bite made him sick?"

"I don't think noffin about it – I nose it. What make him dream bout de goole so much, if tain't cause he bit by de goole bug? Ise heerd bout dem goole bugs fore dis."

"But how do you know he dreams about gold?"

"How I know? Why, cause he talk about it in he sleep – dat's how I nose."

"Well, Jup, perhaps you are right, but to what fortunate circumstance am I to attribute the honour of a visit from you today?"

"What de matter, massa?"

"Did you bring any message from Mr Legrand?"

"No, massa, I bring dis here pissel" – and here Jupiter handed me a note which ran thus:

MY DEAR ——

Why have I not seen you for so long a time? I hope you have not been so foolish as to take offence at any little *brusquerie* of mine – but no, that is improbable.

Since I saw you I have had great cause for anxiety. I have something to tell you, yet scarcely know how to tell it, or whether I should tell it at all.

I have not been quite well for some days past, and poor old Jup annoys me, almost beyond endurance, by his well-meant attentions. Would you believe it? He had prepared a huge stick, the other day, with which to chastise me for giving him the slip, and spending the day, *solus*, among the hills on the mainland. I verily believe that my ill looks alone saved me a flogging.

I have made no addition to my cabinet since we met.

If you can, in any way, make it convenient, come over with Jupiter. *Do* come. I wish to see you *tonight*, upon business of importance. I assure you that it is of the *highest* importance.

Ever yours,

WILLIAM LEGRAND

There was something in the tone of this note which gave me great uneasiness. Its whole style differed materially from that of Legrand. What could he be dreaming of? What new crotchet possessed his excitable brain? What "business of the highest importance" could *he* possibly have to transact? Jupiter's account of him boded no good. I dreaded lest the continued pressure of misfortune had, at length, fairly unsettled the reason of my friend. Without a moment's hesitation, therefore, I prepared to accompany the Negro.

Upon reaching the wharf, I noticed a scythe and three spades, all apparently new, lying in the bottom of the boat in which we were to embark.

"What is the meaning of all this, Jup?" I enquired.

"Him syfe, massa, and spade."

"Very true, but what are they doing here?"

"Him de syfe and de spade what Massa Will sis pon my buying for him in de town, and de Debbil's own lot of money I had to gib for em."

"But what, in the name of all that is mysterious, is your 'Massa Will' going to do with scythes and spades?"

"Dat's more dan I know, and Debbil take me if I don't blieve 'tis more dan he know too. But it's all cum ob de bug."

Finding that no satisfaction was to be obtained of Jupiter, whose whole intellect seemed to be absorbed by "de bug", I now stepped into the boat, and made sail. With a fair and strong breeze we soon ran into the little cove to the northward of Fort Moultrie, and a walk of some two miles brought us to the hut. It was about three in the afternoon when we arrived. Legrand had been awaiting us in eager expectation. He grasped my hand with a nervous *empressement** which alarmed me and strengthened the suspicions already entertained. His countenance was pale even to ghastliness, and his deep-set eyes glared with unnatural lustre. After some enquiries respecting his health, I asked him, not knowing what better to say, if he had yet obtained the *scarabæus* from Lieutenant G——.

"Oh, yes," he replied, colouring violently, "I got it from him the next morning. Nothing should tempt me to part with that *scarabæus*. Do you know that Jupiter is quite right about it?"

"In what way?" I asked, with a sad foreboding at heart.

"In supposing it to be a bug of *real gold*." He said this with an air of profound seriousness, and I felt inexpressibly shocked.

"This bug is to make my fortune," he continued with a triumphant smile, "to reinstate me in my family possessions. Is it any wonder, then, that I prize it? Since Fortune has thought fit to bestow it upon me, I have only to use it properly, and I shall arrive at the gold of which it is the index. Jupiter, bring me that *scarabæus*!"

"What! De bug, massa? I'd rudder not go fer trubble dat bug – you mus git him for your own self." Hereupon Legrand arose, with a grave and stately air, and brought me the beetle from a glass case in which it was enclosed. It was a beautiful *scarabæus*, and, at that time, unknown to naturalists – of course a great prize in a scientific point of view. There were two round, black spots near one extremity of the back, and a long one near the other.

The scales were exceedingly hard and glossy, with all the appearance of burnished gold. The weight of the insect was very remarkable, and, taking all things into consideration, I could hardly blame Jupiter for his opinion respecting it, but what to make of Legrand's agreement with that opinion, I could not, for the life of me, tell.

"I sent for you," said he, in a grandiloquent tone, when I had completed my examination of the beetle, "I sent for you that I might have your counsel and assistance in furthering the views of Fate and of the bug—"

"My dear Legrand," I cried, interrupting him, "you are certainly unwell, and had better use some little precautions. You shall go to bed, and I will remain with you a few days, until you get over this. You are feverish and—"

"Feel my pulse," said he.

I felt it, and, to say the truth, found not the slightest indication of fever.

"But you may be ill and yet have no fever. Allow me this once to prescribe for you. In the first place go to bed. In the next—"

"You are mistaken," he interposed. "I am as well as I can expect to be under the excitement which I suffer. If you really wish me well, you will relieve this excitement."

"And how is this to be done?"

"Very easily. Jupiter and myself are going upon an expedition into the hills, upon the mainland, and, in this expedition, we shall need the aid of some person in whom we can confide. You are the only one we can trust. Whether we succeed or fail, the excitement which you now perceive in me will be equally allayed."

"I am anxious to oblige you in any way," I replied, "but do you mean to say that this infernal beetle has any connection with your expedition into the hills?"

"It has."

"Then, Legrand, I can become a party to no such absurd proceeding."

"I am sorry – very sorry – for we shall have to try it by ourselves."

"Try it by yourselves! The man is surely mad! But stay! How long do you propose to be absent?"

"Probably all night. We shall start immediately, and be back, at all events, by sunrise."

"And will you promise me, upon your honour, that when this freak of yours is over, and the bug business (good God!) settled to your satisfaction, you will then return home and follow my advice implicitly, as that of your physician?"

"Yes, I promise – and now let us be off, for we have no time to lose."

With a heavy heart I accompanied my friend. We started about four o'clock – Legrand, Jupiter, the dog and myself. Jupiter had with him the scythe and spades – the whole of which he insisted upon carrying – more through fear, it seemed to me, of trusting either of the implements within reach of his master than from any excess of industry or complaisance. His demeanour was dogged in the extreme, and "dat d—d bug" were the sole words which escaped his lips during the journey. For my own part, I had charge of a couple of dark lanterns,* while Legrand contented himself with the *scarabæus*, which he carried attached to the end of a bit of whip-cord, twirling it to and fro, with the air of a conjuror, as he went. When I observed this last, plain evidence of my friend's aberration of mind, I could scarcely refrain from tears. I thought it best, however, to humour his fancy, at least for the present, or until I could adopt some more energetic measures with a chance of success. In the mean time I endeavoured, but all in vain, to sound him in regard to the object of the expedition. Having succeeded in inducing me to accompany him, he seemed unwilling to hold conversation upon any topic of minor importance, and to all my questions vouchsafed no other reply than "We shall see!"

We crossed the creek at the head of the island by means of a skiff, and, ascending the high grounds on the shore of the mainland, proceeded in a north-westerly direction, through a tract of country excessively wild and desolate, where no trace of a human footstep was to be seen. Legrand led the way with decision, pausing only for an instant, here and there, to consult what appeared to be certain landmarks of his own contrivance upon a former occasion.

In this manner we journeyed for about two hours, and the sun was just setting when we entered a region infinitely more dreary than any yet seen. It was a species of tableland, near the summit of an almost inaccessible hill, densely wooded from base to pinnacle, and interspersed with huge crags that appeared to lie loosely upon the soil, and in many cases were prevented from precipitating themselves into the valleys below, merely by the support of the trees against which they reclined. Deep ravines, in various directions, gave an air of still sterner solemnity to the scene.

The natural platform to which we had clambered was thickly overgrown with brambles, through which we soon discovered that it would have been impossible to force our way but for the scythe, and Jupiter, by direction of his master, proceeded to clear for us a path to the foot of an enormously tall tulip tree,* which stood, with some eight or ten oaks, upon the level, and far surpassed them all, and all other trees which I had then ever seen,

in the beauty of its foliage and form, in the wide spread of its branches, and in the general majesty of its appearance. When we reached this tree, Legrand turned to Jupiter, and asked him if he thought he could climb it. The old man seemed a little staggered by the question, and for some moments made no reply. At length he approached the huge trunk, walked slowly around it and examined it with minute attention. When he had completed his scrutiny, he merely said:

"Yes, massa, Jup climb any tree he ebber see in he life."

"Then up with you as soon as possible, for it will soon be too dark to see what we are about."

"How far mus go up, massa?" enquired Jupiter.

"Get up the main trunk first, and then I will tell you which way to go – and here – stop! Take this beetle with you."

"De bug, Massa Will! De goole bug!" cried the Negro, drawing back in dismay. "What for mus tote de bug way up de tree? D—n if I do!"

"If you are afraid, Jup, a great big Negro like you, to take hold of a harmless little dead beetle, why you can carry it up by this string – but, if you do not take it up with you in some way, I shall be under the necessity of breaking your head with this shovel."

"What de matter now, massa?" said Jup, evidently shamed into compliance. "Always want for to raise fuss wid old nigger. Was only funnin anyhow. *Me* feered de bug! What I keer for de bug?" Here he took cautiously hold of the extreme end of the string, and, maintaining the insect as far from his person as circumstances would permit, prepared to ascend the tree.

In youth, the tulip tree, or *Liriodendron tulipiferum*, the most magnificent of American foresters, has a trunk peculiarly smooth, and often rises to a great height without lateral branches, but, in its riper age, the bark becomes gnarled and uneven, while many short limbs make their appearance on the stem. Thus the difficulty of ascension, in the present case, lay more in semblance than in reality. Embracing the huge cylinder, as closely as possible, with his arms and knees, seizing with his hands some projections, and resting his naked toes upon others, Jupiter, after one or two narrow escapes from falling, at length wriggled himself into the first great fork, and seemed to consider the whole business as virtually accomplished. The *risk* of the achievement was, in fact, now over, although the climber was some sixty or seventy feet from the ground.

"Which way mus go now, Massa Will?" he asked.

"Keep up the largest branch – the one on this side," said Legrand. The Negro obeyed him promptly, and apparently with but little trouble,

ascending higher and higher, until no glimpse of his squat figure could be obtained through the dense foliage which enveloped it. Presently his voice was heard in a sort of halloo.

"How much fudder is got for go?"

"How high up are you?" asked Legrand.

"Ebber so fur," replied the Negro. "Can see de sky fru de top ob de tree."

"Never mind the sky, but attend to what I say. Look down the trunk and count the limbs below you on this side. How many limbs have you passed?"

"One, two, tree, four, fibe – I done pass fibe big limb, massa, pon dis side."

"Then go one limb higher."

In a few minutes the voice was heard again, announcing that the seventh limb was attained.

"Now, Jup," cried Legrand, evidently much excited, "I want you to work your way out upon that limb as far as you can. If you see anything strange, let me know."

By this time what little doubt I might have entertained of my poor friend's insanity was put finally at rest. I had no alternative but to conclude him stricken with lunacy, and I became seriously anxious about getting him home. While I was pondering upon what was best to be done, Jupiter's voice was again heard.

"Mos feerd for to ventur pon dis limb berry far – 'tis dead limb putty much all de way."

"Did you say it was a *dead* limb, Jupiter?" cried Legrand in a quavering voice.

"Yes, massa, him dead as de doornail – done up for sartain – done departed dis here life."

"What in the name of Heaven shall I do?" asked Legrand, seemingly in the greatest distress.

"Do!" said I, glad of an opportunity to interpose a word. "Why come home and go to bed. Come now! That's a fine fellow. It's getting late, and, besides, you remember your promise."

"Jupiter," cried he, without heeding me in the least, "do you hear me?"

"Yes, Massa Will, hear you ebber so plain."

"Try the wood well, then, with your knife, and see if you think it *very* rotten."

"Him rotten, massa, sure nuff," replied the Negro in a few moments, "but not so berry rotten as mought be. Mought ventur out leetle way pon de limb by myself, dat's true."

"By yourself! What do you mean?"

"Why, I mean de bug. 'Tis *berry* hebby bug. Spose I drop him down fuss, and den de limb won't break wid just de weight ob one nigger."

"You infernal scoundrel!" cried Legrand, apparently much relieved. "What do you mean by telling me such nonsense as that? As sure as you let that beetle fall I'll break your neck. Look here, Jupiter, do you hear me?"

"Yes, massa, needn't hollo at poor nigger dat style."

"Well! Now listen! If you will venture out on the limb as far as you think safe, and not let go the beetle, I'll make you a present of a silver dollar as soon as you get down."

"I'm gwine, Massa Will – deed I is," replied the Negro very promptly. "Mos out to the eend now."

"*Out to the end!*" here fairly screamed Legrand. "Do you say you are out to the end of that limb?"

"Soon be to de eend, massa – o-o-o-o-oh! Lor-gol-a-marcy! What is dis here pon de tree?"

"Well?" cried Legrand, highly delighted. "What is it?"

"Why tain't noffin but a skull – somebody bin lef him head up de tree, and de crows done gobble ebery bit ob de meat off."

"A skull, you say! Very well – how is it fastened to the limb? What holds it on?"

"Sure nuff, massa – mus look. Why dis berry curous sarcumstance, pon my word – dare's a great big nail in de skull, what fastens ob it on to de tree."

"Well now, Jupiter, do exactly as I tell you – do you hear?"

"Yes, massa."

"Pay attention, then – find the left eye of the skull."

"Hum! Hoo! Dat's good! Why dar ain't no eye lef at all."

"Curse your stupidity! Do you know your right hand from your left?"

"Yes, I nose dat – nose all bout dat – 'tis my lef hand what I chops de wood wid."

"To be sure! You are left-handed, and your left eye is on the same side as your left hand. Now, I suppose, you can find the left eye of the skull, or the place where the left eye has been. Have you found it?"

Here was a long pause. At length the Negro asked:

"Is de lef eye of de skull pon de same side as de lef hand of de skull too? Cause de skull ain't got not a bit ob a hand at all – nebber mind! I got de lef eye now – here de lef eye! What mus do wid it?"

"Let the beetle drop through it, as far as the string will reach – but be careful and not let go your hold of the string."

"All dat done, Massa Will; mighty easy ting for to put de bug fru de hole – look out for him dar below!"

During this colloquy no portion of Jupiter's person could be seen, but the beetle, which he had suffered to descend, was now visible at the end of the string, and glistened, like a globe of burnished gold, in the last rays of the setting sun, some of which still faintly illumined the eminence upon which we stood. The *scarabæus* hung quite clear of any branches, and, if allowed to fall, would have fallen at our feet. Legrand immediately took the scythe, and cleared with it a circular space, three or four yards in diameter, just beneath the insect, and, having accomplished this, ordered Jupiter to let go the string and come down from the tree.

Driving a peg, with great nicety, into the ground, at the precise spot where the beetle fell, my friend now produced from his pocket a tape measure. Fastening one end of this at that point of the trunk of the tree which was nearest the peg, he unrolled it till it reached the peg, and thence farther unrolled it, in the direction already established by the two points of the tree and the peg, for the distance of fifty feet – Jupiter clearing away the brambles with the scythe. At the spot thus attained a second peg was driven, and about this, as a centre, a rude circle, about four feet in diameter, described. Taking now a spade himself, and giving one to Jupiter and one to me, Legrand begged us to set about digging as quickly as possible.

To speak the truth, I had no especial relish for such amusement at any time, and, at that particular moment, would most willingly have declined it, for the night was coming on, and I felt much fatigued with the exercise already taken, but I saw no mode of escape, and was fearful of disturbing my poor friend's equanimity by a refusal. Could I have depended, indeed, upon Jupiter's aid, I would have had no hesitation in attempting to get the lunatic home by force, but I was too well assured of the old Negro's disposition to hope that he would assist me, under any circumstances, in a personal contest with his master. I made no doubt that the latter had been infected with some of the innumerable Southern superstitions about money buried, and that his fantasy had received confirmation by the finding of the *scarabæus*, or, perhaps, by Jupiter's obstinacy in maintaining it to be "a bug of real gold". A mind disposed to lunacy would readily be led away by such suggestions – especially if chiming in with favourite preconceived ideas – and then I called to mind the poor fellow's speech about the beetle's being "the index of his fortune". Upon the whole, I was sadly vexed and puzzled, but, at length, I concluded to make a virtue of necessity – to dig

with a good will, and thus the sooner to convince the visionary, by ocular demonstration, of the fallacy of the opinions he entertained.

The lanterns having been lit, we all fell to work with a zeal worthy a more rational cause, and, as the glare fell upon our persons and implements, I could not help thinking how picturesque a group we composed, and how strange and suspicious our labours must have appeared to any interloper who, by chance, might have stumbled upon our whereabouts.

We dug very steadily for two hours. Little was said, and our chief embarrassment lay in the yelpings of the dog, who took exceeding interest in our proceedings. He, at length, became so obstreperous that we grew fearful of his giving the alarm to some stragglers in the vicinity – or, rather, this was the apprehension of Legrand; for myself, I should have rejoiced at any interruption which might have enabled me to get the wanderer home. The noise was, at length, very effectually silenced by Jupiter, who, getting out of the hole with a dogged air of deliberation, tied the brute's mouth up with one of his suspenders, and then returned, with a grave chuckle, to his task.

When the time mentioned had expired, we had reached a depth of five feet, and yet no signs of any treasure became manifest. A general pause ensued, and I began to hope that the farce was at an end. Legrand, however, although evidently much disconcerted, wiped his brow thoughtfully and recommenced. We had excavated the entire circle of four feet diameter, and now we slightly enlarged the limit, and went to the farther depth of two feet. Still nothing appeared. The gold-seeker, whom I sincerely pitied, at length clambered from the pit, with the bitterest disappointment imprinted upon every feature, and proceeded, slowly and reluctantly, to put on his coat, which he had thrown off at the beginning of his labour. In the mean time I made no remark. Jupiter, at a signal from his master, began to gather up his tools. This done, and the dog having been unmuzzled, we turned in profound silence towards home.

We had taken, perhaps, a dozen steps in this direction, when, with a loud oath, Legrand strode up to Jupiter and seized him by the collar. The astonished Negro opened his eyes and mouth to the fullest extent, let fall the spades, and fell upon his knees.

"You scoundrel," said Legrand, hissing out the syllables from between his clenched teeth. "You infernal black villain! Speak, I tell you! Answer me this instant, without prevarication! Which – which is your left eye?"

"Oh, my golly, Massa Will! Ain't dis here my lef eye for sartain?" roared the terrified Jupiter, placing his hand upon his *right* organ of vision, and

holding it there with a desperate pertinacity, as if in immediate dread of his master's attempt at a gouge.

"I thought so! I knew it! Hurrah!" vociferated Legrand, letting the Negro go and executing a series of curvets and caracols,* much to the astonishment of his valet, who, arising from his knees, looked, mutely, from his master to myself, and then from myself to his master.

"Come! We must go back," said the latter, "the game's not up yet" – and he again led the way to the tulip tree.

"Jupiter," said he when we reached its foot, "come here! Was the skull nailed to the limb with the face outward, or with the face to the limb?"

"De face was out, massa, so dat de crows could get at de eyes good, widout any trouble."

"Well, then, was it this eye or that through which you let fall the beetle?" – here Legrand touched each of Jupiter's eyes.

"'Twas dis eye, massa – de lef eye – jis as you tell me" – and here it was his right eye that the Negro indicated.

"That will do – we must try it again."

Here my friend, about whose madness I now saw, or fancied that I saw, certain indications of method, removed the peg which marked the spot where the beetle fell to a spot about three inches to the westward of its former position. Taking, now, the tape measure from the nearest point of the trunk to the peg, as before, and continuing the extension in a straight line to the distance of fifty feet, a spot was indicated, removed, by several yards, from the point at which we had been digging.

Around the new position a circle, somewhat larger than in the former instance, was now described, and we again set to work with the spades. I was dreadfully weary, but, scarcely understanding what had occasioned the change in my thoughts, I felt no longer any great aversion from the labour imposed. I had become most unaccountably interested – nay, even excited. Perhaps there was something, amid all the extravagant demeanour of Legrand – some air of forethought, or of deliberation, which impressed me. I dug eagerly, and now and then caught myself actually looking, with something that very much resembled expectation, for the fancied treasure, the vision of which had demented my unfortunate companion. At a period when such vagaries of thought most fully possessed me, and when we had been at work perhaps an hour and a half, we were again interrupted by the violent howlings of the dog. His uneasiness, in the first instance, had been, evidently, but the result of playfulness or caprice, but he now assumed a bitter and serious tone. Upon Jupiter's again attempting to muzzle him,

he made furious resistance, and, leaping into the hole, tore up the mould frantically with his claws. In a few seconds he had uncovered a mass of human bones, forming two complete skeletons, intermingled with several buttons of metal, and what appeared to be the dust of decayed woollen. One or two strokes of a spade upturned the blade of a large Spanish knife, and, as we dug farther, three or four loose pieces of gold and silver coin came to light.

At sight of these the joy of Jupiter could scarcely be restrained, but the countenance of his master wore an air of extreme disappointment. He urged us, however, to continue our exertions, and the words were hardly uttered when I stumbled and fell forward, having caught the toe of my boot in a large ring of iron that lay half buried in the loose earth.

We now worked in earnest, and never did I pass ten minutes of more intense excitement. During this interval we had fairly unearthed an oblong chest of wood, which, from its perfect preservation and wonderful hardness, had plainly been subjected to some mineralizing process – perhaps that of the bi-chloride of mercury.* This box was three feet and a half long, three feet broad, and two and a half feet deep. It was firmly secured by bands of wrought iron, riveted and forming a kind of open trelliswork over the whole. On each side of the chest, near the top, were three rings of iron – six in all – by means of which a firm hold could be obtained by six persons. Our utmost united endeavours served only to disturb the coffer very slightly in its bed. We at once saw the impossibility of removing so great a weight. Luckily, the sole fastenings of the lid consisted of two sliding bolts. These we drew back – trembling and panting with anxiety. In an instant, a treasure of incalculable value lay gleaming before us. As the rays of the lanterns fell within the pit, there flashed upwards, from a confused heap of gold and of jewels, a glow and a glare that absolutely dazzled our eyes.

I shall not pretend to describe the feelings with which I gazed. Amazement was, of course, predominant. Legrand appeared exhausted with excitement, and spoke very few words. Jupiter's countenance wore, for some minutes, as deadly a pallor as it is possible, in the nature of things, for any Negro's visage to assume. He seemed stupefied – thunderstricken. Presently he fell upon his knees in the pit, and, burying his naked arms up to the elbows in gold, let them there remain, as if enjoying the luxury of a bath. At length, with a deep sigh, he exclaimed, as if in a soliloquy:

"And dis all cum ob de goole bug! De putty goole bug! De poor little goole bug, what I boosed in dat sabage kind ob style! Ain't you shamed ob yourself, nigger? Answer me dat!"

THE GOLD BUG

It became necessary, at last, that I should arouse both master and valet to the expediency of removing the treasure. It was growing late, and it behoved us to make exertion, that we might get everything housed before daylight. It was difficult to say what should be done, and much time was spent in deliberation – so confused were the ideas of all. We, finally, lightened the box by removing two thirds of its contents, when we were enabled, with some trouble, to raise it from the hole. The articles taken out were deposited among the brambles, and the dog left to guard them, with strict orders from Jupiter neither, upon any pretence, to stir from the spot, nor to open his mouth until our return. We then hurriedly made for home with the chest, reaching the hut in safety, but after excessive toil, at one o'clock in the morning. Worn out as we were, it was not in human nature to do more just then. We rested until two, and had supper, starting for the hills immediately afterwards, armed with three stout sacks, which, by good luck, were upon the premises. A little before four we arrived at the pit, divided the remainder of the booty, as equally as might be, among us, and, leaving the holes unfilled, again set out for the hut, at which, for the second time, we deposited our golden burthens, just as the first faint streaks of the dawn gleamed from over the treetops in the east.

We were now thoroughly broken down, but the intense excitement of the time denied us repose. After an unquiet slumber of some three or four hours' duration, we arose, as if by preconcert, to make examination of our treasure.

The chest had been full to the brim, and we spent the whole day, and the greater part of the next night, in a scrutiny of its contents. There had been nothing like order or arrangement. Everything had been heaped in promiscuously. Having assorted all with care, we found ourselves possessed of even vaster wealth than we had at first supposed. In coin there was rather more than four hundred and fifty thousand dollars – estimating the value of the pieces, as accurately as we could, by the tables of the period. There was not a particle of silver. All was gold of antique date and of great variety – French, Spanish and German money, with a few English guineas, and some counters,* of which we had never seen specimens before. There were several very large and heavy coins, so worn that we could make nothing of their inscriptions. There was no American money. The value of the jewels we found more difficulty in estimating. There were diamonds – some of them exceedingly large and fine – a hundred and ten in all, and not one of them small; eighteen rubies of remarkable brilliancy; three hundred and ten emeralds, all very beautiful; and twenty-one sapphires, with an opal.

These stones had all been broken from their settings and thrown loose in the chest. The settings themselves, which we picked out from among the other gold, appeared to have been beaten up with hammers, as if to prevent identification. Besides all this, there was a vast quantity of solid gold ornaments; nearly two hundred massive finger- and ear-rings; rich chains – thirty of these, if I remember; eighty-three very large and heavy crucifixes; five gold censers of great value; a prodigious golden punchbowl, ornamented with richly chased vine leaves and Bacchanalian figures;* with two sword handles exquisitely embossed, and many other smaller articles which I cannot recollect. The weight of these valuables exceeded three hundred and fifty pounds avoirdupois, and in this estimate I have not included one hundred and ninety-seven superb gold watches, three of the number being worth each five hundred dollars, if one. Many of them were very old, and as timekeepers valueless, the works having suffered, more or less, from corrosion – but all were richly jewelled and in cases of great worth. We estimated the entire contents of the chest, that night, at a million and a half of dollars, and upon the subsequent disposal of the trinkets and jewels (a few being retained for our own use), it was found that we had greatly undervalued the treasure.

When, at length, we had concluded our examination, and the intense excitement of the time had, in some measure, subsided, Legrand, who saw that I was dying with impatience for a solution of this most extraordinary riddle, entered into a full detail of all the circumstances connected with it.

"You remember," said he, "the night when I handed you the rough sketch I had made of the *scarabœus*. You recollect also that I became quite vexed at you for insisting that my drawing resembled a death's head. When you first made this assertion I thought you were jesting, but afterwards I called to mind the peculiar spots on the back of the insect, and admitted to myself that your remark had some little foundation in fact. Still, the sneer at my graphic powers irritated me – for I am considered a good artist – and, therefore, when you handed me the scrap of parchment, I was about to crumple it up and throw it angrily into the fire."

"The scrap of paper, you mean," said I.

"No – it had much of the appearance of paper, and at first I supposed it to be such, but when I came to draw upon it, I discovered it at once to be a piece of very thin parchment. It was quite dirty, you remember. Well, as I was in the very act of crumpling it up, my glance fell upon the sketch at which you had been looking, and you may imagine my astonishment when I perceived, in fact, the figure of a death's head just where,

it seemed to me, I had made the drawing of the beetle. For a moment I was too much amazed to think with accuracy. I knew that my design was very different in detail from this – although there was a certain similarity in general outline. Presently I took a candle, and, seating myself at the other end of the room, proceeded to scrutinize the parchment more closely. Upon turning it over, I saw my own sketch upon the reverse, just as I had made it. My first idea, now, was mere surprise at the really remarkable similarity of outline – at the singular coincidence involved in the fact that, unknown to me, there should have been a skull upon the other side of the parchment, immediately beneath my figure of the *scarabæus*, and that this skull, not only in outline, but in size, should so closely resemble my drawing. I say the singularity of this coincidence absolutely stupefied me for a time. This is the usual effect of such coincidences. The mind struggles to establish a connection – a sequence of cause and effect – and, being unable to do so, suffers a species of temporary paralysis. But, when I recovered from this stupor, there dawned upon me gradually a conviction which startled me even far more than the coincidence. I began distinctly, positively, to remember that there had been *no* drawing upon the parchment when I made my sketch of the *scarabæus*. I became perfectly certain of this, for I recollected turning up first one side and then the other in search of the cleanest spot. Had the skull been then there, of course I could not have failed to notice it. Here was indeed a mystery which I felt it impossible to explain, but, even at that early moment, there seemed to glimmer, faintly, within the most remote and secret chambers of my intellect, a glow-worm-like conception of that truth which last night's adventure brought to so magnificent a demonstration. I arose at once, and, putting the parchment securely away, dismissed all further reflection until I should be alone.

"When you had gone, and when Jupiter was fast asleep, I betook myself to a more methodical investigation of the affair. In the first place I considered the manner in which the parchment had come into my possession. The spot where we discovered the *scarabæus* was on the coast of the mainland, about a mile eastward of the island, and but a short distance above high-water mark. Upon my taking hold of it, it gave me a sharp bite, which caused me to let it drop. Jupiter, with his accustomed caution, before seizing the insect, which had flown towards him, looked about him for a leaf, or something of that nature, by which to take hold of it. It was at this moment that his eyes, and mine also, fell upon the scrap of parchment, which I then supposed to be paper. It was lying half

buried in the sand, a corner sticking up. Near the spot where we found it, I observed the remnants of the hull of what appeared to have been a ship's longboat. The wreck seemed to have been there for a very great while, for the resemblance to boat timbers could scarcely be traced.

"Well, Jupiter picked up the parchment, wrapped the beetle in it and gave it to me. Soon afterwards we turned to go home, and on the way met Lieutenant G——. I showed him the insect, and he begged me to let him take it to the fort. On my consenting, he thrust it forthwith into his waistcoat pocket, without the parchment in which it had been wrapped, and which I had continued to hold in my hand during his inspection. Perhaps he dreaded my changing my mind, and thought it best to make sure of the prize at once – you know how enthusiastic he is on all subjects connected with natural history. At the same time, without being conscious of it, I must have deposited the parchment in my own pocket.

"You remember that when I went to the table, for the purpose of making a sketch of the beetle, I found no paper where it was usually kept. I looked in the drawer, and found none there. I searched my pockets, hoping to find an old letter – and then my hand fell upon the parchment. I thus detail the precise mode in which it came into my possession, for the circumstances impressed me with peculiar force.

"No doubt you will think me fanciful – but I had already established a kind of *connection*. I had put together two links of a great chain. There was a boat lying on a sea coast, and not far from the boat was a parchment – *not a paper* – with a skull depicted on it. You will, of course, ask 'Where is the connection?' I reply that the skull, or death's head, is the well-known emblem of the pirate. The flag of the death's head is hoisted in all engagements.

"I have said that the scrap was parchment, and not paper. Parchment is durable – almost imperishable. Matters of little moment are rarely consigned to parchment, since, for the mere ordinary purposes of drawing or writing, it is not nearly so well adapted as paper. This reflection suggested some meaning – some relevancy – in the death's head. I did not fail to observe, also, the *form* of the parchment. Although one of its corners had been, by some accident, destroyed, it could be seen that the original form was oblong. It was just such a slip, indeed, as might have been chosen for a memorandum – for a record of something to be long remembered and carefully preserved."

"But," I interposed, "you say that the skull was not upon the parchment when you made the drawing of the beetle. How then do you

trace any connection between the boat and the skull – since this latter, according to your own admission, must have been designed (God only knows how or by whom) at some period subsequent to your sketching the *scarabæus*?"

"Ah, hereupon turns the whole mystery – although the secret, at this point, I had comparatively little difficulty in solving. My steps were sure, and could afford but a single result. I reasoned, for example, thus: when I drew the *scarabæus*, there was no skull apparent on the parchment. When I had completed the drawing I gave it to you, and observed you narrowly until you returned it. *You*, therefore, did not design the skull, and no one else was present to do it. Then it was not done by human agency. And nevertheless it was done.

"At this stage of my reflections I endeavoured to remember, and *did* remember, with entire distinctness, every incident which occurred about the period in question. The weather was chilly (oh, rare and happy accident!), and a fire was blazing on the hearth. I was heated with exercise and sat near the table. You, however, had drawn a chair close to the chimney. Just as I placed the parchment in your hand, and as you were in the act of inspecting it, Wolf, the Newfoundland, entered, and leapt upon your shoulders. With your left hand you caressed him and kept him off, while your right, holding the parchment, was permitted to fall listlessly between your knees, and in close proximity to the fire. At one moment I thought the blaze had caught it, and was about to caution you, but, before I could speak, you had withdrawn it, and were engaged in its examination. When I considered all these particulars, I doubted not for a moment that *heat* had been the agent in bringing to light, on the parchment, the skull which I saw designed on it. You are well aware that chemical preparations exist, and have existed time out of mind, by means of which it is possible to write upon either paper or vellum, so that the characters shall become visible only when subjected to the action of fire. Zaffre, digested in *aqua regia*,* and diluted with four times its weight of water, is sometimes employed – a green tint results. The regulus* of cobalt, dissolved in spirit of nitre, gives a red. These colours disappear at longer or shorter intervals after the material written on cools, but again become apparent upon the reapplication of heat.

"I now scrutinized the death's head with care. Its outer edges – the edges of the drawing nearest the edge of the vellum – were far more *distinct* than the others. It was clear that the action of the caloric had been imperfect or unequal. I immediately kindled a fire, and subjected every portion of the

parchment to a glowing heat. At first, the only effect was the strengthen-
ing of the faint lines in the skull, but, on persevering in the experiment,
there became visible, at the corner of the slip, diagonally opposite to the
spot in which the death's head was delineated, the figure of what I at first
supposed to be a goat. A closer scrutiny, however, satisfied me that it was
intended for a kid."

"Ha ha!" said I. "To be sure I have no right to laugh at you – a mil-
lion and a half of money is too serious a matter for mirth – but you are
not about to establish a third link in your chain – you will not find any
especial connection between your pirates and a goat – pirates, you know,
have nothing to do with goats: they appertain to the farming interest."

"But I have just said that the figure was *not* that of a goat."

"Well, a kid then – pretty much the same thing."

"Pretty much, but not altogether," said Legrand. "You may have heard
of one *Captain* Kidd.* I at once looked on the figure of the animal as a
kind of punning or hieroglyphical signature. I say signature, because its
position on the vellum suggested this idea. The death's head at the corner
diagonally opposite, had, in the same manner, the air of a stamp, or seal.
But I was sorely put out by the absence of all else – of the body to my
imagined instrument – of the text for my context."

"I presume you expected to find a letter between the stamp and the
signature."

"Something of that kind. The fact is, I felt irresistibly impressed with
a presentiment of some vast good fortune impending. I can scarcely say
why. Perhaps, after all, it was rather a desire than an actual belief – but
do you know that Jupiter's silly words, about the bug being of solid gold,
had a remarkable effect on my fancy? And then the series of accidents and
coincidences – these were so *very* extraordinary. Do you observe how mere
an accident it was that these events should have occurred on the *sole* day
of all the year in which it has been, or may be, sufficiently cool for fire, and
that without the fire, or without the intervention of the dog at the precise
moment in which he appeared, I should never have become aware of the
death's head, and so never the possessor of the treasure?"

"But proceed – I am all impatience."

"Well, you have heard, of course, the many stories current – the thousand
vague rumours afloat about money buried, somewhere on the Atlantic
coast, by Kidd and his associates. These rumours must have had some foun-
dation in fact. And that the rumours have existed so long and so continu-
ously, could have resulted, it appeared to me, only from the circumstance

of the buried treasure still *remaining* entombed. Had Kidd concealed his plunder for a time, and afterwards reclaimed it, the rumours would scarcely have reached us in their present unvarying form. You will observe that the stories told are all about money-seekers, not about money-finders. Had the pirate recovered his money, there the affair would have dropped. It seemed to me that some accident – say the loss of a memorandum indicating its locality – had deprived him of the means of recovering it, and that this accident had become known to his followers, who otherwise might never have heard that treasure had been concealed at all, and who, busying themselves in vain, because unguided attempts, to regain it, had given first birth, and then universal currency, to the reports which are now so common. Have you ever heard of any important treasure being unearthed along the coast?"

"Never."

"But that Kidd's accumulations were immense is well known. I took it for granted, therefore, that the earth still held them, and you will scarcely be surprised when I tell you that I felt a hope, nearly amounting to certainty, that the parchment so strangely found involved a lost record of the place of deposit."

"But how did you proceed?"

"I held the vellum again to the fire, after increasing the heat, but nothing appeared. I now thought it possible that the coating of dirt might have something to do with the failure, so I carefully rinsed the parchment by pouring warm water over it, and, having done this, I placed it in a tin pan, with the skull downwards, and put the pan upon a furnace of lighted charcoal. In a few minutes, the pan having become thoroughly heated, I removed the slip, and, to my inexpressible joy, found it spotted, in several places, with what appeared to be figures arranged in lines. Again I placed it in the pan, and suffered it to remain another minute. On taking it off, the whole was just as you see it now."

Here Legrand, having reheated the parchment, submitted it to my inspection. The following characters were rudely traced, in a red tint, between the death's head and the goat:

53‡‡†305))6*;4826)4‡.)4‡);806*;48†8¶60))85;;]8*;:‡*8†83(88)5*†;46
(;88*96*?;8)*‡(;485);5*†2:*‡(;4956*2(5*−4)8¶8*;4069285);)6†8)4‡‡;1
(‡9;48081;8:8‡ 1;48†85;4)485†528806*81(‡9;48;(88;4(‡?34;48)4‡;161
;:188;‡?;

"But," said I, returning him the slip, "I am as much in the dark as ever. Were all the jewels of Golconda* awaiting me on my solution of this enigma, I am quite sure that I should be unable to earn them."

"And yet," said Legrand, "the solution is by no means so difficult as you might be led to imagine from the first hasty inspection of the characters. These characters, as anyone might readily guess, form a cipher – that is to say, they convey a meaning; but then from what is known of Kidd, I could not suppose him capable of constructing any of the more abstruse cryptographs. I made up my mind, at once, that this was of a simple species – such, however, as would appear, to the crude intellect of the sailor, absolutely insoluble without the key."

"And you really solved it?"

"Readily – I have solved others of an abstruseness ten thousand times greater. Circumstances, and a certain bias of mind, have led me to take interest in such riddles, and it may well be doubted whether human ingenuity can construct an enigma of the kind which human ingenuity may not, by proper application, resolve. In fact, having once established connected and legible characters, I scarcely gave a thought to the mere difficulty of developing their import.

"In the present case – indeed in all cases of secret writing – the first question regards the *language* of the cipher, for the principles of solution, so far, especially, as the more simple ciphers are concerned, depend upon, and are varied by, the genius of the particular idiom. In general, there is no alternative but experiment (directed by probabilities) of every tongue known to him who attempts the solution, until the true one be attained. But, with the cipher now before us all difficulty was removed by the signature. The pun on the word 'Kidd' is appreciable in no other language than the English. But for this consideration I should have begun my attempts with the Spanish and French, as the tongues in which a secret of this kind would most naturally have been written by a pirate of the Spanish Main.* As it was, I assumed the cryptograph to be English.

"You observe there are no divisions between the words. Had there been divisions the task would have been comparatively easy. In such case I should have commenced with a collation and analysis of the shorter words, and, had a word of a single letter occurred, as is most likely (*a* or *I*, for example), I should have considered the solution as assured. But, there being no division, my first step was to ascertain the predominant letters, as well as the least frequent. Counting all, I constructed a table,* thus:

Of the character 8	there are	33
;	"	26
4	"	19
‡)	"	16
*	"	13
5	"	12
6	"	11
† 1	"	8
o	"	6
9 2	"	5
: 3	"	4
?	"	3
¶	"	2
] – .	"	1

"Now, in English, the letter which most frequently occurs is *e*. Afterwards, the succession runs thus: *a o i d h n r s t u y c f g l m w b k p q x z*. E, however, predominates so remarkably that an individual sentence of any length is rarely seen in which it is not the prevailing character.

"Here, then, we have, in the very beginning, the groundwork for something more than a mere guess. The general use which may be made of the table is obvious – but, in this particular cipher, we shall only very partially require its aid. As our predominant character is 8, we will commence by assuming it as the *e* of the natural alphabet. To verify the supposition, let us observe if the 8 be seen often in couples – for *e* is doubled with great frequency in English – in such words, for example, as 'meet', 'fleet', 'speed', 'seen', 'been', 'agree', etc. In the present instance we see it doubled no less than five times, although the cryptograph is brief.

"Let us assume 8, then, as *e*. Now, of all *words* in the language, 'the' is most usual; let us see, therefore, whether there are not repetitions of any three characters, in the same order of collocation, the last of them being 8. If we discover repetitions of such letters, so arranged, they will most probably represent the word 'the'. On inspection, we find no less than seven such arrangements, the characters being ;48. We may, therefore, assume that the semicolon represents *t*, that 4 represents *h*, and that 8 represents *e* – the last being now well confirmed. Thus a great step has been taken.

"But, having established a single word, we are enabled to establish a vastly important point: that is to say, several commencements and terminations of other words. Let us refer, for example, to the last instance but one, in

which the combination ;48 occurs – not far from the end of the cipher. We know that the semicolon immediately ensuing is the commencement of a word, and, of the six characters succeeding this 'the', we are cognizant of no less than five. Let us set these characters down, thus, by the letters we know them to represent, leaving a space for the unknown:

t eeth

"Here we are enabled, at once, to discard the 'th', as forming no portion of the word commencing with the first *t* – since, by experiment of the entire alphabet for a letter adapted to the vacancy, we perceive that no word can be formed of which this *th* can be a part. We are thus narrowed into

t ee

and, going through the alphabet, if necessary, as before, we arrive at the word 'tree', as the sole possible reading. We thus gain another letter, *r*, represented by (, with the words 'the tree' in juxtaposition.

"Looking beyond these words for a short distance, we again see the combination ;48, and employ it by way of *termination* to what immediately precedes. We have thus this arrangement:

the tree;4(‡?34 the

or, substituting the natural letters, where known, it reads thus:

the tree thr‡?3h the

"Now, if, in place of the unknown characters, we leave blank spaces, or substitute dots, we read thus:

the tree thr...h the

when the word 'through' makes itself evident at once. But this discovery gives us three new letters: *o*, *u* and *g*, represented by ‡, ? and 3.

"Looking now, narrowly, through the cipher for combinations of known characters, we find, not very far from the beginning, this arrangement:

83(88, or egree

which, plainly, is the conclusion of the word 'degree', and gives us another letter, *d*, represented by †.

"Four letters beyond the word 'degree', we perceive the combination

;46(;88*

"Translating the known characters, and representing the unknown by dots, as before, we read thus:

th.rtee.

an arrangement immediately suggestive of the word 'thirteen', and again furnishing us with two new characters, *i* and *n*, represented by 6 and*.

"Referring, now, to the beginning of the cryptograph, we find the combination

53‡‡†

"Translating, as before, we obtain

.good

which assures us that the first letter is *A*, and that the first two words are 'A good'.

"To avoid confusion, it is now time that we arrange our key, as far as discovered, in a tabular form. It will stand thus:

5	represents	a
†	"	d
8	"	e
3	"	g
4	"	h
6	"	i
*	"	n
‡	"	o
("	r
;	"	t

"We have, therefore, no less than ten* of the most important letters represented, and it will be unnecessary to proceed with the details of the solution. I have said enough to convince you that ciphers of this nature are readily soluble, and to give you some insight into the rationale of their development. But be assured that the specimen before us appertains to the very simplest species of cryptograph. It now only remains to give you the full translation of the characters upon the parchment, as unriddled. Here it is:

"A good glass in the bishop's hostel in the Devil's seat twenty-one degrees and thirteen minutes north-east and by north main branch seventh limb east side shoot from the left eye of the death's head a beeline from the tree through the shot fifty feet out."

"But," said I, "the enigma seems still in as bad a condition as ever. How is it possible to extort a meaning from all this jargon about 'Devil's seats', 'death's heads' and 'bishop's hotels'?"

"I confess," replied Legrand, "that the matter still wears a serious aspect, when regarded with a casual glance. My first endeavour was to divide the sentence into the natural division intended by the cryptographist."

"You mean, to punctuate it?"

"Something of that kind."

"But how was it possible to effect this?"

"I reflected that it had been a *point* with the writer to run his words together without division, so as to increase the difficulty of solution. Now, a not over-acute man, in pursuing such an object, would be nearly certain to overdo the matter. When, in the course of his composition, he arrived at a break in his subject which would naturally require a pause, or a point, he would be exceedingly apt to run his characters, at this place, more than usually close together. If you will observe the MS, in the present instance, you will easily detect five such cases of unusual crowding. Acting on this hint, I made the division thus:

"A good glass in the bishop's hostel in the Devil's seat – twenty-one degrees and thirteen minutes – north-east and by north – main branch seventh limb east side – shoot from the left eye of the death's head – a beeline from the tree through the shot fifty feet out."

"Even this division," said I, "leaves me still in the dark."

"It left me also in the dark," replied Legrand, "for a few days, during which I made diligent enquiry, in the neighbourhood of Sullivan's Island, for any building which went by the name of the 'Bishop's Hotel' – for, of course, I dropped the obsolete word 'hostel'. Gaining no information on the subject, I was on the point of extending my sphere of search, and proceeding in a more systematic manner, when, one morning, it entered into my head, quite suddenly, that this 'Bishop's Hostel' might have some reference to an old family, of the name of Bessop, which, time out of mind, had held possession of an ancient manor house, about four miles to the northward of the island. I accordingly went over to the plantation, and reinstituted my enquiries among the older Negroes of the place. At length one of the most aged of the women said that she had heard of such a place as 'Bessop's Castle', and thought that she could guide me to it, but that it was not a castle, nor a tavern, but a high rock.

"I offered to pay her well for her trouble, and, after some demur, she consented to accompany me to the spot. We found it without much difficulty, when, dismissing her, I proceeded to examine the place. The 'castle' consisted of an irregular assemblage of cliffs and rocks – one of the latter being quite remarkable for its height as well as for its insulated and artificial appearance. I clambered to its apex, and then felt much at a loss as to what should be next done.

"While I was busied in reflection, my eyes fell upon a narrow ledge in the eastern face of the rock, perhaps a yard below the summit on which I stood. This ledge projected about eighteen inches, and was not more than a foot wide, while a niche in the cliff just above it gave it a rude resemblance to one of the hollow-backed chairs used by our ancestors. I made no doubt that here was the 'Devil's seat' alluded to in the MS, and now I seemed to grasp the full secret of the riddle.

"The 'good glass', I knew, could have reference to nothing but a telescope, for the word 'glass' is rarely employed in any other sense by seamen. Now here, I at once saw, was a telescope to be used, and a definite point of view, *admitting no variation*, from which to use it. Nor did I hesitate to believe that the phrases 'twenty-one degrees and thirteen minutes' and 'north-east and by north' were intended as directions for the levelling of the glass. Greatly excited by these discoveries, I hurried home, procured a telescope and returned to the rock.

"I let myself down to the ledge, and found that it was impossible to retain a seat on it unless in one particular position. This fact confirmed my preconceived idea. I proceeded to use the glass. Of course, the 'twenty-one

degrees and thirteen minutes' could allude to nothing but elevation above the visible horizon, since the horizontal direction was clearly indicated by the words 'north-east and by north'. This latter direction I at once established by means of a pocket compass; then, pointing the glass as nearly at an angle of twenty-one degrees of elevation as I could do it by guess, I moved it cautiously up or down, until my attention was arrested by a circular rift or opening in the foliage of a large tree that overtopped its fellows in the distance. In the centre of this rift I perceived a white spot, but could not, at first, distinguish what it was. Adjusting the focus of the telescope, I again looked, and now made it out to be a human skull.

"On this discovery I was so sanguine as to consider the enigma solved, for the phrase 'main branch, seventh limb, east side', could refer only to the position of the skull on the tree, while 'shoot from the left eye of the death's head' admitted, also, of but one interpretation, in regard to a search for buried treasure. I perceived that the design was to drop a bullet from the left eye of the skull, and that a beeline, or, in other words, a straight line, drawn from the nearest point of the trunk through 'the shot' (or the spot where the bullet fell), and thence extended to a distance of fifty feet, would indicate a definite point – and beneath this point I thought it at least possible that a deposit of value lay concealed."

"All this," I said, "is exceedingly clear, and, although ingenious, still simple and explicit. When you left the 'Bishop's Hotel', what then?"

"Why, having carefully taken the bearings of the tree, I turned homewards. The instant that I left 'the Devil's seat', however, the circular rift vanished, nor could I get a glimpse of it afterwards, turn as I would. What seems to me the chief ingenuity in this whole business is the fact (for repeated experiment has convinced me it *is* a fact) that the circular opening in question is visible from no other attainable point of view than that afforded by the narrow ledge on the face of the rock.

"In this expedition to the 'Bishop's Hotel' I had been attended by Jupiter, who had, no doubt, observed, for some weeks past, the abstraction of my demeanour, and took especial care not to leave me alone. But, on the next day, getting up very early, I contrived to give him the slip, and went into the hills in search of the tree. After much toil I found it. When I came home at night my valet proposed to give me a flogging. With the rest of the adventure I believe you are as well acquainted as myself."

"I suppose," said I, "you missed the spot, in the first attempt at digging, through Jupiter's stupidity in letting the bug fall through the right instead of through the left eye of the skull."

"Precisely. This mistake made a difference of about two inches and a half in the 'shot' – that is to say, in the position of the peg nearest the tree, and had the treasure been *beneath* the 'shot', the error would have been of little moment, but 'the shot', together with the nearest point of the tree, were merely two points for the establishment of a line of direction; of course the error, however trivial in the beginning, increased as we proceeded with the line, and by the time we had gone fifty feet threw us quite off the scent. But for my deep-seated conviction that treasure was here somewhere actually buried, we might have had all our labour in vain."

"I presume the fancy of the skull – of letting fall a bullet through the skull's eye – was suggested to Kidd by the piratical flag. No doubt he felt a kind of poetical consistency in recovering his money through this ominous insignium."

"Perhaps so – still I cannot help thinking that common sense had quite as much to do with the matter as poetical consistency. To be visible from the Devil's seat, it was necessary that the object, if small, should be *white*, and there is nothing like your human skull for retaining and even increasing its whiteness under exposure to all vicissitudes of weather."

"But your grandiloquence, and your conduct in swinging the beetle – how excessively odd! I was sure you were mad. And why did you insist on letting fall the bug, instead of a bullet, from the skull?"

"Why, to be frank, I felt somewhat annoyed by your evident suspicions touching my sanity, and so resolved to punish you quietly, in my own way, by a little bit of sober mystification. For this reason I swung the beetle, and for this reason I let it fall from the tree. An observation of yours about its great weight suggested the latter idea."

"Yes, I perceive – and now there is only one point which puzzles me. What are we to make of the skeletons found in the hole?"

"That is a question I am no more able to answer than yourself. There seems, however, only one plausible way of accounting for them – and yet it is dreadful to believe in such atrocity as my suggestion would imply. It is clear that Kidd – if Kidd indeed secreted this treasure, which I doubt not – it is clear that he must have had assistance in the labour. But, the worst of this labour concluded, he may have thought it expedient to remove all participants in his secret. Perhaps a couple of blows with a mattock* were sufficient, while his coadjutors were busy in the pit; perhaps it required a dozen – who shall tell?"

HOP-FROG*

I never knew anyone so keenly alive to a joke as the king was. He seemed to live only for joking. To tell a good story of the joke kind, and to tell it well, was the surest road to his favour. Thus it happened that his seven ministers were all noted for their accomplishments as jokers. They all took after the king, too, in being large, corpulent, oily men, as well as inimitable jokers. Whether people grow fat by joking, or whether there is something in fat itself which predisposes to a joke, I have never been quite able to determine, but certain it is that a lean joker is a *rara avis in terris*.*

About the refinements, or, as he called them, the "ghost" of wit, the king troubled himself very little. He had an especial admiration for *breadth* in a jest, and would often put up with *length*, for the sake of it. Overniceties wearied him. He would have preferred Rabelais's *Gargantua* to the *Zadig* of Voltaire,* and, upon the whole, practical jokes suited his taste far better than verbal ones.

At the date of my narrative, professing jesters had not altogether gone out of fashion at court. Several of the great continental "powers" still retained their "fools", who wore motley, with caps and bells, and who were expected to be always ready with sharp witticisms, at a moment's notice, in consideration of the crumbs that fell from the royal table.*

Our king, as a matter of course, retained his "fool". The fact is, he *required* something in the way of folly – if only to counterbalance the heavy wisdom of the seven wise men who were his ministers – not to mention himself.

His fool, or professional jester, was not *only* a fool, however. His value was trebled in the eyes of the king by the fact of his being also a dwarf and a cripple. Dwarfs were as common at court, in those days, as fools, and many monarchs would have found it difficult to get through their days (days are rather longer at court than elsewhere) without both a jester to laugh *with*, and a dwarf to laugh *at*. But, as I have already observed, your jesters, in ninety-nine cases out of a hundred, are fat, round and unwieldy

– so that it was no small source of self-gratulation with our king that, in Hop-Frog (this was the fool's name), he possessed a triplicate treasure in one person.

I believe the name "Hop-Frog" was *not* that given to the dwarf by his sponsors at baptism, but it was conferred upon him, by general consent of the several ministers, on account of his inability to walk as other men do. In fact, Hop-Frog could only get along by a sort of interjectional gait – something between a leap and a wriggle – a movement that afforded illimitable amusement, and of course consolation, to the king, for (notwithstanding the protuberance of his stomach and a constitutional swelling of the head) the king, by his whole court, was accounted a capital figure.

But although Hop-Frog, through the distortion of his legs, could move only with great pain and difficulty along a road or floor, the prodigious muscular power which nature seemed to have bestowed upon his arms, by way of compensation for deficiency in the lower limbs, enabled him to perform many feats of wonderful dexterity, where trees or ropes were in question, or anything else to climb. At such exercises he certainly much more resembled a squirrel, or a small monkey, than a frog.

I am not able to say, with precision, from what country Hop-Frog originally came. It was from some barbarous region, however, that no person ever heard of – a vast distance from the court of our king. Hop-Frog, and a young girl very little less dwarfish than himself (although of exquisite proportions, and a marvellous dancer), had been forcibly carried off from their respective homes in adjoining provinces, and sent as presents to the king, by one of his ever-victorious generals.

Under these circumstances, it is not to be wondered at that a close intimacy arose between the two little captives. Indeed, they soon became sworn friends. Hop-Frog, who, although he made a great deal of sport, was by no means popular, had it not in his power to render Trippetta many services, but *she*, on account of her grace and exquisite beauty (although a dwarf), was universally admired and petted – so she possessed much influence, and never failed to use it, whenever she could, for the benefit of Hop-Frog.

On some grand state occasion – I forgot what – the king determined to have a masquerade, and whenever a masquerade, or anything of that kind, occurred at our court, then the talents both of Hop-Frog and Trippetta were sure to be called in play. Hop-Frog, in especial, was so inventive in the way of getting up pageants, suggesting novel characters and arranging costume, for masked balls, that nothing could be done, it seems, without his assistance.

The night appointed for the fête had arrived. A gorgeous hall had been fitted up, under Trippetta's eye, with every kind of device which could possibly give éclat to a masquerade. The whole court was in a fever of expectation. As for costumes and characters, it might well be supposed that everybody had come to a decision on such points. Many had made up their minds (as to what roles they should assume) a week, or even a month, in advance, and, in fact, there was not a particle of indecision anywhere – except in the case of the king and his seven ministers. Why *they* hesitated I never could tell, unless they did it by way of a joke. More probably, they found it difficult, on account of being so fat, to make up their minds. At all events, time flew, and, as a last resource, they sent for Trippetta and Hop-Frog.

When the two little friends obeyed the summons of the king, they found him sitting at his wine with the seven members of his cabinet council, but the monarch appeared to be in a very ill humour. He knew that Hop-Frog was not fond of wine, for it excited the poor cripple almost to madness, and madness is no comfortable feeling. But the king loved his practical jokes, and took pleasure in forcing Hop-Frog to drink and (as the king called it) "to be merry".

"Come here, Hop-Frog," said he as the jester and his friend entered the room. "Swallow this bumper to the health of your absent friends" (here Hop-Frog sighed) "and then let us have the benefit of your invention. We want characters – *characters*, man – something novel – out of the way. We are wearied with this everlasting sameness. Come, drink! The wine will brighten your wits."

Hop-Frog endeavoured, as usual, to get up a jest in reply to these advances from the king, but the effort was too much. It happened to be the poor dwarf's birthday, and the command to drink to his "absent friends" forced the tears to his eyes. Many large, bitter drops fell into the goblet as he took it, humbly, from the hand of the tyrant.

"Ah! Ha ha ha!" roared the latter as the dwarf reluctantly drained the beaker. "See what a glass of good wine can do! Why, your eyes are shining already!"

Poor fellow! His large eyes *gleamed*, rather than shone, for the effect of wine on his excitable brain was not more powerful than instantaneous. He placed the goblet nervously on the table, and looked round upon the company with a half-insane stare. They all seemed highly amused at the success of the king's "joke".

"And now to business," said the prime minister, a *very* fat man.

"Yes," said the king. "Come, Hop-Frog, lend us your assistance. Characters, my fine fellow: we stand in need of characters – all of us – ha ha ha!" – and as this was seriously meant for a joke, his laugh was chorused by the seven.

Hop-Frog also laughed, although feebly and somewhat vacantly.

"Come, come," said the king impatiently, "have you nothing to suggest?"

"I am endeavouring to think of something *novel*," replied the dwarf abstractedly, for he was quite bewildered by the wine.

"Endeavouring!" cried the tyrant fiercely. "What do you mean by *that*? Ah, I perceive. You are sulky, and want more wine. Here, drink this!" – and he poured out another gobletful and offered it to the cripple, who merely gazed at it, gasping for breath.

"Drink, I say!" shouted the monster. "Or by the fiends…"

The dwarf hesitated. The king grew purple with rage. The courtiers smirked. Trippetta, pale as a corpse, advanced to the monarch's seat, and, falling on her knees before him, implored him to spare her friend.

The tyrant regarded her, for some moments, in evident wonder at her audacity. He seemed quite at a loss what to do or say – how most becomingly to express his indignation. At last, without uttering a syllable, he pushed her violently from him, and threw the contents of the brimming goblet in her face.

The poor girl got up as best she could, and, not daring even to sigh, resumed her position at the foot of the table.

There was a dead silence for about half a minute, during which the falling of a leaf, or of a feather, might have been heard. It was interrupted by a low, but harsh and protracted *grating* sound which seemed to come at once from every corner of the room.

"What – what – *what* are you making that noise for?" demanded the king, turning furiously to the dwarf.

The latter seemed to have recovered, in great measure, from his intoxication, and, looking fixedly but quietly into the tyrant's face, merely ejaculated:

"I – I? How could it have been me?"

"The sound appeared to come from without," observed one of the courtiers. "I fancy it was the parrot at the window, whetting his bill upon his cage wires."

"True," replied the monarch, as if much relieved by the suggestion, "but, on the honour of a knight, I could have sworn that it was the gritting of this vagabond's teeth."

Hereupon the dwarf laughed (the king was too confirmed a joker to object to anyone's laughing), and displayed a set of large, powerful and very repulsive teeth. Moreover, he avowed his perfect willingness to swallow as much wine as desired. The monarch was pacified, and, having drained another bumper with no very perceptible ill effect, Hop-Frog entered at once, and with spirit, into the plans for the masquerade.

"I cannot tell what was the association of idea," observed he very tranquilly, and as if he had never tasted wine in his life, "but *just after* Your Majesty had struck the girl and thrown the wine in her face – *just after* Your Majesty had done this, and while the parrot was making that odd noise outside the window, there came into my mind a capital diversion – one of my own country frolics – often enacted among us, at our masquerades; but here it will be new altogether. Unfortunately, however, it requires a company of eight persons, and—"

"Here we *are*!" cried the king, laughing at his acute discovery of the coincidence. "Eight to a fraction – I and my seven ministers. Come! What is the diversion?"

"We call it," replied the cripple, "the 'Eight Chained Ourang-Outangs', and it really is excellent sport if well enacted."

"*We* will enact it," remarked the king, drawing himself up and lowering his eyelids.

"The beauty of the game," continued Hop-Frog, "lies in the fright it occasions among the women."

"Capital!" roared in chorus the monarch and his ministry.

"I will equip you as ourang-outangs," proceeded the dwarf. "Leave all that to me. The resemblance shall be so striking that the company of masqueraders will take you for real beasts – and of course, they will be as much terrified as astonished."

"Oh, this is exquisite!" exclaimed the king. "Hop-Frog! I will make a man of you."

"The chains are for the purpose of increasing the confusion by their jangling. You are supposed to have escaped, en masse, from your keepers. Your Majesty cannot conceive the *effect* produced, at a masquerade, by eight chained ourang-outangs, imagined to be real ones by most of the company, and rushing in with savage cries, among the crowd of delicately and gorgeously habited men and women. The *contrast* is inimitable."

"It *must* be," said the king, and the council arose hurriedly (as it was growing late), to put in execution the scheme of Hop-Frog.

His mode of equipping the party as ourang-outangs was very simple, but effective enough for his purposes. The animals in question had, at the epoch of my story, very rarely been seen in any part of the civilized world, and as the imitations made by the dwarf were sufficiently beast-like and more than sufficiently hideous, their truthfulness to nature was thus thought to be secured.

The king and his ministers were first encased in tight-fitting stockinet* shirts and drawers. They were then saturated with tar. At this stage of the process, some one of the party suggested feathers, but the suggestion was at once overruled by the dwarf, who soon convinced the eight, by ocular demonstration, that the hair of such a brute as the ourang-outang was much more efficiently represented by *flax*. A thick coating of the latter was accordingly plastered upon the coating of tar. A long chain was now procured. First, it was passed about the waist of the king, *and tied*; then about another of the party, and also tied; then about all successively, in the same manner. When this chaining arrangement was complete, and the party stood as far apart from each other as possible, they formed a circle, and to make all things appear natural, Hop-Frog passed the residue of the chain, in two diameters, at right angles, across the circle, after the fashion adopted, at the present day, by those who capture chimpanzees, or other large apes, in Borneo.

The grand saloon in which the masquerade was to take place was a circular room, very lofty, and receiving the light of the sun only through a single window at top. At night (the season for which the apartment was especially designed) it was illuminated principally by a large chandelier, depending by a chain from the centre of the skylight, and lowered, or elevated, by means of a counterbalance as usual, but (in order not to look unsightly) this latter passed outside the cupola and over the roof.

The arrangements of the room had been left to Trippetta's superintendence, but, in some particulars, it seems, she had been guided by the calmer judgement of her friend the dwarf. At his suggestion it was that, on this occasion, the chandelier was removed. Its waxen drippings (which, in weather so warm, it was quite impossible to prevent) would have been seriously detrimental to the rich dresses of the guests, who, on account of the crowded state of the saloon, could not *all* be expected to keep from out its centre – that is to say, from under the chandelier. Additional sconces were set in various parts of the hall, out of the way, and a flambeau, emitting sweet odour, was placed in the right hand of each of the caryatids* that stood against the wall – some fifty or sixty altogether.

The eight ourang-outangs, taking Hop-Frog's advice, waited patiently until midnight (when the room was thoroughly filled with masqueraders) before making their appearance. No sooner had the clock ceased striking, however, than they rushed, or rather rolled in, all together – for the impediment of their chains caused most of the party to fall, and all to stumble as they entered.

The excitement among the masqueraders was prodigious, and filled the heart of the king with glee. As had been anticipated, there were not a few of the guests who supposed the ferocious-looking creatures to be beasts of *some* kind in reality, if not precisely ourang-outangs. Many of the women swooned with affright, and had not the king taken the precaution to exclude all weapons from the saloon, his party might soon have expiated their frolic in their blood. As it was, a general rush was made for the doors, but the king had ordered them to be locked immediately upon his entrance, and, at the dwarf's suggestion, the keys had been deposited with *him*.

While the tumult was at its height, and each masquerader attentive only to his own safety (for, in fact, there was much *real* danger from the pressure of the excited crowd), the chain by which the chandelier ordinarily hung, and which had been drawn up on its removal, might have been seen very gradually to descend, until its hooked extremity came within three feet of the floor.

Soon after this, the king and his seven friends having reeled about the hall in all directions, found themselves, at length, in its centre, and, of course, in immediate contact with the chain. While they were thus situated, the dwarf, who had followed closely at their heels, inciting them to keep up the commotion, took hold of their own chain at the intersection of the two portions which crossed the circle diametrically and at right angles. Here, with the rapidity of thought, he inserted the hook from which the chandelier had been wont to depend, and, in an instant, by some unseen agency, the chandelier chain was drawn so far upwards as to take the hook out of reach, and, as an inevitable consequence, to drag the ourang-outangs together in close connection, and face to face.

The masqueraders, by this time, had recovered, in some measure, from their alarm, and, beginning to regard the whole matter as a well-contrived pleasantry, set up a loud shout of laughter at the predicament of the apes.

"Leave them to *me!*" now screamed Hop-Frog, his shrill voice making itself easily heard through all the din. "Leave them to *me*. I fancy *I* know them. If I can only get a good look at them, *I* can soon tell who they are."

Here, scrambling over the heads of the crowd, he managed to get to the wall, when, seizing a flambeau from one of the caryatids, he returned, as he went, to the centre of the room – leaping, with the agility of a monkey, upon the king's head – and thence clambered a few feet up the chain – holding down the torch to examine the group of ourang-outangs, and still screaming: "*I* shall soon find out who they are!"

And now, while the whole assembly (the apes included) were convulsed with laughter, the jester suddenly uttered a shrill whistle, when the chain flew violently up for about thirty feet – dragging with it the dismayed and struggling ourang-outangs, and leaving them suspended in mid-air between the skylight and the floor. Hop-Frog, clinging to the chain as it rose, still maintaining his relative position in respect to the eight maskers, and still (as if nothing were the matter) continued to thrust his torch down towards them, as though endeavouring to discover who they were.

So thoroughly astonished were the whole company at this ascent that a dead silence, of about a minute's duration, ensued. It was broken by just such a low, harsh, *grating* sound as had before attracted the attention of the king and his councillors when the former threw the wine in the face of Trippetta. But, on the present occasion, there could be no question as to *whence* the sound issued. It came from the fang-like teeth of the dwarf, who ground them and gnashed them as he foamed at the mouth, and glared, with an expression of maniacal rage, into the upturned countenances of the king and his seven companions.

"Ah ha!" said at length the infuriated jester. "Ah ha! I begin to see who these people *are*, now!" Here, pretending to scrutinize the king more closely, he held the flambeau to the flaxen coat which enveloped him, and which instantly burst into a sheet of vivid flame. In less than half a minute the whole eight ourang-outangs were blazing fiercely, amid the shrieks of the multitude who gazed at them from below, horror-stricken, and without the power to render them the slightest assistance.

At length the flames, suddenly increasing in virulence, forced the jester to climb higher up the chain, to be out of their reach, and, as he made this movement, the crowd again sank, for a brief instant, into silence. The dwarf seized his opportunity, and once more spoke:

"I now see *distinctly*," he said, "what manner of people these maskers are. They are a great king and his seven privy councillors – a king who does not scruple to strike a defenceless girl, and his seven councillors who abet him in the outrage. As for myself, I am simply Hop-Frog, the jester – and *this is my last jest*."

Owing to the high combustibility of both the flax and the tar to which it adhered, the dwarf had scarcely made an end of his brief speech before the work of vengeance was complete. The eight corpses swung in their chains, a fetid, blackened, hideous and indistinguishable mass. The cripple hurled his torch at them, clambered leisurely to the ceiling and disappeared through the skylight.

It is supposed that Trippetta, stationed on the roof of the saloon, had been the accomplice of her friend in his fiery revenge, and that, together, they effected their escape to their own country, for neither was seen again.

THE JOURNAL
OF JULIUS RODMAN*

BEING AN ACCOUNT OF THE FIRST PASSAGE
ACROSS THE ROCKY MOUNTAINS OF NORTH
AMERICA EVER ACHIEVED BY CIVILIZED MAN

CHAPTER I

Introductory

What we must consider an unusual piece of good fortune has enabled us to present our readers, under this head, with a narrative of very remarkable character, and certainly of very deep interest. The journal which follows not only embodies a relation of *the first* successful attempt to cross the gigantic barriers of that immense chain of mountains which stretches from the Polar Sea in the north to the Isthmus of Darien* in the south, forming a craggy and snow-capped rampart throughout its whole course, but, what is of still greater importance, gives the particulars of a tour, beyond these mountains, through an immense extent of territory which, *at this day*, is looked upon as totally untravelled and unknown, and which, in every map of the country to which we can obtain access, is marked as "an unexplored region".* It is, moreover, the *only* unexplored region within the limits of the continent of North America. Such being the case, our friends will know how to pardon us for the slight amount of *unction** with which we have urged this journal upon the public attention. For our own parts, we have found, in its perusal, a degree and a species of interest such as *no* similar narrative ever inspired. Nor do we think that our relation to these papers, as the channel through which they will be first made known, has had more than a moderate influence in begetting this interest. We feel assured that all our readers will unite with us in thinking the adventures here recorded unusually entertaining and important. The peculiar character of the gentleman who was the leader and soul of the expedition, as well as its historian, has imbued what he has written with a vast deal of romantic fervour, very different from the lukewarm and statistical air which pervades most records of the kind. Mr James E. Rodman, from whom we obtained the MS, is well known to many of the readers of this magazine, and partakes, in some degree, of that temperament which embittered the earlier

portion of the life of his grandfather, Mr Julius Rodman, the writer of the narrative. We allude to an hereditary hypochondria.* It was the instigation of this disease which, more than anything else, led him to attempt the extraordinary journey here detailed. The hunting and trapping designs, of which he speaks himself in the beginning of his journal, were, as far as we can perceive, but excuses made to his own reason for the audacity and novelty of his attempt. There can be no doubt, we think (and our readers will think with us) that he was urged solely by a desire to seek, in the bosom of the wilderness, that peace which his peculiar disposition would not suffer him to enjoy among men. He fled to the desert as to a friend. In no other view of the case can we reconcile many points of his record with our ordinary notions of human action.

As we have thought proper to omit two pages of the MS, in which Mr R. gives some account of his life previous to his departure up the Missouri, it may be as well to state here that he was a native of England, where his relatives were of excellent standing, where he had received a good education, and from which country he emigrated to this, in 1784 (being then about eighteen years of age), with his father and two maiden sisters. The family first settled in New York, but afterwards made their way to Kentucky, and established themselves, almost in hermit fashion, on the banks of the Mississippi, near where Mills Point* now makes into the river. Here old Mr Rodman died, in the fall of 1790, and, in the ensuing winter, both his daughters perished of the smallpox, within a few weeks of each other. Shortly afterwards (in the spring of 1791), Mr Julius Rodman, the son, set out upon the expedition which forms the subject of the following pages. Returning from this in 1794, as hereinafter stated, he took up his abode near Abingdon, in Virginia, where he married and had three children, and where most of his descendants now live.

We are informed by Mr James Rodman that his grandfather had merely kept an outline diary of his tour, during the many difficulties of its progress, and that the MSS with which we have been furnished were not written out in detail, from that diary, until many years afterwards, when the tourist was induced to undertake the task at the instigation of M. Andre Michau, the botanist and author of the *Flora Boreali-Americana*, and of the *Histoire des chênes d'Amerique*. M. Michau, it will be remembered, had made an offer of his services to Mr Jefferson, when that statesman first contemplated sending an expedition across the Rocky Mountains. He was engaged to prosecute the journey, and had even proceeded on his way as far as Kentucky, when he was overtaken by an order from the French

minister, then at Philadelphia, requiring him to relinquish the design, and to pursue elsewhere the botanical enquiries on which he was employed by his government.* The contemplated undertaking then fell into the hands of Messieurs Lewis and Clark, by whom it was successfully accomplished.

The MS when completed, however, never reached M. Michau, for whose inspection it had been drawn up, and was always supposed to have been lost on the road by the young man to whom it was entrusted for delivery at M. M.'s temporary residence, near Monticello.* Scarcely any attempt was made to recover the papers, Mr Rodman's peculiar disposition leading him to take but little interest in the search. Indeed, strange as it may appear, we doubt, from what we are told of him, whether he would have ever taken any steps *to make public* the results of his most extraordinary tour: we think that his only object in retouching his original diary was to oblige M. Michau. Even Mr Jefferson's exploring project, a project which, at the time it was broached, excited almost universal comment, and was considered a perfect *novelty*, drew from the hero of our narrative only a few general observations, addressed to the members of his family. He never made his own journey a subject of conversation, seeming, rather, to avoid the topic. He died before the return of Lewis and Clark, and the diary, *which had been given into the hands of the messenger for delivery to M. Michau,* was found, about three months ago, in a secret drawer of a bureau which had belonged to Mr Julius R. We do not learn by whom it was placed there – Mr R.'s relatives all exonerate *him* from the suspicion of having secreted it – but, without intending any disrespect to the memory of that gentleman, or to Mr James Rodman (to whom we feel under especial obligation), we cannot help thinking that the supposition of the narrator's having, by some means, reprocured the package from the messenger, and concealed it where it was discovered, is very reasonable, and not at all out of keeping with the character of that morbid sensibility which distinguished the individual.

We did not wish, by any means, to alter the *manner* of Mr Rodman's narration, and have, therefore, taken very few liberties with the MS, and these few only in the way of abridgement. The style, indeed, could scarcely be improved – it is simple and very effective, giving evidence of the deep delight with which the traveller revelled in the majestic novelties through which he passed, day after day. There is a species of *affectionateness* which pervades his account, even of the severest hardships and dangers, which lets us at once into the man's whole idiosyncrasy. He was possessed with a burning love of Nature, and worshipped her, perhaps, more in her dreary

and savage aspects than in her manifestations of placidity and joy. He stalked through that immense and often terrible wilderness with an evident rapture at his heart which we envy him as we read. He was, indeed, *the man* to journey amid all that solemn desolation which he, plainly, so loved to depict. His was the proper spirit to perceive; his the true ability to feel. We look, therefore, upon his MS as a rich treasure – in its way absolutely unsurpassed – indeed, never equalled.

That the events of this narrative have hitherto lain *perdus*,* that even the *fact* of the Rocky Mountains having been crossed by Mr Rodman prior to the expedition of Lewis and Clark has never been made public, or at all alluded to in the works of any writer on American geography (for it certainly never has been thus alluded to, as far as we can ascertain), must be regarded as very remarkable – indeed, as exceedingly strange. The only reference to the journey at all of which we can hear in any direction is said to be contained in an unpublished letter of M. Michau's, in the possession of Mr W. Wyatt, of Charlottesville, Virginia. It is there spoken of in a casual way, and collaterally, as "a gigantic idea wonderfully carried out". If there has been any further allusion to the journey, we know nothing of it.

Before entering upon Mr Rodman's own relation, it will not be improper to glance at what has been done by others, in the way of discovery, upon the north-western portion of our continent. If the reader will turn to a map of North America, he will be better enabled to follow us in our observations.

It will be seen that the continent extends from the Arctic Ocean, or from about the 70th parallel of north latitude, to the 9th, and from the 56th meridian west of Greenwich, to the 168th. The whole of this immense extent of territory has been visited by civilized man, in a greater or less degree, and indeed a very large portion of it has been permanently set-tled. But there is an exceedingly wide tract which is still marked upon all our maps as *unexplored*, and which, until this day, has always been so considered. This tract lies within the 60th parallel on the south, the Arctic Ocean on the north, the Rocky Mountains on the west, and the possessions of Russia on the east.* *To Mr Rodman, however, belongs the honour of having traversed this singularly wild region in many directions, and the most interesting particulars of the narrative now published have reference to his adventures and discoveries therein.*

Perhaps the earliest travels of any extent made in North America by white people were those of Hennepin and his friends in 1698* – but as his researches were mostly in the south, we do not feel called upon to speak of them more fully.

Mr Irving, in his *Astoria*,* mentions the attempt of Captain Jonathan Carver as being the first ever made to cross the continent from the Atlantic to the Pacific Ocean, but in this he appears to be mistaken, for we find, in one of the journals of Sir Alexander Mackenzie, that two different enterprises were set on foot, with that especial object in view, by the Hudson Bay Fur Company, the one in 1758, the other as early as 1749, both of which are supposed to have entirely failed, as no accounts of the actual expeditions are extant. It was in 1763, shortly after the acquisition of the Canadas by Great Britain, that Captain Carver undertook the journey. His intention was to cross the country, between the forty-third and forty-sixth degrees of north latitude, to the shores of the Pacific. His object was to ascertain the breadth of the continent at its broadest part, and to determine upon some place, on the western coast, where government might establish a post to facilitate the discovery of a north-west passage, or a communication between Hudson's Bay and the Pacific Ocean. He had supposed that the Columbia, then termed the Oregon, disembogued itself somewhere about the straits of Annian,* and it was here that he expected the post to be formed. He thought, also, that a settlement in this neighbourhood would disclose new sources of trade, and open a more direct communication with China, and the British possessions in the East Indies, than the old route afforded by the Cape of Good Hope. He was baffled, however, in his attempt to cross the mountains.

In point of time, the next important expedition, in the northern portion of America, was that of Samuel Hearne, who, with the object of discovering copper mines, pushed north-westwardly during the years 1769, '70, '71 and '72, from the Prince of Wales Fort, in Hudson's Bay, as far as the shores of the Arctic Ocean.*

We have, after this, to record a second attempt of Captain Carver's, which was set on foot in 1774, and in which he was joined by Richard Whitworth, a Member of Parliament, and a man of wealth. We only notice this enterprise on account of the extensive scale on which it was projected, for in fact it was never carried into execution. The gentlemen were to take with them fifty or sixty men, artificers and mariners, and, with these, make their way up one of the branches of the Missouri, explore the mountains for the source of the Oregon, and sail down that river to its supposed mouth, near the straits of Annian. Here a fort was to be built, as well as vessels for the purpose of further discovery. The undertaking was stopped by the breaking out of the American Revolution.*

As early as 1775, the fur trade had been carried by the Canadian missionaries, north and west to the banks of the Saskatchawine River,* in 53 north latitude, 102 west longitude, and, in the beginning of 1776, Mr Joseph Frobisher* proceeded, in this direction, as far as 55 N. and 103 W.

In 1778, Mr Peter Bond, with four canoes, pushed on to the Elk River, about thirty miles south of its junction with the Lake of the Hills.*

We have now to mention another attempt, which was baffled at its very outset, to cross the broadest portion of the continent from ocean to ocean. This attempt is scarcely known by the public to have been made at all, and is mentioned by Mr Jefferson* alone, and by him only in a cursory way. Mr J. relates that Ledyard called upon him in Paris, panting for some new enterprise, after his successful voyage with Captain Cook, and that he (Mr J.) proposed to him that he should go by land to Kamchatka, cross in some of the Russian vessels to Nootka Sound, fall down into the latitude of the Missouri, and then, striking through the country, pass down that river to the United States. Ledyard agreed to the proposal provided the permission of the Russian government could be obtained. Mr Jefferson succeeded in obtaining this, and the traveller, setting out from Paris, arrived at St Petersburg after the empress had left that place to pass the winter at Moscow. His finances not permitting him to make unnecessary stay at St P., he continued on his route with a passport from one of the ministers, and, at two hundred miles from Kamchatka, was arrested by an officer of the empress, who had changed her mind, and now forbade his proceeding. He was put into a close carriage, and driven day and night, without stopping, till he reached Poland, where he was set down and dismissed. Mr Jefferson, in speaking of Ledyard's undertaking, erroneously calls it "the *first* attempt to explore the western part of our northern continent".

The next enterprise of moment was the remarkable one of Sir Alexander Mackenzie, which was prosecuted in 1789.* He started from Montreal, pushed through the Utawas River, Lake Nipissing, Lake Huron, around the northern shore of Lake Superior, through what is called the Grand Portage, thence along Rain River, the Lake of the Woods, Bonnet Lake, the upper part of Dog-Head Lake, the south coast of Lake Winnipeg, through Cedar Lake and past the mouth of the Saskatchawine, to Sturgeon Lake; thence again, by portage,* to the Missinipe, and through Black Bear, Primo's and Buffalo Lakes, to a range of high mountains running NE and SW – then taking Elk River to the Lake of the Hills – then passing through Slave River to Slave Lake – around the northern shore of this latter to Mackenzie's River, and down this, lastly, to the Polar Sea – an immense

journey, during which he encountered dangers innumerable and hardships of the severest kind. In the whole of his course down Mackenzie's River to its embouchure,* he passed along the bottom of the eastern declivity of the Rocky Mountains, but never crossed these barriers. In the spring of 1793, however, starting from Montreal and pursuing the route of his first journey as far as the mouth of the Unjigah or Peace River, he then turned off to the westward, up this stream, pushed through the mountains in latitude 56, then proceeded to the south until he struck a river which he called the Salmon (now Frazer's) and, following this, finally reached the Pacific in about the 40th parallel of N.L.

The memorable expedition of Captains Lewis and Clark was in progress during the years 1804, '5 and '6. In 1803, the act for establishing trading houses with the Indian tribes being about to expire, some modifications of it (with an extension of its views to the Indians on the Missouri) were recommended to Congress by a confidential message from Mr Jefferson, of 18th January. In order to prepare the way, it was proposed to send a party to trace the Missouri to its source, cross the Rocky Mountains and follow the best water communication which offered itself thence to the Pacific Ocean.* This design was fully carried out, Captain Lewis exploring (but not first "discovering" as Mr Irving relates) the upper waters of the Columbia River, and following the course of that stream to its embouchure. The headwaters of the Columbia were visited by Mackenzie as early as 1793.

Coincident with the exploring tour of Lewis and Clark up the Missouri was that of Major Zebulon M. Pike up the Mississippi, which he succeeded in tracing to its source in Itasca Lake. Upon his return from this voyage he penetrated, by the orders of government, from the Mississippi westwardly, during the years 1805, '6 and '7, to the headwaters of the Arkansas (beyond the Rocky Mountains in latitude 40 N.), passing along the Osage and Kanzas rivers, and to the source of the Platte.*

In 1810, Mr David Thompson, a partner of the North West Fur Company, set out from Montreal, with a strong party, to cross the continent to the Pacific. The first part of the route was that of Mackenzie in 1793. The object was to anticipate a design of Mr John Jacob Astor's – to wit, the establishment of a trading post at the mouth of the Columbia.* Most of his people deserted him on the eastern side of the mountains, but he finally succeeded in crossing the chain, with only eight followers, when he struck the northern branch of the Columbia, and descended that river from a point much nearer its source than any white man had done before.

In 1811, Mr Astor's own remarkable enterprise* was carried into effect
– at least so far as the journey across the country is concerned. As Mr
Irving has already made all readers well acquainted with the particulars
of this journey, we need only mention it in brief. The design we have just
spoken of. The track of the party (under command of Mr Wilson Price
Hunt*) was from Montreal, up the Utawas, through Lake Nipissing, and
a succession of small lakes and rivers, to Michilimackinac, or Mackinaw
– thence by Green Bay, Fox and Wisconsin rivers, to the Prairie du Chien
– thence down the Mississippi to St Louis – thence up the Missouri, to
the village of the Arickara Indians,* between the 46th and 47th parallels
of N. latitude, and fourteen hundred and thirty miles above the mouth
of the river – thence, bending to the south-west across the desert, over
the mountains about where the headwaters of the Platte and Yellowstone
take rise, and, along the south branch of the Columbia, to the sea. Two
small return parties from this expedition made most perilous and eventful
passages across the country.

The travels of Major Stephen H. Long are the next important ones in
point of time. This gentleman, in 1823, proceeded to the source of St
Peter's River, to Lake Winnipeg, to the Lake of the Woods, etc., etc.* Of
the more recent journeys of Captain Bonneville and others it is scarcely
necessary to speak, as they still dwell in the public memory. Captain B.'s
adventures have been well related by Mr Irving.* In 1832, he passed from
Fort Osage across the Rocky Mountains, and spent nearly three years in
the regions beyond. Within the limits of the United States there is very
little ground which has not, of late years, been traversed by the man of
science, or the adventurer. But in those wide and desolate regions which
lie north of our territory, and to the westward of Mackenzie's River, the
foot of no civilized man, with the exception of Mr Rodman and his very
small party, has ever been known to tread. In regard to the question of
the *first* passage across the Rocky Mountains, it will be seen, from what
we have already said, that the credit of the enterprise should never have
been given to Lewis and Clark, since Mackenzie succeeded in it, in the year
1793, and that, in point of fact, Mr Rodman was the first who overcame
those gigantic barriers, crossing them as he did in 1792. Thus it is not
without good reason that we claim public attention for the extraordinary
narrative which ensues.

EDS GM*

CHAPTER II

After the death of my father, and both sisters, I took no further interest in our plantation at the Point, and sold it, at a complete sacrifice, to M. Junôt. I had often thought of trapping up the Missouri, and resolved now to go on an expedition up that river, and try to procure peltries,* which I was sure of being able to sell at Petite Côte to the private agents of the North West Fur Company.* I believed that much more property might be acquired in this way, with a little enterprise and courage, than I could make by any other means. I had always been fond, too, of hunting and trapping, although I had never made a business of either, and I had a great desire to explore some portion of our western country, about which Pierre Junôt had often spoken to me. He was the eldest son of the neighbour who bought me out, and was a man of strange manners and somewhat eccentric turn of mind, but still one of the best-hearted fellows in the world, and certainly as courageous a man as ever drew breath, although of no great bodily strength. He was of Canadian descent, and having gone, once or twice, on short excursions for the Fur Company, in which he had acted as *voyageur*,* was fond of calling himself one, and of talking about his trips. My father had been very fond of Pierre, and I thought a good deal of him myself; he was a great favourite, too, with my younger sister, Jane, and I believe they would have been married had it been God's will to have spared her.

When Pierre discovered that I had not entirely made up my mind what course to pursue after my father's death, he urged me to fit out a small expedition for the river, in which he would accompany me, and he had no difficulty in bringing me over to his wishes. We agreed to push up the Missouri as long as we found it possible, hunting and trapping as we went, and not to return until we had secured as many peltries as would be a fortune for us both. His father made no objection, and gave him about three hundred dollars, when we proceeded to Petite Côte for the purpose of getting our equipments, and raising as many men as we could for the voyage.

Petite Côte* is a small place on the north bank of the Missouri, about twenty miles from its junction with the Mississippi. It lies at the foot of a range of low hills, and upon a sort of ledge, high enough above the river to be out of reach of the June freshets.* There are not more than five or six houses, and these of wood, in the upper part of the place, but, nearer to the east, there is a chapel and twelve or fifteen good dwellings, running

parallel with the river. There are about a hundred inhabitants, mostly Creoles of Canadian descent. They are extremely indolent, and make no attempt at cultivating the country around them, which is a rich soil, except now and then when a little is done in the way of gardening. They live principally by hunting, and trading with the Indians for peltries, which they sell again to the North West Company's agents. We expected to meet with no difficulty here in getting recruits for our journey, or equipments, but were disappointed in both particulars, for the place was too poor in every respect to furnish all that we wanted, so as to render our voyage safe and efficient.*

We designed to pass through the heart of a country infested with Indian tribes, of whom we knew nothing except by vague report, and whom we had every reason to believe ferocious and treacherous. It was therefore particularly necessary that we should go well provided with arms and ammunition, as well as in some force as regards numbers, and if our voyage was to be a source of profit, we must take with us canoes of sufficient capacity to bring home what peltries we might collect. It was the middle of March when we first reached Petite Côte, and we did not succeed in getting ready until the last of May. We had to send twice down the river to the Point for men and supplies, and neither could be obtained except at great cost. We should have failed at last in getting many things absolutely requisite, if it had not so happened that Pierre met with a party on its return from a trip up the Mississippi, and engaged six of its best men, besides a canoe or piroque* – purchasing, at the same time, most of the surplus stores and ammunition.

This seasonable aid enabled us to get fairly ready for the voyage before 1st June. On the third of this month (1791) we bid adieu to our friends at Petite Côte, and started on our expedition. Our party consisted in all of fifteen persons. Of these, five were Canadians from Petite Côte, and had all been on short excursions up the river. They were good boatmen, and excellent companions, as far as singing French songs went, and drinking, at which they were pre-eminent – although, in truth, it was a rare thing to see any of them so far the worse for liquor as to be incapable of attending to duty. They were always in a good humour, and always ready to work, but as hunters I did not think them worth much, and as fighting men I soon discovered they were not to be depended upon. There were two of these five Canadians who engaged to act as interpreters for the first five or six hundred miles up the river (should we proceed so far) and then we hoped to procure an Indian occasionally to interpret, should it be necessary, but

we had resolved to avoid, as far as possible, any meetings with the Indians, and rather to trap ourselves than run the great risk of trading, with so small a party as we numbered. It was our policy to proceed with the greatest caution, and expose ourselves to notice only when we could not avoid it.

The six men whom Pierre had engaged from aboard the return Mississippi boat were as different a set from the Canadians as could well be imagined. Five of them were brothers, by the name of Greely* (John, Robert, Meredith, Frank and Poindexter), and bolder- or finer-looking persons it would have been difficult to find. John Greely was the eldest and stoutest of the five, and had the reputation of being the strongest man, as well as best shot in Kentucky – from which state they all came. He was full six feet in height, and of most extraordinary breadth across the shoulders, with large, strongly knit limbs. Like most men of great physical strength, he was exceedingly good-tempered, and on this account was greatly beloved by us all. The other four brothers were all strong, well-built men, too, although not to be compared with John. Poindexter was as tall, but very gaunt, and of a singularly fierce appearance, but, like his elder brother, he was of peaceable demeanour. All of them were experienced hunters and capital shots. They had gladly accepted Pierre's offer to go with us, and we made an arrangement with them which ensured them an equal share with Pierre and myself in the profits of the enterprise – that is to say, we divided the proceeds into three parts: one of which was to be mine, one Pierre's and one shared among the five brothers.

The sixth man whom we enlisted from the return boat was, also, a good recruit. His name was Alexander Wormley, a Virginian, and a very strange character. He had originally been a preacher of the Gospel, and had afterwards fancied himself a prophet, going about the country with a long beard and hair, and in his bare feet, haranguing everyone he met. This hallucination was now diverted into another channel, and he thought of nothing else than of finding gold mines in some of the fastnesses of the country. Upon this subject he was as entirely mad as any man could well be, but upon all others was remarkably sensible and even acute. He was a good boatman and a good hunter, and as brave a fellow as ever stepped, besides being of great bodily strength and swiftness of foot. I counted much upon this recruit, on account of his enthusiastic character, and in the end I was not deceived, as will appear.

Our other two recruits were a Negro belonging to Pierre Junôt, named Toby, and a stranger whom we had picked up in the woods near Mills Point, and who joined our expedition upon the instant as soon as we mentioned

our design. His name was Andrew Thornton, also a Virginian, and I believe of excellent family, belonging to the Thorntons of the northern part of the state. He had been from Virginia about three years, during the whole of which time he had been rambling about the western country, with no other companion than a large dog of the Newfoundland species. He had collected no peltries, and did not seem to have any object in view more than the gratification of a roving and adventurous propensity. He frequently amused us, when sitting around our campfires at night, with the relation of his adventures and hardships in the wilderness – recounting them with a straightforward earnestness which left us no room to doubt their truth, although, indeed, many of them had a marvellous air. Experience afterwards taught us that the dangers and difficulties of the solitary hunter can scarcely be exaggerated, and that the real task is to depict them to the hearer in sufficiently distinct colours. I took a great liking to Thornton from the first hour in which I saw him.

I have only said a few words respecting Toby, but he was not the least important personage of our party. He had been in old M. Junôt's family for a great number of years, and had proved himself a faithful Negro. He was rather too old to accompany such an expedition as ours, but Pierre was not willing to leave him. He was an able-bodied man, however, and still capable of enduring great fatigue. Pierre himself was probably the feeblest of our whole company, as regards bodily strength, but he possessed great sagacity, and a courage which nothing could daunt. His manners were sometimes extravagant and boisterous, which led him to get into frequent quarrels, and had once or twice seriously endangered the success of our expedition, but he was a true friend, and in that one point I considered him invaluable.

I have now given a brief account of all our party, as it was when we left Petite Côte.* To carry ourselves and accoutrements, as well as to bring home what peltries might be obtained, we had two large boats. The smallest of these was a piroque made of birchbark, sewed together with the fibres of the roots of the spruce tree, the seams payed* with pine resin, and the whole so light that six men could carry it with ease. It was twenty feet long, and could be rowed with from four to twelve oars, drawing about eighteen inches water when loaded to the gunwale, and, when empty, not more than ten. The other was a keelboat* which we had made at Petite Côte (the canoe having been purchased by Pierre from the Mississippi party). It was thirty feet long, and, when loaded to the gunwale, drew two feet water. It had a deck for twenty feet of its length forward, forming a cuddy

cabin,* with a strong door, and of sufficient dimensions to contain our whole party with close crowding, as the boat was very broad. This part of it was bulletproof, being wadded with oakum between two coatings of oak plank, and in several positions we had small holes bored, through which we could have fired upon an enemy in case of attack, as well as observe their movements; these holes, at the same time, gave us air and light, when we closed the door, and we had secure plugs to fit them when necessary. The remaining ten feet of the length was open, and here we could use as many as six oars – but our main dependence was upon poles which we employed by walking along the deck. We had also a short mast, easily shipped and unshipped, which was stepped* about seven feet from the bow, and upon which we set a large square sail when the wind was fair, taking in mast and all when it was ahead.

In a division made in the bow, under deck, we deposited ten kegs of good powder, and as much lead as we considered proportionate, one tenth ready-moulded in rifle bullets. We had also stowed away here a small brass cannon and carriage, dismounted and taken to pieces, so as to lie in little compass,* thinking that such a means of defence might possibly come into play at some period of our expedition. This cannon was one of three which had been brought down the Missouri by the Spaniards two years previously, and lost overboard from a piroque, some miles above Petite Côte. A sandbar had so far altered the channel at the place where the canoe capsized that an Indian discovered one of the guns, and procured assistance to carry it down to the settlement, where he sold it for a gallon of whiskey. The people at Petite Côte then went up and procured the other two. They were very small guns, but of good metal, and beautiful workmanship, being carved and ornamented with serpents like some of the French field pieces. Fifty iron balls were found with the guns, and these we procured. I mention the way in which we obtained this cannon because it performed an important part in some of our operations, as will be found hereafter. Besides it, we had fifteen spare rifles, boxed up, and deposited forward with the other heavy goods. We put the weight here, to sink our bows well in the water, which is the best method, on account of the snags and sawyers* in the river.

In the way of other arms we were sufficiently provided, each man having a stout hatchet, and knife, besides his ordinary rifle and ammunition. Each boat was provided with a camp kettle, three large axes, a towing line, two oilcloths to cover the goods when necessary and two large sponges for bailing. The piroque had also a small mast and sail (which I omitted

to mention), and carried a quantity of gum, birchbark and watape,* to make repairs with. She also had in charge all the Indian goods which we had thought necessary to bring with us, and which we purchased from the Mississippi boat. It was not our design to trade with the Indians, but these goods were offered us at a low rate, and we thought it better to take them, as they might prove of service. They consisted of silk and cotton handkerchiefs; thread, lines and twine; hats, shoes and hose; small cutlery and ironmongery; calicoes and printed cottons; Manchester goods; twist and carrot tobacco; milled blankets;* and glass toys, beads, etc., etc. All these were done up in small packages, three of which were a man's load. The provisions were also put up so as to be easily handled, and a part was deposited in each boat. We had, altogether, two hundredweight of pork, six hundredweight of biscuit and six hundredweight of pemmican.* This we had made at Petite Côte, by the Canadians, who told us that it was used by the North West Fur Company in all their long voyages, when it is feared that game may not prove abundant. It is manufactured in a singular manner. The lean parts of the flesh of the larger animals is cut into thin slices, and placed on a wooden grate over a slow fire, or exposed to the sun (as ours was), or sometimes to the frost. When it was sufficiently dried in this way, it is pounded between two heavy stones, and will then keep for years. If, however, much of it is kept together, it ferments upon the breaking up of the frost in the spring, and, if not well exposed to the air, soon decays. The inside fat, with that of the rump, is melted down and mixed, in a boiling state, with the pounded meat, half and half; it is then squeezed into bags, and is ready to eat without any further cooking, being very palatable without salt, or vegetables. The best pemmican is made with the addition of marrow and dried berries, and is a capital article of food.* Our whiskey was in carboys, of five gallons each, and we had twenty of these, a hundred gallons in all.

When everything was well on board, with our whole company, including Thornton's dog, we found that there was but little room to spare, except in the big cabin, which we wished to preserve free of goods, as a sleeping place in bad weather; we had nothing in here except arms and ammunition, with some beaver traps and a carpet of bearskins. Our crowded state suggested an expedient which ought to have been adopted at all events: that of detaching four hunters from the party to course along the riverbanks, and keep us in game, as well as to act in capacity of scouts, to warn us of the approach of Indians. With this object we procured two good horses, giving one of them in charge of Robert and Meredith Greely, who were to

keep upon the south bank, and the other in charge of Frank and Poindexter (Greely) who were to course along the north side. By means of the horses they could bring in what game was shot.

This arrangement relieved our boats very considerably, lessening our number to eleven. In the small boat were two of the men from Petite Côte, with Toby and Pierre Junôt. In the large one were the Prophet (as we called him), or Alexander Wormley, John Greely, Andrew Thornton, three of the Petite Côte men and myself, with Thornton's dog.

Our mode of proceeding was sometimes with oars, but not generally: we most frequently pulled ourselves along by the limbs of trees on shore, or, where the ground permitted it, we used a towline, which is the easiest way, some of us being on shore to haul, while some remained on board, to set the boat offshore with poles. Very often we poled altogether. In this method (which is a good one when the bottom is not too muddy, or full of quicksands, and when the depth of water is not too great), the Canadians are very expert, as well as at rowing. They use long, stiff and light poles, pointed with iron; with these they proceed to the bow of the boat, an equal number of men at each side; the face is then turned to the stern, and the pole inserted in the river, reaching the bottom; a firm hold being thus taken, the boatmen apply the heads of the poles to the shoulder, which is protected by a cushion, and, pushing in this manner, while they walk along the gunwale, the boat is urged forward with great force. There is no necessity for any steersman while using the pole, for the poles direct the vessel with wonderful accuracy.

In these various modes of getting along, now and then varied with the necessity of wading and dragging our vessels by hand, in rapid currents, or through shallow water, we commenced our eventful voyage up the Missouri River. The skins which were considered as the leading objects of the expedition were to be obtained, principally, by hunting and trapping, as privately as possible, and without direct trade with the Indians, whom we had long learnt to know as, in the main, a treacherous race, not to be dealt with safely in so small a party as ours. The furs usually collected by previous adventurers upon our contemplated route included beaver, otter, marten, lynx, mink, musquash, bear, fox, kit fox, wolverine, raccoon, fisher,* wolf, buffalo, deer and elk, but we proposed to confine ourselves to the more costly kinds.

The morning on which we set out from Petite Côte was one of the most inspiring, and delicious, and nothing could exceed the hilarity of our whole party. The summer had hardly yet commenced, and the wind, which

blew a strong breeze against us, at first starting, had all the voluptuous softness of spring. The sun shone clearly, but with no great heat. The ice had disappeared from the river, and the current, which was pretty full, concealed all those marshy and ragged alluvia* which disfigure the borders of the Missouri at low water. It had now the most majestic appearance, washing up among the willows and cottonwood on one side, and rushing, with a bold volume, by the sharp cliffs on the other. As I looked up the stream (which here stretched away to the westward, until the waters apparently met the sky in the great distance) and reflected on the immensity of territory through which those waters had probably passed, a territory as yet altogether unknown to white people, and perhaps abounding in the magnificent works of God, I felt an excitement of soul such as I had never before experienced, and secretly resolved that it should be no slight obstacle which should prevent my pushing up this noble river farther than any previous adventurer had done. At that moment I seemed possessed of an energy more than human, and my animal spirits rose to so high a degree that I could with difficulty content myself in the narrow limits of the boat. I longed to be with the Greelys on the bank, that I might give full vent to the feelings which inspired me by leaping and running in the prairie. In these feelings Thornton participated strongly, evincing a deep interest in our expedition, and an admiration of the beautiful scenery around us, which rendered him from that moment a particular favourite with myself. I never, at any period of my life, felt so keenly as I then did the want of some friend to whom I could converse freely, and without danger of being misunderstood. The sudden loss of all my relatives by death had saddened but not depressed my spirits, which appeared to seek relief in a contemplation of the wild scenes of nature, and these scenes and the reflections which they encouraged could not, I found, be thoroughly enjoyed without the society of some one person of reciprocal sentiments. Thornton was precisely the kind of individual to whom I could unburthen my full heart, and unburthen it of all its extravagant emotion, without fear of incurring a shadow of ridicule, and even in the certainty of finding a listener as impassioned as myself. I never, before or since, met with anyone who so fully entered into my own notions respecting natural scenery, and this circumstance alone was sufficient to bind him to me in a firm friendship. We were as intimate, during our whole expedition, as brothers could possibly be, and I took no steps without consulting him. Pierre and myself were also friends, but there was not the tie of reciprocal thought between us – that strongest of all mortal

bonds. His nature, although sensitive, was too volatile to comprehend all the devotional fervour of my own.

The incidents of the first day of our voyage had nothing remarkable in them, except that we had some difficulty in forcing our way, towards nightfall, by the mouth of a large cave on the south side of the river. This cave had a very dismal appearance as we passed it, being situated at the foot of a lofty bluff, full two hundred feet high, and jutting somewhat over the stream. We could not distinctly perceive the depth of the cavern, but it was about sixteen or seventeen feet high, and at least fifty in width.* The current ran past it with great velocity, and as, from the nature of the cliff, we could not tow, it required the utmost exertion to make our way by it – which we at length effected by getting all of us, with the exception of one man, into the large boat. This one remained in the piroque, and anchored it below the cave. By uniting our force, then, in rowing, we brought the large boat up beyond the difficult pass, paying out a line to the piroque as we proceeded, and by this line hauling it up after us, when we had fairly ascended. We passed, during the day, Bonhomme and Osage Femme rivers, with two small creeks, and several islands of little extent. We made about twenty-five miles, notwithstanding the headwind, and encamped at night on the north bank, and at the foot of a rapid called "Diable".

4th June – Early this morning, Frank and Poindexter Greely came into our camp with a fat buck, upon which we all breakfasted in high glee, and afterwards pushed on with spirit. At the Diable rapid, the current sets with much force against some rocks which jut out from the south, and render the navigation difficult. A short distance above this we met with several quicksand bars, which put us to trouble; the banks of the river here fall in continually, and, in the process of time, must greatly alter the bed. At eight o'clock we had a fine fresh wind from the eastward, and, with its assistance, made rapid progress, so that by night we had gone perhaps thirty miles, or more. We passed, on the north, the river Du Bois, a creek called Charité* and several small islands. The river was rising fast as we came to, at night, under a group of cottonwood trees, there being no ground near at hand upon which we were disposed to encamp. It was beautiful weather, and I felt too much excited to sleep, so, asking Thornton to accompany me, I took a stroll into the country, and did not return until nearly daylight. The rest of our crew occupied the cabin, for the first time, and found it quite roomy enough for five or six more persons. They had been disturbed, in the night, by a strange noise overhead, on deck, the origin of which they had not been able to ascertain, as, when some of the party rushed out to

see, the disturber had disappeared. From the account given of the noise, I concluded that it must have proceeded from an Indian dog, who had scented our fresh provisions (the buck of yesterday) and was endeavouring to make off with a portion. In this view I felt perfectly satisfied, but the occurrence suggested the great risk we ran in not posting a regular watch at night, and it was agreed to do so for the future.

*

Having thus given, in Mr Rodman's own words, the incidents of the two first days of the voyage, we forbear to follow him minutely in his passage up the Missouri to the mouth of the Platte,* at which he arrived on 10th August. The character of the river throughout this extent is so well known, and has been so frequently described, that any further account of it is unnecessary, and the journal takes note of little else, at this portion of the tour, than the natural features of the country – together with the ordinary boating and hunting occurrences. The party made three several halts for the purpose of trapping, but met with no great success, and finally concluded to push farther into the heart of the country, before making any regular attempts at collecting peltries. Only two events, of moment, are recorded, for the two months which we omit. One of these was the death of a Canadian, Jacques Lauzanne, by the bite of a rattlesnake; the other was the encountering a Spanish commission* sent to intercept and turn the party back, by order of the commandant of the province. The officer in charge of the detachment, however, was so much interested in the expedition, and took so great a fancy to Mr Rodman, that our travellers were permitted to proceed. Many small bodies of Osage and Kanzas Indians hovered occasionally about the boats, but evinced nothing of hostility. We leave the voyagers for the present, therefore, at the mouth of the river Platte, on 10th August 1791 – their number having been reduced to fourteen.

CHAPTER III

Having reached the mouth of the river Platte, our voyagers encamped for three days, during which they were busily occupied in drying and airing their goods and provisions, making new oars and poles, and repairing the birch canoe, which had sustained material injury. The hunters brought in an abundance of game, with which the boats were loaded to repletion. Deer was had for the asking, and turkeys and fat grouse were met with

in great plenty. The party, moreover, regaled on several species of fish, and, at a short distance from the riverbanks, found an exquisite kind of wild grape. No Indians had been seen for better than a fortnight, as this was the hunting season, and they were doubtless engaged in the prairies, taking buffalo. After perfectly recruiting, the voyagers broke up their encampment, and pushed on up the Missouri. We resume the words of the journal.

14th August – We started with a delightful breeze from the SE, and kept along by the southern shore, taking advantage of the eddy, and going at a great rate, notwithstanding the current, which, in the middle, was unusually full and strong. At noon, we stopped to examine some remarkable mounds on the south-western shore, at a spot where the ground seems to have sunk considerably to an extent of three hundred acres, or more. A large pond is in the vicinity, and appears to have drained the low tract. This is covered with mounds of various sizes, and shapes, all formed of sand and mud, the highest being nearest the river. I could not make up my mind whether these hillocks were of natural or artificial construction. I should have supposed them made by the Indians, but for the general appearance of the soil, which had apparently been subjected to the violent action of water.* We stayed at this spot the rest of the day, having made altogether twenty miles.

15th August – Today we had a heavy, disagreeable headwind, and made only fifteen miles, with great labour, encamping at night beneath a bluff on the north shore, this being the first bluff on that side which we had seen since leaving the Nodaway River.* In the night it came on to rain in torrents, and the Greelys brought in their horses, and ensconced themselves in the cabin. Robert swam the river with his horse from the south shore, and then took the canoe across for Meredith. He appeared to think nothing of either of these feats, although the night was one of the darkest and most boisterous I ever saw, and the river was much swollen. We all sat in the cabin very comfortably, for the weather was quite cool, and were kept awake for a long time by the anecdotes of Thornton, who told story after story of his adventures with the Indians on the Mississippi. His huge dog appeared to listen with profound attention to every word that was said. Whenever any particularly incredible circumstance was related, Thornton would gravely refer to him as a witness. "Nep," he would say, "don't you remember that time?" – or, "Nep can swear to the truth of that – can't you, Nep?" – when the animal would roll up his eyes immediately, loll out his monstrous tongue and wag his great head up and down, as much as

to say: "Oh it's every bit as true as the Bible." Although we all knew that this trick had been taught the dog, yet for our lives we could not forbear shouting with laughter whenever Thornton would appeal to him.

16th August – Early this morning passed an island, and a creek about fifteen yards wide, and, at a farther distance of twelve miles, a large island in the middle of the river. We had now, generally, high prairie, and timbered hills on the north, with low ground on the south, covered with cottonwood. The river was excessively crooked, but not so rapid as before we passed the Platte. Altogether there is less timber than formerly; what there is, is mostly elm, cottonwood, hickory and walnut, with some oak. Had a strong wind nearly all day, and, by means of the eddy and this, we made twenty-five miles before night. Our encampment was on the south, upon a large plain, covered with high grass, and bearing a great number of plum trees and currant bushes. In our rear was a steep woody ridge, ascending which we found another prairie extending back for about a mile, and stopped again by a similar woody ridge, followed by another vast prairie, going off into the distance as far as the eye can reach. From the cliffs just above us we had one of the most beautiful prospects in the world.*

17th August – We remained at the encampment all day, and occupied ourselves in various employments. Getting Thornton, with his dog, to accompany me, I strolled to some distance to the southward, and was enchanted with the voluptuous beauty of the country. The prairies exceeded in beauty anything told in the tales of the *Arabian Nights*.* On the edges of the creeks there was a wild mass of flowers which looked more like art than nature, so profusely and fantastically were their vivid colours blended together. Their rich odour was almost oppressive. Every now and then we came to a kind of green island of trees, placed amid an ocean of purple, blue, orange and crimson blossoms, all waving to and fro in the wind. These islands consisted of the most majestic forest oaks, and, beneath them, the grass resembled a robe of the softest green velvet, while up their huge stems there clambered, generally, a profusion of grapevines, laden with delicious ripe fruit. The Missouri, in the distance, presented the most majestic appearance, and many of the real islands with which it was studded were entirely covered with plum bushes, or other shrubbery, except where crossed in various directions by narrow, mazy paths, like the alleys in an English flower garden, and in these alleys we could always see either elks or antelopes, who had no doubt made them. We returned, at sunset, to the encampment, delighted with our excursion. The night was warm, and we were excessively annoyed by mosquitoes.

18th August – Today passed through a narrow part of the river, not more than two hundred yards wide, with a rapid channel, much obstructed with logs and driftwood. Ran the large boat on a sawyer, and half filled her with water before we could extricate her from the difficulty. We were obliged to halt, in consequence, and overhaul our things. Some of the biscuit was injured, but none of the powder. Remained all day – having only made five miles.

19th August – We started early this morning and made great headway. The weather was cool and cloudy, and at noon we had a drenching shower. Passed a creek on the south, the mouth of which is nearly concealed by a large sand island of singular appearance. Went about fifteen miles beyond this. The highlands now recede from the river, and are probably from ten to twenty miles apart. On the north is a good deal of fine timber, but on the south very little. Near the river are beautiful prairies, and along the banks we procured four or five different species of grape, all of good flavour and quite ripe; one is a large purple grape of excellent quality. The hunters came into camp, at night, from both sides of the river, and brought us more game than we well knew what to do with – grouse, turkeys, two deer, an antelope and a quantity of yellow birds with black-striped wings – these latter proved delicious eating. We made about twenty miles during the day.

20th August – The river, this morning, was full of sandbars and other obstructions, but we proceeded with spirit, and reached the mouth of a pretty large creek, before night, at a distance of twenty miles from our last encampment. The creek comes in from the north, and has a large island opposite its mouth. Here we made our camp, with the resolution of remaining four or five days to trap beaver, as we saw great signs of them in the neighbourhood. This island was one of the most fairy-looking* situations in the world, and filled my mind with the most delightful and novel emotions. The whole scenery rather resembled what I had dreamt of when a boy than an actual reality. The banks sloped down very gradually into the water, and were carpeted with a short soft grass of a brilliant green hue, which was visible under the surface of the stream for some distance from the shore, especially on the north side, where the clear creek fell into the river. All round the island, which was probably about twenty acres in extent, was a complete fringe of cottonwood, the trunks loaded with grapevines in full fruit, and so closely interlocking with each other that we could scarcely get a glimpse of the river between the leaves. Within this circle the grass was somewhat higher, and of a coarser texture, with a pale-yellow or white streak down the middle of each blade, and giving

out a remarkably delicious perfume, resembling that of the vanilla bean, but much stronger, so that the whole atmosphere was loaded with it. The common English sweetgrass is no doubt of the same genus, but greatly inferior in beauty and fragrance. Interspersed among it in every direction were myriads of the most brilliant flowers in full bloom, and most of them of fine odour – blue, pure white, bright yellow, purple, crimson, gaudy scarlet, and some with streaked leaves like tulips. Little knots of cherry trees and plum bushes grew in various directions about, and there were many narrow, winding paths which circled the island, and which had been made by elk or antelopes. Nearly in the centre was a spring of sweet and clear water, which bubbled up from among a cluster of steep rocks, covered from head to foot with moss and flowering vines. The whole bore a wonderful resemblance to an artificial flower garden, but was infinitely more beautiful – looking rather like some of those scenes of enchantment which we read of in old books. We were all in ecstasy with the spot, and prepared our camp in the highest glee, amid its wilderness of sweets.

[The party remained here a week, during which time, the neighbouring country to the north was explored in many directions, and some peltries obtained, especially upon the creek mentioned. The weather was fine, and the enjoyment of the voyagers suffered no alloy, in their terrestrial Paradise. Mr Rodman, however, omitted no necessary precautions, and sentries were regularly posted every night, when all hands assembled at camp and made merry. Such feasting and drinking were never before known, the Canadians proving themselves the very best fellows in the world at a song, or over a flagon. They did nothing but eat, and cook, and dance, and shout French carols at the top of their voice. During the day they were chiefly entrusted with the charge of the encampment, while the steadier members of the party were absent upon hunting or trapping expeditions. In one of these Mr Rodman enjoyed an excellent opportunity of observing the habits of the beaver,* and his account of this singular animal is highly interesting – the more so as it differs materially, in some points, from the ordinary descriptions.

He was attended, as usual, by Thornton and his dog, and had traced up a small creek to its source in the highlands about ten miles from the river. The party came at length to a place where a large swamp had been made by the beavers, in damming up the creek. A thick grove of willows occupied one extremity of the swamp, some of them overhanging the water at a spot where several of the animals were observed. Our adventurers crept stealthily round to these willows, and, making Neptune lie down at

a little distance, succeeded in climbing, unobserved, into a large and thick tree, where they could look immediately down upon all that was going on.

The beavers were repairing a portion of their dam, and every step of their progress was distinctly seen. One by one the architects were perceived to approach the edge of the swamp, each with a small branch in his mouth. With this he proceeded to the dam, and placed it carefully, and longitudinally, on the part which had given way. Having done this, he dived immediately, and in a few seconds reappeared above the surface with a quantity of stiff mud, which he first squeezed so as to drain it of its moisture in a great degree, and then applied with its feet and tail (using the latter as a trowel) to the branch which he had just laid upon the breach. He then made off among the trees, and was quickly succeeded by another of the community, who went through precisely the same operation.

In this way the damage sustained by the dam was in a fair way of being soon repaired. Messieurs Rodman and Thornton observed the progress of the work for more than two hours, and bear testimony to the exquisite skill of the artisans. But as soon as a beaver left the edge of the swamp in search of a branch, he was lost sight of among the willows, much to the chagrin of the observers, who were anxious to watch his further operations. By clambering a little higher up in the tree, however, they discovered everything. A small sycamore had been felled, apparently, and was now nearly denuded of all its fine branches, a few beavers still nibbling off some that remained, and proceeding with them to the dam. In the mean time a great number of the animals surrounded a much older and larger tree, which they were busily occupied in cutting down. There were as many as fifty or sixty of the creatures around the trunk, of which number six or seven would work at once, leaving off one by one, as each became weary, a fresh one stepping in to the vacated place. When our travellers first observed the sycamore, it had been already cut through to a great extent, but only on the side nearest the swamp, upon the edge of which it grew. The incision was nearly a foot wide, and as cleanly made as if done with an axe, and the ground at the bottom of the tree was covered with fine longitudinal slips, like straws, which had been nibbled out, and not eaten, as it appears that these animals only use the bark for food. When at work some sat upon the hind legs, in the posture so common with squirrels, and gnawed at the wood, their forefeet resting upon the edge of the cut, and their heads thrust far into the aperture. Two of them, however, were entirely within the incision, lying at length, and working with great eagerness for a short time, when they were relieved by their companions.

Although the position of our voyagers was anything but comfortable, so great was their curiosity to witness the felling of the sycamore that they resolutely maintained their post until sunset, an interval of eight hours from the time of ascending. Their chief embarrassment was on Neptune's account, who could with difficulty be kept from plunging in the swamp after the plasterers who were repairing the dam. The noise he made had several times disturbed the nibblers at the tree, who would every now and then start, as if all actuated by one mind, and listen attentively for many minutes. As evening approached, however, the dog gave over his freaks, and lay quiet, while the beavers went on uninterruptedly with their labour.

Just as the sun began to set, a sudden commotion was observed among the woodcutters, who all started from the tree, and flew round to the side which was untouched. In an instant afterwards it was seen to settle down gradually on the gnawed side, till the lips of the incision met, but still it did not fall, being sustained partially by the unsundered bark. This was now attacked with zeal by as many nibblers as could find room to work at it, and very quickly severed, when the huge tree, to which the proper inclination had already been so ingeniously given, fell with a tremendous crash, and spread a great portion of its topmost branches over the surface of the swamp. This matter accomplished, the whole community seemed to think a holiday was deserved, and, ceasing work at once, began to chase each other about in the water, diving and slapping the surface with their tails.

The account here given of the method employed by the beaver in its woodcutting operations is more circumstantial than any we have yet seen, and seems to be conclusive in regard to the question of *design* on the animal's part. The intention of making the tree fall towards the water appears here to be obvious. Captain Bonneville, it will be remembered, discredits the alleged sagacity of the animal in this respect, and thinks it has no further aim than to get the tree down, without any subtle calculation in respect to its mode of descent.* This attribute, he thinks, has been ascribed to it from the circumstance that trees in general, which grow near the margin of water, either lean bodily towards the stream or stretch their most ponderous limbs in that direction, in search of the light, space and air which are there usually found. The beaver, he says, attacks, of course, those trees which are nearest at hand, and on the banks of the stream or pond, and these, when cut through, naturally preponderate towards the water. This suggestion is well timed, but by no means conclusive against the design of the beaver, whose sagacity, at best, is far beneath that which is positively ascertained in respect to many classes of inferior animals

– infinitely below that of the lion ant, of the bee and of the coralliferi.*
The probability is that, were two trees offered to the choice of the beaver,
one of which preponderated to the water, and the other did not, he would,
in felling the first, omit as unnecessary the precautions just described, but
observe them in felling the second.

In a subsequent portion of the journal other particulars are given
respecting the habits of the singular animal in question, and of the mode
of trapping it employed by the party, and we give them here for the sake
of continuity. The principal food of the beavers is bark, and of this they
put by regularly a large store for winter provision, selecting the proper
kind with care and deliberation. A whole tribe, consisting sometimes of
two or three hundred, will set out together upon a foraging expedition,
and pass through groves of trees all apparently similar, until a particular
one suits their fancy. This they cut down, and, breaking off its most tender
branches, divide them into short slips of equal length and divest these
slips of their bark, which they carry to the nearest stream leading to their
village, thence floating it home. Occasionally the slips are stored away for
the winter without being stripped of the bark, and, in this event, they are
careful to remove the refuse wood from their dwellings, as soon as they
have eaten the rind, taking the sticks to some distance. During the spring
of the year the males are never found with the tribe at home, but always by
themselves, either singly, or in parties of two or three, when they appear
to lose their usual habits of sagacity, and fall an easy prey to the arts of
the trapper. In summer they return home, and busy themselves, with the
females, in making provision for winter. They are described as exceedingly
ferocious animals when irritated.

Now and then they may be caught upon shore, especially the males
in spring, who are then fond of roving to some distance from the water
in search of food. When thus caught, they are easily killed with a blow
from a stick, but the most certain and efficacious mode of taking them
is by means of the trap. This is simply constructed to catch the foot of
the animal. The trapper places it usually in some position near the shore,
and just below the surface of the water, fastening it by a small chain to a
pole stuck in the mud. In the mouth of the machine is placed one end of
a small branch, the other end rising above the surface, and well soaked in
the liquid bait whose odour is found to be attractive to the beaver. As soon
as the animal scents it, he rubs his nose against the twig, and, in so doing,
steps upon the trap, springs it, and is caught. The trap is made very light,
for the convenience of portage, and the prey would easily swim off with

it but for its being fastened to the pole by a chain – no other species of fastening could resist his teeth. The experienced trapper readily detects the presence of beaver in any pond or stream, discovering them by a thousand appearances which would afford no indication to the unpractised observer.

Many of the identical woodcutters whom the two voyagers had watched so narrowly from the treetop fell afterwards a victim to trap, and their fine furs became a prey to the spoilers, who made sad havoc in the lodge at the swamp. Other waters in the neighbourhood also afforded the travellers much sport, and they long remembered the island at the creek's mouth, by the name of Beaver Island, in consequence. They left this little Paradise in high spirits on the 27th of the month, and, pursuing their hitherto some-what uneventful voyage up the river, arrived, by 1st September, without any incident of note, at the mouth of a large river on the south, to which they gave the name of Currant River, from some berries abounding upon its margin, but which was, beyond doubt, the Quicourre.* The principal objects of which the journal takes notice in this interval are the numerous herds of buffalo which darkened the prairies in every direction, and the remains of a fortification on the south shore of the river, nearly opposite the upper extremity of what has been since called Bonhomme Island.* Of these remains a minute description is given, which tallies in every important particular with that of Captains Lewis and Clark. The travellers had passed the Little Sioux, Floyd's, the Great Sioux, White Stone and Jacques rivers on the north, with Wawandysenche Creek and White Paint River on the south,* but at neither of these streams did they stop to trap for any long period. They had also passed the great village of the Omahas,* of which the journal takes no notice whatever. This village, at the time, consisted of full three hundred houses, and was inhabited by a numerous and powerful tribe, but it is not immediately upon the banks of the Missouri, and the boats probably went by it during the night – for the party had begun to adopt this mode of progress, through fear of the Sioux.* We resume the narrative of Mr Rodman, with 2nd September.]

2nd September – We had now reached a part of the river where, accord-ing to all report, a great deal of danger was to be apprehended from the Indians, and we became extremely cautious in our movements. This was the region inhabited by the Sioux, a warlike and ferocious tribe, who had, upon several occasions, evinced hostility to the whites, and were known to be constantly at war with all the neighbouring tribes. The Canadians had many incidents to relate respecting their savage propensities, and I had much apprehension lest these cowardly creatures should take an

opportunity of deserting, and retracing their way to the Mississippi. To lessen the chances of this, I removed one of them from the piroque, and supplied his place by Poindexter Greely. All the Greelys came in from the shore, turning loose the horses. Our arrangement was now as follows: in the piroque, Poindexter Greely, Pierre Junôt, Toby and one Canadian; in the large boat, myself, Thornton, Wormley, John, Frank, Robert and Meredith Greely, and three Canadians, with the dog. We set sail about dusk, and, having a brisk wind from the south, made good headway, although, as night came on, we were greatly embarrassed* by the shoals. We continued our course without interruption, however, until a short time before daybreak, when we ran into the mouth of a creek, and concealed the boats among the underwood.

3rd and 4th September – During both of these days it rained and blew with excessive violence, so that we did not leave our retreat at all. The weather depressed our spirits very much, and the narratives of the Canadians about the terrible Sioux did not serve to raise them. We all congregated in the cabin of the large boat, and held a council in regard to our future movements. The Greelys were for a bold push through the dangerous country, maintaining that the stories of the voyagers were mere exaggerations, and that the Sioux would only be a little troublesome, without proceeding to hostility. Wormley and Thornton, however, as well as Pierre (all of whom had much experience in the Indian character), thought that our present policy was the best, although it would necessarily detain us much longer on our voyage than would otherwise be the case. My own opinion coincided with theirs – in our present course we might escape any collision with the Sioux – and I did not regard the delay as a matter of consequence.

5th September – We set off at night, and proceeded for about ten miles, when the day began to appear, and we hid the boats as before, in a narrow creek, which was well adapted to the purpose, as its mouth was almost blocked up by a thickly wooded island. It again came on to rain furiously, and we were all drenched to the skin before we could arrange matters for turning in, in the cabin. Our spirits were much depressed by the bad weather, and the Canadians especially were in a miserable state of dejection. We had now come to a narrow part of the river where the current was strong, and the cliffs on both sides overhung the water, and were thickly wooded with lynn,* oak, black walnut, ash and chestnut. Through such a gorge we knew it would be exceedingly difficult to pass without observation, even at night, and our apprehensions of attack were

greatly increased. We resolved not to recommence our journey until late, and then to proceed with the most stealthy caution. In the mean time we posted a sentry on shore, and one in the piroque, while the rest of us busied ourselves in overhauling the arms and ammunition, and preparing for the worst.

About ten o'clock we were getting ready to start, when the dog gave a low growl, which made us all fly to our rifles, but the cause of the disturbance proved to be a single Indian of the Ponca tribe,* who came up frankly to our sentry on shore, and extended his hand. We brought him on board, and gave him whiskey, when he became very communicative, and told us that his tribe, who lived some miles lower down the river, had been watching our movements for several days past, but that the Poncas were friends and would not molest the whites, and would trade with us upon our return. They had sent him now to caution the whites against the Sioux, who were great robbers, and who were lying in wait for the party at a bend of the river, twenty miles farther up. There were three bands of them, he said, and it was their intention to kill us all, in revenge for an insult sustained by one of their chiefs, many years previously, at the hands of a French trapper.

CHAPTER IV

[We left our travellers, on 5th September, apprehending a present attack from the Sioux.* Exaggerated accounts of the ferocity of this tribe had inspired the party with an earnest wish to avoid them, but the tale told by the friendly Ponca made it evident that a collision must take place. The night voyages were therefore abandoned as impolitic, and it was resolved to put a bold face upon the matter, and try what could be effected by blustering. The remainder of the night of the 5th was spent in warlike demonstration. The large boat was cleared for action as well as possible, and the fiercest aspect assumed which the nature of the case would permit. Among other preparations for defence, the cannon was got out from below, and placed forward upon the cuddy deck, with a load of bullets, by way of canister shot.* Just before sunrise the adventurers started up the river in high bravado, aided by a heavy wind. That the enemy might perceive no semblance of fear or mistrust, the whole party joined the Canadians in an uproarious boat song at the top of their voices, making the woods reverberate, and the buffaloes stare.

The Sioux, indeed, appear to have been Mr Rodman's bugbears par excellence, and he dwells upon them and their exploits with peculiar emphasis. The narrative embodies a detailed account of the tribe – an account which we can only follow in such portions as appear to possess novelty, or other important interest. *Sioux* is the French term for the Indians in question – the English have corrupted it into *Sues*. Their primitive name is said to be *Darcotas*. Their original seats were on the Mississippi, but they had gradually extended their dominions, and, at the date of the journal, occupied almost the whole of that vast territory circumscribed by the Mississippi, the Saskatchawine, the Missouri and the Red River of Lake Winnipeg. They were subdivided into numerous clans. The Darcotas proper were the Winowacants, called the Gens du Lac by the French – consisting of about five hundred warriors, and living on both sides of the Mississippi, in the vicinity of the Falls of St Anthony. Neighbours of the Winowacants, and residing north of them on the river St Peter's, were the Wappatomies, about two hundred men. Still farther up the St Peter's lived a band of one hundred, called the Wappytooties, among themselves, and by the French the Gens des Feuilles. Higher up the river yet, and near its source, resided the Sissytoonies, in number two hundred or thereabouts. On the Missouri dwelt the Yanktons and the Tetons. Of the first tribe there were two branches, the northern and southern, of which the former led an Arab life in the plains at the sources of the Red, Sioux and Jacques rivers, being in number about five hundred. The southern branch kept possession of the tract lying between the river Des Moines on the one hand, and the rivers Jacques and Sioux on the other. But the Sioux most renowned for deeds of violence are the Tetons, and of these there were four tribes – the Saonies, the Minnakenozzies, the Okydandies and the Bois-Brulés. These last, a body of whom were now lying in wait to intercept the voyagers, were the most savage and formidable of the whole race, numbering about two hundred men, and residing on both sides of the Missouri near the rivers called by Captains Lewis and Clark the White and Teton. Just below the Chayenne River were the Okydandies, one hundred and fifty. The Minnakenozzies – two hundred and fifty – occupied a tract between the Chayenne and the Watarhoo, and the Saonies, the largest of the Teton bands, counting as many as three hundred warriors, were found in the vicinity of the Warreconne.*

Besides these four divisions – the regular Sioux – there were five tribes of seceders called Assiniboins:* the Menatopae Assiniboins, two hundred, on Mouse River, between the Assiniboin and the Missouri; the Gens de

Feuilles Assiniboins, two hundred and fifty, occupying both sides of White River; the Big Devils, four hundred and fifty, wandering about the heads of Porcupine and Milk rivers; with two other bands whose names are not mentioned, but who roved on the Saskatchawine, and numbered together about seven hundred men. These seceders were often at war with the parent or original Sioux.

In person, the Sioux generally are an ugly, ill-made race, their limbs being much too small for the trunk, according to our ideas of the human form – their cheekbones are high, and their eyes protruding and dull. The heads of the men are shaved, with the exception of a small spot on the crown, whence a long tuft is permitted to fall in plaits upon the shoulders; this tuft is an object of scrupulous care, but is now and then cut off, upon an occasion of grief or solemnity. A full-dressed Sioux chief presents a striking appearance. The whole surface of the body is painted with grease and coal. A shirt of skins is worn as far down as the waist, while round the middle is a girdle of the same material, and sometimes of cloth, about an inch in width; this supports a piece of blanket or fur passing between the thighs. Over the shoulders is a white-dressed buffalo mantle, the hair of which is worn next the skin in fair weather, but turned outwards in wet. This robe is large enough to envelope the whole body, and is frequently ornamented with porcupine quills (which make a rattling noise as the warrior moves) as well as with a great variety of rudely painted figures, emblematical of the wearer's military character. Fastened to the top of the head is worn a hawk's feather, adorned with porcupine quills. Leggings of dressed antelope skin serve the purpose of pantaloons, and have seams at the sides, about two inches wide, and bespotted here and there with small tufts of human hair, the trophies of some scalping excursion. The moccasins are of elk or buffalo skin, the hair worn inwards; on great occasions the chief is seen with the skin of a polecat dangling at the heel of each boot. The Sioux are indeed partial to this noisome* animal, whose fur is in high favour for tobacco pouches and other appendages.

The dress of a chieftain's squaw is also remarkable. Her hair is suffered to grow long, is parted across the forehead, and hangs loosely behind, or is collected into a kind of net. Her moccasins do not differ from her husband's, but her leggings extend upwards only as far as the knee, where they are met by an awkward shirt of elk skin depending to the ankles, and supported above by a string going over the shoulders. This shirt is usually confined to the waist by a girdle, and over all is thrown a buffalo mantle like that of the men. The tents of the Teton Sioux are described

as of neat construction, being formed of white-dressed buffalo hide, well secured and supported by poles.

The region infested by the tribe in question extends along the banks of the Missouri for some hundred and fifty miles or more, and is chiefly prairie land, but is occasionally diversified by hills. These latter are always deeply cut by gorges or ravines, which in the middle of summer are dry, but form the channels of muddy and impetuous torrents during the season of rain. Their edges are fringed with thick woods, as well at top as at bottom, but the prevalent aspect of the country is that of a bleak lowland, with rank herbage, and without trees. The soil is strongly impregnated with mineral substances in great variety – among others with Glauber salts, copperas, sulphur and alum,* which tinge the water of the river and impart to it a nauseous odour and taste. The wild animals most usual are the buffalo, deer, elk and antelope. We again resume the words of the journal.]

6th September – The country was open, and the day remarkably pleasant: so that we were all in pretty good spirits notwithstanding the expectation of attack. So far, we had not caught even a glimpse of an Indian, and we were making rapid way through their dreaded territory. I was too well aware, however, of the savage tactics to suppose that we were not narrowly watched, and had made up my mind that we should hear something of the Tetons at the first gorge which would afford them a convenient lurking place.

About noon a Canadian bawled out "The Sioux! The Sioux!" – and directed attention to a long, narrow ravine, which intersected the prairie on our left, extending from the banks of the Missouri as far as the eye could reach, in a southwardly course. This gully was the bed of a creek, but its waters were now low, and the sides rose up like huge regular walls on each side. By the aid of a spyglass I perceived at once the cause of the alarm given by the voyageur. A large party of mounted savages were coming down the gorge in Indian file, with the evident intention of taking us unawares. Their calumet feathers* had been the means of their detection, for every now and then we could see some of these bobbing up above the edge of the gully, as the bed of the ravine forced the wearer to rise higher than usual. We could tell that they were on horseback by the motion of these feathers. The party was coming upon us with great rapidity, and I gave the word to pull on with all haste so as to pass the mouth of the creek before they reached it. As soon as the Indians perceived by our increased speed that they were discovered, they immediately raised a yell, scrambled out of the gorge and galloped down upon us, to the number of about one hundred.

Our situation was now somewhat alarming. At almost any other part of the Missouri which we had passed during the day, I should not have cared so much for these freebooters, but, just here, the banks were remarkably steep and high, partaking of the character of the creek banks, and the savages were enabled to overlook us completely, while the cannon, upon which we had placed so much reliance, could not be brought to bear upon them at all. What added to our difficulty was that the current in the middle of the river was so turbulent and strong that we could make no headway against it except by dropping arms and employing our whole force at the oars. The water near the northern shore was too shallow even for the pirogue, and our only mode of proceeding, if we designed to proceed at all, was by pushing in within a moderate stone's throw of the left or southern bank, where we were completely at the mercy of the Sioux, but where we could make good headway by means of our poles and the wind, aided by the eddy. Had the savages attacked us at this juncture I cannot see how we could have escaped them. They were all well provided with bows and arrows, and small round shields, presenting a very noble and picturesque appearance. Some of the chiefs had spears, with fanciful flags attached, and were really gallant-looking men. The portrait here annexed is that of the commander-in-chief of the party which now interrupted us, and was sketched by Thornton, at a subsequent period.

Either good luck upon our own parts, or great stupidity on the parts of the Indians, relieved us very unexpectedly from the dilemma. The savages, having galloped up to the edge of the cliff just above us, set up another yell, and commenced a variety of gesticulations, whose meaning we at once knew to be that we should stop and come on shore. I had expected this demand, and had made up my mind that it would be most prudent to pay no attention to it at all, but proceed on our course. My refusal to stop had at least one good effect, for it appeared to mystify the Indians most wonderfully, who could not be brought to understand the measure in the least, and stared at us, as we kept on our way without answering them, in the most ludicrous amazement. Presently they commenced an agitated

conversation among themselves, and at last finding that nothing could be made of us, fairly turned their horses' heads to the southward and galloped out of sight, leaving us as much surprised as rejoiced at their departure.

In the mean time we made the most of the opportunity, and pushed on with might and main, in order to get out of the region of steep banks before the anticipated return of our foes. In about two hours we again saw them in the south, at a great distance, and their number much augmented. They came on at full gallop, and were soon at the river, but our position was now much more advantageous, for the banks were sloping, and there were no trees to shelter the savages from our shot. The current, moreover, was not so rapid as before, and we were enabled to keep in mid-channel. The party, it seems, had only retreated to procure an interpreter, who now appeared upon a large grey horse, and, coming into the river as far as he could without swimming, called out to us in bad French to stop, and come on shore. To this I made one of the Canadians reply that, to oblige our friends the Sioux, we would willingly stop, for a short time, and converse, but that it was inconvenient for us to come on shore, as we could not do so without incommoding our great medicine* (here the Canadian pointed to the cannon), who was anxious to proceed on his voyage, and whom we were afraid to disobey.

At this they began again their agitated whisperings and gesticulations among themselves, and seemed quite at a loss what to do. In the mean time the boats had been brought to anchor in a favourable position, and I was resolved to fight now, if necessary, and endeavour to give the freebooters so warm a reception as would inspire them with wholesome dread for the future. I reflected that it was nearly impossible to keep on good terms with these Sioux, who were our enemies at heart, and who could only be restrained from pillaging and murdering us by a conviction of our prowess. Should we comply with their present demands, go on shore, and even succeed in purchasing a temporary safety by concessions and donations, such conduct would not avail us in the end, and would be rather a palliation than a radical cure of the evil. They would be sure to glut their vengeance sooner or later, and, if they suffered us to go on our way now, might hereafter attack us at a disadvantage, when it might be as much as we could do to repel them, to say nothing of inspiring them with awe. Situated as we were here, it was in our power to give them a lesson they would be apt to remember, and we might never be in so good a situation again. Thinking thus, and all except the Canadians agreeing with me in opinion, I determined to assume a bold stand, and rather provoke

hostilities than avoid them. This was our true policy. The savages had no firearms which we could discover, except an old carabine* carried by one of the chiefs, and their arrows would not prove very effective weapons when employed at so great a distance as that now between us. In regard to their number, we did not care much for that. Their position was one which would expose them to the full sweep of our cannon.

When Jules (the Canadian) had finished his speech about incommoding our great medicine, and when the consequent agitation had somewhat subsided among the savages, the interpreter spoke again and propounded three queries. He wished to know, first, whether we had any tobacco, or whiskey, or fire-guns; secondly, whether we did not wish the aid of the Sioux in rowing our large boat up the Missouri as far as the country of the Ricarees,* who were great rascals; and, thirdly, whether our great medicine was not a very large and strong green grasshopper.

To these questions, propounded with profound gravity, Jules replied, by my directions, as follows. First, that we had plenty of whiskey, as well as tobacco, with an inexhaustible supply of fire-guns and powder – but that our great medicine had just told us that the Tetons were greater rascals than the Ricarees – that they were our enemies – that they had been lying in wait to intercept and kill us for many days past – that we must give them nothing at all, and hold no intercourse with them whatever; we should therefore be afraid to give them anything, even if so disposed, for fear of the anger of the great medicine, who was not to be trifled with. Secondly, that, after the character just given the Sioux Tetons, we could not think of employing them to row our boat; and, thirdly, that it was a good thing for them (the Sioux) that our great medicine had not overheard their last query, respecting the "large green grasshopper", for, in that case, it might have gone very hard with them (the Sioux). Our great medicine was anything but a large green grasshopper, and *that* they should soon see, to their cost, if they did not immediately go, the whole of them, about their business.

Notwithstanding the imminent danger in which we were all placed, we could scarcely keep our countenances in beholding the air of profound admiration and astonishment with which the savages listened to these replies, and I believe that they would have immediately dispersed, and left us to proceed on our voyage, had it not been for the unfortunate words in which I informed them that they were greater rascals than the Ricarees. This was, apparently, an insult of the last atrocity, and excited them to an incontrollable degree of fury. We heard the words "Ricaree! Ricaree!" repeated, every now and then, with the utmost emphasis and excitement,

and the whole band, as well as we could judge, seemed to be divided into two factions: the one urging the immense power of the great medicine, and the other the outrageous insult of being called greater rascals than the Ricarees. While matters stood thus, we retained our position in the middle of the stream, firmly resolved to give the villains a dose of our canister shot, upon the first indignity which should be offered us.

Presently, the interpreter on the grey horse came again into the river, and said that he believed we were no better than we should be – that all the palefaces who had previously gone up the river had been friends of the Sioux, and had made them large presents – that they, the Tetons, were determined not to let us proceed another step unless we came on shore and gave up all our fire-guns and whiskey, with half of our tobacco – that it was plain we were allies of the Ricarees (who were now at war with the Sioux), and that our design was to carry them supplies, which we should not do – lastly, that they did not think very much of our great medicine, for he had told us a lie in relation to the designs of the Tetons, and was positively nothing but a great green grasshopper, in spite of all that we thought to the contrary. These latter words, about the great green grass-hopper, were taken up by the whole assemblage as the interpreter uttered them, and shouted out at the top of the voice, that the great medicine himself might be sure to hear the taunt. At the same time, they all broke into wild disorder, galloping their horses furiously in short circles, using contemptuous and indecent gesticulations, brandishing their spears, and drawing their arrows to the head.

I knew that the next thing would be an attack, and so determined to anticipate it at once, before any of our party were wounded by the discharge of their weapons – there was nothing to be gained by delay, and everything by prompt and resolute action. As soon as a good opportunity presented itself, the word was given to fire, and instantly obeyed. The effect of the discharge was very severe, and answered all our purposes to the full. Six of the Indians were killed, and perhaps three times as many badly wounded. The rest were thrown into the greatest terror and confusion, and made off into the prairie at full speed, as we drew up our anchors, after reloading the gun, and pulled boldly in for the shore. By the time we had reached it, there was not an unwounded Teton within sight.

I now left John Greely, with three Canadians, in charge of the boats, landed with the rest of the men, and, approaching a savage who was severely but not dangerously wounded, held a conversation with him, by means of Jules. I told him that the whites were well disposed to the Sioux, and

to all the Indian nations; that our sole object in visiting his country was to trap beaver, and see the beautiful region which had been given the red men by the Great Spirit; that when we had procured as many furs as we wished, and seen all we came to see, we should return home; that we had heard that the Sioux, and especially the Tetons, were a quarrelsome race, and that therefore we had brought with us our great medicine for protection; that he was now much exasperated with the Tetons on account of their intolerable insult in calling him a green grasshopper (which he was not); that I had had great difficulty in restraining him from a pursuit of the warriors who had fled, and from sacrificing the wounded who now lay around us; and that I had only succeeded in pacifying him by becoming personally responsible for the future good behaviour of the savages. At this portion of my discourse the poor fellow appeared much relieved, and extended his hand in token of amity. I took it, and assured him and his friends of my protection as long as we were unmolested, following up this promise by a present of twenty carrots of tobacco, some small hardware, beads and red flannel, for himself and the rest of the wounded.

While all this was going on, we kept a sharp look out for the fugitive Sioux. As I concluded making the presents, several gangs of these were observable in the distance, and were evidently seen by the disabled savage, but I thought it best to pretend not to perceive them, and shortly afterwards returned to the boats. The whole interruption had detained us full three hours, and it was after three o'clock when we once more started on our route. We made extraordinary haste, as I was anxious to get as far as possible from the scene of action before night. We had a strong wind at our back, and the current diminished in strength as we proceeded, owing to the widening of the stream. We therefore made great way, and by nine o'clock had reached a large and thickly wooded island, near the northern bank, and close by the mouth of a creek. Here we resolved to encamp, and had scarcely set foot on shore when one of the Greelys shot and secured a fine buffalo, many of which were upon the place. After posting our sentries for the night, we had the hump for supper, with as much whiskey as was good for us. Our exploit of the day was then freely discussed, and by most of the men was treated as an excellent joke, but I could by no means enter into any merriment upon the subject. Human blood had never, before this epoch, been shed at my hands, and although reason urged that I had taken the wisest, and what would no doubt prove in the end the most merciful course, still conscience, refusing to hearken even to reason herself, whispered pertinaciously within my ear: "It is human blood which thou hast

shed." The hours wore away slowly – I found it impossible to sleep. At length the morning dawned, and with its fresh dews, its fresher breezes and smiling flowers, there came a new courage, and a bolder tone of thought, which enabled me to look more steadily upon what had been done, and to regard in its only proper point of view the urgent necessity of the deed.

7th September – Started early, and made great way, with a strong cold wind from the east. Arrived about noon at the upper gorge of what is called the Great Bend,* a place where the river performs a circuit of full thirty miles, while by land the direct distance is not more than fifteen hundred yards. Six miles beyond this is a creek about thirty-five yards wide, coming in from the south. The country here is of peculiar character: on each side of the river the shore is strewed thickly with round stones washed from the bluffs, and presenting a remarkable appearance for miles. The channel is very shallow, and much interrupted with sandbars. Cedar is here met with more frequently than any other species of timber, and the prairies are covered with a stiff kind of prickly pear, over which our men found it no easy matter to walk in their moccasins.

About sunset, in endeavouring to avoid a rapid channel, we had the misfortune to run the larboard side of the large boat on the edge of a sandbar, which so heeled us over that we were very near getting filled with water, in spite of the greatest exertion. As it was, much damage was done to the loose powder, and the Indian goods were all more or less injured. As soon as we found the boat careering,* we all jumped into the water, which was here up to our armpits, and by main force held the sinking side up. But we were still in a dilemma, for all our exertions were barely sufficient to keep from capsizing, and we could not spare a man to do anything towards pushing off. We were relieved, very unexpectedly, by the sinking of the whole sandbar from under the boat, just as we were upon the point of despair. The bed of the river in this neighbourhood is much obstructed by these shifting sands, which frequently change situations with great rapidity, and without apparent cause. The material of the bars is a fine hard yellow sand, which, when dry, is of a brilliant glass-like appearance, and almost impalpable.

8th September – We were still in the heart of the Teton country, and kept a sharp lookout, stopping as seldom as possible, and then only upon the islands, which abounded with game in great variety – buffaloes, elk, deer, goats, black-tailed deer and antelopes, with plover and brant* of many kinds. The goats are uncommonly tame, and have *no* beard. Fish is not so abundant here as lower down the river. A white wolf was killed by John

Greely in a ravine upon one of the smaller islands. Owing to the difficult navigation, and the frequent necessity of employing the towline, we did not make great progress this day.

9th September – Weather growing sensibly colder, which made us all anxious of pushing our way through the Sioux country, as it would be highly dangerous to form our winter encampment in their vicinity. We aroused ourselves to exertion, and proceeded rapidly, the Canadians singing and shouting as we went. Now and then we saw, in the extreme distance, a solitary Teton, but no attempt was made to molest us, and we began to gather courage from this circumstance. Made twenty-eight miles during the day, and encamped at night, in high glee, on a large island well stocked with game, and thickly covered with cottonwood.

[We omit the adventures of Mr Rodman from this period until 10th April. By the last of October, nothing of importance happening in the interval, the party made their way to a small creek which they designated as Otter Creek,* and, proceeding up this about a mile to an island well adapted for their purpose, built a log fort and took up their quarters for the winter. The location is just above the old Ricara* villages. Several parties of these Indians visited the voyagers, and behaved with perfect friendliness – they had heard of the skirmish with the Tetons, the result of which hugely pleased them. No further trouble was experienced from any of the Sioux. The winter wore away pleasantly, and without accident of note. On 10th April the party resumed their voyage.]

CHAPTER V

10th April 1792 – The weather was now again most delicious, and revived our spirits exceedingly. The sun began to have power, and the river was quite free of ice, so the Indians assured us, for a hundred miles ahead. We bade adieu to Little Snake [a chief of the Ricarees who had shown the voyagers many evidences of friendship during the winter] and his band, with unfeigned regret, and set out, after breakfast, on our voyage. Perrine [an agent of the Hudson Bay Fur Company on his way to Petite Côte] accompanied us with three Indians for the first ten miles, when he took leave of us and made his way back to the village, where (as we afterwards heard) he met with a violent death from the hands of a squaw to whom he offered some insult. Upon parting with the agent, we pushed on vigorously up the river, and made great way, notwithstanding a rapid current. In the

afternoon, Thornton, who had been complaining for some days past, was taken seriously ill, so much so that I urged the return of the whole party to the hut, there to wait until he should get better, but he resisted this offer so strongly that I was forced to yield. We made him a comfortable bed in the cabin, and paid him every attention, but he had a raging fever, with occasional delirium, and I was much afraid that we should lose him. In the mean time we still pushed ahead with resolution, and by night had made twenty miles – an excellent day's work.

11th April – Still beautiful weather. We started early, and had a good wind, which aided us greatly – so that, but for Thornton's illness, we should all have been in fine spirits. He seemed to grow much worse, and I scarcely knew how to act. Everything was done for his comfort which could be done; Jules, the Canadian, made him some tea, from prairie herbs, which had the effect of inducing perspiration, and allayed the fever very sensibly. We stopped at night on the mainland to the north, and three hunters went out into the prairie by moonlight, returning at one in the morning, without their rifles, and with a fat antelope.

They related that, having proceeded many miles across the country, they reached the banks of a beautiful rivulet, where they were much surprised and alarmed at discovering a large war party of the Saonie Sioux, who immediately took them prisoners, and carried them a mile on the other side of the stream to a kind of park, or enclosure, walled with mud and sticks, in which was a large herd of antelopes. These animals were still coming into the park, the gates of which were so contrived as to prevent escape. This was an annual practice of the Indians. In the autumn, the antelopes retire for food and shelter from the prairie to the mountainous regions on the south of the river. In the spring they recross it in great numbers, and are then easily taken by being enticed into a strong enclosure as above described.

The hunters (John Greely, the Prophet and a Canadian) had scarcely any hope of escape from the clutches of the Indians (who numbered as many as fifty), and had well-nigh made up their minds to die. Greely and the Prophet were disarmed and tied hand and foot; the Canadian, however, was suffered, for some reason not perfectly understood, to remain unbound, and was only deprived of his rifle, the savages leaving him in possession of his hunter's knife (which possibly they did not perceive, as it was worn in a sort of sheath in the side of his legging) and treating him otherwise with a marked difference from their demeanour to the others. This circumstance proved the source of the party's deliverance.

It was, perhaps, nine o'clock at night when they were first taken. The moon was bright, but, as the air was unusually cool for the season, the savages had kindled two large fires at a sufficient distance from the park not to frighten the antelopes, who were still pouring into it continually. At these fires they were occupied in cooking their game when the hunters so unexpectedly came upon them from round a clump of trees. Greely and the Prophet, after being disarmed and bound with strong thongs of buffalo hide, were thrown down under a tree at some distance from the blaze, while the Canadian was permitted to seat himself, in charge of two savages, by one of the fires, the rest of the Indians forming a circle round the other and larger one. In this arrangement, the time wore away slowly, and the hunters were in momentary expectation of death; the cords of the two who were bound caused them, also, infinite pain, from the tightness with which they were fastened. The Canadian had endeavoured to hold a conversation with his guards, in the hope of bribing them to release him, but could not make himself understood. About midnight, the congregation around the large fire were suddenly disturbed by the dash of several large antelopes in succession through the midst of the blaze. These animals had burst through a portion of the mud wall which confined them, and, mad with rage and affright, had made for the light of the fire, as is the habit of insects at night in like circumstances. It seems, however, that the Saonies had never heard of any similar feat of these usually timid creatures, for they were in great terror at the unexpected interruption, and their alarm increased to perfect dismay as the whole captured herd came rushing and bounding upon them, after the lapse of a minute or so from the outbreak of the first few. The hunters described the scene as one of the most singular nature. The beasts were apparently frantic, and the velocity and impetuosity with which they flew, rather than leapt, through the flames, and through the midst of the terrified savages, was said by Greely (a man not in the least prone to exaggerate) to have been not only an imposing but even a terrible spectacle. They carried everything before them in their first plunges, but, having cleared the large fire, they immediately dashed at the small one, scattering the brands and blazing wood about; then returned, as if bewildered, to the large one, and so backwards and forwards until the decline of the fires, when, in small parties, they scampered off like lightning to the woods.

Many of the Indians were knocked down in this furious mêlée, and there is no doubt that some of them were seriously, if not mortally, wounded by the sharp hoofs of the agile antelopes. Some threw themselves flat on the

ground, and so avoided injury. The Prophet and Greely, not being near the fires, were in no danger. The Canadian was prostrated at the first onset by a kick which rendered him senseless for some minutes. When he came to himself he was nearly in darkness, for the moon had gone behind a heavy thundercloud, and the fires were almost out, or only existed in brands scattered hither and thither. He saw no Indians near him, and, instantly arousing himself to escape, made, as well as he could, for the tree where his two comrades were lying. Their thongs were soon cut, and the three set off at full speed in the direction of the river, without stopping to think of their rifles, or of anything beyond present security. Having run for some miles, and finding no one in pursuit, they slackened their pace, and made their way to a spring for a draught of water. Here it was they met with the antelope which, as I mentioned before, they brought with them to the boats. The poor creature lay panting, and unable to move, by the border of the spring. One of its legs was broken, and it bore evident traces of fire. It was no doubt one of the herd which had been the means of deliverance. Had there been even a chance of its recovery the hunters would have spared it in token of their gratitude, but it was miserably injured, so they put it at once out of its misery, and brought it home to the boats, where we made an excellent breakfast upon it next morning.

12th, 13th, 14th and 15th April – During these four days we kept on our course without any adventure of note. The weather was very pleasant during the middle of the day, but the nights and mornings were exceedingly cold, and we had sharp frosts. Game was abundant. Thornton still continued ill, and his sickness perplexed and grieved me beyond measure. I missed his society very much, and now found that he was almost the only member of our party in whom I could strictly confide. By this I merely mean that he was almost the only one to whom I could, or would, freely unburthen my heart, with all its wild hopes, and fantastic wishes – not that any individual among us was unworthy of implicit faith. On the contrary, we were all like brothers, and a dispute, of any importance, never occurred. One interest seemed to bind all; or rather we appeared to be a band of voyagers *without* interest in view – mere travellers for pleasure. What ideas the Canadians might have held upon this subject I cannot, indeed, exactly say. These fellows talked a great deal, to be sure, about the profits of the enterprise, and especially about their expected share of it, yet I can scarcely think they cared much for these points, for they were the most simple-minded, and certainly the most obliging set of beings upon the face of the earth. As for the rest of the crew, I have no doubt in the world that the pecuniary

benefit to be afforded by the expedition was the last thing upon which they speculated. Some singular evidences of the feeling which more or less pervaded us all occurred during the prosecution of the voyage. Interests which, in the settlements, would have been looked upon as of the highest importance were here treated as matters unworthy of a serious word, and neglected, or totally discarded upon the most frivolous pretext. Men who had travelled thousands of miles through a howling wilderness, beset by horrible dangers, and enduring the most heart-rending privations for the ostensible purpose of collecting peltries, would seldom take the trouble to secure them when obtained, and would leave behind them without a sigh an entire cache of fine beaver skin rather than forgo the pleasure of pushing up some romantic-looking river, or penetrating into some craggy and dangerous cavern, for minerals whose use they knew nothing about, and which they threw aside as lumber at the first decent opportunity.

In all this my own heart was very much with the rest of the party, and I am free to say that, as we proceeded on our journey, I found myself less and less interested in the main business of the expedition, and more and more willing to turn aside in pursuit of idle amusement – if indeed I am right in calling by so feeble a name as amusement that deep and most intense excitement with which I surveyed the wonders and majestic beauties of the wilderness. No sooner had I examined one region than I was possessed with an irresistible desire to push forward and explore another. As yet, however, I felt as if in too close proximity to the settlements for the full enjoyment of my burning love of nature, and of *the unknown*. I could not help being aware that *some* civilized footsteps, although few, had preceded me in my journey – that *some* eyes before mine own had been enraptured with the scenes around me. But for this sentiment, ever obtruding itself, I should no doubt have loitered more frequently on the way, turning aside to survey the features of the region bordering upon the river, and perhaps penetrating deeply, at times, into the heart of the country to the north and south of our route. But I was anxious to *go on* – to get, if possible, beyond the extreme bounds of civilization – to gaze, if I could, upon those gigantic mountains of which the existence had been made known to us only by the vague accounts of the Indians. These ulterior hopes and views I communicated fully to no one of our party save Thornton. He participated in all my most visionary projects, and entered completely into the spirit of romantic enterprise which pervaded my soul. I therefore felt his illness as a bitter evil. He grew worse daily, while it was out of our power to render him any effectual assistance.

16th April – Today we had a cold rain with a high wind from the north, obliging us to come to anchor until late in the afternoon. At four o'clock, p.m., we proceeded, and made five miles by night. Thornton was much worse.

17th and 18th April – During both these days we had a continuance of raw, unpleasant weather, with the same cold wind from the north. We observed many large masses of ice in the river, which was much swollen and very muddy. The time passed unpleasantly, and we made no way. Thornton appeared to be dying, and I now resolved to encamp at the first convenient spot, and remain until his illness should terminate. We accordingly, at noon this day, drew the boats up a large creek coming in from the south, and formed an encampment on the mainland.

25th April – We remained at the creek until this morning, when, to the great joy of us all, Thornton was sufficiently recovered to go on. The weather was fine, and we proceeded gaily through a most lovely portion of the country without encountering a single Indian, or meeting with any adventure out of the usual course until the last of the month, when we reached the country of the Mandans, or rather of the Mandans, the Minnetarees and the Ahnahaways,* for these three tribes all live in the near vicinity of each other, occupying five villages. Not a great many years ago the Mandans were settled in nine villages, about eighty miles below, the ruins of which we passed without knowing what they were – seven on the west and two on the east of the river, but they were thinned off by the smallpox and their old enemies the Sioux, until reduced to a mere handful, when they ascended to their present position. [Mr R. gives here a tolerably full account of the Minnetarees and Ahnahaways or Wassatoons, but we omit it, as differing in no important particular from the ordinary statements respecting these nations.] The Mandans received us with perfect friendliness, and we remained in their neighbourhood three days, during which we overhauled and repaired the piroque, and otherwise refitted. We also obtained a good supply of a hard corn, of a mixed colour, which the savages had preserved through the winter in holes, near the front of their lodges. While with the Mandans we were visited by a Minnetaree chief, called Waukerassah, who behaved with much civility, and was of service to us in many respects. The son of this chief we engaged to accompany us as interpreter as far as the great fork. We made the father several presents, with which he was greatly pleased.* On the first of May we bade adieu to the Mandans, and went on our way.

1st May – The weather was mild, and the surrounding country began to assume a lovely appearance with the opening vegetation, which was now

much advanced. The cottonwood leaves were quite as large as a crown, and many flowers were full blown. The low grounds began to spread out here more than usual, and were well supplied with timber. The cottonwood and common willow, as well as red willow, abounded, with rose bushes in great plenty. Beyond the low grounds on the river, the country extended in one immense plain without wood of any kind. The soil was remarkably rich. The game was more abundant than we had ever yet seen it. We kept a hunter ahead of us on each bank, and today they brought in an elk, a goat, five beavers and a great number of plovers. The beavers were very tame and easily taken. This animal is quite a *bonne bouche** as an article of food, especially the tail, which is of a somewhat glutinous nature, like the fins of the halibut. A beaver tail will suffice for a plentiful dinner for three men. We made twenty miles before night.

2nd May – We had a fine wind this morning, and used our sails until noon, when it became rather too much for us, and we stopped for the day. Our hunters went out and shortly returned with an immense elk, whom Neptune had pulled down after a long chase, the animal having been only slightly wounded by a buckshot. He measured six feet in height. An antelope was also caught about dusk. As soon as the creature saw our men, it flew off with the greatest velocity, but after a few minutes stopped, and returned on its steps, apparently through curiosity – then bounded away again. This conduct was repeated frequently, each time the game coming nearer and nearer, until at length it ventured within rifle distance, when a shot from the Prophet brought it down. It was lean and with young. These animals, although of incredible swiftness of foot, are still bad swimmers, and thus frequently fall a victim to the wolves in their attempts to cross a stream. Today made twelve miles.

3rd May – This morning we made great headway, and by night had accomplished full thirty miles. The game continued to be abundant. Buffaloes, in vast numbers, lay dead along the shore, and we saw many wolves devouring the carcasses. They fled always at our approach. We were much at a loss to account for the death of the buffaloes, but some weeks afterwards the mystery was cleared up. Arriving at a pass of the river where the bluffs were steep and the water deep at their base, we observed a large herd of the huge beasts swimming across, and stopped to watch their motions. They came in a sidelong manner down the current, and had apparently entered the water from a gorge, about half a mile above, where the bank sloped into the stream. Upon reaching the land on the west side of the river they found it impossible to ascend the cliffs, and the water

was beyond their depth. After struggling for some time, and endeavouring in vain to get a foothold in the steep and slippery clay, they turned and swam to the eastern shore, where the same kind of inaccessible precipices presented themselves, and where the ineffectual struggle to ascend was repeated. They now turned a second time, a third, a fourth and a fifth – always making the shore at very nearly the same places. Instead of suffering themselves to go down with the current in search of a more favourable landing (which might have been found a quarter of a mile below), they seemed bent upon maintaining their position, and, for this purpose, swam with their breasts at an acute angle to the stream and used violent exertions to prevent being borne down. At the fifth time of crossing, the poor beasts were so entirely exhausted that it was evident they could do no more. They now struggled fearfully to scramble up the bank, and one or two of them had nearly succeeded when, to our great distress (for we could not witness their noble efforts without commiseration), the whole mass of loose earth above caved in, and buried several of them in its fall, without leaving the cliff in better condition for ascent. Upon this the rest of the herd commenced a lamentable kind of lowing or moaning – a sound conveying more of a dismal sorrow and despair than anything which it is possible to imagine – I shall never get it out of my head. Some of the beasts made another attempt to swim the river, struggled a few minutes, and sank – the waves above them being dyed with the red blood that gushed from their nostrils in the death agony. But the greater part, after the moaning described, seemed to yield supinely to their fate, rolled over on their backs and disappeared. The whole herd were drowned – not a buffalo escaped. Their carcasses were thrown up in half an hour afterwards upon the flat grounds a short distance below, where, but for their ignorant obstinacy, they might so easily have landed in safety.

4th May – The weather was delightful, and, with a fair warm wind from the south, we made twenty-five miles before night. Today Thornton was sufficiently recovered to assist in the duties of the boat. In the afternoon he went out with me into the prairie on the west, where we saw a great number of early spring flowers of a kind never seen in the settlements. Many of them were of a rare beauty and delicious perfume. We saw also game in great variety, but shot none, as we were sure the hunters would bring in more than was wanted for use, and I was averse to the wanton destruction of life. On our way home we came upon two Indians of the Assiniboin nation, who accompanied us to the boats. They had evinced nothing like distrust on the way, but, on the contrary, had been frank and

bold in demeanour; we were therefore much surprised to see them, upon coming within a stone's throw of the piroque, turn, both of them, suddenly round, and make off into the prairie at full speed. Upon getting a good distance from us, they stopped and ascended a knoll which commanded a view of the river. Here they lay on their bellies, and, resting their chins on their hands, seemed to regard us with the deepest astonishment. By the aid of a spyglass I could minutely observe their countenances, which bore evidence of both amazement and terror. They continued watching us for a long time. At length, as if struck with a sudden thought, they arose hurriedly and commenced a rapid flight in the direction from which we had seen them issue at first.

5th May – As we were getting under way very early this morning, a large party of Assiniboins suddenly rushed upon the boats, and succeeded in taking possession of the piroque before we could make any effectual resistance. No one was in it at the time except Jules, who escaped by throwing himself into the river, and swimming to the large boat, which we had pushed out into the stream. These Indians had been brought upon us by the two who had visited us the day before, and the party must have approached us in the most stealthy manner imaginable, as we had our sentries regularly posted, and even Neptune failed to give any token of their vicinity.

We were preparing to fire upon the enemy when Misquash (the new interpreter – son of Waukerassah) gave us to understand that the Assiniboins were friends and were now making signals of amity. Although we could not help thinking that the highway robbery of our boat was but an indifferent way of evincing friendship, still we were willing to see what these people had to say, and desired Misquash to ask them why they had behaved as they did. They replied with many protestations of regard, and we at length found that they really had no intention of molesting us any further than to satisfy an ardent curiosity which consumed them, and which they now entreated us to appease. It appeared that the two Indians of the day before, whose singular conduct had so surprised us, had been struck with sudden amazement at the sooty appearance of our Negro, Toby. They had never before seen or heard of a blackamoor, and it must therefore be confessed that their astonishment was not altogether causeless. Toby, moreover, was as ugly an old gentleman as ever spoke – having all the peculiar features of his race: the swollen lips, large white protruding eyes, flat nose, long ears, double head,* pot belly and bow legs. Upon relating their adventure to their companions, the two savages could obtain no credit for the wonderful story, and were about losing caste for ever, as liars and double-dealers,

when they proposed to conduct the whole band to the boats by way of vindicating their veracity. The sudden attack seemed to have been the mere result of impatience on the part of the still incredulous Assiniboins, for they never afterwards evinced the slightest hostility, and yielded up the piroque as soon as we made them understand that we would let them have a good look at old Toby. The latter personage took the matter as a very good joke, and went ashore at once, *in naturalibus*,* that the inquisitive savages might observe the whole extent of the question. Their astonishment and satisfaction were profound and complete. At first they doubted the evidence of their own eyes, spitting upon their fingers and rubbing the skin of the Negro to be sure that it was not painted. The wool on the head elicited repeated shouts of applause, and the bandy legs were the subject of unqualified admiration. A jig dance on the part of our ugly friend brought matters to a climax. Wonder was now at its height. Approbation could go no further. Had Toby but possessed a single spark of ambition he might then have made his fortune for ever by ascending the throne of the Assiniboins, and reigning as King Toby the First.

This incident detained us until late in the day. After interchanging some civilities and presents with the savages, we accepted the aid of six of the band in rowing us about five miles on our route – a very acceptable assistance, and one for which we did not fail to thank Toby. We made, today, only twelve miles, and encamped at night on a beautiful island which we long remembered for the delicious fish and fowl which its vicinity afforded us. We stayed at this pleasant spot two days, during which we feasted and made merry, with very little care for the morrow,* and with very little regard to the numerous beaver which disported around us. We might have taken at this island one or two hundred skins without difficulty. As it was, we collected about twenty. The island is at the mouth of a tolerably large river* coming in from the south, and at a point where the Missouri strikes off in a due westerly direction. The latitude is about 48.

8th May – We proceeded with fair winds and fine weather, and after making twenty or twenty-five miles, reached a large river coming in from the north. Where it debouches,* however, it is very narrow – not more than a dozen yards wide, and appears to be quite choked up with mud. Upon ascending it a short distance, a fine bold stream is seen, seventy or eighty yards wide, and very deep, passing through a beautiful valley, abounding in game. Our new guide told us the name of this river, but I have no memorandum of it.* Robert Greely shot here some geese which build their nests upon trees.

9th May – In many places a little distant from the riverbanks, today, we observed the ground encrusted with a white substance which proved to be a strong salt. We made only fifteen miles, owing to several petty hindrances, and encamped at night on the mainland, among some clumps of cottonwood and rabbit-berry bushes.*

10th May – Today the weather was cold, and the wind strong, but fair. We made great headway. The hills in this vicinity are rough and jagged, showing irregular broken masses of rock, some of which tower to a great height, and appear to have been subject to the action of water. We picked up several pieces of petrified wood and bone, and coal was scattered about in every direction. The river gets very crooked.

11th May – Detained the greater part of the day by squalls and rain. Towards evening it cleared up beautifully with a fair wind, of which we took advantage, making ten miles before encamping. Several fat beavers were caught, and a wolf was shot upon the bank. He seemed to have strayed from a large herd which were prowling about us.

12th May – Landed today at noon, after making ten miles, upon a small steep island, for the purpose of overhauling some of our things. As we were about taking our departure, one of the Canadians, who led the van of the party and was several yards in advance, suddenly disappeared from our view with a loud scream. We all ran forward immediately, and laughed heartily upon finding that our man had only tumbled into an empty cache, from which we soon extricated him. Had he been alone, however, there is much room for question if he would have got out at all. We examined the hole carefully but found nothing in it beyond a few empty bottles; we did not even see anything serving to show whether French, British or Americans had concealed their goods here, and we felt some curiosity upon this point.

13th May – Arrived at the junction of the Yellowstone with the Missouri,* after making twenty-five miles during the day. Misquash here left us, and returned home.

CHAPTER VI

The character of the country through which we had passed for the last two or three days was cheerless in comparison with that to which we had been accustomed. In general it was more level, the timber being more abundant on the skirts of the stream, with little or none at all in the distance. Wherever bluffs appeared upon the margin we descried

THE JOURNAL OF JULIUS RODMAN

indications of coal, and we saw one extensive bed of a thick bituminous nature which very much discoloured the water for some hundred yards below it. The current is more gentle than hitherto, the water clearer, and the rocky points and shoals fewer, although such as we had to pass were as difficult as ever. We had rain incessantly, which rendered the banks so slippery that the men who had the towing lines could scarcely walk. The air too was disagreeably chilly, and upon ascending some low hills near the river we observed no small quantity of snow lying in the clefts and ridges. In the extreme distance on our right we had perceived several Indian encampments which had the appearance of being temporary, and had been only lately abandoned. This region gives no indication of any permanent settlement, but appears to be a favourite hunting ground with the tribes in the vicinity – a fact rendered evident by the frequent traces of the hunt, which we came across in every direction. The Minnetarees of the Missouri, it is well known, extend their excursions in pursuit of game as high as the great fork, on the south side, while the Assiniboins go up still higher. Misquash informed us that between our present encampment and the Rocky Mountains we should meet with no lodges except those of the Minnetarees that reside on the lower or south side of the Saskatchawine.

The game had been exceedingly abundant, and in great variety – elk, buffalo, bighorn,* mule deer, bears, foxes, beaver, etc., etc., with wildfowl innumerable. Fish was also plentiful. The width of the stream varied considerably from two hundred and fifty yards to passes where the current rushed between bluffs not more than a hundred feet apart. The face of these bluffs generally was composed of a light yellowish freestone,* intermingled with burnt earth, pumice stone and mineral salts. At one point the aspect of the country underwent a remarkable change, the hills retiring on both sides to a great distance from the river, which was thickly interspersed with small and beautiful islands, covered with cottonwood. The low grounds appeared to be very fertile, those on the north wide and low, and opening into three extensive valleys. Here seemed to be the extreme northern termination of the range of mountains through which the Missouri had been passing for so long a time, and which are called the Black Hills* by the savages. The change from the mountainous region to the level was indicated by the atmosphere, which now became dry and pure – so much so indeed that we perceived its effects upon the seams of our boats, and our few mathematical instruments.

As we made immediate approach to the forks* it came on to rain very hard, and the obstructions in the river were harassing in the extreme.

The banks in some places were so slippery, and the clay so soft and stiff, that the men were obliged to go barefooted, as they could not keep on their moccasins. The shores also were full of pools of stagnant water, through which we were obliged to wade, sometimes up to our armpits. Then again we had to scramble over enormous shoals of sharp-pointed flints, which appeared to be the wreck of cliffs that had fallen down en masse. Occasionally we came to a precipitous gorge or gully, which it would put us to the greatest labour to pass, and in attempting to push by one of these the rope of the large boat (being old and much worn) gave way and permitted her to be swung round by the current upon a ledge of rock in the middle of the stream, where the water was so deep that we could only work in getting her off by the aid of the piroque, and so were full six hours in effecting it.

At one period we arrived at a high wall of black rock on the south, towering above the ordinary cliffs for about a quarter of a mile along the stream, after which there was an open plain, and, about three miles beyond this again, another wall of a light colour on the same side, fully two hundred feet high, then another plain or valley, and then still another wall of the most singular appearance arises on the north, soaring in height probably two hundred and fifty feet, and being in thickness about twelve, with a very regular artificial character. These cliffs present indeed the most extraordinary aspect, rising perpendicularly from the water. The last-mentioned are composed of very white soft sandstone, which readily receives the impression of the water. In the upper portion of them appears a sort of frieze or cornice formed by the intervention of several thin horizontal strata of a white freestone, hard and unaffected by the rains. Above them is a dark rich soil, sloping gradually back from the water to the extent of a mile or thereabouts, when other hills spring up abruptly to the height of full five hundred feet more.

The face of these remarkable cliffs, as might be supposed, is chequered with a variety of lines formed by the trickling of the rains upon the soft material, so that a fertile fancy might easily imagine them to be gigantic monuments reared by human art, and carved over with hieroglyphical devices. Sometimes there are complete niches (like those we see for statues in common temples) formed by the dropping out bodily of large fragments of the sandstone, and there are several points where staircases and long corridors appear, as accidental fractures in the freestone cornice happen to let the rain trickle down uniformly upon the softer material below. We passed these singular bluffs in a bright moonlight and their effect upon

my imagination I shall never forget. They had all the air of enchanted structures (such as I have dreamt of), and the twittering of myriads of martins, which have built their nests in the holes that everywhere perforate the mass, aided this conception not a little. Besides the main walls there are, at intervals, inferior ones, of from twenty to a hundred feet high, and from one to twelve or fifteen feet thick, perfectly regular in shape, and perpendicular. These are formed of a succession of large black-looking stones, apparently made up of loam, sand and quartz, and absolutely symmetrical in figure, although of various sizes. They are usually square, but sometimes oblong (always parallelepipedal*) and are lying one above the other as exactly and with as perfect regularity as if placed there by some mortal mason, each upper stone covering and securing the point of junction between two lower ones, just as bricks are laid in a wall. Sometimes these singular erections run in parallel lines, as many as four abreast; sometimes they leave the river and go back until lost amid the hills; sometimes they cross each other at right angles, seeming to enclose large artificial gardens, the vegetation within which is often of a character to preserve the illusion. Where the walls are thinnest, there the bricks are less in size, and the converse. We regarded the scenery presented to our view at this portion of the Missouri as altogether the most surprising, if not the most beautiful, which we had yet seen. It left upon my own mind an impression of novelty – of singularity – which can never be effaced.

Shortly before reaching the fork we came to a pretty large island on the northern side, one mile and a quarter from which is a low ground on the south very thickly covered with fine timber. After this there were several small islands, at each of which we touched for a few minutes as we passed. Then we came to a very black-looking bluff on the north, and then to two other small islands, about which we observed nothing remarkable. Going a few miles farther we reached a tolerably large island situated near the point of a steep promontory, afterwards passing two others, smaller. All these islands are well timbered. It was at night on 13th May that we were shown by Misquash the mouth of the large river, which in the settlements goes by the name of the Yellowstone, but by the Indians is called the Ahmateaza.* We made our camp on the south shore in a beautiful plain covered with cottonwood.

14th May – This morning we were all awake and stirring at an early hour, as the point we had now reached was one of great importance, and it was requisite that, before proceeding any farther, we should make

some survey by way of ascertaining which of the two large streams in view would afford us the best passage onward. It seemed to be the general wish of the party to push up one of these rivers as far as practicable, with a view of reaching the Rocky Mountains, when we might perhaps hit upon the headwaters of the large stream Aregan,* described by all the Indians with whom we had conversed upon the subject as running into the great Pacific Ocean. I was also anxious to attain this object, which opened to my fancy a world of exciting adventure, but I foresaw many difficulties which we must necessarily encounter if we made the attempt with our present limited information in respect to the region we should have to traverse, and the savages who occupied it, about which latter we only knew indeed that they were generally the most ferocious of the North American Indians. I was afraid, too, that we might get into the wrong stream, and involve ourselves in an endless labyrinth of troubles which would dishearten the men. These thoughts, however, did not give me any long uneasiness, and I set to work at once to explore the neighbourhood, sending some of the party up the banks of each stream to estimate the comparative volume of water in each, while I myself, with Thornton and John Greely, proceeded to ascend the high grounds in the fork, whence an extensive prospect of the surrounding region might be attained. We saw here an immense and magnificent country spreading out on every side into a vast plain, waving with glorious verdure, and alive with countless herds of buffaloes and wolves, intermingled with occasional elk and antelope. To the south the prospect was interrupted by a range of high, snow-capped mountains, stretching from south-east to north-west, and terminating abruptly. Behind these again was a higher range, extending to the very horizon in the north-west. The two rivers presented the most enchanting appearance as they wound away their long snake-like lengths in the distance, growing thinner and thinner until they looked like mere faint threads of silver as they vanished in the shadowy mists of the sky. We could glean nothing, from their direction so far, as regards their ultimate course, and so descended from our position much at a loss what to do.

The examination of the two currents gave us but little more satisfaction. The north stream was found to be the deeper, but the south was the wider, and the volume of water differed but little. The first had all the colour of the Missouri, but the latter had the peculiar round gravelly bed which distinguishes a river that issues from a mountainous region. We were finally determined by the easier navigation of the north branch

to pursue this course, although from the rapidly increasing shallowness we found that in a few days, at farthest, we should have to dispense with the large boat. We spent three days at our encampment, during which we collected a great many fine skins, and deposited them with our whole stock on hand, in a well-constructed cache on a small island in the river a mile below the junction.* We also brought in a great quantity of game, and especially of deer, some haunches of which we pickled or corned for future use. We found great abundance of the prickly pear in this vicinity, as well as chokeberries* in great plenty upon the low grounds and ravines. There were also many yellow and red currants (not ripe) with gooseberries. Wild roses were just beginning to open their buds in the most wonderful profusion. We left our encampment in fine spirits on the morning of

18th May – The day was pleasant, and we proceeded merrily, notwithstanding the constant interruptions occasioned by the shoals and jutting points with which the stream abounds. The men, one and all, were enthusiastic in their determination to persevere, and the Rocky Mountains were the sole theme of conversation. In leaving our peltries behind us, we had considerably lightened the boats, and we found much less difficulty in getting them forward through the rapid currents than would otherwise have been the case. The river was crowded with islands, at nearly all of which we touched. At night we reached a deserted Indian encampment, near bluffs of a blackish clay. Rattlesnakes disturbed us very much, and before morning we had a heavy rain.

19th May – We had not proceeded far before we found the character of the stream materially altered, and very much obstructed by sandbars, or rather ridges of small stones, so that it was with the greatest difficulty we could force a passage for the larger boat. Sending two men ahead to reconnoitre, they returned with an account of a wider and deeper channel above, and once again we felt encouraged to persevere. We pushed on for ten miles and encamped on a small island for the night. We observed a peculiar mountain in the distance to the south, of a conical form, isolated, and entirely covered with snow.

20th May – We now entered into a better channel, and pursued our course with little interruption for sixteen miles, through a clayey country of peculiar character, and nearly destitute of vegetation. At night we encamped on a very large island, covered with tall trees, many of which were new to us. We remained at this spot for five days to make some repairs in the piroque.

During our sojourn here an incident of note occurred. The banks of the Missouri in this neighbourhood are precipitous, and formed of a peculiar blue clay, which becomes excessively slippery after rain. The cliffs, from the bed of the stream back to the distance of a hundred yards, or thereabouts, form a succession of steep terraces of this clay, intersected in numerous directions by deep and narrow ravines, so sharply worn by the action of water at some remote period of time as to have the appearance of artificial channels. The mouths of these ravines, where they debouch upon the river, have a very remarkable appearance, and look from the opposite bank, by moonlight, like gigantic columns standing erect upon the shore. To an observer from the uppermost terrace the whole descent towards the stream has an indescribably chaotic and dreary air. No vegetation of any kind is seen.

John Greely, the Prophet, the interpreter Jules and myself started out after breakfast one morning to ascend to the topmost terrace on the south shore for the purpose of looking around us – in short, to see what could be seen. With great labour, and by using scrupulous caution, we succeeded in reaching the level grounds at the summit opposite our encampment. The prairie here differs from the general character of that kind of land in being thickly overgrown for many miles back with cottonwood, rose bushes, red willow and broad-leaved willow, the soil being unsteady, and at times swampy, like that of the ordinary low grounds – it consists of a black-looking loam, one third sand, and when a handful of it is thrown into water, it dissolves in the manner of sugar, with strong bubbles. In several spots we observed deep incrustations of common salt, some of which we collected and used.

Upon reaching these level grounds we all sat down to rest, and had scarcely done so when we were alarmed by a loud growl immediately in our rear, proceeding from the thick underwood. We started to our feet at once in great terror, for we had left our rifles at the island, that we might be unencumbered in the scramble up the cliffs, and the only arms we had were pistols and knives. We had scarcely time to say a word to each other before two enormous brown bears (the first we had yet encountered during the voyage) came rushing at us open-mouthed from a clump of rose bushes. These animals are much dreaded by the Indians, and with reason, for they are indeed formidable creatures, possessing prodigious strength, with untameable ferocity, and the most wonderful tenacity of life. There is scarcely any way of killing them by a bullet, unless the shot be through the brains, and these are defended by two large muscles covering the side

of the forehead, as well as by a projection of a thick frontal bone. They have been known to live for days with half a dozen balls through the lungs, and even with very severe injuries in the heart. So far we had never met with a brown bear, although often with its tracks in the mud or sand, and these we had seen nearly a foot in length, exclusive of the claws, and full eight inches in width.

What to do was now the question. To stand and fight, with such weapons as we possessed, was madness, and it was folly to think of escape by flight in the direction of the prairie, for not only were the bears running towards us from that quarter, but, at a very short distance back from the cliffs, the underwood of briar bushes, dwarf willow, etc., was so thick that we could not have made our way through it at all, and if we kept our course along the river between the underwood and the top of the cliff, the animals would catch us in an instant, for as the ground was boggy we could make no progress upon it, while the large flat foot of the bear would enable him to travel with ease. It seemed as if these reflections (which it takes some time to embody in words) flashed all of them through the minds of all of us in an instant – for every man sprang at once to the cliffs, without sufficiently thinking of the hazard that lay there.

The first descent was some thirty or forty feet, and not very precipitous; the clay here also partook in a slight degree of the loam of the upper soil, so that we scrambled down with no great difficulty to the first terrace, the bears plunging after us with headlong fury. Arrived here, we had not a moment for hesitation. There was nothing left for us now but to encounter the enraged beasts upon the narrow platform where we stood, or to go over the second precipice. This was nearly perpendicular, sixty or seventy feet deep, and composed entirely of the blue clay which was now saturated with late rains, and as slippery as glass itself. The Canadian, frightened out of his senses, leapt to the edge at once, slid with the greatest velocity down the cliff and was hurled over the third descent by the impetus of his course. We then lost sight of him, and of course supposed him killed, for we could have no doubt that his terrific slide would be continued from precipice to precipice until it terminated with a plunge over the last into the river – a fall of more than a hundred and fifty feet.

Had Jules not gone in this way it is more than probable that we should all have decided, in our extremity, upon attempting the descent, but his fate caused us to waver, and in the mean time the monsters were upon us. This was the first time in all my life I had ever been brought to close quarters with a wild animal of any strength or ferocity, and I have no

scruple to acknowledge that my nerves were completely unstrung. For some moments I felt as if about to swoon, but a loud scream from Greely, who had been seized by the foremost bear, had the effect of arousing me to exertion, and when once fairly aroused I experienced a kind of wild and savage pleasure from the conflict.

One of the beasts, upon reaching the narrow ledge where we stood, had made an immediate rush at Greely, and had borne him to the earth, where he stood over him, holding him with his huge teeth lodged in the breast of his overcoat – which, by the greatest good fortune, he had worn, the wind being chilly. The other, rolling rather than scrambling down the cliff, was under so much headway when he reached our station that he could not stop himself until the one half of his body hung over the precipice; he staggered in a sidelong manner, and his right legs went over while he held on in an awkward way with his two left. While thus situated he seized Wormley by the heel with his mouth, and for an instant I feared the worst, for in his efforts to free himself from the grasp the terrified struggler aided the bear to regain his footing. While I stood helpless, as above described, through terror, and watching the event without ability to render the slightest aid, the shoe and moccasin of W. were torn off in the grasp of the animal, who now tumbled headlong down to the next terrace, but stopped himself, by means of his huge claws, from sliding farther. It was now that Greely screamed for aid, and the Prophet and myself rushed to his assistance. We both fired our pistols at the bear's head, and my own ball, I am sure, must have gone through some portion of his skull, for I held the weapon close to his ear. He seemed more angry, however, than hurt; the only good effect of the discharge was in his quitting his hold of Greely (who had sustained no injury) and making at us. We had nothing but our knives to depend upon, and even the refuge of the terrace below was cut off from us by the presence of another bear there. We had our backs to the cliff, and were preparing for a deadly contest, not dreaming of help from Greely (whom we supposed mortally injured) when we heard a shot, and the huge beast fell at our feet, just when we felt his hot and horribly fetid breath in our faces. Our deliverer, who had fought many a bear in his lifetime, had put his pistol deliberately to the eye of the monster, and the contents had entered the brain.

Looking now downwards, we discovered the fallen bruin* making ineffectual efforts to scramble up to us – the soft clay yielded to his claws, and he fell repeatedly and heavily. We tried him with several shots, but did no harm, and resolved to leave him where he was for the crows. I

do not see how he could ever have made his escape from the spot. We crawled along the ledge on which we stood for nearly half a mile before we found a practicable path to the prairie above us, and did not get to camp until late in the night. Jules was there all alive, but cruelly bruised – so much so indeed that he had been unable to give any intelligible account of his accident or of our whereabouts. He had lodged in one of the ravines upon the third terrace, and had made his way down its bed to the river shore.

COMMONLY CITED WORKS

IRV *Astoria, or, Enterprise beyond the Rocky Mountains*, by the American writer Washington Irving (1783–1859), published in Philadelphia in 1836. For the Astoria expedition, see note to p. 265.

LEW *History of the Expedition under the Command of Captains Lewis and Clark, to the Sources of the Missouri*, published in two volumes in Philadelphia in 1814, and consisting principally of the journals kept by Meriwether Lewis (1774–1809) and William Clark (1770–1838) themselves, shaped into a coherent narrative by the financier Nicholas Biddle (1786–1844) and "prepared for the press" by the journalist Paul Allen (1775–1826). For the Lewis and Clark expedition, see note to p. 265.

MOR1 The 'First Voyage' in *Narrative of Four Voyages*, published in New York in 1832, the ghost-written memoir of the American sea captain, explorer and trader Benjamin Morrell (1795–c.1839), who made a number of voyages to the Atlantic, the Southern Ocean and the Pacific Islands. Morrell's ghost writer was the American author Samuel Woodworth (1784–1842). The 'First Voyage' is an account of a trading and sealing expedition undertaken to the Southern Ocean by the sealer *Wasp*, captained by Morrell, and the schooner *Henry*, captained by Robert Johnson, in 1822, with a further remit to "ascertain the practicality, under favourable circumstances, of penetrating to the South Pole".

MOR4 The 'Fourth Voyage' in the above work, an account of a sealing expedition to the South Atlantic and Pacific led by Morrell on the schooner *Antarctic* between September 1829 and August 1831.

NOTE ON THE TEXT

For details of the original publication of the tales in this collection, as well as of the sources from which the texts are taken (if different), see the first note for each story. The publisher would like to acknowledge the assistance in the preparation of this edition of the annotations in the following volumes, from which some factual information has been taken: *The Collected Writings of Edgar Allan Poe*, vol. i: *Imaginary Voyages*, ed. Burton R. Pollin (1981; New York: Gordian Press, 1994), used for *The Narrative of Arthur Gordon Pym of Nantucket* and *The Journal of Julius Rodman*, particularly in relation to Poe's sources; *The Collected Works of Edgar Allan Poe*, vol. ii: *Tales and Sketches*, ed. Thomas Ollive Mabbott (Cambridge, MA: Belknap Press of Harvard University Press, 1978), used for 'Loss of Breath', 'Mystification', 'How to Write a *Blackwood* Article' and 'A Predicament'; and *The Collected Works of Edgar Allan Poe*, vol. iii: *Tales and Sketches*, ed. Thomas Ollive Mabbott (Cambridge, MA: Belknap Press of Harvard University Press, 1978), used for 'The Balloon Hoax', 'The Cask of Amontillado', 'The Gold Bug' and 'Hop-Frog'. Spelling and punctuation have been standardized, modernized and made consistent throughout.

NOTES

p. 3, *The Narrative of Arthur Gordon Pym of Nantucket*: For details of the publication history of this novel, see Extra Material.

p. 5, *Preface*: Added for the volume edition of the novel, published in July 1838. See Extra Material.

p. 5, *Mr Poe... city of Richmond*: For Poe's relationship with Thomas Willis White (1788–1843) and employment with the *Southern Literary Messenger*, see Extra Material.

p. 7, *Nantucket*: An island thirty miles south of Cape Cod off the coast of Massachusetts, and formerly a major whaling centre.

p. 7, *Edgarton New Bank*: The town of Edgartown is on Martha's Vineyard, another island south of Cape Cod, thirty miles west of Nantucket.

p. 7, *New Bedford*: A city on the south coast of Massachusetts. New Bedford was an important whaling port in the nineteenth century.

p. 7, *Tinian*: One of the Northern Mariana Islands in the western Pacific Ocean.

p. 7, *She had a half-deck... sloop-fashion*: A half-deck is a deck covering half the length of a ship, extending from the mainmast aft (that is, towards the stern). A cuddy is a small cabin in the stern, although Poe appears to treat this term as synonymous with "half-deck". A sloop is a sailing boat with a single mast, whose sails are rigged fore and aft, that is, along the line of the keel (a structural beam running along the bottom of the vessel) as opposed to perpendicular to it. (Vessels whose sails are arranged in the latter fashion are said to be "square-rigged".)

p. 8, *jib and mainsail*: The sails fore and aft, respectively, of the mast on a sloop (see previous note).

p. 9, *bilge water*: Water that collects in the bilge, the lowest part of the hull.

p. 10, *no reef in either jib or mainsail*: A reef is a section of a sail that can be taken in or rolled up. The point here is that the sails have not been "reefed" and are therefore entirely exposed to the wind.

p. 10, *bows*: The front end of a ship.

p. 10, *broach to*: Veer suddenly to windward.

p. 10, *the sea behind fell combing over our counter*: That is, the waves behind the vessel broke over the stern.

p. 10, *let it go by the run*: That is, loosened it and let it fall freely.

p. 10, *by the board*: Overboard.

p. 10, *Under the jib only*: The English playwright William Evans Burton (1804–60), reviewing the novel in his own literary journal, *Burton's Gentleman's Magazine*, in September 1838, pointed out the impossibility of sailing under the jib in the absence of the mainmast: "A cabin boy of a month's standing would have been ashamed of such a phrase!" In 1839, Burton became Poe's employer – see Extra Material.

p. 11, *close-hauled*: That is, with its sails set as close to the wind as possible, typically at an angle of between thirty and forty-five degrees relative to the wind direction.

p. 11, *New London*: A seaport in Connecticut.

p. 12, *in stays*: A vessel is said to be "in stays" when, during tacking (changing course), the bows are pointed directly into the wind.

p. 12, *jolly-boat*: A small ship's boat, typically clinker-built, that is, with a hull consisting of overlapping planks.

p. 12, *main-chains*: Brackets on the side of a ship that serve as anchoring points for the mainmast shrouds (ropes supporting the mainmast).

p. 13, *air boxes*: Air tanks used to aid buoyancy.

p. 15, *the Messieurs Enderby, I believe, of Liverpool*: A reference to Samuel Enderby & Sons, a major whaling and sealing company founded in London (not Liverpool) in 1775 by the entrepreneur Samuel Enderby (1717–97).

p. 15, *the brig Grampus*: A brig is a sailing vessel with two masts (a foremast and a mainmast), both of which are square-rigged, but with a lower fore-and-aft sail on the mainmast. (For fore-and-aft and square rigging, see fifth note to p. 7.) The name *Grampus* was likely taken from the novel *Miriam Coffin, or, The Whale Fishermen* (1835) by the American writer Joseph C. Hart (1798–1855), which concerns the Nantucket whaling industry, and in which the character Jethro Coffin decides upon the *Grampus* as the most suitable name for a whaler: "The *Thunderer* sounds well – but it won't do – it's pagan. *King Philip* or *Anawan* might answer upon a pinch, but such titles savour of man worship. The *Grampus* – yea, that's it – I have hit it at last! *Grampus* – *Grampus*, ay, that will do. Her name is decided on" (Volume I, Chapter I).

p. 17, *Long Tom*: Likely a reference to the character Long Tom Coffin, a towering coxswain from the nautical adventure novel *The Pilot: A Tale of*

the Sea (1823) by the American author James Fenimore Cooper (1789–1851), the point being that Peterson believes that he has mistaken a veteran seaman of Long Tom's ilk for his own grandson. A "Long Tom" was also a kind of long-barrelled naval gun.

p. 17, *combings*: Raised borders around the edges of a ship's hatches and scuttles, designed to prevent entry of water.

p. 18, *dark lantern*: A lantern with a sliding front to shut off the light.

p. 19, *sea biscuit*: A form of hard, dry biscuit eaten by sailors on sea voyages.

p. 19, *under weigh*: Sometimes erroneously used in place of "under way" in a nautical context, due to association with "weighing anchor", that is, raising the anchor in preparation for beginning a voyage.

p. 19, *aboveboard*: In fact a gambling term – to play "above board" is to have one's cards visible above the level of the table, thereby avoiding suspicion of cheating – with no nautical meaning.

p. 20, *the expedition… the Columbia*: For the Lewis and Clark expedition, see note to p. 265. Lewis and Clark's own written account of the journey, published in 1814, was later one of the principal sources for Poe's unfinished *The Journal of Julius Rodman* (1840), included in this edition.

p. 21, *larboard*: Port (the left side of a ship when one is facing forward).

p. 21, *the burning sand plains of Zahara*: The Sahara Desert.

p. 25, *the blade of my penknife*: The 1838 edition read "the penblade of my knife", presumably a compositor's error.

p. 27, *mumbled*: Chewed.

p. 30, *orlop deck*: The lowest deck.

p. 30, *a gill*: A quarter of a pint.

p. 34, *handspike*: A kind of crowbar used on board a ship consisting of a wooden rod tipped with iron.

p. 34, *companionway*: Steps (or a ladder) leading from the deck to the cabins below.

p. 34, *chronometer*: A highly accurate timepiece indicating Greenwich Mean Time. By comparing the time provided by a chronometer with the local time, calculated through observation of the stars, mariners were able to establish a vessel's longitude.

p. 35, *concerned in the mutiny, twenty-seven*: The second and final instalment of the novel to appear in the *Southern Literary Messenger*, published in February 1837, ended here. See Extra Material.

p. 35, *line manager*: A man responsible for the rope attached to the harpoon on a whaling vessel, and specifically for ensuring that it did not become tangled or caught when the harpoon was fired.

p. 35, *Dirk Peters*: The character of Dirk Peters was influenced by the fur trapper and interpreter Pierre Dorion, Jr (1782–1814), who was a Metis, that is, a person in Canada of mixed indigenous and European ancestry. (His mother was Yankton Sioux – for whom see first note to p. 295.) He is best remembered as a guide for the Astoria expedition of 1810–13 – see note to p. 265. Poe took information about Dorion from IRV.

p. 35, *the tribe of Upsarokas… Black Hills*: The Apsáalooke, known as the Crow, are a Native American tribe historically associated with the area around the Yellowstone River in Montana. The Black Hills, a mountain range in western South Dakota and north-eastern Wyoming, represented the eastern limit of their territory.

p. 36, *Lewis River*: A tributary of the Snake River in Wyoming, named after Meriwether Lewis (for whom see note to p. 265).

p. 39, *salt junk*: Salt meat eaten by sailors on long voyages.

p. 41, *the back of a letter… from Mr Ross*: An error of continuity: the reverse of Augustus's note was previously "a dreary and unsatisfactory blank" (Chapter III).

p. 41, *pea jacket*: A short double-breasted jacket, typically worn by sailors.

p. 42, *main hatchway*: The hatchway adjacent to the mainmast.

p. 43, *Many years elapsed… this fact*: Another error of continuity: Augustus will be dead a few weeks after these events; it is therefore impossible for him to apprise Pym of his near despair "many years" later.

p. 46, *When lying to… beam ends*: To "lie to" is to remain stationary in the water during a gale. Poe provides a detailed description of lying to in Chapter VII. A headsail is any sail, such as a jib (see note to p. 8), set forward of the foremast. A vessel is thrown upon its "beam ends" when it is knocked to one side by the wind so that its horizontal beams are touching the water.

p. 47, *schooner*: A small seagoing vessel with two masts, both fore-and-aft rigged. (For fore-and-aft rigging, see fifth note to p. 7.)

p. 47, *foresail*: The largest and lowest sail on the foremast of a square-rigged ship, such as a brig.

p. 48, *oil casks*: Whaling vessels are usually fitted with iron oil tanks – why the *Grampus* was not I have never been able to ascertain. [POE'S NOTE]

p. 48, *five sail*: That is, five sailing vessels.

p. 50, *a flaw of wind*: A squall.

p. 50, *foretopsail*: A sail above the foresail (see second note to p. 47).

p. 50, *trysail*: A fore-and-aft sail (see fifth note to p. 7) raised in heavy weather.

p. 50, *Simms*: Perhaps named after the writer William Gilmore Simms (1806–70), best known for his historical novels set in the American South. An unfavourable review by Poe of Simms's *The Partisan* (1835) appeared in the *Southern Literary Messenger* in January 1836, although he would later, in a review of *The Wigwam and the Cabin* (1845) published in the *Broadway Journal* in October 1845, describe Simms as "the best novelist which this country has, upon the whole, produced".

p. 50, —— *Greely*: Perhaps named after the American newspaper editor Horace Greeley (1811–72), founder of *The New-Yorker* (1834) and the *New York Tribune* (1841). Poe reused the name in *The Journal of Julius Rodman*, included in this edition, albeit for a more sympathetic character.

p. 51, *A sail was thrummed, and got under the bows*: That is, pieces of rope yarn were sewn into a spare sail to create a mat with a rough surface, which was then passed under the bottom of the ship to stop the leak.

p. 51, *Spoke two small schooners*: That is, communicated with two schooners.

p. 51, *Norfolk*: A city in Virginia.

p. 52, *on the other side there were five*: In fact, due to the defection of Greely and Allen, described in the entry for 7th July in the previous chapter, there are now seven men in the mate's party.

p. 53, *throwing round... take them aback*: That is, arranging the sails in such a way that they counteract each other, bringing the vessel to a standstill. A sail is taken "aback" when it is turned so that the wind strikes it on its leeward side and it is therefore pushed back against the mast. As Poe goes on to explain, this technique is impossible in gale conditions, in which the sails must be either severely reefed or taken down altogether.

p. 53, *when the wind is ahead*: That is, when the wind is blowing from the direction in which the vessel is heading.

p. 54, *scud*: To run "before a gale" (with the gale blowing from behind) with no sails.

p. 54, *her head... across the vessel*: That is, the vessel is turned slightly into the wind, in a position that allows one sail to catch just enough wind to stabilize it and prevent it from drifting. This sail is pulled tight ("hauled flat aft") and set diagonally across the vessel, thereby countering the effect of the wind on the bows and keeping the vessel stationary.

p. 55, *erysipelas*: An acute bacterial infection of the skin characterized by a raised bright-red rash, which often led to serious complications in the era before antibiotics.

p. 56, *scuppers*: Holes in the side of a ship on the level of the deck designed to carry water overboard.

p. 56, *stockinet*: A knitted, highly elastic fabric.

p. 60, *This friend was no other than Tiger*: This is the last appearance of the dog Tiger in the events of the narrative (although he is referred to once more in Chapter IX).

p. 61, *shipped a sea*: That is, was flooded by a large wave.

p. 61, *caboose*: The ship's kitchen.

p. 61, *sprung*: Cracked, split.

p. 61, *the heel of this mast had been stepped between decks*: That is, instead of being placed in a sturdy foundation ("stepped") in the keel, the base of the mast (the "heel") has been attached to an intermediate deck, thereby freeing up space in the after-hold at the expense of structural stability. This sentence, along with the remainder of the paragraph, is paraphrased from 'The Loss of the *Peggy*', an account that appeared in *Interesting and Authentic Narratives of the Most Remarkable Shipwrecks, Fires, Famines, Calamities, Providential Deliverances and Lamentable Disasters on the Seas, in Most Parts of the World* (1836), compiled by R. Thomas. It concerns a ship that sank after encountering a gale while crossing the Atlantic between the Irish port of Waterford and New York in October 1785. In the remainder of this chapter Poe makes further use of this source, as well as of another narrative from Thomas's collection, 'Loss of the Ship *Albion*', and 'Loss of His Majesty's Ship *Centaur*', found in *The Mariner's Chronicle: Containing Narratives of the Most Remarkable Disasters at Sea, Such as Shipwrecks, Storms, Fires and Famines* (1834).

p. 62, *the weather lanyards*: The ropes used to secure the sails on the side of the ship from which the wind is blowing (the "weather" side).

p. 62, *The necessary preparations... the aid of both pumps*: This passage is taken almost verbatim from 'The Loss of the *Peggy*' – see fourth note to p. 61.

p. 62, *bowsprit*: A spar (pole) projecting from a ship's bows.

p. 63, *windlass*: A winch used for weighing anchor.

p. 63, *sternpost*: The principal vertical wooden support at the rear of a ship (the stern), which supports the rudder.

p. 66, *the sun was... an hour high*: That is, it was an hour after sunrise.

p. 69, *weather forechains*: Forechains are the foremast's equivalent of the main-chains (see third note to p. 12). The reference here is to those on the "weather" side of the vessel (see first note to p. 62).

p. 70, *in nine long years*: In fact the narrative of the novel terminates after only another eight months in the life of Pym.

p. 70, *hermaphrodite brig*: A two-masted vessel with a square-rigged foremast (as on a brig) and fore-and-aft-rigged mainmast (as on a schooner). For fore-and-aft and square rigging, see fifth note to p. 7.

p. 70, *foretopmast*: The topmost section of the foremast.

p. 71, *No person was seen upon her decks*: The following four paragraphs were influenced by the third chapter, titled 'Heat and Thirst: A Scene in Jamaica', of *Tom Cringle's Log* (1833), an autobiographical novel of maritime adventure by the Scottish author Michael Scott (1789–1835), first serialized in *Blackwood's Magazine* in 1829 and then published in book form in 1833.

p. 71, *yaw*: An erratic deviation from a direct course.

p. 72, *nicest*: Most scrupulous.

p. 72, *cathead*: A large wooden beam on either side of a ship's bow, used to support the anchor when it is being raised or lowered, as well as for carrying it during a voyage.

p. 73, *yellow fever*: A tropical disease affecting the liver and kidneys, one of the symptoms of which is jaundice (hence the "saffron-like hue").

p. 76, *mania a potu*: Literally, "madness from drink" (Latin).

p. 84, *Gallipago*: Galápagos.

p. 84, *In a subsequent portion... species of tortoise*: Poe's description of the Galápagos tortoise in this paragraph is taken from MOR1 (Chapter IX). Poe makes extensive use of material from MOR1 and MOR4 from Chapter XIV onwards.

p. 85, *In a bag... supply of water*: Galápagos tortoises have no such thing, although the error is faithful to MOR1: "They carry with them a constant supply of water, in a bag at the root of the neck, which contains about two gallons, and on tasting that found in those we killed on board, it proved perfectly fresh and sweet."

p. 86, *recruited*: Restored, reinvigorated.

p. 86, *grateful*: Pleasing to the senses; welcome.

p. 87, *northward*: The meaning here is obviously "northerly", although "northward" suggests the opposite, that is, "southerly".

p. 87, *lie along*: Lean, tilt.

p. 88, *He proved to be much smaller than we had supposed*: The tortoise was described in the previous chapter as female.

p. 92, *thickly covered... nutritious food*: Poe's source for the mariners' consumption of barnacles, as well as, two paragraphs later, of crabs, was

perhaps 'Loss of the Brig *Polly*', another account that appeared in Thomas's *Remarkable Shipwrecks* (see fourth note to p. 61).

p. 93, *rakish-looking*: "Having a streamlined or sleek appearance, suggestive of speed" (*OED*).

p. 93, *an act of fiendish barbarity... the human species*: The case of the brig *Polly*, of Boston, is one so much in point, and her fate, in many respects, so remarkably similar to our own, that I cannot forbear alluding to it here. This vessel, of one hundred and thirty tons burden, sailed from Boston, with a cargo of lumber and provisions, for Santa Croix, on 12th December 1811, under the command of Captain Casneau. There were eight souls on board besides the captain – the mate, four seamen and the cook, together with a Mr Hunt, and a Negro girl belonging to him. On the fifteenth, having cleared the shoal of Georges, she sprang a leak in a gale of wind from the south-east, and was finally capsized, but, the masts going by the board, she afterwards righted. They remained in this situation, without fire, and with very little provision, for the period of one hundred and ninety-one days (from 15th December to 20th June), when Captain Casneau and Samuel Badger, the only survivors, were taken off the wreck by the *Fame*, of Hull, Captain Featherstone, bound home from Rio Janeiro. When picked up, they were in latitude 28° N., longitude 13° W., *having drifted above two thousand miles*! On 9th July the *Fame* fell in with the brig *Dromero*, Captain Perkins, who landed the two sufferers in Kennebeck. The narrative from which we gather these details ends in the following words: "It is natural to enquire how they could float such a vast distance upon the most frequented part of the Atlantic and not be discovered all this time. *They were passed by more than a dozen sail, one of which came so nigh them that they could distinctly see the people on deck and on the rigging looking at them, but, to the inexpressible disappointment of the starving and freezing men, they stifled the dictates of compassion, hoisted sail, and cruelly abandoned them to their fate.*" [POE'S NOTE] This note begins as a very close paraphrase of, and ends as a direct quotation from, 'Loss of the Brig *Polly*' (see note to p. 92). Saint Croix is one of the Virgin Islands, then a Danish colony known as the Danish West Indies. Poe incorrectly transcribed the name of the *Polly*'s captain, which is given as "Cazneau" in the source, as well as that of the *Dromo*. "Kennebeck" should also be "Kennebunk", a coastal town in Maine.

p. 93, *hauling her wind*: Changing her course to sail closer to the wind, that is, in a direction closer to that from which the wind is blowing.

p. 93, CHAPTER XIV: Poe makes extensive use in this chapter of material from MOR1.

p. 93, *her draught of water... she was destined*: That is, the *Jane Guy* sits too low in the water and is therefore at risk of striking coral reefs. (A vessel's "draught" is the depth of water necessary for it to float.)

p. 93, *barque-rigged*: A barque is a vessel with three masts, two of which, the fore- and mainmasts, are square-rigged, and the other, the mizenmast (aft of the mainmast) is fore-and-aft rigged. (For fore-and-aft and square rigging, see fifth note to p. 7.)

p. 94, *carronades... long twelves*: Respectively, short, large-calibre cannon and long-barrelled naval guns for firing twelve-pound shells.

p. 94, *Kerguelen's Land*: The Kerguelen Islands, an archipelago in the southern Indian Ocean around 2,300 miles south-east of the Cape of Good Hope, discovered by the French navigator Yves-Joseph de Kerguelen-Trémarec (1734–97) in 1772 and later explored by the English naval captain James Cook (1728–79) during his third voyage (1776–79). It consists of the island of Kerguelen (also known as Desolation Island, as Poe – taking his information from MOR1 – later explains) and nearly 300 islets. Most of the information about the Kerguelen Islands and their fauna in this chapter comes from MOR1, Chapter IV.

p. 94, *Cape St Roque*: Cape São Roque, the easternmost point of Brazil.

p. 95, *We continued... spermaceti*: Much of this paragraph and the next are a close paraphrase of material from Chapter IV of *Voyage of the United States Frigate Potomac* (1835) by the American journalist and explorer Jeremiah N. Reynolds (1799–1858). The spermaceti is the sperm whale.

p. 96, *On 13th October longitude 48° E.*: Prince Edward Island is the smaller of the two Prince Edward Islands in the southern Indian Ocean, around 1,200 miles south-east of the Cape of Good Hope. Île de la Possession, or Possession Island, is one of the five Crozet Islands, around 600 miles east of the Prince Edward Islands. Both groups were discovered in 1772 by the French explorer Marion du Fresne (1724–72), but were only later, in 1776, given their present names – respectively, that of Prince Edward, Duke of Kent and Strathearn (1767–1820), son of George III, and that of Marion du Fresne's second in command, Julien-Marie Crozet (1728–82) – by Captain Cook, who was informed of the islands' existence by Crozet, who had survived the decimation of the Marion du Fresne expedition by the Maoris.

p. 96, *Christmas Harbour*: Port-Christmas, at the northern tip of the main island of the Kerguelen group. It was given its name by Cook, whose vessels arrived in the bay on Christmas Day 1776.

p. 97, *into which... ten to three*: That is, the entrance to the basin has a depth of four fathoms (around 7.3 metres), and therefore vessels with a

shallower draught (the depth of the hull below the waterline) can enter safely. The depth of the water inside the basin ranges from three to ten fathoms.

p. 97, *with her best bower ahead*: That is, with the larger of the two bow anchors (known as the "best bower") positioned forward of the vessel.

p. 97, *sea elephants*: Elephant seals.

p. 97, *The royal penguin*: The description that follows, taken from MOR1, is in fact of the king penguin (which Morrell calls "the royal or king penguin"). Royal penguins, which closely resemble the macaroni penguins mentioned later in the paragraph, are notable for their orange-coloured bills and long, yellow-orange crests, and are found only on Macquarie Island, equidistant from New Zealand and Antarctica.

p. 97, *sea hens... the albatross*: "Sea hen" is a nickname for several species; here the most likely candidate is the brown skua, also known as the southern great skua, a large, predatory Antarctic seabird. "Sea swallow" is another name for the common tern. The Port Egmont hen is a large skua, named after the first British settlement in the Falkland Islands (see seventh note to p. 102). Port Egmont in turn was named after John Perceval, 2nd Earl of Egmont (1711–70), First Lord of the Admiralty at the time of its founding in 1765. "Cape pigeon" is another name for the pintado petrel, a common seabird of the Southern Ocean. "The nelly" is a sailors' and whalers' nickname for the giant petrel (in fact two species: the southern giant petrel and the northern giant petrel, both found in the Southern Ocean). "Mother Carey's chickens" are storm petrels, seabirds believed to warn of coming storms. ("Mother Carey" was the personification of the harsh and unforgiving sea in the maritime folklore of the eighteenth and nineteenth centuries.) "Mother Carey's geese" are giant petrels (see "nelly" above) – referred to as "great petrel" by Poe.

p. 98, *The albatross... South Sea birds*: The lengthy digression on the subject of albatross "rookeries" that occurs over the next several paragraphs is taken from MOR1, Chapter III.

p. 100, CHAPTER XV: This chapter is heavily dependent on material from Morrell, particularly MOR4. See especially Chapter II.

p. 100, *Marion's Island, one of Crozet's group*: Marion Island is the larger of the two Prince Edward Islands, named after its discoverer, Marion du Fresne (see first note to p. 96). As was common at the time, Poe here uses the term "Crozet's group" to refer to both archipelagos combined, that is, the western Prince Edward Islands and the eastern Crozet Islands.

p. 100, *the islands of Tristan da Cunha*: A group of volcanic islands in the South Atlantic, around 1,700 miles from the Cape of Good Hope and 3,800 miles west of the Kerguelen Islands. They are named after their discoverer, the Portuguese explorer Tristão da Cunha (*c*.1460–*c*.1540). The largest of the three islands is also called Tristan da Cunha.

p. 100, *by the Dutch in 1643, and by the French in 1767*: The Dutch East India Company ship *Heemstede*, captained by Claes Gerritsz Bierenbroodspot (*c*.1579–1650), landed on Tristan da Cunha in February 1643. In 1767, the islands were surveyed by the crew of the French naval corvette *Heure du Berger*.

p. 102, *taken possession of by the British government*: The British sent a garrison from Cape Colony (then in the possession of the British) to Tristan da Cunha in 1816 in order to prevent Napoleon Bonaparte (1769–1821), the self-declared emperor of the French, who had been exiled to the remote South Atlantic island of St Helena after his defeat at the Battle of Waterloo in June 1815, from attempting to use it as a base. St Helena is 1,500 miles north of Tristan da Cunha.

p. 102, *Van Diemen's Land*: The former name of Tasmania.

p. 102, *an Englishman of the name of Glass*: The Scottish corporal William Glass (1786–1853) was part of the garrison sent to Tristan da Cunha in 1816. When the British withdrew a year later, he was granted permission to stay by the governor of Cape Colony, Lord Charles Somerset (1767–1831). Many of Glass's descendants remain on the island today; his surname remains common among the inhabitants.

p. 102, *5th November*: The *Jane Guy* left the Kerguelen Islands on 12th November and reached Tristan da Cunha fifteen days later; the date here should, therefore, be 5th December.

p. 102, *a group of islands called the Auroras*: For the section dealing with the elusive Aurora islands, Poe draws once again from MOR 1, Chapter III.

p. 102, *the Spanish corvette Atrevida*: The *Atrevida*, along with its twin, the *Descubierta*, was a Spanish naval corvette built for the Malaspina expedition (1789–94), a five-year maritime scientific exploration led by the explorers and Spanish naval officers Alejandro Malaspina (1754–1810), an Italian, commander of the *Descubierta*, and José de Bustamante y Guerra (1759–1825), commander of the *Atrevida*. The survey of the non-existent Auroras was conducted because the Spanish government feared that their location presented a danger to trade between the Spanish colony of Lima in Peru and the port of Cadiz in south-western Spain. The phantom islands continued to appear on maps until the second half of the nineteenth century.

p. 102, *the port of Soledad in the Malninas*: The "Malninas" are the Falkland Islands, known in Spanish as Islas Malvinas, an archipelago in the South Atlantic around 300 miles east of the southern Patagonian coast. Puerto Soledad was a Spanish military outpost on the largest island, East Falkland (itself known in Spanish as Isla Soledad), later renamed first Anson's Harbour and then Port Louis by the British.

p. 103, *Captain James Weddell*: The British explorer and seal hunter James Weddell (1787–1834), who set a record for navigation into the Antarctic. The Weddell Sea, an arm of the Atlantic off the coast of Antarctica, is named after him.

p. 103, *Staten Land*: Isla de los Estados, eighteen miles off the eastern tip of Tierra del Fuego, at the southern extremity of South America. It was named after the Staten-Generaal, the parliament of the Netherlands, by the Dutch explorers Jacob le Maire (*c.*1585–1616) and Willem Schouten (*c.*1567–1625) in 1615.

p. 103, *there have been not a few... oddly in dispute*: Among the vessels which at various times have professed to meet with the Auroras may be mentioned the ship *San Miguel*, in 1769, the ship *Aurora*, in 1774, the brig *Pearl*, in 1779, and the ship *Dolores*, in 1790. They all agree in giving the mean latitude fifty-three degrees south. [POE'S NOTE]

p. 103, *Georgia*: South Georgia, an island in the South Atlantic around 870 miles east of the Falkland Islands.

p. 103, *in 1822... schooner* Wasp: Here Poe acknowledges indirectly his source for most of the information about the Auroras: MOR1.

p. 104, CHAPTER XVI: Poe's principal source in this chapter was the *Address on the Subject of a Surveying and Exploring Expedition to the Pacific Ocean and the South Seas* by Jeremiah N. Reynolds (for whom see note to p. 95), which the author had delivered to the US House of Representatives in April 1836 as part of a lobbying campaign on behalf of a proposed government-sponsored expedition to the Pacific. Poe reviewed the *Address* favourably in the January 1837 edition of the *Southern Literary Messenger*, stating his belief that Reynolds was "a man of the loftiest principles and of unblemished character" and that he would be "entitled to the lion's share" of any glory that might accrue from the endeavour. In the event, however, Reynolds quarrelled with the Secretary of the Navy, Mahlon Dickerson (1770–1853), and the naval officer Charles Wilkes (1798–1877) was instead given command of what became the United States Exploring Expedition, also known as the Wilkes expedition, of 1838–42. Poe refers to, though does not name, the Wilkes expedition in the 'Note' at the end of the novel.

p. 104, *the Strait of Magellan*: A sea route separating mainland South America to the north and the islands of Tierra del Fuego to the south, connecting the Atlantic and Pacific oceans. It was discovered in 1520 by the Spanish expedition led by the Portuguese navigator Ferdinand Magellan (c.1480–1521).

p. 104, *That of Captain Cook... the Adventure*: The description that follows is of Cook's second voyage, between July 1772 and July 1775, whose purpose was to circumnavigate the globe as far south as possible in order to establish the existence or otherwise of the hypothetical continent, Terra Australis Incognita ("unknown land of the south"), whose existence had been presumed by European cartographers since the early modern period and speculated upon since antiquity. "Lieutenant Furneaux" is the British navigator and officer of the Royal Navy Tobias Furneaux (1735–81).

p. 105, *Palmer's Land lies south of the Shetland*: Palmer Land is a section of the Antarctic Peninsula, the northernmost part of mainland Antarctica. It is named after the American sealer Nathaniel Palmer (1799–1877), who explored the area in 1820. The South Shetland Islands are around ninety miles north of the Antarctic Peninsula. They were discovered in 1819 by the English sea captain William Smith (c.1790–1847), and are named after the Shetland Islands in northern Scotland.

p. 105, *In 1803... circumnavigating the globe*: The first Russian circumnavigation of the globe was achieved by two ships, the *Nadezhda* and the *Neva*, commanded, respectively, by the Russian naval officers Adam Johann von Krusenstern (1770–1846) and Yuri Fyodorovich Lisyansky (1773–1837). Poe transcribes both names incorrectly. (The latter is spelt "Lisiansky" in Reynolds's *Address* – for which see first note to p. 104.) "Alexander of Russia" is Alexander I (1777–1825).

p. 106, *Sandwich Land and the South Orkneys*: The South Sandwich Islands are a group of uninhabited volcanic islands in the South Atlantic, around 430 miles south-east of South Georgia (see fourth note to p. 103) and 1,100 miles north-east of the Antarctic Peninsula. Several of them were discovered by Cook during his second voyage (see third note to p. 104); Cook named them after John Montagu, 4th Earl of Sandwich (1718–92), then First Lord of the Admiralty. The South Orkney Islands are around 375 miles north-east of the Antarctic Peninsula. They were discovered in 1821 by Nathaniel Palmer (see first note to p. 105) and the English sealer George Powell (1794–1824).

P. 106, *On 11th January 1823... as far south as possible*: Poe here returns briefly to MOR1, Chapter IV.

p. 106, *I found the variation to be 14° 27' easterly, per azimuth…*: The "variation" is the angle difference between true north and magnetic north. This can be calculated "per azimuth", that is, by comparing the observed direction of a celestial object (such as the sun or the stars), measured clockwise around the horizon from 0° to 360°, with the direction indicated by a magnetic compass. Magnetic variation can be significant and unpredictable at high latitude, such as in the polar regions.

p. 107, *In 1831… the cutter Tula*: The English explorer John Biscoe (1794–1843) led the expedition that first sighted the section of Antarctica known as Enderby Land, as well as the part of the Antarctic Peninsula known as Graham Land (named after Sir James Graham, First Lord of the Admiralty at the time of Biscoe's voyage). He also discovered Adelaide Island, off the west coast of Graham Land, named in honour of Adelaide of Saxe-Meiningen (1792–1849), wife of William IV (1765–1837), and the nearby Biscoe Islands. In fact, the descriptions of the vessels are the wrong way round: the *Lively* was a cutter and the *Tula* a brig. For Samuel Enderby & Sons, see first note to p. 15. With this sentence, Poe returns to his principal source for this chapter, Reynolds's *Address* (see first note to p. 104).

P. 108, CHAPTER XVII: Poe's principal source in this chapter was MOR1, Chapter IV.

p. 108, *a press of sail*: As much sail as possible.

p. 108, *Here we found… per azimuth*: Poe here paraphrases the passage from MOR1, Chapter IV, that he quoted directly in the previous chapter.

p. 109, *we warped our way*: That is, the ship was hauled along manually by means of a rope or cable attached to a fixed point, such as an anchor or an object on shore (or, in this case, the ice floe).

p. 109, *Peter Vredenburgh*: Poe here re-employs the name previously used in that of the firm, Lloyd & Vredenburgh, "engaged in repairing and fitting out the brig *Grampus*" (Chapter II).

p. 110, *gunwale*: The upper edge of a ship's side.

p. 112, *This morning*: The terms *morning* and *evening*, which I have made use of to avoid confusion in my narrative, as far as possible, must not, of course, be taken in their ordinary sense. For a long time past we had had no night at all, the daylight being continual. The dates throughout are according to nautical time, and the bearing must be understood as per compass. I would also remark, in this place, that I cannot, in the first portion of what is here written, pretend to strict accuracy in respect to dates, or latitudes and longitudes, having kept no regular journal until after the

period of which this first portion treats. In many instances I have relied altogether upon memory. [POE'S NOTE]

p. 113, *a group of very large islands*: Many of the details of the description of these islands and their inhabitants in this chapter are taken from the account of the "Massacre Islands" in MOR4, Chapter v.

p. 113, *They were about... long woolly hair*: Pollin believes that the full stop after "frame" here is likely a compositor's error, and should be a comma, thereby eliminating the sentence fragment beginning "Their complexion". For Pollin, see Note on the Text.

p. 115, *biche de mer*: That is, bêche-de-mer, or sea cucumber, a long, slug-like echinoderm (a kind of marine invertebrate), consumed as a delicacy in East Asia. Poe provides a detailed discussion of the subject (taken from MOR4, Chapter v) in Chapter xx. For the etymology of the term, see first note to p. 123.

p. 116, *a swivel*: A swivel gun: a gun or cannon mounted on a swivel.

p. 117, *gum arabic*: A gum exuded by certain species of acacia, used in food as well as in glue and incense.

p. 117, *the whole hundred and ten savages of the canoes*: Poe forgets that ten were left behind as hostages at the end of the previous chapter.

p. 119, *their friends the pelicans*: Poe clearly intended to write "penguins" rather than "pelicans" here – see Chapter xiv.

p. 119, *canvas-back*: A North American diving duck, whose name refers to the colour of its back feathers.

p. 119, *paracutas*: Barracudas.

p. 119, *Lord Auckland Islands*: The Auckland Islands, an archipelago of New Zealand, 289 miles south of South Island (the larger of the two main islands of New Zealand). The Auckland Islands were discovered in 1806 by the British sealer and whaler Abraham Bristow (*c.*1771–1846), who named them after the British diplomat and politician William Eden, 1st Baron Auckland (1745–1814), a friend of his father.

p. 121, *brown celery and scurvy grass*: "Brown" celery appears to be Poe's invention. Scurvy grass is a plant of the cabbage family that, due to its high concentration of vitamin C, was formerly eaten by sailors as a means of staving off scurvy.

p. 122, *piculs*: A picul is a traditional Asian unit of weight, defined as a load as heavy as the average man could carry. The precise weight varied both geographically and historically, although today a picul is considered to be 60.4 kilograms (equivalent to "133⅓ lbs", the weight given in the long quotation from MOR4 that follows).

p. 122, *a modern history of a voyage to the South Seas*: The following quotation is taken verbatim from MOR4 (Chapter v), although only the second, third and fourth paragraphs represent Morrell's narrative. The first (beginning "It is that *mollusca* from the Indian Seas") is presented by Morrell as a direct quotation from a paper by "the learned and scientific Doctor Pascalis", that is, the French scholar, physician and naturalist Felix Ouvière Pascalis (1762–1833). Poe has removed the quotation marks around this paragraph that appear in his source.

p. 123, *the French name bouche de mer (a nice morsel from the sea)*: Pascalis's etymology is incorrect. The French *biche de mer*, used by Morrell and Poe, is a calque of the Portuguese *bicho-do-mar*, meaning "sea worm". The variant *bêche-de-mer*, meaning, literally, "sea spade", has become standard in French, and is also the form used in English.

p. 123, *the celebrated Cuvier calls it Gasteropeda pulmonifera*: The reference is to the French naturalist Georges Cuvier (1769–1832), and especially to his *Le Règne animal distribué d'après son organisation* (*The Animal Kingdom, Distributed According to Its Organization*), first published in 1817, although no discussion of the sea cucumber appears in that work. The cod Latin name *Gasteropeda pulmonifera* is perhaps Pascalis's garbled recollection of the term *Gastropoda pulmonata*, a class that includes several air-breathing snails, and therefore not sea cucumbers, which extract oxygen from water.

p. 123, *gendering*: Breeding.

p. 123, *zoophytes*: Plant-like animals such as coral, sea anemones or sponges.

p. 124, *Batavia*: The former name for Jakarta.

p. 124, *Peterson*: This name was previously given as that of Pym's grandfather (Chapter II).

p. 125, *grape and canister*: Different types of shot to be fired from a cannon or large gun. Grape shot consisted of a cluster of iron balls – resembling a bunch of grapes – held together by a canvas bag or metal framework. When fired from a cannon, the balls would diverge into a wide pattern, greatly increasing the target area. Canister shot consisted of a metal cylinder containing numerous smaller projectiles, such as musket balls or iron fragments. When fired, the canister would burst open at the cannon's muzzle, dispersing the contents like shrapnel.

p. 125, *her anchor apeak*: An anchor is "apeak" when it is almost vertical, with its chain pulled tight and leading straight down to the seabed, as when the ship is directly above it.

p. 125, *the bowie knife... southern country*: A bowie knife is a large knife with a blade between ten and fifteen inches long, curved and double-edged

towards the point. It is named after the American frontiersman and folk hero James Bowie (1799–1836), who was famously involved in the "Sandbar Fight" of 19th September 1827, a formal duel between two men, Samuel Levi Wells III and Thomas Maddox, of Alexandria, Louisiana, that descended into a violent altercation involving several participants. Bowie, present as a supporter of Wells, stabbed and killed Major Norris Wright, a supporter of Maddox, with a large knife that had been made for him by his brother, Rezin Bowie (1793–1841). Following this notorious incident such knives came to be associated with the more lawless parts of the United States.

p. 126, *filbert*: Hazelnuts.

p. 127, *blackness of darkness*: "Raging waves of the sea, foaming out their own shame; wandering stars, to whom is reserved the blackness of darkness for ever" (Jude 1:13).

p. 128, *We took courage... wooded ravine*: This sentence originally contained an apparently erroneous instance of the word "what": "and what, by dint of cutting steps". It has been omitted here for sense.

p. 129, *The means*: This passage was likely suggested to Poe by the excerpts from *Incidents of Travel in Egypt, Arabia Petraea, and the Holy Land* (1837) by the American explorer John Lloyd Stephens (1805–52) that had appeared in the *New-Yorker* and the *New-York Mirror* in April 1837, notably the section describing "deserted quarries" in Syene (now Aswan) in Upper Egypt (Volume I, Chapter VII).

p. 130, *the only living white men upon the island*: Peters was introduced as a "half-breed Indian" in the Preface, and is described in Chapter IV as the son of "an Indian squaw" and "a fur-trader".

p. 131, *bight*: A bend or indentation in a coastline.

p. 131, *That they would... for an instant*: Poe's source for this and the following paragraph was Morrell's account of the "Massacre Islands" (MOR4, Chapter V).

p. 131, *get springs upon the cable*: That is, attach additional ropes or cables ("springs") to the anchor chain ("cable") in order to rotate the ship.

p. 132, *star and double-headed shot*: A piece of star shot consisted of a number of metal rods connected at one end to a circular link, like keys around a keyring. When projected through the air the rods would be splayed out in a star shape. A piece of double-headed shot consisted of two linked iron balls.

p. 134, *They had already made a complete wreck of the vessel*: Poe's source for this and the following paragraph was the account of the destruction of the *Tonquin* in IRV (Chapter XI). The *Tonquin* sailed on a trading mission from Fort Astoria to Vancouver Island in June 1811, but all but four members

of its crew were killed after a dispute arose with the Tla-o-qui-aht natives. The vessel was then destroyed and sunk when the survivors deliberately detonated its powder magazine. For the Astoria expedition, see note to p. 265.

p. 135, CHAPTER XXIII: In the first edition, both this and the next chapter are numbered "XXIII". Many critics have concluded – from its close relationship with the novel's concluding 'Note' – that this, the first of the two, was inserted by Poe at a later point in the writing process.

p. 137, *On 15th February... more lamentable*: This day was rendered remarkable by our observing in the south several huge wreaths of the greyish vapour I have spoken of. [POE'S NOTE] See Chapter XVII: "The sky was usually clear, with now and then a slight appearance of thin vapour in the southern horizon."

p. 139, *indentures*: Indentations.

p. 142, *the descriptions... degraded Babylon*: The ancient city of Babylon, the capital of Mesopotamia (in modern-day Iraq) from the early second millennium to the early first millennium BC and of the Chaldean empire in the seventh and sixth centuries BC, began to decline after its invasion by the forces of the Persian king Cyrus the Great (d. *c*.530 BC) in 539 BC, and, after a succession of further conquests and periods of destruction, was finally abandoned in the seventh century AD, during the early Islamic period. Its ruins became a popular destination for European travellers in the eighteenth century, including the French astronomer Pierre Joseph de Beauchamp (1752–1801), author of the memoir *Mémoire sur les découvertes à faire dans la géographie de l'Asie* (1790), and the German explorer Carsten Niebuhr (1733–1815), author of *Beschreibung von Arabien* (1772), published in English as *Description of Arabia* (1792), and *Reisebeschreibung nach Arabien und andern umliegenden Ländern* (1774), published in English as *Travels through Arabia, and Other Countries in the East* (1792).

p. 142, *tumuli*: Burial mounds.

p. 142, *Scoria*: Solidified lava. The correct plural form is "scoriae".

p. 142, *intermingled with others of marl*: The marl was also black; indeed, we noticed no light-coloured substances of any kind upon the island. [POE'S NOTE]

p. 145, *osier*: Willow.

p. 146, *1st March*: For obvious reasons I cannot pretend to strict accuracy in these dates. They are given principally with a view to perspicuity of narrative, and as set down in my pencil memorandum. [POE'S NOTE]

p. 150, *the governmental expedition... the Southern Ocean*: The Wilkes expedition – see first note to p. 104.

NOTES

p. 151, *a word or two concerning them all*: Poe's source for the philological analysis that follows was *A Hebrew and English Lexicon of the Old Testament* (1863), translated from the Latin original of the German scholar Wilhelm Gesenius (1786–1842) by the American scholar Edward Robinson (1794–1863).

p. 151, *Ethiopian*: That is, Ethiopic, or Ge'ez, an ancient Semitic language of Ethiopia, from which the modern Ethiopian languages such as Amharic are descended.

p. 152, *I have graven... within the rock*: Poe presents the final sentence as a quotation, although in fact it is of his own composition, albeit a close echo of Job 19:24: "That they were graven with an iron pen and lead in the rock for ever!"

p. 153, *Loss of Breath*: First published in its final, revised form – upon which the text in the present edition is based – in the *Broadway Journal* of 3rd January 1846. An earlier version of the story appeared as 'A Decided Loss' in Philadelphia's *Saturday Courier* of 10th November 1832.

p. 153, *Blackwood*: *Blackwood's Magazine*, founded in Edinburgh by the publisher William Blackwood (1776–1834), and published between 1817 and 1980. By the 1840s *Blackwood's* had become particularly associated with sensation and horror fiction. See 'How to Write a *Blackwood* Article', also included in this edition.

p. 153, *O breathe not... Moore's Melodies*: From the first line of 'Oh! Breathe Not His Name', from the first volume (1808) of the *Irish Melodies* by the Irish poet Thomas Moore (1779–1852), commemorating the Irish nationalist leader Robert Emmet (1778–1803), who was hanged after leading a rebellion against the British in Dublin in 1803: "Oh! Breathe not his name, let it sleep in the shade, / Where cold and unhonoured his relics are laid" (ll. 1–2).

p. 155, *Salmanezer... fifth part of a century*: In the 720s BC, Shalmaneser V (*fl.* eighth century BC), king of the empire of Assyria, laid siege to Samaria, capital of Israel, following the rebellion of its king, Hoshea (*c.*732–724 BC). See 2 Kings 17. According to the *Bibliotheca historica* of the Greek historian Diodorus Siculus (*fl.* first century BC), Sardanapalus, the last king of Assyria, said to have lived in the seventh century BC, defended the empire's capital Nineveh, in modern-day Iraq, for seven years against an alliance of Medes, Persians and Babylonians, before the city fell. In fact Sardanapalus is a legendary figure; the historical fall of Nineveh occurred in 612 BC, under Sin-shar-ishkun. In Greek mythology, the city of Troy was besieged by the Greeks for ten years (two lustra) following the abduction by the Trojan

345

prince Paris of Helen, the wife of Menelaus, king of Sparta. See Homer's *Iliad*. According to the *Histories* of the ancient Greek historian Herodotus (b. *c*.484 BC), Psamtik I, king of ancient Egypt, who reigned between 664 and 610 BC, carried out a twenty-nine-year siege of the city of Ashdod in modern-day Israel (II, 157). "Aristaeus" is perhaps the semi-legendary poet Aristeas of Proconnesus, whom Herodotus discusses elsewhere (IV, 13–16); he is not mentioned in reference to the story of Psamtik I's siege of Ashdod.

p. 155, *whippersnapper!*: "A diminutive or insignificant person" (*OED*).

p. 155, *et le chemin… la philosophie véritable*: "The road of the passions has led me to true philosophy" (French). The reference is to the epistolary novel *Julie, ou la nouvelle Héloïse* (1761) by the Genevan-born philosopher and writer Jean-Jacques Rousseau (1712–78) (Part II, Letter III), about a love affair between the aristocratic maiden Julie d'Étanges and her tutor, a commoner known as Saint-Preux. Lord Eduard Bomston is a wealthy English peer and a friend of Julie's father.

p. 156, *pas de Zephyr*: A light and airy ballet step. Zephyr is the god of the west wind in Greek mythology.

p. 156, *lachrymatory*: Tear-inducing.

p. 156, *water dog*: A dog that swims well, especially one that is trained to retrieve waterfowl.

p. 157, *William Godwin… the only realities*: From the novel *Mandeville: A Tale of the Seventeenth Century* (1817) by the English philosopher and novelist William Godwin (1756–1836): "Invisible things are the only realities; invisible things alone are the things that shall remain" (Volume III, Chapter III).

p. 157, *Anaxagoras… snow is black*: According to the Greek philosopher Sextus Empiricus (*fl.* third century AD), in his *Outlines of Pyrrhonism* – a history of scepticism, a school of philosophy founded by Pyrrho (*c*.360–*c*.272 BC) – the Greek philosopher Anaxagoras (*c*.500–*c*.428 BC) "argued against the whiteness of snow because snow is frozen water and water is black; therefore, snow is black" (I, 33).

p. 157, *Metamora*: *Metamora, or, The Last of the Wampanoags* (1829), a play by the American playwright John Augustus Stone (1801–34).

p. 157, *a similar proceeding of Demosthenes*: According to the *Institutio oratoria* (*Institutes of Oratory*) of the Roman author Quintilian (*c*.35–*c*.96 AD), the Athenian statesman Demosthenes (384–322 BC) is said to have practised his oratory on the seashore, where he was forced to compete with the sound of the waves, in order to overcome a speech impediment (X, 3).

p. 158, *the bull of Phalaris*: Phalaris (d. *c*.554 BC), the notoriously cruel tyrant of the city of Acragas in Sicily, is said to have had built a bronze bull in which his victims were roasted alive, their agonized cries resembling the creature's bellowing.

p. 159, *galvanic battery*: A cell that produces electricity from chemical reactions, named after the Italian scientist Luigi Galvani (1737–98), best known for making the muscles of dead frogs' legs twitch in an electric field. In the nineteenth century, scientists made use of galvanic batteries in the attempt to revive corpses.

p. 159, *the Hippocratian pathology*: The ancient Greek physician Hippocrates (*c*.460–377 BC), regarded as the father of medicine, is considered the first person to have believed that disease occurs naturally, such as a consequence of environment, diet or living habits, rather than as punishment by the gods. Specifically, he is said to have believed that disease was caused by poor diet: that vapours excreted by undigested food were absorbed into the body, causing illness.

p. 160, *the Omnipresence of the Deity*: A long religious poem by the English poet and minister Robert Montgomery (1807–55), published in 1828.

p. 160, *à la Catalani*: That is, in the manner of the Italian opera singer Angelica Catalani (1780–1849).

p. 160, *the means of elevating... possession of Babylon*: According to Herodotus (see first note to p. 155), when Cyrus the Great (d. *c*.530 BC), king of Persia and founder of the Achaemenid dynasty, was succeeded by his elder son, Cambyses II (d. 522 BC), the latter secretly arranged for the murder of his younger brother, Smerdis, whom he feared as a potential competitor. Then, while Cambyses was away from Susa (the winter capital of the Achaemenid empire) on a military campaign in Egypt, the throne was seized by a Magian – a Zoroastrian priest – also named Smerdis, who claimed to be his namesake, of whose demise few were aware. The deception was eventually exposed by the nobleman Otanes, who observed that the man claiming to be king had no ears, identifying him as the other Smerdis, whose ears had been cut off as a punishment (III, 1–38, 61–88). Thus, far from being the means by which he was elevated, the loss of his ears was in fact the means by which the false Smerdis was forced from the throne (and killed). Herodotus also relates the story of the Persian nobleman Zopyrus, who, during the siege of the rebellious city of Babylon led by the Achaemenid king Darius the Great (*c*.550–486 BC) – the successor of the false Smerdis and one of the conspirators in his downfall – cut off his own nose and ears and presented himself to Darius with the suggestion

that he infiltrate the Babylonian camp while posing as a deserter. Having secured Darius's agreement, Zopyrus put his plan into action, and was able to win the trust of the Babylonians, quickly being put in command of their forces, a position from which he deliberately led them to defeat. Having reconquered the city, Darius rewarded Zopyrus by making him satrap (governor) of Babylonia (III, 150–60).

p. 160, *The mail-robber... in the suburbs*: The reference is to the real-life mail-robber George Wilson, who was sentenced to death for robbing the US Mail in Pennsylvania in May 1830. In June of the same year, Wilson received a pardon from the US president Andrew Jackson (1767–1845). However, Wilson, refused the pardon, resulting in a Supreme Court ruling in January 1833 that a pardon that is not accepted by the intended recipient cannot be applied. Nevertheless, Wilson escaped execution, subsequently accepted another presidential pardon, this time from Martin Van Buren (1782–1862), and was ultimately released in January 1841.

p. 161, *Mark Antony composed a treatise upon getting drunk*: The Roman general Mark Antony (*c.*83–30 BC), remembered as one of the triumvirs who ruled Rome following the assassination of Julius Caesar in 44 BC and as the lover of the Egyptian queen Cleopatra (69–30 BC), was the author of a now lost treatise, *De sua ebrietate*, a title meaning "On his drunkenness".

p. 161, *Pinxit availed himself... Marsyas Flayed Alive*: In Greek mythology, Marsyas was a satyr from Phrygia in Asia Minor who challenged the god Apollo to a flute-playing contest and was then tied to a tree and flayed alive for his hubris. The episode has been represented many times in painting and other media. "*Pinxit*" is Latin for "he painted".

p. 161, *Marston's Malcontent... open house*: *The Malcontent* is a play by the English dramatist and poet John Marston (1576–1634), written in 1603. The quotation, however, is from the same author's *Antonio and Mellida*, written in around 1599 (Act III, Sc. 2, l. 204).

p. 162, *His studies have been confined to the poetry of Crabbe*: A pun: crabs walk sideways, not forwards. George Crabbe (1754–1832) was an English poet, best known for narrative poems such as 'The Village' (1783) and 'The Borough' (1810).

p. 162, *pas de papillon*: "Butterfly step" (French). A step in ballet.

p. 162, *Pelion upon Ossa*: Mountains in Thessaly. In Greek mythology, the giants Otus and Ephialtes piled Pelion on Ossa as part of a plan to storm Olympus, home of the gods. See, for instance, Homer's *Odyssey*, XI, l. 315. Proverbially, to "pile Pelion on Ossa" is to worsen an already difficult situation by the addition of a new problem.

p. 162, *shot towers*: A tower in which shot was made. Molten lead was poured through sieves at the top, falling into water at the bottom.

p. 162, *Lombardy poplars*: The Lombardy poplar is a deciduous tree that can grow up to thirty metres in height.

p. 162, *South on the Bones*: *A Short Description of the Bones* (1825) by the English surgeon John Flint South (1797–1882).

p. 162, *Captain Barclay, who walked against Time*: Robert Barclay Allardice (1779–1854), known as "Captain Barclay", famously walked 1,000 miles in 1,000 hours to win a wager of 1,000 guineas at Newmarket between 1st June and 12th July 1809.

p. 162, *Windham and Allbreath... Phiz*: Windham may be the English Whig statesman William Windham (1750–1810); Allbreath appears to be fictitious. "Phiz" was the soubriquet of Hablot Knight Browne (1815–82), illustrator of most of the novels of Charles Dickens (1812–70).

p. 162, *He died gloriously... Hieronymus*: "*Tenera res in feminis fama pudicitiæ, et quasi flos pulcherrimus, cito ad levem marcescit auram, levique flatu corrumpitur – maxime, etc.*" – Hieronymus ad Salvinam. [POE'S NOTE] The Latin means: "A reputation for chastity in women is a delicate thing, and like the most beautiful flower it withers at the slightest blast, and is greatly corrupted by a light breeze." The quotation is taken from a letter sent by the theologian St Jerome (347–420 AD) (Hieronymus), best known for his Latin translation of the Bible, the Vulgate, to Salvina, a Roman noblewoman, on the death of her husband, Nebridius.

p. 164, *this remark is from Epictetus... relieving them in others*: One of the *Fragments* of the Stoic philosopher Epictetus (*c.*55–*c.*135 AD): "In prosperity it is very easy to find a friend; in adversity, nothing is so difficult" (122; trans. Thomas Wentworth Higginson, 1890).

p. 164, *Like Brutus, I paused for a reply*: An allusion to the speech delivered to the masses by Brutus in Shakespeare's *Julius Caesar*, following the assassination of the Roman dictator, in which Brutus was one of the leading conspirators: "Who is here so vile that will not love his country? If any, speak, for him have I offended. I pause for a reply" (Act III, Sc. 2, ll. 34–36).

p. 165, *among the ancient Hebrews... "Amen!"*: See *Zillah: A Tale of the Holy City* (1828) by the English poet and novelist Horace Smith (1779–1849): "The Jews having imbibed the strange notion that the gates of heaven would be opened to him who answered *Amen* with all his might, the whole immense multitude chanted this word, at the conclusion of every prayer, with such a stentorian energy that the solemn roar of their innumerable voices, reverberating from the lofty front and encircling walls of the Temple,

sounded like a rolling peal of thunder, and seemed even to shake the very foundations of the sacred edifice" (Volume I, Chapter V).

p. 165, *when a great plague… "to the proper God"*: According to the Greek author Diogenes Laërtius (*fl.* third century AD) in his history of ancient Greek philosophy, *Lives and Opinions of Eminent Philosophers*, when the semi-mythical Cretan philosopher Epimenides (*fl.* sixth century BC) was brought from Crete to Athens to assist in the combating of a plague, "he took some black sheep and some white ones and led them up to the Areopagus, and from thence he let them wherever they chose, having ordered the attendants to follow them, and wherever any one of them lay down they were to sacrifice him to the God who was the patron of the spot, and so the evil was stayed" (I, 10; trans. C.D. Yonge, 1915).

p. 167, *Mystification*: First published as 'Von Jung, the Mystific' in the June 1837 edition of the *American Monthly Magazine*. The story first appeared under the title 'Mystification' in the *Boston Pearl and Galaxy* of 3rd June 1837. The text in the present edition is based on the version that appeared in the *Broadway Journal* of 27th December 1845.

p. 167, *Slid… Ned Knowles*: The words of the young gallant Edward Kno'well in the comedy *Every Man in His Humour* (1598) by the English dramatist and poet Ben Jonson (1572–1637) (Act IV, Sc. 5). "Passado" and "montant" are fencing terms meaning, respectively, "a forward thrust with the foil, the rear foot being advanced at the same time" and "a blow or cut directed upwards" (*OED*). "'Slid" is an abbreviated oath, short for "God's lid".

p. 169, *Tieck… exemplifications*: The German writer Johann Ludwig Tieck (1773–1853), a key figure in the early Romantic movement in Germany, was the author of a number of fairy tales and other fantastical stories.

p. 170, *Heraclitus*: The pre-Socratic Greek philosopher Heraclitus (*c.*535–*c.*475 BC), who was considered a depressive and a misanthrope, and who was known as "the weeping philosopher".

p. 170, *art mystifique*: This term is Poe's invention. "*Mystifique*" is not a word in French.

p. 171, *dolce far niente*: "Sweet idleness" (Italian).

p. 171, *pot-houses*: Taverns.

p. 171, *duello*: "Duel" (Italian). The term is also used in English to refer to the custom or practice of duelling.

p. 171, *rencontres*: "Encounters" (French).

p. 171, *fanfaronnade*: "Boasting" (French).

p. 171, *sermonic manner of Coleridge*: The English Romantic poet Samuel Taylor Coleridge (1772–1834) worked as a Unitarian preacher between 1794

and 1799. He later returned to the Anglican faith, and produced a number of religious works, including *Lay Sermons* (1817), *Aids to Reflection* (1825) and *The Constitution of Church and State* (1830).

p. 172, *upon the tapis*: That is, under consideration. From the French "*sur le tapis*", meaning, literally, "on the tablecloth".

p. 173, *There were the Ordonnance... bound by Derome*: The first of the works listed here is *Traité contre les duels avec l'edit de Philippes le Bel de l'an 1306* (1610) – whose title means "Treaty against duels with the edict of Philip the Fair of the year 1306" – by the French historian Jean Savaron (1566–1622). "Philip the Fair" is Philip IV (1268–1314), king of France from 1285 to 1314. The second is *The Theater of Honour and Knighthood* (1623), an English translation of the French work *Le Théatre d'honneur et de chevalerie* (1620) by André Favyn. The third is *Le Vray et ancien usage des duels, confirmé par l'exemple des plus illustres combats et deffys qui se soient fairs en la Chrestianté* (1617) – whose title means "The true and ancient custom of duelling, confirmed by the example of the most illustrious fights and challenges that have been fought in Christianity" – by the French poet and writer Vital d'Audiguier (1565–1624). The last is *Mémoires... contenant les anecdotes de la cour de France, sous les rois Henry II, François II, Henry III et IV, touchant les duels* – whose title means "Memoirs... containing anecdotes from the court of France, under kings Henry II, Francis II, Henry III and IV, relating to duels" – by the French soldier and biographer Pierre de Bourdeille, seigneur de Brantôme (*c*.1540–1614), published posthumously in 1722. The date of 1666, given by Poe, refers to the publication of the first, four-volume edition of Brantôme's memoirs (which did not include the above volume), which was published at Leyden in 1665–66 by "Jean Sambix le Jeune", a pseudonym of the publisher Daniel Elzevier (1626–80), one of a celebrated family of Dutch booksellers and publishers of the seventeenth and early eighteenth centuries, whose books were particularly associated with a number of distinctive and elegant typefaces. "Derome" is Nicolas-Denis Derome (1731–88), the most famous of a French family of bookbinders.

p. 174, *a thick octavo... aliterque*: This work, whose title means "The law of duelling, written and unwritten and otherwise", is fictitious.

p. 174, *Injuriæ... et per se*: "Injuries by application, by construction and by themselves" (Latin).

p. 174, *cartel*: "A written challenge, a letter of defiance" (*OED*).

p. 175, *the nonsense verses of Du Bartas*: A reference to the French Huguenot courtier and poet Guillaume de Salluste du Bartas (1544–90), remembered

for his religious poetry, in particular *La Sepmaine, ou, creation du monde* (1578), and *La Seconde semaine* (1584), though not for nonsense verse, as suggested by Poe.

p. 177, *How to Write a Blackwood Article*: A satirical companion piece to Poe's story 'A Predicament'. Both were originally published in the Baltimore-based *American Museum of Literature and the Arts* in November 1838, under the titles 'The Psyche Zenobia' and 'The Scythe of Time'. When they were republished in Poe's *Tales of the Grotesque and Arabesque* (1840), the names were changed to, respectively, 'How to Write a *Blackwood* Article' and 'A Predicament'. The texts in the present edition are based on the versions that appeared in the *Broadway Journal* of 12th July 1845.

p. 177, *In the name… Turkish fig-pedlar*: From 'Johnson's Ghost', a chapter pastiching the style of the English polymath Samuel Johnson (1709–84) in *Rejected Addresses*, a book of literary parodies by the brothers James (1775–1839) and Horace Smith (1779–1849), published in 1812: "A swelling opening is too often succeeded by an insignificant conclusion. Parturient mountains have now produced muscipular abortions, and the auditor who compares incipient grandeur with final vulgarity is reminded of the pious hawkers of Constantinople, who solemnly perambulate her streets, exclaiming, 'In the name of the Prophet – figs!'"

p. 179, *Zenobia*: Zenobia was queen of the Roman colony of Palmyra, in present-day Syria, between around 267 and 272 AD. She invaded most of Rome's eastern provinces before finally being defeated by the emperor Aurelian (*c*.215–75 AD).

p. 179, *mantelet… auriculas*: A mantelet is a kind of cape or shawl. An agraffe is an ornamental clasp or fastener. Auriculas are Alpine primroses.

p. 179, *"a Greek"*: A slang term for a cheat or "a person of loose habits" (*OED*).

p. 179, *puncheon*: A large cask.

p. 179, *the RSA… Useful Knowledge*: The Royal Society of Arts (RSA) was founded – as the Society for the Encouragement of Arts, Manufactures and Commerce – in London in 1754 by the English drawing master William Shipley (1715–1803). The Society for the Diffusion of Useful Knowledge (SDUK) was founded in London in 1826 by the Whig statesman and social reformer Henry Peter Brougham, 1st Baron Brougham and Vaux (1778–1868).

p. 180, *the "fitness of things"*: A phrase – often in the extended form "the eternal fitness of things" – associated with the English philosopher and cleric Samuel Clarke (1675–1729), and which refers to the notion that morality, like mathematics, is inherent in the nature of the world.

p. 180, *spell "cant" with a capital K*: A reference to the German philosopher Immanuel Kant (1724–1804).

p. 180, *Gulley's New Compendium of Slang-Whang*: Fictitious. "Slang-whang" is an American term for invective or bombast.

p. 181, *a few cases*: All of the works subsequently listed are genuine, all but one appearing in *Blackwood's*: 'The Buried Alive', a tale of horror by the Scottish novelist John Galt (1779–1839) published in *Blackwood's* in October 1821; *Confessions of an English Opium-Eater* by the English writer Thomas De Quincey (1785–1859), serialized in the *London Magazine* in September and October 1821, appearing in book form in 1822; 'The Involuntary Experimentalist', about a man who, while helping to fight a fire at a Dublin distillery, falls and becomes trapped in a "large, copper boiler", published in *Blackwood's* in October 1837; *Passages from the Diary of a Late Physician*, a series of sensational but fictional case histories by the English lawyer, novelist and politician Samuel Warren (1807–77), published in *Blackwood's* between 1830 and 1837, appearing in book form in two volumes in 1832, with a third following in 1837; and 'The Man in the Bell', a tale about a man trapped beneath the clapper of a cathedral bell by the Irish writer William Maginn (1794–1842), published in *Blackwood's* in November 1821.

p. 181, *a rummer of Hollands and water*: That is, a large glass of Dutch gin and water.

p. 182, *'Truth is strange,' you know, 'stranger than fiction'*: From the epic poem *Don Juan* (1819–24) by the English Romantic poet Lord Byron (1788–1824): "'Tis strange – but true; for truth is always strange; / Stranger than fiction" (XIV, 101, ll. 1–2).

p. 182, *Brandreth's pills*: Laxative pills that claimed to purge "the effete materials or impure parts of the blood". They were invented by the English-born Benjamin Brandreth (1809–80).

p. 183, *the Ionic… Alcmaeon*: The Ionian and Eleatic were two schools of pre-Socratic Greek philosophy, originating in, respectively, the central part of the west coast of Asia Minor (Ionia) and a city (Elea) on the coast of the Tyrrhenian Sea in the modern-day Italian province of Salerno. Archytas (*fl.* 400–350 BC), from Tarentum (now Taranto) in southern Italy, was a Greek philosopher, Pythagorean mathematician and close friend of Plato. Gorgias of Leontini (*c.*483–*c.*376 BC) was a Greek sophist and rhetorician originally from Sicily. Alcmaeon (*fl.* sixth century BC), from Croton (now Crotone) in southern Italy, was a Greek philosopher and physiologist, remembered as a pioneer of the dissection of human bodies for the purposes of research.

p. 183, *Locke*: The English philosopher John Locke (1632–1704), author of *An Essay concerning Human Understanding* (1690), the founding document of empiricism.

p. 183, *Kritik... Naturwissenschaft*: Respectively, Kant's *Critique of Pure Reason*, published in German in 1781 and in English in 1838, translated by Francis Haywood (1796–1858), and *Metaphysical Foundations of Natural Science*, published in German in 1786 and in English in 1832, translated by John Richardson. For Kant, see also second note to p. 180.

p. 183, *the Dial*: A magazine published between 1840 and 1844 that was the mouthpiece of Transcendentalism, a philosophical and literary school that developed in New England in the 1830s as a reaction against rationalism, and that included prominent figures such as Ralph Waldo Emerson (1803–82) and Henry David Thoreau (1817–62).

p. 183, *Channing's poems... show of Can*: William Ellery Channing II (1817–1901) was an American Transcendentalist poet of whose work Poe was highly critical in *Graham's Magazine* in August 1843. The (inaccurate) quotation is from the poem 'Thoughts': "Thou meetest a common man, / With a delusive show of *can*" (II, ll. 17–18). For the Transcendentalists, see previous note.

p. 184, *bel-esprit-ism*: A "*bel esprit*" (meaning, literally, "fine mind") is a brilliant wit.

p. 184, *three Muses... singing*: According to the *Periegesis Hellados* (*Description of Greece*) of the Greek traveller and geographer Pausanias (*fl.* 143–76 AD), only three Muses – goddesses presiding over the arts and sciences – were originally worshipped at Mount Helicon in Boeotia: Melete, Mneme and Aoede (IX, 29). Over time the number of Muses increased to nine – see Homer's *Odyssey*, XXIV, l. 60. The nine (Clio, Euterpe, Thalia, Melpomene, Terpsichore, Erato, Polymnia, Urania and Calliope) were first listed by name in the *Theogony* of the Greek poet Hesiod (*fl. c.*700 BC) (l. 77).

p. 184, *The river Alpheus... its waters*: In Greek mythology, Alpheus was a hunter who fell in love with the nymph Arethusa. When Arethusa fled from him and went to the island of Ortygia (on the eastern coast of Sicily) – where she was transformed into a well – Alpheus turned himself into a river that flowed under the Peloponnese (the mountainous southern peninsula of Greece) all the way to the island, where he was reunited with her.

p. 184, *Epidendrum flos aeris*: A kind of orchid identified in South East Asia by the German botanist Johann Gerhard König (1728–85) in 1753.

p. 184, *Ju-Kiao-Li*: *Iu-Kiao-Li, or, The Two Fair Cousins* (1827) was an English adaptation by the Church of Ireland bishop Thomas Percy (1729–1811) of a French translation by the sinologist Jean-Pierre Abel-Rémusat (1788–1832) of a Chinese novel of uncertain authorship thought to have been written in the early seventeenth century, in the late Ming period.

p. 184, *Chickasaw*: The name of a Native American tribe originally from Mississippi and Alabama, and their language.

p. 185, *Aussi tendre… tragedy of that name*: A reference to the tragedy *Zaïre* – known in English as *The Tragedy of Zara* – by the French Enlightenment writer, dramatist and poet Voltaire (1694–1778), whose real name was François-Marie Arouet, first performed in 1732. Set during the Crusades, the play concerns Zaïre, a Christian slave girl raised in the palace of the sultan of Jerusalem, Orosmane, with whom she falls in love.

p. 185, *Van muerte… Miguel de Cervantes*: These lines are in fact from a poem by the Valencian poet Juan Escrivá (*fl.* 1500) that appeared in *Cancionero general de Hernando del Castillo*, an anthology of lyric poetry first printed in Valencia in 1511. They are quoted by the Spanish writer Miguel de Cervantes (1547–1616) in his novel *Don Quixote*, published between 1605 and 1615, about a confused old man who, fixated with stories of romance, comes to believe he is a knight on a heroic quest. In the episode in question, Countess Trifaldi, waiting woman to Princess Antonomasia, explains to Don Quixote that the young knight Don Clavijo recited the poem to her as part of a ruse to gain access to the princess, with disastrous consequences (II, 38).

p. 185, *Il pover' uomo… from Ariosto*: Not, in fact, from *Orlando furioso* by the Italian poet Ludovico Ariosto (1474–1533), originally published in 1516 and printed in its final form in 1532, but from an earlier romantic epic, *Orlando innamorato*, by the Italian author Matteo Maria Boiardo (1440–94), published between 1483 and 1495, of which Ariosto's poem is a continuation. Specifically, it is a misquotation from the version of *Orlando innamorato* that was extensively revised by the Tuscan poet Francesco Berni (*c.*1497–1535) in 1531: "Così colui, del colpo non accorto, / andava combattendo, ed era morto," translated by John Hoole (1727–1803), in his preface to his English version of *Orlando furioso* (1783), as follows: "So the fierce knight, with vigour yet unbroke, / Fought on, tho' dead, unconscious of the stroke" (LIII, 60, ll. 7–8).

p. 185, *Und sterb'… from Schiller*: The quotation is in fact from 'Das Veilchen' ('The Violet'), a poem from *Erwin und Elmire* (1775), a singspiel (light opera) by Johann Wolfgang von Goethe (1749–1832), and not by his friend and fellow German playwright and poet Friedrich von Schiller (1759–1805).

p. 185, *Molucca*: The Moluccas are an Indonesian archipelago formerly known as the Spice Islands.

p. 185, *en mosaïques*: Literally, "in mosaics" (French).

p. 185, *Tortoni's*: A famous café on Boulevard des Italiens in Paris.

p. 185, *ignoratio elenchi*: "Ignorance of proof" (Latin), a logical fallacy also known as "irrelevant conclusion", that is, an argument that fails to address the issue in question.

p. 186, *Lucan... anemone words*: The phrase is not found in the work of the Roman poet Lucan (39–65 AD); rather, it is a Latin translation of a phrase from the dialogue *Lexiphanes* by the ancient Greek rhetorician and satirist Lucian (120–80 AD), part of the advice given by Lycinus to the bombastic Lexiphanes: "And no dallying with unsubstantial flowers of speech; accustom yourself, like the athletes, to solid food" (XXIII; trans. H.W. Fowler and F.G. Fowler, 1905).

p. 186, *insomnia Jovis... inflated*: Rather than being from the work of the Roman senator and poet Silius Italicus (*c.*26–*c.*101 AD), the phrase is in fact a Latin translation from *On the Sublime* by the Greek author Longinus (*fl.* first century AD), one of the seminal works of literary criticism: "When Homer nods like this, we must be content to say that he dreams as Zeus might dream" (IX; trans. Herbert Lord Havell, 1890).

p. 186, *Demosthenes... that's slain*: The Greek quotation is actually from a fragment by the Greek dramatist Menander (*c.*342–*c.*290 BC) found in *Noctes Atticæ* (*Attic Nights*), a commonplace book compiled by the Roman author and grammarian Aulus Gellius (*fl.* second century AD). It was mistakenly attributed to the Athenian statesman Demosthenes (384–322 BC) by the English statesman and philosopher Francis Bacon (1561–1626) in his *Apophthegms New and Old* (1625): "Demosthenes when he fled from the battle, and that it was reproached to him, said 'that he that flies might fight again'" (169). The translation provided by Poe is slightly misquoted from *Hudibras* (1663–78), a long, mock-heroic and satirical poem by the English writer Samuel Butler (1613–80) (III, 3, ll. 243–44). For Demosthenes, see also fourth note to p. 157.

p. 189, *A Predicament*: For details of the original publication of this story, as well as of the text used in this edition, see first note to p. 177.

p. 189, *What chance... Comus*: From *Comus* by the English poet John Milton (1608–74), a masque first performed in 1634 about a virtuous lady who, separated from her brothers and lost in the woods, encounters the evil necromancer Comus, who imprisons her in his palace (l. 277).

p. 191, *Edina*: Edinburgh.

p. 191, *the fitness of things... Jo-Go-Slow*: The first of the narrator's garbled recapitulations of the advice she received from Blackwood in 'How to Write a *Blackwood* Article'. For the "fitness of things", see first note to p. 180. For the novel *Iu-Kiao-Li, or, The Two Fair Cousins*, see fifth note to p. 184.

p. 192, *mantelet... auricula*: For these terms, see second note to p. 179.

p. 192, *three Furies... Fiddling*: Blackwood's statement was about the Muses, not the Furies (three goddesses of vengeance and punishment in Greek mythology).

p. 192, *river Alfred... beneath the sea*: Blackwood referred to the "river Alpheus".

p. 193, *the Prussian Isis... perfectly scentless*: The exemplar suggested by Blackwood referred to the "Persian Iris".

p. 194, *happydandy... the roots*: The narrator misremembers the name *Epidendrum flos aeris*, used by Blackwood.

p. 194, *ossi tender que beefsteak*: The narrator's muddled recollection of Blackwood's reference to Voltaire's *Zaïre*.

p. 195, *ignoramus... enemy-werrybor'em*: For "*ignoratio elenchi*", see eighth note to p. 185. For "*insomnia Jovis*", see second note to p. 186. For "*anemonæ verborum*", see first note to p. 186.

p. 196, *scythe of time*: The original title of this story. See first note to p. 177. For the literary use of the phrase, see for instance Shakespeare's Sonnet 12: "And nothing 'gainst Time's scythe can make defence" (l. 13).

p. 196, *the grateful sermonic harangues of Dr Ollapod*: Dr Ollapod is a character in the comedy *The Poor Gentleman* (1801) by the English dramatist George Colman the Younger (1762–1836). "Ollapod", or "olla podrida", is a kind of Spanish and Portuguese stew; in an extended sense, the term refers to any kind of diverse mixture of elements.

p. 196, *verses of the poet... darry, widdy!*: For Blackwood's quotation from Cervantes (in fact Escrivá), see second note to p. 185.

p. 198, *words of Ariosto... erry morty*: For Blackwood's quotation from Ariosto (in fact Boiardo), see third note to p. 185.

p. 198, *words of Demosthenes... to fly*: For Blackwood's quotation from Demosthenes (in fact Menander), see third note to p. 186.

p. 198, *the German of Schiller... duk she!*: For Blackwood's quotation from Schiller (in fact Goethe), see fourth note to p. 185.

p. 199, *The Balloon Hoax*: For an account of this fabricated story's original appearance as a news article in the *New York Sun* of 13th April 1844, see Extra Material. It later appeared under the title 'The Balloon Hoax' in

The Works of the Late Edgar Allan Poe, vol. i: *Tales*, ed. Rufus Wilmot Griswold (New York: J.S. Redfield, 1850). The text in the present edition is based on this version.

p. 199, *SC*: South Carolina. Sullivan's Island is the setting of Poe's 'The Gold Bug', included in this edition.

p. 199, *Mr Mason... Mr Harrison Ainsworth*: Respectively, the Irish flautist and balloonist Thomas Monck Mason (1803–89), who famously accompanied the English balloonist Charles Green (1785–1870) on a flight in a balloon named the *Great Nassau* from London's Vauxhall Gardens to Weilburg in Nassau, Germany, in November 1836, subsequently publishing *Account of the Late Aeronautical Expedition from London to Weilburg* (1836); the English balloonist and politician Robert Hollond (1808–77), who provided the financial backing for Green's flight as well as taking part in it; the English-born aviation pioneer William Samuel Henson (1812–88); and the English historical novelist William Harrison Ainsworth (1805–82), author, of, among others, *Jack Sheppard* (1839), about an eighteenth-century burglar (referred to later in the story), *The Tower of London* (1840) and *The Lancashire Witches* (1849).

p. 199, *quidnuncs*: Gossips, busybodies.

p. 199, *Sir Everard Bringhurst... Lord Bentinck's*: Both fictitious.

p. 200, *Two very decided failures... Sir George Cayley*: In 1843 Henson (see third note to p. 199) published his design for a fixed-wing monoplane known as the "aerial steam carriage"; in the same year, he and his fellow inventor John Stringfellow (1799–1883) formed the Aerial Transit Company to invite investment in the project. The English engineer Sir George Cayley (1773–1857), known as the "father of British aeronautics", created the concept of an aeroplane as a fixed-wing flying machine in 1799, and later, in 1853, constructed the first manned gliders. Poe took most of the technical information in this and the following paragraphs from an article in the Philadelphia newspaper *Alexander's Express Messenger* of 21st February 1844, which outlined the failure of Henson's recent experiments at the National Gallery of Practical Science, known as the "Adelaide Gallery", established by the American inventor Jacob Perkins (1766–1849) at Adelaide Street, off the Strand in central London, in 1832. It also described Cayley's recent unsuccessful attempts to fly a balloon, which had been made at the Polytechnic Institution (now the University of Westminster) on London's Regent Street, founded in 1838 and of which he was the chairman. In turn, the *Express Messenger* article was largely derived from a pamphlet written by Mason, *Remarks on the Ellipsoidal*

Balloon Propelled by the Archimedean Screw, Described as the New Aerial Machine (1843).

p. 201, *the Archimedean screw*: The Archimedean screw, attributed to the ancient Greek mathematician and inventor Archimedes (*c.*287–212 BC), was originally a device for lifting water consisting of a rotating spiral or helix enclosed within a cylinder. When adapted to move air instead of water, the screw shape ensures a continuous and smooth displacement of air, which, pushed backwards, generates forward thrust.

p. 201, *Willis's Rooms*: Socially exclusive assembly rooms on King Street, St James's, central London, founded by William Almack (1741–81) and known originally as Almack's Assembly Rooms. On Almack's death the rooms were inherited by his niece, Elizabeth Willis, and thereafter became known as Willis's Rooms.

p. 201, *gores*: Wedge-shaped or triangular pieces of cloth.

p. 201, *battledore*: Either a wooden, paddle-shaped implement used to beat clothes during washing or a racket used in the game of the same name, similar to badminton.

p. 202, *the British Channel*: The English Channel.

p. 202, *aerostation*: The science or art of operating aerostats, that is, lighter-than-air craft such as hot-air balloons.

p. 202, *Penstruthal, in Wales*: Fictitious.

p. 202, *gum caoutchouc*: Rubber.

p. 203, *Charles Green*: See third note to p. 199.

p. 203, *The supporting power being estimated at 2,500 pounds*: Poe's source for much of the information in this and the following two paragraphs was Mason's *Account of the Late Aeronautical Expedition from London to Weilburg* – see third note to p. 199.

p. 203, *slack-lime*: Calcium hydroxide produced by combining quicklime – an alkaline powder formed from dehydrated lime that is traditionally used in the manufacture of building materials – with water, releasing significant heat.

p. 204, *Weal-Vor House*: Fictitious.

p. 205, *the Bristol Channel*: An inlet of the Atlantic between South Wales and the south-western peninsula of England. It is named after the English city and port of Bristol.

p. 206, *Cape Clear*: An island off the south-west coast of County Cork in Ireland.

p. 207, *beat up... lying to*: To "beat up" is to sail into the wind in a zigzag pattern (also known as "tacking"). For "lying to", see note to p. 46, as

well as Poe's detailed description in Chapter VII of *Arthur Gordon Pym*, included in this edition.

p. 207, *geneva*: Dutch gin.

p. 208, *Cotopaxi*: A volcanic mountain in Ecuador, whose peak is 19,347 feet high.

p. 208, *Omne ignotum pro magnifico*: "Every unknown thing is taken for something great" (Latin). From the *Agricola* of the Roman historian Tacitus (*c*.56–*c*.120 AD), about the life of the Roman general Gnaeus Julius Agricola (40–93 AD) (I, 30).

p. 208, *at 25,000 feet... concave*: *Note* – Mr Ainsworth has not attempted to account for this phenomenon, which, however, is quite susceptible of explanation. A line dropped from an elevation of 25,000 feet, perpendicularly to the surface of the earth (or sea), would form the perpendicular of a right-angled triangle, of which the base would extend from the right angle to the horizon, and the hypotenuse from the horizon to the balloon. But the 25,000 feet of altitude is little or nothing in comparison with the extent of the prospect. In other words, the base and hypotenuse of the supposed triangle would be so long, when compared with the perpendicular, that the two former may be regarded as nearly parallel. In this manner the horizon of the aeronaut would appear to be *on a level* with the car. But, as the point immediately beneath him seems, and is, at a great distance below him, it seems, of course, also, at a great distance below the horizon. Hence the impression of *concavity*, and this impression must remain, until the elevation shall bear so great a proportion to the extent of prospect that the apparent parallelism of the base and hypotenuse disappears – when the earth's real convexity must become apparent. [POE'S NOTE]

p. 209, *one of the New York-line packets*: That is, a ship carrying mail, passengers or cargo that travelled regularly across the Atlantic between New York and the north-western English port of Liverpool.

p. 209, *Fort Moultrie*: A military base on Sullivan's Island off the coast of South Carolina, where Poe himself had served in 1828. See Extra Material.

p. 211, *The Cask of Amontillado*: First published in the November 1846 edition of *Godey's Lady's Book*, the source for the text in the present edition. Amontillado is a kind of dry sherry, named after the Andalusian town of Montilla, where it was originally produced.

p. 213, *the carnival season*: Carnival is a festival held during the week before Lent in Roman Catholic countries, typically comprising parades, street parties and other, circus-like entertainments, and in which people often don elaborate costumes and take part in masquerades.

p. 213, *a pipe*: A cask for wine equal to two hogsheads, or 477 litres.

p. 214, *encrusted with nitre*: Nitre is potassium nitrate, or saltpetre, a crystalline substance that forms on damp surfaces in underground or poorly ventilated spaces, such as cellars, caves or crypts.

p. 214, *roquelaire*: A man's knee-length cloak. The term "roquelaire", or "roquelaure", is a borrowing from French, and refers to the French nobleman Antoine Gaston de Roquelaure (1656–1738).

p. 215, *Médoc*: A red wine produced in the region of the same name in south-western France.

p. 215, *A huge human foot d'or... in the heel*: The Montresor coat of arms consists principally of a golden foot ("foot d'or") against a blue background ("field azure"), expressed in the specialized language of heraldry. In heraldic terms, an animal is "rampant" when it is represented as standing on its hind legs with its right foreleg raised above the left. (The presumably limbless serpent is perhaps represented in an equivalently confrontational posture.)

p. 215, *Nemo me impune lacessit*: "No one attacks me with impunity" (Latin), the national motto of Scotland.

p. 216, *a flacon of De Grâve*: A small stoppered bottle of wine from the Graves area of the Bordeaux region in south-western France.

p. 216, *the masons*: That is, the Freemasons, a powerful secret society that evolved from the medieval guild of stonemasons and whose members today are mainly professionals and businessmen. It is known for its pseudo-religious use of rituals and ancient symbols.

p. 218, *In pace requiescat!*: "Rest in peace!" (Latin).

p. 219, *The Gold Bug*: Originally published in two instalments in Philadelphia's *Dollar Newspaper* on 21st and 28th June 1843 – see Extra Material. The text in the present edition follows that published in Poe's *Tales*, published in June 1845 by Wiley & Putnam.

p. 219, *What ho!... All in the Wrong*: These words are not, in fact, from *All in the Wrong* (1761), a comic play by the Irish author Arthur Murphy (1727–1805), but appear to be of Poe's composition. They refer to the phenomenon of "tarantism", an irrepressible urge to dance, which, in early modern Italy, was popularly believed to be caused by the bite of the tarantula.

p. 221, *the marsh hen*: Another name for the moorhen.

p. 221, *Fort Moultrie*: See second note to p. 209.

p. 221, *Swammerdam*: The Dutch naturalist Jan Swammerdam (1637–80), author of *Historia insectorum generalis* (1669), published in English as *The Book of Nature, or, The History of Insects* in 1758.

p. 222, *manumitted*: Released from slavery.

p. 222, *bivalve*: An aquatic mollusc with a hinged shell, such as an oyster or a mussel.

p. 222, *scarabæus*: The name of a genus of beetle. Some beetles of the scarab family were considered sacred in ancient Egypt.

p. 224, *caput hominis*: "Head of a man" (Latin).

p. 224, *cuts*: Woodcuts.

p. 227, *empressement*: "Eagerness" (French).

p. 229, *dark lanterns*: See note to p. 18.

p. 229, *tulip tree*: Trees of the species *Liriodendron tulipifera* (referred to incorrectly by Poe as *Liriodendron tulipiferum* later), native to North America, which produce large flowers resembling tulips.

p. 235, *curvets and caracols*: Respectively, leaps and half-turns (when performed by horses).

p. 236, *some mineralizing process... bi-chloride of mercury*: "Bi-chloride of mercury" is mercury(II) chloride, a compound of mercury and chlorine used as a preservative in the nineteenth century. By reacting with organic materials in wood, mercury(II) chloride creates chemical bonds, rendering it harder and more durable, as well as resistant to decay and pests – that is, more mineral-like.

p. 237, *counters*: In a numismatic context, the term "counter" usually means "an imitation coin of brass or inferior metal; a token used to represent real coin" (*OED*). The significance of the inclusion of these relatively low-quality items in a hoard whose contents are otherwise highly valuable is unclear.

p. 238, *Bacchanalian figures*: Bacchanalia was the Roman festival of Bacchus, also known to the Greeks as Dionysus, the god of fertility, wine and ecstasy. Such festivals were associated with wild and orgiastic revelry.

p. 241, *Zaffre, digested in aqua regia*: Zaffre is an impure oxide of cobalt, used as a blue pigment in pottery and glass, for instance. *Aqua regia* is a mixture of nitric and hydrochloric acids capable of dissolving gold – hence its name, which means "royal water".

p. 241, *regulus*: The purer, more metallic component of a mineral, obtained by smelting.

p. 242, *Captain Kidd*: The Scottish privateer and pirate William Kidd (*c*.1645–1701), famous among other things for the buried treasure it is claimed he left behind.

p. 244, *Golconda*: A ruined Indian city, used proverbially to mean a place of great wealth.

p. 244, *the Spanish Main*: The former name for the territories controlled by the Spanish empire in the Americas, from Florida in the north to the northern coast of Brazil in the south, as well as the Caribbean. In a more restricted sense it referred to an area of the northern coast of South America that spanned roughly the Isthmus of Panama to the delta of the Orinoco River. The term was in use between *c.*1520 and *c.*1730.

p. 244, *a table*: There are several inaccuracies in the following table. In fact there are 34 instances of *8* (not 33), 27 of *;* (not 26), 15 of *‡* (not 16), 14 of *** (not 13) and 7 of *1* (not 8).

p. 248, *no less than ten*: In fact, eleven: *?*, standing for *u*, is omitted.

p. 251, *mattock*: A tool like a pickaxe.

p. 253, *Hop-Frog*: First published as 'Hop-Frog, or, The Eight Chained Ourang-Outangs' in the Boston-based newspaper the *Flag of Our Union* of 17th March 1849. The text in the present edition is based on this version.

p. 255, *rara avis in terris*: "A rare bird in the world" (Latin). From the *Satires* of the Roman poet Juvenal (*c.*60–*c.*140 AD) (VI, l. 165).

p. 255, *He would have preferred... Zadig of Voltaire*: That is, he would have preferred the broad humour of *Gargantua and Pantagruel*, a series of satirical and ribald novels by the French writer François Rabelais (*c.*1494–1553), published between 1532 and 1564, which follow the adventures of two giants, Gargantua and his son Pantagruel, in the process ridiculing the mores of the author's day, to the subtle comedy of Voltaire's philosophical novella *Zadig, ou, La Destinée* (1747) – published in English as *Zadig, or, The Book of Fate* in 1749 – about a Zoroastrian philosopher in ancient Babylonia. For Voltaire, see first note to p. 185.

p. 255, *crumbs that fell from the royal table*: See Luke 16:21.

p. 260, *stockinet*: See second note to p. 56.

p. 260, *caryatids*: Stone pillars carved in the form of female figures. The name refers to the priestesses of Artemis at Karyai in ancient Laconia, in the Peloponnese.

p. 265, *The Journal of Julius Rodman*: First published in six instalments in *Burton's Gentleman's Magazine* – of which Poe was then the assistant editor – between January and June 1840. The text in the present edition is based on this version. Twelve instalments were planned, but the novel was abandoned by Poe following his dismissal from the magazine in May 1840 (for which see Extra Material). Poe made use of two principal models for the expedition described in the fictitious journal that follows. The first was that led by the American explorers Meriwether Lewis (1774–1809) and William Clark (1770–1838) across the territory, consisting of the

western half of the Mississippi River basin, acquired by the United States from France in the Louisiana Purchase of 1803 – for which see first note to p. 269 – and then through the Pacific Northwest. The "Corps of Discovery" left St Louis, Missouri, in May 1804, eventually reaching the Pacific coast, via the Columbia River – which flows from the Rocky Mountains in British Columbia into the Pacific in present-day Oregon and Washington – in November 1805. The second was the Astoria expedition of 1810–13, financed by the New York businessman John Jacob Astor (1763–1848), which was an attempt to establish a trading outpost for Astor's newly founded Pacific Fur Company at the mouth of the Columbia River. The expedition consisted of two groups: one travelling overland from St Louis and across the Rocky Mountains, and another group sailing around Cape Horn to reach the Columbia River by sea. The post, Fort Astoria, was established in 1811, the first permanent US settlement on the Pacific coast. Poe's chief sources were IRV and LEW.

p. 267, *Isthmus of Darien*: Historical name for the Isthmus of Panama, the narrow strip of land that links North and South America, with the Caribbean Sea to the north and the Pacific to the south.

p. 267, *particulars of a tour... "an unexplored region"*: This section of the account was never completed by Poe. The story terminates with Rodman and his companions still to the east of the Rocky Mountains.

p. 267, *unction*: Fervency; passion; earnestness.

p. 268, *hereditary hypochondria*: Such a condition was attributed to Meriwether Lewis by the American statesman Thomas Jefferson (1743–1826) in his 'Life of Captain Lewis', included as an introduction to LEW. For the Lewis and Clark expedition, see note to p. 265.

p. 268, *Mills Point*: Founded by James Mills in 1819, Mills Point later, in 1837, came to be known as Hickman.

p. 269, *induced to undertake the task... employed by his government*: "Andre Michau" is the French botanist and explorer André Michaux (1746–1802), author of two works on the plants of North America: *Histoire des chênes de l'Amérique* (1803) – about the oak trees found on the continent – and *Flora Boreali-Americana* (1803), a survey of American plant life. In 1793, Michaux was chosen to lead an expedition to explore the Missouri River and beyond, an endeavour he himself had suggested to Jefferson, a long-term enthusiast for such a scheme – and which was being planned by the Philadelphia-based American Philosophical Society (APS). However, in his capacity as an agent for the government of the new-found French Republic, Michaux was secretly directed by his country's envoy to the United States, Edmond-Charles Genêt

(1763–1834), known as Citizen Genêt, to use the expedition to promote French political interests, namely to foster alliances with Native Americans in the Mississippi Valley to bolster France's ambitions against its former ally Spain, which then controlled all of the land west of the Mississippi River extending to the Rocky Mountains. (This territory, known as "Spanish Louisiana", had been ceded to Spain by France in 1763 at the conclusion of the French and Indian War – see first note to p. 271 – in compensation for Spain's loss to Great Britain of Spanish Florida. It remained under Spanish control until 1800, when it was ceded back to France, before being sold to the United States in the Louisiana Purchase of 1803.) It is untrue, therefore, that Michaux was required "to pursue elsewhere the botanical enquiries on which he was employed by his government". When revealed, Michaux's dual role as explorer and agent compromised his position as a neutral scientific explorer in the eyes of the proposed expedition's sponsors, and the enterprise was cancelled. This passage is a close paraphrase of Jefferson's 'Life of Captain Lewis' (see first note to p. 268).

p. 269, *delivery at M. M.'s temporary residence, near Monticello*: Michaux left the United States in 1796; the MS could not, therefore, have been delivered to him at Monticello "many years afterwards". (Rodman returned from his expedition in 1794.) Monticello, outside Charlottesville, Virginia, was the plantation owned by Jefferson.

p. 270, *perdus*: "Lost" (French).

p. 270, *This tract… Russia on the east*: The area here described is roughly equivalent to what is now the Yukon Territory of north-western Canada. The "possessions of Russia on the east" must be Alaska, purchased from Russia in 1867, which in fact represents the north-*west* extremity of the American continent.

p. 270, *those of Hennepin and his friends in 1698*: The Franciscan missionary Louis Hennepin (1626–1704) played a significant role in the exploration of North America during the late seventeenth century. In 1679 he joined an expedition led by the French explorer René-Robert Cavelier, Sieur de La Salle (1643–87) to explore the interior of the continent. Together they explored the Great Lakes, before, in February 1690, Hennepin was sent by La Salle to explore along the Mississippi River, a journey that resulted in Hennepin's capture by the Dakota people, with whom he lived for several months. He later described his travels in *Description de la Louisiane* (1683) and *Nouvelle découverte d'un très grand pays situé dans l'Amérique* (1697), the latter published in English in 1698 as *A New Discovery of a Vast Country in America*. For the Dakota, see first note to p. 295.

p. 271, *Mr Irving, in his Astoria*: Except for the material in the first sentence about the Scottish fur trader and explorer Sir Alexander Mackenzie (1764–1820), Poe's source for this paragraph was IRV (Chapter III). At the conclusion of the French and Indian War (1754–63) – part of the wider Seven Years War (1756–63) – in which the colonies belonging to the British Empire fought those belonging to the French, France ceded New France (modern-day Canada), including the provinces of Quebec, parts of Ontario and other areas, to Britain, along with all of its territories east of the Mississippi River. In 1766, Jonathan Carver (1710–80), a captain who had served in a Massachusetts colonial unit during the war, embarked on an expedition commissioned by the American-born British Army officer Robert Rogers (1731–95) to explore the newly acquired territories, notably the upper reaches of the Mississippi River and the lands westward. Starting from Fort Michilimackinac in Michigan, Carver travelled west through the Great Lakes region to the Mississippi and then upriver to the territory controlled by the Sioux Indians – for whom see first note to p. 295 – where he spent the winter of 1766–67. In 1767 he joined a group that had been sent out by Rogers to find a route to the Pacific Ocean, but the attempt was abandoned. He later published *Travels through America in the Years 1766, 1767, and 1768* (1778). In 1793, Mackenzie became the first European to reach the Pacific Ocean by land along a northern route, crossing the Rocky Mountains from Fort Chipewyan in what is now Alberta to the Pacific coast of what is now British Columbia. An expedition led by Mackenzie four years earlier, in 1789, had followed the river now named the Mackenzie north-west to the Arctic Ocean. He recounted his experiences of both expeditions in *Voyages from Montreal, on the River St Laurence, through the Continent of North America, to the Frozen and Pacific Oceans, in the Years 1789 and 1793* (1801), in the introductory section of which, 'A General History of the Fur Trade from Canada to the North-West', he stated: "Of these trading commanders, I understood that two attempted to penetrate to the Pacific Ocean, but the utmost extent of their journey I could never learn, which may be attributed, indeed, to a failure of the undertaking." He mentions no dates, however; these – 1749 and 1758 – are apparently Poe's embellishment.

p. 271, *the Columbia… straits of Annian*: For the Columbia, see note to p. 265. A river "disembogues" when it reaches the sea. The "straits of Annian" are the Strait of Anián, a navigable waterway that was believed to connect the Pacific Ocean with the Arctic or Atlantic, and that was the subject of geographical speculation between the sixteenth and the eighteenth

centuries. A passage between the Pacific and the Arctic was eventually found in the form of the Bering Strait, which separates the eastern tip of Siberia from Alaska, and which was discovered by the Danish explorer Vitus Bering (1681–1741) in 1728.

p. 271, *the next important expedition... the Arctic Ocean*: The English explorer and fur-trader Samuel Hearne (1745–92) was the first European to traverse northern Canada to the Arctic Ocean, on an expedition that departed from the Prince of Wales Fort near Churchill, Manitoba, on the western shore of Hudson Bay in Canada – originally built by the Hudson's Bay Company to protect its fur trade interests in the region – in December 1770, and whose objective was to locate a rumoured source of copper. Hearne reached the Arctic Ocean at the mouth of the Coppermine River – which he named – in July 1771. Hearne's *Journey from Prince of Wales' Fort to the Northern Ocean* appeared posthumously in 1795.

p. 271, *We have... American Revolution*: This paragraph is taken from IRV (Chapter III). The proposed expedition of Carver and the English politician Richard Whitworth (*c.*1734–1811) was thwarted due to the outbreak of the War of American Independence in April 1775.

p. 272, *Saskatchawine River*: The Saskatchewan River, a major waterway in western Canada, flowing through the modern-day provinces of Alberta, Saskatchewan and Manitoba. It is formed by the confluence of two main branches: the North Saskatchewan and the South Saskatchewan, which merge near Prince Albert, Saskatchewan. It then flows eastward across the prairies and empties into Lake Winnipeg, Manitoba.

p. 272, *Mr Joseph Frobisher*: The English-born Canadian fur trader Joseph Frobisher (1740–1810), one of the early pioneers of the Canadian fur trade, who played a significant role in expanding European commerce into the western regions of Canada and was instrumental in the formation of the North West Company, a major fur-trading enterprise founded in Montreal in 1783–84 that was a fierce rival of the Hudson's Bay Company until, in 1821, the two concerns were forcibly merged by order of the British government.

p. 272, *In 1778... Lake of the Hills*: Poe means the American explorer Peter Pond (1739–1807), another of the founders of the North West Company (see previous note). He has apparently misread his source, Mackenzie's 'A General History' (see first note to p. 271).

p. 272, *mentioned by Mr Jefferson*: The following story is taken from Jefferson's 'Life of Captain Lewis' (see first note to p. 268). "Ledyard" is the American explorer John Ledyard (1751–89), who, between 1776

and 1780, accompanied James Cook on his third and final voyage. The journey described in this paragraph took place between December 1786, when Ledyard departed from London, and February 1788, when he was deported to Poland. The Kamchatka Peninsula is a rugged and remote land mass in the Russian Far East, extending into the Pacific Ocean. Nootka Sound is a large inlet on the western coast of Vancouver Island in British Columbia, Canada.

p. 272, *The next enterprise... in 1789*: For Mackenzie's expeditions of 1789 and 1793, see first note to p. 271. On both occasions the starting point was Fort Chipewyan in what is now Alberta, not Montreal.

p. 272, *portage*: The carrying of a boat and its cargo between two navigable waterways.

p. 273, *embouchure*: The mouth of a river.

p. 273, *The memorable expedition... the Pacific Ocean*: The act in question was the Trade and Intercourse Act, originally passed in 1796, which authorized the US government to establish trading posts at which Native Americans could buy and sell goods under fair and regulated conditions. On 18th January 1803, President Jefferson recommended to Congress that the system be extended to new territories along the Missouri River and beyond, enabling trade and diplomacy with Native American tribes in regions soon to be acquired from France in the Louisiana Purchase (for which see first note to p. 269). Poe took the information in this passage from Jefferson's 'Life of Captain Lewis' (see first note to p. 268). For the Lewis and Clark expedition, see note to p. 265.

p. 273, *Coincident... the source of the Platte*: The American soldier and explorer Zebulon Montgomery Pike (1779–1813) led two expeditions through the Louisiana Purchase territory: the first, in 1805–06, reconnoitred the upper northern reaches of the Mississippi, and the second, in 1806–07, explored south-west to the frontier of the Spanish settlements of New Mexico and Texas. He later published *The Expeditions of Zebulon Montgomery Pike to Headwaters of the Mississippi River, through Louisiana Territory, and in New Spain, during the Years 1805–6–7* (1810). Lake Itasca in modern-day Minnesota is indeed the source of the Mississippi, although in fact Pike believed it to be Leech Lake in the same state. The Platte originates, in the form of two tributaries, the North Platte and the South Platte, near the Rockies in northern Colorado. The two branches converge in western Nebraska near what is today the city of North Platte. The Platte then meets the Missouri River in eastern Nebraska, near what is now the city of Omaha.

p. 273, *In 1810, Mr David Thompson... mouth of the Columbia*: Poe's source for this paragraph was IRV (Chapter X). In 1811, the English-born Canadian fur trader David Thompson (1770–1857) became the first European to navigate the full length of the Columbia River, a journey undertaken on behalf of the North West Company, a rival to Astor's Pacific Fur Company.

p. 274, *Mr Astor's own remarkable enterprise*: See note to p. 265.

p. 274, *Mr Wilson Price Hunt*: The American explorer Wilson Price Hunt (1783–1842) led the overland portion of the Astoria expedition – see note to p. 265.

p. 274, *Arickara Indians*: Later, in Chapter IV, referred to as the "Ricarees". See second note to p. 300.

p. 274, *The travels of Major Stephen H. Long... etc., etc.*: In 1823, the American explorer Stephen Harriman Long (1784–1864) led a military and scientific expedition to explore the upper Mississippi River and the Red River of the North, aiming to survey the border between the United States and British Canada following the Treaty of Ghent, which, signed in December 1814 at the conclusion of the War of 1812 between the United States and Great Britain, negated territorial gains made by both sides during the conflict and restored the borders established by the 1783 Treaty of Paris (the agreement that ended the War of American Independence). The expedition travelled through modern-day Minnesota, North Dakota and Manitoba, exploring the Red River Basin and documenting the area's flora, fauna and indigenous cultures. Long had previously, in 1819–20, led an expedition to map the Great Plains and the Rocky Mountains, travelling through what is now Nebraska, Kansas, Colorado and Wyoming, reaching the Rockies near what is now the city of Denver, Colorado.

p. 274, *Of the more recent journeys... related by Mr Irving*: In 1832, the French-born American military officer, explorer and fur trader Benjamin Bonneville (1796–1878) led an expedition to the Pacific Northwest, partly to assess British influence in the region on behalf of his sponsor, Jacob Astor (see note to p. 265). The journey encompassed the Rocky Mountains, the Great Salt Lake area, the Snake River and parts of present-day Idaho, Wyoming and Oregon. Washington Irving later wrote up and embellished Bonneville's notes in the form of *The Rocky Mountains, or, Scenes, Incidents and Adventures in the Far West, Digested from the Journal of Captain B.L.E. Bonneville*, generally known as *The Adventures of Captain Bonneville*, published in 1837.

p. 274, EDS GM: That is, the editors of *Burton's Gentleman's Magazine*: William Evans Burton and Poe himself (although, obviously, the footnotes

are entirely Poe's work, an authentication device for the wholly fictitious *Journal*). For Burton, see seventh note to p. 10. For Poe's relationship with Burton and employment with *Burton's Gentleman's Magazine*, see Extra Material.

p. 275, *peltries*: Animal pelts.

p. 275, *Petite Côte… North West Fur Company*: "Petite Côte" is what is now the city of St Charles, Missouri, founded around 1769 as "Les Petites Côtes" (meaning "the little hills") by the French Canadian fur trader Louis Blanchette (1739–93). (See also Poe's next footnote.) For the North West Company, see second note to p. 272.

p. 275, *voyageur*: A Canadian boatman employed by the fur companies to carry goods to and from trading posts.

p. 275, *Petite Côte*: Now St Charles – eds *GM*. [POE'S NOTE]

p. 275, *freshets*: Flooding from heavy rain or melting snow.

p. 276, *Petite Côte is a small place… safe and efficient*: This paragraph is mostly a paraphrase of a passage in LEW (Chapter 1) although the phrase "Creoles of Canadian descent" is taken from a passage in IRV (Chapter XV) describing the Metis Dorion, the model for Dirk Peters in *Arthur Gordon Pym* (see third note to p. 35).

p. 276, *piroque*: More commonly "pirogue" – a canoe hollowed from the trunk of a single tree.

p. 277, *Greely*: Also the name of one of the mutineers in *Arthur Gordon Pym* (see fifth note to p. 50).

p. 278, *I have now given… Petite Côte*: Mr Rodman has not given any description of himself, and the account of his party is by no means complete without a portraiture of its leader. "He was about twenty-five years of age," says Mr James Rodman in a memorandum now before us, "when he started up the river. He was a remarkably vigorous and active man, but short in stature, not being more than five feet three or four inches high, strongly built, with legs somewhat bowed. His physiognomy was of a Jewish cast, his lips thin and his complexion saturnine" – eds *GM*. [POE'S NOTE]

p. 278, *payed*: "Pay" is a nautical term meaning to smear or cover a wooden surface – usually with pitch or tar – in order to make it watertight.

p. 278, *keelboat*: A long, narrow, shallow-draught boat with a keel to provide stability. Such vessels were commonly used in the eighteenth and nineteenth centuries for transporting goods and passengers on rivers and other inland waterways.

p. 279, *cuddy cabin*: A small cabin in the stern – see also fifth note to p. 7.

p. 279, *stepped*: For the "stepping" of a ship's mast, see fourth note to p. 61.

p. 279, *in little compass*: In a compact or confined space.

p. 279, *snags and sawyers*: Respectively, submerged trees or roots lodged in the riverbed capable of puncturing or damaging a vessel's hull, and tree trunks floating in a river that are still partially attached to their roots and bob up and down in the water due to the current, in a manner that resembles the motion of a saw.

p. 280, *watape*: The fibrous roots of certain trees, particularly the spruce, traditionally used by indigenous peoples in the construction of canoes.

p. 280, *Manchester goods; twist and carrot tobacco; milled blankets*: Manchester, known as "Cottonopolis", was the centre of the English cotton industry. To facilitate transportation, storage and distribution, tobacco was often tightly twisted into rope-like strands, from which small pieces could be cut off for chewing or smoking, or compressed into a dense, carrot-shaped form. "Milling" is another term for "fulling", that is, thickening cloth and making it more durable by means of various mechanical processes.

p. 280, *pemmican*: The following description is taken almost verbatim from a footnote to the section headed 'Some Account of the Chepewyan Indians', part of Mackenzie's 'A General History' (see first note to p. 271).

p. 280, *six hundredweight of pemmican... capital article of food*: The *pemmican* here described by Mr Rodman is altogether new to us, and is very different from that with which our readers have no doubt been familiarized in the journals of Parry, Ross, Back and other northern voyagers. This, if we remember, was prepared by long-continued boiling of the lean meat (carefully excluding fat) until the soup was reduced to a very small proportion of its original bulk, and assumed a pulpy consistency. To this residue, many spices and much salt were added, and great nutriment was supposed to be contained in little bulk. The positive experience of an American surgeon, however, who had an opportunity of witnessing, and experimenting upon, the digestive process through an open wound in the stomach of a patient, has demonstrated that bulk is, in itself, an essential in this process, and that consequently the condensation of the nutritive property of food involves, in a great measure, a paradox – eds *GM*. [POE'S NOTE] The method described in this note is apparently of Poe's invention. The "northern voyagers" mentioned are the British Arctic explorers Sir William Edward Parry (1790–1855), author of *Journal of a Voyage for the Discovery of a Northwest Passage from the Atlantic to the Pacific, Performed in the Years 1819–20* (1821), *Journal of a Second Voyage for the Discovery of a Northwest Passage* (1824) and *Narrative of an Attempt to Reach the North Pole* (1828); Sir John Ross (1777–1856), author of *A Voyage*

of Discovery, Made under the Orders of the Admiralty, in His Majesty's Ships Isabella and Alexander, for the Purpose of Exploring Baffin's Bay, and Inquiring into the Probability of a Northwest Passage (1819) and *Narrative of a Second Voyage in Search of a Northwest Passage, and of a Residence in the Arctic Regions during the Years 1829–1833* (1835); and Sir George Back (1796–1878), author of *Narrative of the Arctic Land Expedition to the Mouth of the Great Fish River, and along the Shores of the Arctic Ocean, in the Years 1833, 1834 and 1835* (1836) and *Narrative of an Expedition in HMS Terror, Undertaken with a View to Geographical Discovery on the Arctic Shores, in the Years 1836–37* (1838). The "American surgeon" is the US Army surgeon William Beaumont (1785–1853), who became known as the "father of gastric physiology" as a result of his work with a Canadian voyageur (for which term see third note to p. 275), Alexis St Martin (1802–80), who, following a gunshot wound in 1822, was left with a hole, or fistula, in his stomach that enabled Beaumont to observe digestive processes closely and to perform experiments on digestion. Beaumont published an account of his work with St Martin as *Experiments and Observations on the Gastric Juice, and the Physiology of Digestion* (1838).

p. 281, *musquash… fisher*: "Musquash" is another term for a muskrat, a large North American rodent named for its musky odour. A kit fox is a small nocturnal fox that inhabits the deserts and plains of the south-western United States. A wolverine is a carnivorous mammal larger than other weasels and martens though belonging to the same family. It is native to the northern parts of Europe, Asia and America. A fisher is a large brown marten found in North American woodland.

p. 282, *alluvia*: Deposits of clay, silt and sand left by floodwater.

p. 283, *a large cave… at least fifty in width*: The cave here mentioned is that called the "Tavern" by the traders and boatmen. Some grotesque images are painted on the cliffs, and commanded, at one period, great respect from the Indians. In speaking of this cavern, Captain Lewis says that it is a hundred and twenty feet wide, twenty feet high and forty deep, and that the bluffs overhanging it are nearly three hundred feet high. We wish to call attention to the circumstance that, in every point, Mr R.'s account *falls short* of Captain Lewis's. With all his evident enthusiasm, our traveller is never prone to the exaggeration of facts. In a great variety of instances like the present, it will be found that his statements respecting quantity (in the full sense of the term) always fall within the truth, as this truth is since ascertained. We regard this as a remarkable trait in his mind, and it is assuredly one which should entitle his observations to the highest credit, when they

concern regions about which we know nothing beyond these observations. In all points which relate to *effects*, on the contrary, Mr Rodman's peculiar temperament leads him into excess. For example, he speaks of the cavern now in question, as of a "dismal appearance", and the colouring of his narrative respecting it is derived principally from the sombre hue of his own spirit at the time of passing the rock. It will be as well to bear these distinctions in mind as we read his journal. His facts are never heightened; his impressions from these facts must have, to ordinary perceptions, a tone of exaggeration. Yet there is no falsity in this exaggeration, except in view of a general sentiment upon the thing seen and described. As regards his own mind, the apparent gaudiness of colour is the absolute and only true tint – eds *GM*. [POE'S NOTE] The relevant passage is in LEW, Chapter 1.

p. 283, *the river Du Bois, a creek called Charité*: La Charette? Du Bois is no doubt Wood River – eds *GM*. [POE'S NOTE] In fact this passage is based on one from LEW: "We encamped on the south side, having ascended ten miles, and the next day, 25th May, passed on the south side the mouth of Wood River, on the north, two small creeks and several islands, and stopped for the night at the entrance of a creek on the north side, called by the French La Charrette, ten miles from our last encampment" (Chapter 1). "*Charrette*" is French for "cart".

p. 284, *the mouth of the Platte*: See third note to p. 273.

p. 284, *a Spanish commission*: At the time of Rodman's expedition (1792), Spain controlled all of the land west of the Mississippi River extending to the Rocky Mountains. For the history of "Spanish Louisiana", see first note to p. 269.

p. 285, *mounds of various sizes... action of water*: These mounds are now well understood to indicate the position of the ancient city of the Ottoes, who were once a very powerful tribe. Being reduced by continual hostilities, they sought protection of the Pawnees, and migrated to the south of the Platte, about thirty miles from its mouth – eds *GM*. [POE'S NOTE] The Otoe and the Pawnee are Native American tribes historically associated with the Great Plains region of what is now the United States.

p. 285, *the Nodaway River*: A tributary of the Missouri that flows through the states of modern-day Iowa and Missouri, roughly parallel to the Platte.

p. 286, *From the cliffs... in the world*: The Council Bluffs – eds *GM*. [POE'S NOTE] On 3rd August 1804, Lewis and Clark held a council with representatives of the Otoe and Missouria tribes at this location on the western bank of the Missouri, in what is now Nebraska. Designed to establish diplomatic relations, establish US sovereignty and encourage peaceful trade, it was one

of the first official meetings between representatives of the United States and Native American tribes following the Louisiana Purchase (for which see first note to p. 269). The meeting gave its name to the Council Bluffs, Iowa, located on the opposite side of the river.

p. 286, *the Arabian Nights*: A collection of stories taken from Middle Eastern and Indian folklore, including the tales of Aladdin, Ali Baba and Sinbad the Sailor, which was compiled sometime in the Middle Ages. It was first published in English in 1706.

p. 287, *fairy-looking*: That is, enchanted or ethereal in appearance.

p. 288, *the habits of the beaver*: Poe derived the following paragraphs concerning beavers from Irving's *The Adventures of Captain Bonneville* (Chapter XXVI). For Bonneville, see fifth note to p. 274.

p. 290, *Captain Bonneville... mode of descent*: The explicit reference to Bonneville here is itself taken almost verbatim from Irving's *The Adventures of Captain Bonneville*: "Captain Bonneville, however, discredits on the whole the alleged sagacity of the beaver in this particular, and thinks the animal has no other aim than to get the tree down, without any of the subtle calculation as to its mode or direction of falling" (Chapter XXVI).

p. 291, *the lion ant... the coralliferi*: The lion ant, or ant lion, is an insect resembling a dragonfly. Poe found the term "coralliferi" in *A Synopsis of Natural History* (1839) by Céran Lemonnier, translated by Thomas Wyatt: "Animals united in great numbers to form composite animals, protected and sustained by solid matters called *polypiers*, internal or external." Examples given include sponges and coral.

p. 292, *the Quicourre*: The Niobrara River, which reaches the Missouri near modern-day Niobrara, Nebraska. The name used by Poe is derived from the French name "L'Eau Qui Court", meaning "the river that runs". See IRV (Chapter XVIII).

p. 292, *Bonhomme Island*: So named in LEW: "On the 22nd we made about eighteen miles, passing several small farms on the bank of the river, a number of islands and a large creek on the south side, called Bonhomme, or Goodman's river" (Chapter I). The island gave its name to what is now Bon Homme County in South Dakota.

p. 292, *the Little Sioux... on the south*: The "Great Sioux" is better known as the Big Sioux River, which forms the border between South Dakota and Iowa. "White Stone" is the Vermillion River in South Dakota, called "Whitestone" by Lewis and Clark in their *History of the Expedition* on the understanding that this was the meaning of the name used by the Native Americans (Chapter II). "Jacques" is the James River in North

Dakota and South Dakota, known in French as "Rivière aux Jacques". "Wawandysenche" is Poe's spelling of "Waucandipeeche", mentioned by Lewis and Clark: "We descended to the river and passed a small creek on the south, called, by the Mahas, Waucandipeeche ('Great Spirit is bad')" (Chapter II). "White Paint River" is likely what is now Bazile Creek, in Knox County, Nebraska.

p. 292, *the Omahas*: A Native American people who historically inhabited the upper Missouri River region, specifically in present-day Nebraska and parts of Iowa.

p. 292, *the Sioux*: A group of Native American tribes from the Great Plains region, historically one of the most powerful and influential indigenous groups in North America. Poe provides a "detailed account of the tribe", derived from LEW (Chapter V), early in the following chapter. See first note to p. 295.

p. 293, *embarrassed*: Impeded.

p. 293, *lynn*: The linden, or lime.

p. 294, *the Ponca tribe*: A Native American people closely related to the Omaha (see fourth note to p. 292) and based in the late eighteenth century at the confluence of the Niobrara and Missouri rivers.

p. 294, *a present attack from the Sioux*: The party's encounter with the Sioux in this chapter is derived from IRV (Chapter XVIII), although this opening editorial section, including the "detailed account of the tribe" that follows in the next paragraph, is based on material from LEW (Chapter V).

p. 294, *canister shot*: See first note to p. 125.

p. 295, *Sioux is the French term... the Warreconne*: The name "Sioux" is derived from the French name "Nadouessioux", itself derived from the word *nadoweisiw* in the language of the Ojibwa, long-standing rivals of the Sioux, which means "adders" (and therefore "enemies"). The term "Sioux" was adopted by Europeans and became widely used to refer to the large group of Native American tribes of the Great Plains. The natives encountered by Rodman and his companions in this chapter are the Sicangu Lakota, whose name means, literally, "burnt thighs nation", and who were called by the French the Brûlé, meaning "burnt". (Following his source, Chapter V of LEW, Poe calls the Brûlé the "Bois-Brulés", although this is in fact the name of an unrelated tribe of Metis – for whom see third note to p. 35.) The Sicangu Lakota are a subdivision of the Lakota, or the Teton Sioux, one of the three major groups of the Sioux, along with the Dakota and the Nakota. The Lakota inhabited the region along the Missouri River in present-day South Dakota. The various "clans" listed by Poe in

this paragraph are as follows. The "Winowacants" are the Mdewakanton, a subdivision of the Dakota, whose name means "dwellers of the spirit lake" (hence "Gens du Lac"), who lived near the Falls of St Anthony on the Mississippi, now in the city of Minneapolis, Minnesota. It is likely that the terms "Wappatomies" and "Wappytooties" – or "Wahpatone" and "Wahpatootas", as they appear in Poe's source – represent different transliterations of the name of the same group, namely the Wakhpetonwan, a Dakota tribe who lived along the Minnesota River (also called the St Peter's River), a tributary of the Mississippi in what is now Minnesota. The name "Wakhpetonwan" means "dwellers among the leaves" – hence the French name given in Poe's source: "Gens des Feuilles" ("people of the leaves"). The "Sissytoonies" are another Dakota band, historically located near the upper Minnesota River. The Yanktons belonged to the Nakota group of the Sioux, occupying lands near the Missouri River between the Big Sioux River, a tributary of the Missouri, to the west, and the Des Moines River, a tributary of the Mississippi, to the east. The "four tribes" of the Teton listed are the Saône, the Miniconjou, the Oglala and the Brûlé – for the last of whom, and the Teton in general, see above.

p. 295, *Assiniboins*: The Assiniboine people – whose name is derived from the Ojibwe term *asiniibwaan*, meaning "stone boilers" – were originally part of the Dakota nation, but broke from their parent group sometime before the seventeenth century and migrated to the north-west. They are historically associated with Saskatchewan, Alberta and Manitoba in Canada, and Montana and North Dakota in the United States.

p. 296, *noisome*: Foul-smelling.

p. 297, *Glauber salts, copperas, sulphur and alum*: "Glauber salts" are sodium sulphate, discovered by the German–Dutch chemist Johann Rudolf Glauber (1604–70) in 1625 and with a variety of applications, including in medicine (it was used as a laxative), in glass manufacturing and in textile-dyeing processes. Copperas is ferrous sulphate, also known as "green vitriol", used in dyeing, tanning and making ink, among other things. Alum, or potash alum, is a compound also used in dyeing and tanning.

p. 297, *calumet feathers*: A calumet was a ceremonial pipe used by many Native American tribes, often consisting of a wooden stem adorned with colourful feathers, beads and other decorations of cultural or spiritual significance. According to Lewis and Clark: "the men of consideration wear a hawk's feather, or calumet feather worked with porcupine quills, and fastened to the top of the head" (Chapter IV). Elsewhere they refer to

"the feathers of the great eagle or calumet bird" (Chapter XVI), suggesting that "calumet feathers" mean specifically eagle feathers. (Poe previously stated: "Fastened to the top of the head is worn a hawk's feather.")

p. 299, *medicine*: A spell, charm or fetish believed by some indigenous North American peoples to possess magical powers.

p. 300, *carabine*: A kind of short rifle or musket used by cavalry. The name is more usually spelt "carbine".

p. 300, *the Ricarees*: The Arikara people, a Native American tribe who lived along the Missouri in what are now North and South Dakota.

p. 303, *the Great Bend*: Now called the Big Bend, a large meander (winding curve) of the Missouri, located in South Dakota.

p. 303, *careering*: Likely a malapropism – or misprint – for "careening", that is, tilting.

p. 303, *brant*: Small geese.

p. 304, *which they designated as Otter Creek*: In fact, Poe took the name from LEW: "At fourteen and a half miles we stopped for the night on a sandbar, opposite a creek on the north, called Otter Creek, twenty-two yards in width, and containing more water than is common for creeks of that size" (Chapter IV).

p. 304, *Ricara*: Previously "Ricaree". See second note to p. 300.

p. 309, *the Mandans... the Ahnahaways*: The Mandan and the Minnetarees, also known as the Hidatsa, are closely related, Siouan-language Native American tribes who historically lived along both banks of the upper Missouri River in present-day North and South Dakota. The Ahnahaways, otherwise known as the Awaxawis, and called by the Mandan "Wattasoon" (not "Wassatoons", as Poe subsequently calls them), were an offshoot of the Hidatsa. This passage paraphrases a section in LEW (Chapter V).

p. 309, *a Minnetaree chief... he was greatly pleased*: The chief Waukerassah is mentioned by Captains Lewis and Clark, whom he also visited. [POE'S NOTE] See LEW: "A Minnetaree chief, the first who has visited us, came down to the fort: his name was Waukerassa" (Chapter V).

p. 310, *bonne bouche*: Literally, "a good taste in the mouth" (French); a dainty morsel.

p. 312, *double head*: The meaning of this term is unclear. The suggestion is perhaps that Toby, along with the rest of "his race", has a markedly broad or pronounced forehead, giving the impression of two parts to the head.

p. 313, *in naturalibus*: Literally, "in the natural" (Latin), that is, naked.

p. 313, *we feasted and made merry, with very little care for the morrow*: See 1 Corinthians 15:32.

p. 313, *a tolerably large river*: Likely the Little Missouri, which rises in north-eastern Wyoming, flowing north-eastward before meeting the Missouri in what is now Dunn County in North Dakota.

p. 313, *debouches*: Emerges into a wider space, in this case the Missouri.

p. 313, *Our new guide… memorandum of it*: Probably White Earth River – eds GM. [POE'S NOTE] The White Earth River is a tributary of the Missouri in north-western North Dakota.

p. 314, *rabbit-berry bushes*: North American shrubs of the oleaster family bearing scarlet berries.

p. 314, *the junction of the Yellowstone with the Missouri*: The Yellowstone meets the Missouri near what is now the city of Williston in north-western North Dakota. The Yellowstone River is the largest tributary of the Missouri.

p. 315, *bighorn*: Wild sheep with large, curved horns found in mountainous areas of North America.

p. 315, *freestone*: A type of sedimentary rock, specifically sandstone or limestone, that can be easily shaped or carved, making it a desirable material for building or sculpting.

p. 315, *Black Hills*: See fourth note to p. 35.

p. 315, *the forks*: The junction of the Yellowstone and the Missouri rivers.

p. 317, *parallelepipedal*: Corrected from Poe's "parrallelipedal", a neologism derived from his source, LEW: "These stones are almost invariably regular parallelipeds of unequal sizes in the wall" (Chapter IX). A parallelepiped is a three-dimensional figure whose faces are all parallelograms.

p. 317, *the Yellowstone… the Ahmateaza*: There appears to be some discrepancy here which we have not thought it worthwhile to alter, as, after all, Mr Rodman may not be in the wrong. The Ahmateaza (according to the narrative of Lewis and Clark) is the name given by the Minnetarees not to the Yellowstone, but to the Missouri itself. [POE'S NOTE] The reference to the Missouri as the "Ahmateahza" occurs at the point in LEW at which the travellers reach the junction of the Missouri and the Marias River in what is today Montana: "We crossed and fixed our camp in the point formed by the junction of the river with the Missouri. It now became an interesting question which of these two streams is what the Minnetarees call Ahmateahza or the Missouri, which they described as approaching very near to the Columbia" (Chapter IX).

p. 318, *the large stream Aregan*: That is, the Columbia, "then termed the Oregon", as Poe stated in Chapter I. For the Columbia, see note to p. 265.

p. 319, *in a well-constructed cache… below the junction*: Caches are holes very frequently dug by the trappers and fur traders, in which to deposit their

furs or other goods during a temporary absence. A dry and retired situation is first selected. A circle about two feet in diameter is then described – the sod within this carefully removed and laid by. A hole is now sunk perpendicularly to the depth of a foot, and afterwards gradually widened until the excavation becomes eight or ten feet deep, and six or seven feet wide. As the earth is dug up, it is cautiously placed on a skin, so as to prevent any traces upon the grass, and, when all is completed, is thrown into the nearest river, or otherwise effectually concealed. This cache is lined throughout with dried sticks and hay, or with skins, and within it almost any species of backwoods property may be safely and soundly kept for years. When the goods are in, and well covered with buffalo hide, earth is thrown upon the whole, and stamped firmly down. Afterwards the sod is replaced, and a private mark made upon the neighbouring trees, or elsewhere, indicating the precise location of the depot – eds *GM*. [POE'S NOTE]

p. 319, *chokeberries*: Sour berries from a North American shrub of the same name belonging to the rose family.

p. 322, *bruin*: A bear, from the Dutch for "brown". "Bruin" was the name of a bear in a cycle of medieval beast fables centring on the hero Reynard the Fox that first appeared in written form in twelfth-century France.

Extra Material

on

Edgar Allan Poe's

*The Narrative of
Arthur Gordon Pym*

and Other Tales

Edgar Allan Poe's Life

Edgar Allan Poe was born in a lodging house in Boston, Massachusetts, on 19th January 1809. His mother, Eliza (née Arnold, 1787–1811), an actress and a celebrated beauty, had arrived in the United States from England in 1796, going on to play more than two hundred parts in the theatre over the course of her brief career. On 14th March 1806 she had married an aspiring actor, David Poe, Jr (1784–*c*.1811), in Richmond, Virginia – her first husband, Charles Hopkins, another thespian, having died the previous year. Her new husband failed to match Eliza's success on the stage, however, and was a heavy drinker. Their first child, Henry, was born in January 1807. Due to his parents' itinerant lifestyle, at the age of two the young boy was sent to be cared for by his paternal grandparents, Elizabeth (1756–1835) and "General" David Poe (1743–1816), in Baltimore, Maryland. (The senior David Poe was not in fact a general, although he had served as deputy quartermaster general for the city of Baltimore during the War of American Independence.) After his own birth, Edgar too was cared for by his paternal grandparents for several months, returning to his parents in Richmond in the summer of 1809. A third child, Rosalie, was born in December 1810. By this time, both of Edgar's parents were suffering from tuberculosis, and the family's financial situation was dire.

In spring 1811 David Poe abandoned his family. The reason for his disappearance is unclear, although there was speculation that Rosalie was not his. Then, in November, Eliza died. Later in his life, Poe reported in a letter that

his father passed away only a few weeks after his mother – whether this is true or not, the three children were now in effect orphans. "I have many occasional dealings with adversity," he wrote, "but the want of parental affection has been the heaviest of my trials."

After their mother's death, the children were separated: Rosalie was thereafter raised by a family named the Mackenzies, while Edgar was taken in by the twenty-five-year-old Frances ("Fanny") Allan (1784–1829), who had visited the dying Eliza in response to a plea for help that had appeared in the *Richmond Enquirer* during her final illness, and had taken an interest in the young boy. She was the wife of John Allan (1779–1834), a Scottish-born merchant, who resided above the premises of Ellis & Allan on the corner of Thirteenth Street and Main Street in Richmond. The Allans proved to be kindly foster parents – Fanny, in particular, pampered her new charge. The change in Edgar's circumstances was reflected in the name he was christened with on 7th January 1812: Edgar Allan Poe.

London In June 1815, in a move made necessary by a decline in John Allan's fortunes, the family left for Liverpool aboard the *Lothair*, arriving in England on 29th July. After a tour of Scotland, they reached London in October, taking lodgings on Southampton Row. In April 1816, Edgar began attending a boarding school in Sloane Street, where he proved an able learner: "Edgar is a fine boy and reads Latin pretty sharply," wrote John Allan in June 1818. In July of the same year, he was moved to the Manor House School in Stoke Newington, then a rural village north-east of the capital, whose headmaster, the Reverend John Bransby, later described Edgar as "quick and clever", claiming that he "would have been a very good boy if he had not been spoilt by his parents" – evidence of the doting affection that Fanny Allan had for her foster son. Edgar's time at the Manor House School – which he subsequently described as "sad, lonely and unhappy" – later inspired the short story 'William Wilson' (1839).

Due to a drop in tobacco prices in London, the Allans *Return to* returned to Richmond in the summer of 1820, lodging *Richmond* initially with John Allan's business partner, Charles Ellis, who was perhaps instrumental in persuading him to remain in his post and not to abandon trade in favour of a career in farming, as he had planned to do. Edgar was sent to a local school, Richmond Academy, where, as well as acquitting himself capably in both his academic work and as a sportsman, he proved himself, in the words of one teacher, to be a "born poet", whose verses were written "*con amore* and not as mere tasks". According to one contemporary, however, he was "self-willed, capricious, inclined to be imperious, and though of generous impulses, not steadily kind, or even amiable"; another remarked that he was "retiring in disposition and singularly unsociable in manner". During this period Edgar began to form his first romantic attachments: first to the mother of a school friend, the thirty-year-old Jane Stanard, who inspired the poem 'To Helen' ("Helen, thy beauty is to me"), which appeared in the 1831 collection *Poems*, and whose death in spring 1824 affected him profoundly, and then to the fifteen-year-old Elmira Royster, who lived opposite his school. Meanwhile, Edgar had to contend with new-found domestic difficulties, as Fanny's health deteriorated and relations with his foster father began to show signs of strain. John Allan complained that Edgar "possesses not a spark of affection for us, not a particle of gratitude for all my care and kindness towards him", while Edgar later described his surrogate parent as "a man of gross and brutal temperament".

In February 1826, Edgar began attending the schools *University;* of Ancient Languages and Modern Languages at the *First Book of* newly founded University of Virginia in Charlottesville. *Poems* Though he excelled in his scholarly endeavours, he once again showed himself to be somewhat aloof, forming no close friendships with his fellow students, one of whom remembered him as having "a sad, melancholy

face always – and even a smile... seemed to be forced". The same student also referred to Edgar's tendency to "put himself under the influence" of alcohol as a means of medicating the "nervous excitability" that plagued him, while another described his "passion" for gambling.

Increasingly resentful of his errant charge, who had by now amassed debts of $2,000, at the end of 1826 John Allan announced that he would no longer subsidize Edgar's university career, as a consequence of which relations between foster father and son reached a new low. In the following March, the disgruntled and penniless young man – his mood worsened by the revelation that Elmira Royster was engaged to be married to another man – left the home of the Allans and travelled to Boston. It was here that, with the help of a young printer, Calvin Frederick Stephen Thomas, he published fifty copies of his first book of verse, *Tamerlane and Other Poems*.

The Army Failing to secure any stable employment in Boston, in May 1826 Poe elected to enlist in the US Army, which he did under the pseudonym "Edgar A. Perry". Over the next two years he served first in an artillery battery off Boston Harbor, then at Fort Moultrie on Sullivan's island off the coast of South Carolina, and finally at Fortress Monroe on the Virginia Peninsula, where, in early 1829, he was made regimental sergeant major, the highest non-commissioned rank. By this time tiring of life as a common soldier, however, he sought his foster father's consent in securing a discharge, in order that he might then apply to West Point, the officers' academy on the west bank of the Hudson River in New York State. His request coincided with the final illness of Fanny Allan, however – Poe learnt of her death on 1st March and returned to Richmond the following day, only to find that the funeral had already taken place. He later wrote to Allan: "*Your* love I never valued – but she I believed loved me as her own child." His resolve perhaps weakened by his loss, John Allan acceded to Poe's entreaty, and in April the

young man left the army, submitting his application to West Point soon afterwards.

In May 1829 Poe travelled to Baltimore to visit his elder brother, Henry, in order to become more closely acquainted with his paternal grandfather's family. "General" Poe was now dead; his widow, along with Henry, Poe's aunt Maria Clemm (1790–1871) and her six-year-old daughter Virginia (1822–47), were living in poverty. Henry, according to Poe's account a drunkard, was dying of consumption; both his grandmother and Maria Clemm were also in poor health. Nevertheless, Poe formed a profound attachment to both Maria and Virginia. From Baltimore Poe travelled by steamer to Philadelphia, where he presented the manuscript of a new collection of poems to Isaac Lea of the publishing house Carey, Lea & Carey, only to receive a standard rejection letter a few weeks later. He therefore offered it instead to the Baltimore firm of Hatch & Dunning, who published *Al Aaraaf, Tamerlane and Minor Poems*, by "Edgar A. Poe", in December 1829. *Meeting with Virginia Clemm; Second Book of Poems*

The parlous state of Poe's finances compelled him to return to Richmond in early 1830. Then, in May, he left for West Point, where he lodged with three fellow cadets at 28 South Barracks. A contemporary remembered him as "shy, proud, sensitive and unsociable… He spent more time in reading than in study." Another, Cadet Gibson, stated: "Very early in his brief career at the Point he established a high reputation for genius, and poems and squibs of local interest were daily issued from Number 28." Characteristically, however, Poe quickly grew weary of life as an officer cadet – but his efforts to resign were thwarted by John Allan, whose parental permission was required if his wayward foster son was to receive an honourable discharge. Newly remarried, and eager to free himself of the burden that Edgar had become, Allan went so far as to attempt to sever relations with him – something that, in a letter to his surrogate parent, Poe responded to with predictable self-pity: "It was my crime *West Point*

to have no one on earth who cared for me or loved me."
In the absence of Allan's blessing, therefore, from early
1831 Poe set about deliberately attempting to provoke
his superiors into expelling him from the academy. His
persistent heavy drinking, combined with his failure to
attend to his duties, led to a court martial at the end
of January, as a result of which he was charged with
"gross neglect of duty" and "disobedience of orders",
and dismissed.

Third Book of On 19th February he left for New York, where –
Poems; Early miserable, impecunious and plagued by ill health – he
Fiction stayed for three months. It was here, in April, that his
third book of poetry, entitled simply *Poems* – financed
in part by some of his West Point colleagues, each of
whom contributed seventy-five cents towards the cost
– was published, by the printer Elam Bliss. In May, Poe
returned to Baltimore, where his brother Henry died in
August. During this time he became increasingly dependent
on his aunt, Maria Clemm, nicknamed "Muddy", who
shouldered the burden of keeping the household together
(she was later described as the "ever-vigilant guardian of
the home" by a neighbour), and deepened his attachment
to the eight-year-old Virginia, whom he called "Sis" or
"Sissie". Unable to find work, and receiving no answer to
the begging letters he sent to his erstwhile guardian, John
Allan, he now turned his hand to fiction as a means of
earning a living – Poe always believed that his true vocation
was as a poet – with the result that 'Metzengerstein', a
Gothic tale "in imitation of the German" appeared in
Philadelphia's *Saturday Courier* in January 1832. Despite
this, and the four further sensational or supernatural tales
that appeared in the same publication over the course of
the year, plus an unknown quantity of journalistic hack
work, Poe was forced to turn to his foster father for help
one final time, in April 1833. "For God's sake pity me,"
he wrote, "and save me from destruction." Allan did not
reply, and communication between the two ceased for ever.

In autumn 1833 Poe won a competition in the weekly
periodical the *Baltimore Saturday Visiter* for his story
'MS Found in a Bottle', a nautical tale with a supernatural
flavour, and was awarded fifty dollars. It was published
in the magazine in October. As a result, he made the
acquaintance of John P. Kennedy, one of the *Visiter*'s
editorial committee, who became his de facto patron.
In the month in which this story was printed, it was
announced in the *Visiter* that a collection entitled
Tales of the Folio Club, containing seventeen pieces
by Poe – satires on various literary styles – was to be
published by subscription. The proposed volume never
in fact materialized, however, due to the unwillingness
of American publishers to take on work by one of their
compatriots – the lack of copyright legislation ensuring
that it was more profitable to produce pirated editions
of works by British authors. Nevertheless, the individual
tales – including 'The Duc de L'Omelette', 'Lionizing'
and 'King Pest' – appeared in the *Philadelphia Saturday
Courier* and the *Southern Literary Messenger* between
1832 and 1836.

In March 1834 John Allan died, leaving nothing to *Death of
John Allan;
the Southern
Literary
Messenger* Poe in his will, provoking a typically resentful and self-
indulgent response from his former charge in which
he bemoaned his poverty and friendlessness. Penniless
as ever, Poe turned for help to Kennedy, who, in the
spring of 1835, recommended him to Thomas Willis
White, the editor of the new monthly *Southern Literary
Messenger*, based in Richmond, who agreed to publish
a characteristically macabre new story, 'Berenice'. In
correspondence Poe told White that he believed that the
best stories contained "the ludicrous heightened into
the grotesque, the fearful coloured into the horrible,
the witty exaggerated into the burlesque, the singular
wrought out into the strange and mystical", as well
as offering him a great deal of unsolicited editorial
advice. As a consequence, in June White offered Poe

a job as a staff writer and critic on the magazine – his first ever secure employment – at sixty dollars per month. After some prevarication, Poe accepted and returned to Richmond. However, White was soon complaining about his "rather dissipated" and unreliable new employee. Meanwhile, Poe's stories continued to appear – including 'Morella' (April 1835) and 'Hans Phaall – A Tale' (June 1835).

Poe abandoned his new post in September on learning to his horror that his beloved Virginia, now thirteen, was to be taken in by his cousin, Neilson Poe. Fearful of losing his "darling little wifey" – who was half his age – he returned to Baltimore, where it is conjectured that he married her in secret. Either way, Virginia's proposed relocation to the home of her relative did not take place. He then requested of White that he be allowed to return to his job on the *Messenger*. White agreed so long as Poe promised to abstain from alcohol. "No man is safe who drinks before breakfast," he warned him.

Marriage to Virginia Poe returned to Richmond in October, bringing with him Maria and Virginia, the trio presenting themselves as a mother and daughter accompanied by their unmarried cousin. No longer tormented by the prospect of losing Virginia, Poe temporarily gave up drinking, and was made editor of the *Messenger* by White. In the spring of 1836, in a service performed by the Presbyterian minister Amasa Converse, Poe married Virginia formally, lying about her age – one witness stated on oath that she was twenty-one. By September, Poe had fallen back into the habit of immoderate drinking, and was given notice by White, but was able to persuade the editor to reconsider. White imposed certain conditions, but Poe proved unable to keep them, and so was finally dismissed in January 1837 – the same month in which the first instalment of a novel, *The Narrative of Arthur Gordon Pym of Nantucket*, appeared in the *Messenger*. "I am as sick of his writings as I am of him," White wrote.

At the end of February 1837, Poe and his family left for *Philadelphia;* New York, where they stayed for an unhappy year, during *the Burton's Gentleman's* which Poe succeeded in publishing only two stories. *Magazine* Furthermore, serialization of *Arthur Gordon Pym* in the *Messenger* ceased after only two instalments. At the beginning of 1838, therefore, Poe, accompanied as ever by his wife and Maria, relocated to Philadelphia, at the time the largest city in the United States as well as the hub of the country's publishing industry. The family were now desperately poor. That summer, *Arthur Gordon Pym* was published in volume form by Harper & Brothers, but received mixed reviews and made no money – Poe himself dismissed it as "a very silly book". 'Ligeia', a story inspired by a dream, was published in September in the *American Museum of Literature and the Arts* – Poe later called it "my *best* tale".

Still in straitened circumstances, in the spring of 1839 Poe offered his services as assistant to William E. Burton, a comic actor from England who was editor of the eponymously named and Philadelphia-based *Burton's Gentleman's Magazine*. Burton accepted, proposing to pay him ten dollars a day for two hours' work. He was formally employed in June, and quickly gained a reputation for the vicious, scathing reviews he wrote of the work of other writers. "I intend to put up with nothing that I can *put down*," he wrote to a correspondent in August. Many of his finest stories appeared in the *Burton's Gentleman's Magazine* in this period, including 'The Fall of the House of Usher' (September 1839) and 'William Wilson' (October 1839). At the end of the year, twenty-five of Poe's tales, including these two, were collected as *Tales of the Grotesque and Arabesque*, published in two volumes by Lea & Blanchard (the successor firm of Carey, Lea & Carey, who had previously rejected Poe's second book of poetry). The two volumes did not sell well, however, and Poe received no payment.

Plans for the
Penn Magazine The perennial problem of Poe's heavy drinking
continued to interfere with his working life, however,
resulting in the breakdown in his relationship with Burton
and his dismissal in May 1840. In response Poe hatched
a plan to establish his own journal, the *Penn Magazine*,
which he said would inhabit "the loftiest regions of
literature", and thus began to contact editors, publishers
and journalists in order to build up a subscription list.
The first edition was planned for early 1841; however, in
late 1840 Poe was bedridden for a month with what he
described as a "severe illness", and so publication was
pushed back to March – but then a financial crisis in
February forced him to abandon the project altogether.

Poe once again offered his services to the *Burton's
Gentleman's Magazine*, now under the ownership of
George Rex Graham, a Philadelphia lawyer with little
journalistic experience, and retitled *Graham's Lady's and
Gentleman's Magazine*. He consequently became editor
of the book reviews in spring 1841 at a salary of eight
hundred dollars per year. Over the next two years nine
more of his stories appeared in the magazine, including
the pioneering detective tale 'The Murders in the Rue
Morgue' (April 1841) and 'A Descent into the Maelstrom'
(May 1841). Despite now enjoying the highest income
he had ever received, he considered the appointment a
temporary one, and after a few months tried – with the
help of the writer Frederick W. Thomas, one of his few
close friends – to secure a position with the Department
of the Treasury in Washington DC. This plan foundered,
however, and in autumn 1841 he agreed to stay in his role
with *Graham's* – whose circulation had increased from
five to twenty-five thousand, due in no small part to the
presence in its pages of Poe's fiction and journalism –
for a further year. At this time he proposed to Lea &
Blanchard another collection of his short fiction, which
would comprise the contents of *Tales of the Grotesque
and Arabesque* plus eight newer stories, and was to

be called *Phantasy Pieces*. Lea & Blanchard, however, declined, on the basis that they were still burdened with unsold copies of the former work.

In January 1842 Virginia began to cough up blood, a *Resignation* sign of the tuberculosis that would eventually claim her *from Graham's* life. "Mrs Poe is again dangerously ill with haemorrhage *Magazine* from the lungs. It is folly to hope," Poe despaired. He later wrote that "at each accession of the disorder I loved her more dearly and clung to her life with more desperate pertinacity". In his misery he turned to drink once more, and, in the spring, resigned from *Graham's*, claiming to be disgusted with the "namby-pamby character" of the magazine – although in reality he was forced to leave because of the irregularity of his own behaviour. In the summer he went to New York, ostensibly to look for journalistic work. The expedition, however, degenerated into a drinking "spree" (his own term for such binges), during which he went missing. In the words of Mary Devereaux, an old flame he had decided in his inebriation to visit, Poe was eventually found "in the woods on the outskirts of Jersey City, wandering about like a crazy man". Despite his misfortunes, he produced some of his greatest stories during this year: 'The Masque of the Red Death' (published in May 1842), 'The Mystery of Marie Rogêt' (published in November 1842) and 'The Tell-Tale Heart' (published in January 1843).

In the next year, 1843, with his drinking now the gossip of Philadelphia and his family once again in dire financial straits, Poe sought to secure a clerkship at the Philadelphia Custom House, something that he hoped would give him the security he needed to launch his journal, now to be called *The Stylus* – which, he claimed, would "far surpass all American journals of its kind". The attempt to secure an administrative position came to nothing, although at this time Poe was fortunate enough to make the acquaintance of Thomas C. Clarke, editor of the Philadelphia *Saturday Museum*, who agreed to finance

the proposed magazine. Poe travelled to Washington to look for subscribers – while there, he also entertained the fanciful notion of securing an audience with the US president, John Tyler, as part of his ongoing efforts to obtain an administrative position with the federal government. As before, however, in practice the trip was nothing more than another humiliating alcoholic "spree".

Back in Philadelphia, Poe began writing 'The Raven'. Meanwhile, his adventure yarn 'The Gold Bug' won a prize of one hundred dollars in the city's *Dollar Newspaper*, and was published in two instalments on 21st and 28th June. The story was described in the *Saturday Museum* as "the most remarkable piece of American fiction that has been published within the last fifteen years". Other major stories were written at this time but published later, including 'The Premature Burial' (published in July 1844) and 'The Purloined Letter' (published in December 1844). In November Poe began a series of lectures, the first of which was held at the Julianna Street Church in Philadelphia on the subject of "American poetry". He was typically acerbic in his pronouncements, singling out the poet Rufus Wilmot Griswold, his successor at *Graham's* and already a literary rival, whose anthology *Poets and Poetry of America* (1842) was, he said, the best of those available, but still showed a "miserable want of judgement – the worst specimens being chosen instead of the best". This contributed to a literary feud that continued to rage even after Poe's death.

New York;
'The Raven' In April 1844, Poe and Virginia moved again to New York, staying at a boarding house on Greenwich Street, where they were joined a short while later by Maria. Almost immediately on arrival, Poe sold a story to the *New York Sun* about a man, Monck Mason – the name of a real-life balloonist – who had apparently crossed the Atlantic in three days aboard a hot-air balloon. The story, a hoax, appeared on 13th April, but was retracted two days later. In June the family moved to a farmhouse five

miles outside the city, where it was hoped that the country air might improve Virginia's health. With the family as indigent as ever, Maria Clemm took it upon herself to find work for Poe, travelling into the city and calling on Nathaniel P. Willis, editor of the new *Evening Mirror*. As a result, Poe became a "mechanical paragraphist" on the newspaper, a relatively lowly copy-writing position. In the winter, the family moved back to Greenwich Street in order that Poe might be closer to his place of work.

'The Raven' was published in the *Evening Mirror* on 29th January 1845, and quickly became a sensation. The *New York Express* claimed that it transcended "anything that has been done even by the best poets of the age". It earned Poe the acclaim he had craved all his life. He began to appear at New York literary salons, and for the time being succeeded in remaining sober. Poe himself became known as "the Raven" – not least because of his custom of dressing entirely in black. For its author, the poem was calculated to achieve commercial success: "'The Raven' has had a great 'run'," he wrote to Frederick W. Thomas, "but I wrote it for the express purpose of running." He also wrote an essay, 'The Philosophy of Composition', published in April 1846, in which he elucidated in great technical detail the poetic processes involved in bringing the poem into existence.

Buoyed by this success, Poe left his job on the *Evening Mirror* and joined the *Broadway Journal* as editor soon afterwards (February 1845). In its pages he repeatedly attacked the eminent American poet Henry Wadsworth Longfellow, accusing him, not for the first time, of plagiarism, calling him a "determined imitator and a dextrous adapter of the ideas of other people" (specifically Tennyson). Although Longfellow did not respond, and while such diatribes may have been merely a publicity stunt designed to draw attention to the *Broadway Journal*, Poe's repeated assaults on his literary contemporary came to be known as "the Longfellow War", one of the

The Broadway Journal; the "Longfellow War"

most notorious literary feuds in American history. Poe levelled the accusation of plagiarism at other poets during this period, including James Russell Lowell and Richard Henry Stoddard.

Soon, however, Poe – complaining of being "dreadfully unwell" – expressed a desire to give up his post on the *Broadway Journal*, where, once again, his drinking had made him unreliable. Although his partner, Charles Frederick Briggs – who had come to regard Poe as a liability, describing him as "a drunken sot" and the "most purely selfish of human beings" – was more than happy to see him go, Poe quickly changed his mind, desiring instead to be given "entire control" of the magazine in order to turn it into "the great literary journal of the future". Thus in October he bought Briggs out and became proprietor, with full editorial authority. Only six weeks later, however, he sold half his interest to a man named Thomas H. Lane, and, after another month, went on one of his debauched "sprees". Lane closed the magazine in January 1846. Appropriately enough, Poe's story 'The Imp of the Perverse' – about the impulse to perform self-destructive actions "merely because we feel we should not" – was published during this period (in the July 1845 issue of *Graham's*).

Frances Sargent Osgood and Elizabeth F. Ellet Meanwhile, in March 1845, Poe made the acquaintance of the poet Frances Sargent Osgood, whom he had praised in his lecture on American poetry, and with whom he embarked on what seemed to be a romantic dalliance. Poe printed several of her poems in the *Broadway Journal*, responding with some of his own, including 'To F——s S. O——d' and 'To F——', both of which had originally been written for other women. 'For Her These Lines Are Penned…' – which appeared in the *Evening Mirror* on 21st February 1846 – even contained within it the name "Frances Sargent Osgood", obtained by taking the first letter of the first line, the second of the second line, and so on. The admiration was clearly mutual – one

writer remembered how Osgood had been put under Poe's "wizard spell" – although it is unlikely that the relationship was sexual: indeed, it may even have been purely platonic, not least because it was conducted with the knowledge of Virginia, who seemed in fact to approve of the association on the basis that it kept her husband sober, as well as of Osgood's spouse, the painter Samuel Stillman Osgood.

Scandal ensued in early 1846, however, when Elizabeth F. Ellet, another poet and perhaps Osgood's rival for Poe's attentions, claimed that Virginia had shown her an indiscreet letter from Osgood to Poe, and advised Ellet to retrieve her correspondence from him. When two other literary women, Margaret Fuller and Anne Lynch, subsequently demanded that Poe return Osgood's letters, Poe retaliated by suggesting that Ellet "look after her *own* letters". Poe was then threatened by Ellet's brother, Colonel William Lummis, who did not believe the former's claim to have already returned his sister's letters. In response Poe attempted to borrow a pistol – to use in self-defence – from the writer Thomas Dunn English, but the conversation devolved into a fist fight when English stated that he did not believe that Poe had ever possessed any correspondence from Ellet. Poe subsequently persuaded his doctor to write an apologetic letter to Ellet in which he attributed his behaviour to temporary insanity. In July, under threat of legal action from Osgood's husband, Ellet sent a letter of apology to Osgood, in which she said that the note she had seen must have been a forgery created by Poe himself. The scandal abated, although the flirtation between Poe and Osgood – as well as between Poe and Ellet – was at an end.

1845 also saw the publication first of *Tales* (June) and then of *The Raven and Other Poems* (November), the first poetry collection published by Poe since 1831. Then, in the spring of 1846, Poe began to publish a series of critical articles under the title 'The Literati of New York

Move to Fordham

397

City' for the magazine *Godey's Lady's Book*, in which he attacked many of the prominent literary figures of the day with typical brutality. Some of his targets were minded to reciprocate, including Thomas Dunn English, who responded with a piece in the *New York Mirror* in which he accused Poe of, among other things, forgery and plagiarism. In turn, Poe set about suing the newspaper for libel. At this time he and his family moved to a cottage in the village of Fordham, thirteen miles north of New York, where their poverty was acute enough to compel Maria to dig up and cook the turnips that were intended as fodder for the cattle. Meanwhile, Poe's claim of temporary insanity during the Ellet affair had become the subject of gossip, leading to much speculation in the press, with the Baltimore *Saturday Visiter* claiming that he was suffering from "mental derangement" and had been consigned to an asylum in Utica. Poe's physical well-being also became the focus of attention, with New York's *Morning Express* stating on 15th December that the writer and his wife were both "dangerously ill with the consumption" and so poor as to be "barely able to obtain the necessaries of life". Several papers – including the *Mirror*, the publication being sued by Poe – appealed for financial contributions on his family's behalf. Such publicity brought Poe's plight to the attention of a woman named Marie Louise Shew, who became Virginia's nurse during her final days.

Death of Virginia Virginia Poe died on 30th January 1847. Several weeks later Poe wrote: "I was overwhelmed by a sorrow so poignant as to deprive me for several weeks of all power of thought or action." Shew, believing Poe to be suffering from madness produced by a lesion on the brain, nursed him back to health. The day before Virginia's funeral, Poe's libel case against the *Mirror* was heard before the New York Superior Court. During the hearing English called Poe "a notorious liar" and "a common drunkard" – nevertheless, the court found in Poe's favour, and he was awarded $225.06 in damages and $101.42 in costs.

Thereafter, with Shew's help, his health slowly recovered from the blow dealt by his wife's death, to the extent that by the summer he was able to visit Washington and Philadelphia in yet another attempt to launch *The Stylus*. As so often, however, he resorted to the bottle when separated from the restraining influences of home.

On 3rd February 1848, Poe gave a lecture on the subject *Eureka* of "The Cosmography of the Universe" at the Society Library on Leonard Street and Broadway, in which he expounded on his theories about the origins and nature of the cosmos to sixty somewhat bemused audience members (inclement weather having ensured only sparse attendance). The lecture put a strain on Poe's relationship with Shew, who, considering the ideas it described to be heretical, left him in the early summer. Poe subsequently adapted the lecture into *Eureka: A Prose Poem*, published in March 1848 by George P. Putnam. Around this time Poe also composed 'Ulalume' and 'The Bells', two of his best-known poems.

Poe's behaviour became increasingly erratic in the *Annie* period following Virginia's death, as demonstrated by *Richmond and* his somewhat hysterical and simultaneous pursuit of two *Sarah Helen Whitman* unobtainable women. In summer 1848, while visiting a married friend named Jane E. Locke (yet another woman to whom he had written passionate letters) in Lowell, Massachusetts, he was introduced to, and immediately smitten with, a married woman named Nancy Locke ("Annie") Richmond. Very soon afterwards, in September, he proposed marriage to a widow named Sarah Helen Whitman, a poet and spiritualist from Providence, Rhode Island, who had come to his attention by writing him a Valentine's poem earlier in the year. Whitman declined – on the basis that she was responsible for the care of her elderly mother – but Poe persisted, only to be met with further refusal, or at any rate prevarication. When Richmond, aware of Poe's relationship with the other woman, recommended that he marry Whitman, he was

grief-stricken by her apparent willingness to countenance his romantic attachment to another – thus, in November, in an apparent bid to end his life, Poe purchased two ounces of laudanum before boarding a train from Lowell to Boston. The suicide attempt succeeded only in making Poe severely ill, and two days later he travelled to Providence to visit Whitman, apparently in a state of mental disorder. After he had recuperated, Whitman finally agreed to marry him – on the condition that he stop drinking. However, when, during a visit made by the couple to a Providence library, an anonymous note was handed to Whitman notifying her that Poe had reneged on his promise to stay sober, she broke off the engagement.

*Richmond;
Engagement to
Elmira Shelton* In early 1849 Poe completed the poem 'The Bells' and began writing 'Annabel Lee', but by April had become unwell and depressed once more: "My life seems wasted – the future looks a dreary blank," he wrote. On 29th June he set off on a steamboat to Philadelphia, en route to Richmond, where he was to deliver a series of lectures, but relapsed into dipsomaniacal ways on the journey. The events of the following two or three days in the former city – where he mislaid the suitcase containing his lecture notes – are obscured by an alcoholic miasma. For instance, he told Maria Clemm that he had been arrested for drunkenness, although there is no record of this having taken place. Meanwhile George Lippard, a Philadelphia journalist, reported that a penniless Poe had visited him wearing only one shoe. Poe attributed his erratic behaviour on this occasion to "*mania a potu*" – that is, delirium tremens. He eventually made it to Richmond, where he recovered somewhat, as well as reacquainting himself with his sister Rosalie. He also called on his boyhood sweetheart Elmira Royster, now Elmira Shelton and a widow. Rumours began to circulate

*Griswold's
Obituary and
'Memoir of the
Author'* that they were engaged, although Shelton later denied that this was the case. As is often the case with Poe, it is difficult to determine the truth of what happened.

In September, Poe, still in Richmond, was invited to travel to Philadelphia to edit a volume of poems by the wife of a piano manufacturer, an uncongenial job he accepted for the money, with the intention of then travelling on to New York, where he planned to make further preparations for the launch of *The Stylus*. He expected to be away from Richmond for a total of two weeks. The day before his departure he visited Shelton, who judged that he was too ill to travel. Nevertheless, early the next morning, 27th September, he boarded the steamboat for Baltimore – forgetting to take his luggage with him. The next six days are shrouded in mystery. As his cousin, Neilson Poe, subsequently wrote to Maria Clemm: "At what time he arrived in [Baltimore], where he spent the time he was here, or under what circumstances, I have been unable to ascertain." Poe was found insensible in a Baltimore inn called Gunner's Hall, clad in a straw hat and strange clothes (not those he had been wearing on leaving Richmond) on 3rd October. The inn was at that time doubling as a polling station for congressional elections that were taking place in Maryland on that day. One popular theory is that Poe, in his inebriated state, had somehow become involved in electoral fraud by being persuaded to don a different set of garments in order to vote more than once for a particular candidate. Whatever the explanation, Poe – after his cousin, Henry Herring, who coincidentally arrived on the scene, had refused to take responsibility for him – was removed from the tavern to the city's Washington College Hospital, where, delirious and full of self-reproach, he died four days later. The official cause of death was given as "phrenitis" – inflammation of the brain. A funeral was held the next day, 8th October, attended by only four mourners, including Herring and Neilson Poe.

An obituary appeared in the *New York Tribune* on 9th October 1849, signed "Ludwig", the pseudonym of Poe's long-standing adversary Rufus Wilmot Griswold, which stated that "few will be grieved" by Poe's death since

Last Days and Mysterious Death

"he had few or no friends". At this time Griswold also claimed that it was Poe's wish that he (Griswold) be made his literary executor – whether this is the case or not, it is true that Maria Clemm transferred power of attorney to Griswold on 20th October. As a result, a three-volume collection of Poe's works was published from January 1850, edited by Griswold, James Russell Lowell and Nathaniel Parker Willis. The third volume was prefaced by a vituperative 'Memoir of the Author' written by Griswold, which contained many fabrications – including that Poe was expelled from the University of Virginia and that he attempted to seduce his foster father John Allan's second wife – and in which he represented the author as a lunatic, a drug addict and a drunkard. Although it was denounced by many who had known Poe, including Sarah Helen Whitman, Charles Frederick Briggs and George Rex Graham, Griswold's character assassination coloured the writer's posthumous reputation throughout the nineteenth century.

Edgar Allan Poe's Works

Tamerlane and Other Poems Poe published his first, forty-page book of verse, entitled *Tamerlane and Other Poems*, at his own expense in June or July 1827, with the help of a Boston printer named Calvin Frederick Stephen Thomas, about whom little is known. Only one hundred copies were printed, and the volume received no critical attention during the author's lifetime. Indeed, so small was the volume's print run, and so limited was its distribution, that, writing in 1850 – the year after Poe's death – the editor and critic Rufus Wilmot Griswold questioned whether it had existed at all. (A copy was eventually found in 1859.) The book contained ten poems, including the long title piece, about the Turko-Mongol conqueror Tamerlane (1336–1405). In the book's preface the anonymous author (called simply "a Bostonian" on the cover), referring to himself in the

third person, asserted that "failure will not at all influence him in a resolution already adopted".

The author's second collection, *Al Aaraaf, Tamerlane and Minor Poems*, which included revised versions of five of the poems from the first volume, was published by the Baltimore firm of Hatch & Dunning in December 1829 and ascribed to "Edgar A. Poe". The extent of the print run is unknown, although it is likely that five hundred copies or fewer were produced. The book contains the first published version of Poe's longest poem, 'Al Aaraaf' (422 lines), which took as its inspiration the discovery in 1572 by the Danish astronomer Tycho Brahe of a supernova, which Poe equated with Al Aaraaf, a place described in the Koran as, in Poe's words, "a medium between Heaven and Hell". Critics mostly reacted negatively to the volume, although John Neal, editor of the *Yankee and Boston Literary Gazette*, opined that if the author "would but do himself justice he might make a beautiful and perhaps a magnificent poem". *Al Aaraaf, Tamerlane and Minor Poems*

Al Aaraaf, Tamerlane and Minor Poems was followed just over a year later, in the spring of 1831, by a third collection of poetry, entitled simply *Poems*, printed by Elam Bliss of New York, probably in a run of between five hundred and a thousand copies. Poe dedicated it to his former colleagues in "the US Corps of Cadets" – some of whom had contributed seventy-five cents each towards the cost. The book described itself as a "second edition", since it contained many poems that had appeared in previous collections, notably 'Tamerlane' and 'Al Aaraaf', as well as six previously unpublished pieces, including early versions of 'To Helen' and 'Israfel'. The volume also included a preface, 'Letter to Mr —', in which Poe outlined his belief that a poem "is opposed to a work of science by having, for its immediate object, *pleasure*, not truth". *Poems*

Having switched his attention to fiction in the early 1830s, partly for pragmatic reasons, Poe had begun to devise a plan for a volume of short stories under the *The Narrative of Arthur Gordon Pym of Nantucket*

title *Tales of the Folio Club*. However, the collection was turned down by the publishers Harper & Brothers, who suggested to Poe that "a single work" – that is, a novel – might appeal to "the ordinary comprehension of the generality of readers". Thus he began composing what would be his only novel – a seafaring adventure yarn with supernatural elements about a stowaway aboard a whaling ship – arranging with his employer, Thomas Willis White, editor of the Richmond-based *Southern Literary Messenger*, to have the story, titled *The Narrative of Arthur Gordon Pym of Nantucket*, serialized in the periodical. However, only two instalments appeared before Poe was fired from his position on the *Messenger* in January 1837. Economic necessity later forced Poe to complete the novel, which was published in two volumes by Harper & Brothers in July 1838, presented as an account by Pym himself – Poe's name did not appear. Contemporary reviewers were unimpressed, with many criticizing its violence as well as the attempt to trick readers into believing it was a true story. Poe himself called it "a very silly book". Nevertheless, *Arthur Gordon Pym* has proven to be a highly influential work, with eminent authors such as Jorge Luis Borges, H.G. Wells and Arthur Conan Doyle among its admirers.

Tales of the Grotesque and Arabesque In late 1839, the Philadelphia firm Lea & Blanchard produced a collection of twenty-five of Poe's short stories, comprising those that were to have been included in the abandoned *Tales of the Folio Club* – including 'MS Found in a Bottle' and 'Metzengerstein' – plus several more, notably 'The Fall of the House of Usher', 'William Wilson' and 'Ligeia'. All of the pieces included in the two volumes, titled *Tales of the Grotesque and Arabesque* and dated 1840, had previously appeared in print, in a variety of publications including the *Southern Literary Messenger* and *Burton's Gentleman's Magazine*. "If in many of my productions terror has been the thesis,

I maintain that terror is not of Germany, but of the soul,"
Poe wrote in his preface, responding to the criticisms of
"'Germanism' and gloom" in his fiction. The author was
beginning to receive considerable praise for his own work
at this time, something that he craved, and many of the
reviews of the collection were positive: Poe had "placed
himself in the foremost rank of American writers",
according to the reviewer of *Alexander's Weekly*. The
book failed to sell, however, and Poe received no payment.
A year later he approached Lea & Blanchard with a
proposal for a second, expanded edition – to be titled
Phantasy Pieces and incorporating newer stories such as
'The Murders in the Rue Morgue' and 'A Descent into
the Maelstrom' – but the publisher declined.

The next collection of Poe's fiction to be published was *Tales*
Tales, which appeared in June 1845 under the imprint
of the New York-based Wiley & Putnam. The selection
of twelve stories – which, as well as 'The Murders in the
Rue Morgue', included two other adventures featuring
Poe's detective C. Auguste Dupin, 'The Mystery of Marie
Rogêt' and 'The Purloined Letter', as well as now-famous
pieces such as 'The Gold-Bug' and 'The Black Cat' – was
made by an editor, Evert Augustus Duyckinck, although
Poe expressed dissatisfaction with the choices, believing
that they represented an insufficient "diversity of subject,
thought and especially tone and manner of handling".
Nevertheless, the collection was a critical success, with the
American Review hailing it as "one of the most original
and peculiar [volumes] ever published in the United States".

Only four months later, in November 1845, *The Raven* *The Raven and*
and Other Poems, the first collection of Poe's verse to be *Other Poems*
published for fourteen years, appeared, courtesy again of
Wiley & Putnam. The title work had appeared in the New
York *Evening Mirror* on 29th January 1845, and had proved
wildly popular, enabling Poe to enjoy a taste of the popular
and critical approbation he felt so keenly that he needed.
The new volume, which contained thirty poems, reprinted

several works that had appeared in previous collections, notably 'Tamerlane' and 'Al Aaraaf', alongside a number of hitherto unpublished pieces. In his preface Poe wrote: "With me poetry has been not a purpose, but a passion." Anticipating brisk sales following the success of *Tales*, the publisher increased the print run of *The Raven and Other Poems* from 750 to about 1,500 copies. The collection, however, failed to make a significant commercial impact.

Eureka The last of Poe's works to be issued in his lifetime was *Eureka: A Prose Poem*, which appeared in July 1848, published by George P. Putnam (the successor firm of Wiley & Putnam). A work of non-fiction, it was based on a lecture titled "The Cosmography of the Universe" that Poe gave at New York's Society Library on 3rd February of the same year. Two months after the lecture, Poe approached Putnam with a proposal to adapt its contents into a treatise on the origins, expansion and ultimate collapse of the cosmos, a work whose impact would eclipse that of Newton's theory of gravitation. Putnam was impressed, and agreed to print five hundred copies (a tenth of the quantity suggested by Poe). Poe presented it in his preface "as an art product alone: let us say as a romance – or, if I be not urging too lofty a claim, as a poem". Despite its eccentricity, and the fact that Poe had no formal scientific training to draw on, some see *Eureka* – and the lecture – as predicting aspects of modern cosmology, including the Big Bang theory (in Poe's description of a "primordial particle" created by God) and relativity (in Poe's claim that "space and duration are one"). Poe considered it his greatest work, although the critics failed to agree, with many dismissing it as baffling and absurd.

Edgar Allan Poe's Works

Correspondence:
The Collected Letters of Edgar Allan Poe, ed. J.W.
 Ostrom, B.R. Pollin and J.A. Savoye, 2 vols., 3rd edn.
 (New York: Gordian Press, 2008)

Biographies:
Peter Ackroyd, *Poe: A Life Cut Short* (London: Chatto &
 Windus, 2008)
Hervey Allen, *Israfel: The Life and Times of Edgar Allan
 Poe*, 2 vols. (New York: George H. Doran, 1927)
Jeffrey Meyers, *Edgar Allan Poe: His Life and Legacy*
 (New York: Charles Scribner's Sons, 1992)
Una Pope-Hennessy, *Edgar Allan Poe, 1809–1849:
 A Critical Biography* (New York: Haskell House, 1934)
Arthur Hobson Quinn, *Edgar Allan Poe: A Critical
 Biography* (New York: D. Appleton–Century, 1941)

Additional Recommended Background Material:
Kevin J. Hayes, ed., *The Cambridge Companion to Edgar
 Allan Poe* (Cambridge: Cambridge University Press,
 2002)
I.M. Walker, ed., *Edgar Allan Poe: The Critical Heritage*
 (London: Routledge, 1986)

Websites:
The Edgar Allan Poe Society of Baltimore, available at
 eapoe.org
The Poe Museum, available at poemuseum.org

EVERGREENS SERIES

Beautifully produced classics, affordably priced

Alma Classics is committed to making available a wide range of literature from around the globe. Most of the titles are enriched by an extensive critical apparatus, notes and extra reading material, as well as a selection of photographs. The texts are based on the most authoritative editions and edited using a fresh, accessible editorial approach. With an emphasis on production, editorial and typographical values, Alma Classics aspires to revitalize the whole experience of reading classics.

On the ORIGIN of SPECIES — Charles Darwin

Daniel Defoe — Moll Flanders

CHARLES DICKENS — A Christmas Carol

DAVID COPPERFIELD — CHARLES DICKENS

GREAT EXPECTATIONS — by CHARLES DICKENS

HARD TIMES — CHARLES DICKENS

CHARLES DICKENS — OLIVER TWIST

CHARLES DICKENS — TALE OF TWO CITIES

The DOUBLE — Fyodor Dostoevsky

Fyodor Dostoevsky — The GAMBLER

The IDIOT — Fyodor Dostoevsky

NOTES from UNDERGROUND — Fyodor DOSTOEVSKY

Middlemarch — GEORGE ELIOT

The MILL on the FLOSS — George Eliot

PRAISE of FOLLY — ERASMUS

The BEAUTIFUL and DAMNED — F. SCOTT FITZGERALD

The GREAT GATSBY — F. SCOTT FITZGERALD

TENDER is the NIGHT — F. SCOTT FITZGERALD

GUSTAVE FLAUBERT — MADAME BOVARY

NORTH and SOUTH — ELIZABETH GASKELL

THE SORROWS OF YOUNG WERTHER — GOETHE

Dead SOULS — Nikolai GOGOL

Nikolai GOGOL — Petersburg TALES

THOMAS HARDY — FAR FROM THE MADDING CROWD

THOMAS HARDY — JUDE THE OBSCURE

THOMAS HARDY — TESS OF THE D'URBERVILLES

Nathaniel Hawthorne — The Scarlet LETTER

THE PORTRAIT OF A LADY — HENRY JAMES

THREE MEN IN A BOAT — JEROME K. JEROME

DUBLINERS — JAMES JOYCE

ULYSSES — JAMES JOYCE

FRANZ — METAMORPHOSIS AND OTHER STORIES — KAFKA

FRANZ KAFKA — THE TRIAL

LADY CHATTERLEY'S LOVER — D. H. LAWRENCE

SONS AND LOVERS — D. H. LAWRENCE

Mikhail Lermontov — A Hero of Our Time

For our complete list and latest offers

visit

almabooks.com/evergreens

101-PAGE CLASSICS
Great Rediscovered Classics

This series has been created with the aim to redefine and enrich the classics canon by promoting unjustly neglected works of enduring significance. These works, beautifully produced and mostly in translation, will intrigue and inspire the literary connoisseur and the general reader alike.

THE PERFECT COLLECTION OF LESSER-KNOWN WORKS BY MAJOR AUTHORS

almabooks.com/101-pages

GREAT POETS SERIES

Each volume is based on the most authoritative text, and reflects Alma's commitment to provide affordable editions with valuable insight into the great poets' works.

Selected Poems
Blake, William
ISBN: 9781847498212
£7.99 • PB • 288 pp

The Rime of the Ancient Mariner
Coleridge, Samuel Taylor
ISBN: 9781847497529
£7.99 • PB • 256 pp

Complete Poems
Keats, John
ISBN: 9781847497567
£9.99 • PB • 520 pp

Paradise Lost
Milton, John
ISBN: 9781847498038
£7.99 • PB • 320 pp

Sonnets
Shakespeare, William
ISBN: 9781847496089
£4.99 • PB • 256 pp

Leaves of Grass
Whitman, Walt
ISBN: 9781847497550
£8.99 • PB • 288 pp

MORE POETRY TITLES

Dante Alighieri: *Inferno, Purgatory, Paradise, Rime, Vita Nuova, Love Poems*;
Alexander Pushkin: *Lyrics Vol. 1 and 2, Love Poems, Ruslan and Lyudmila*;
François Villon: *The Testament and Other Poems*; Cecco Angiolieri: *Sonnets*;
Guido Cavalcanti: *Complete Poems*; Emily Brontë: *Poems from the Moor*;
Anonymous: *Beowulf*; Ugo Foscolo: *Sepulchres*; W.B. Yeats: *Selected Poems*;
Charles Baudelaire: *The Flowers of Evil*; Sándor Márai: *The Withering World*;
Antonia Pozzi: *Poems*; Giuseppe Gioacchino Belli: *Sonnets*; Dickens: *Poems*

WWW.ALMABOOKS.COM/POETRY